"Elizabeth Chadwick writes a powerful love story
...splendid!"
—*Romantic Times*

RELUCTANT KISS

"You shouldn't have come here," he murmured and bent forward, encircling her waist and lifting her against him.

Kat's heart was beating so fast she felt smothered as his lips closed over hers. She hardly noticed when they moved to his bed, so bemused was she by his kiss. The first one, the accidental one, had been pleasant, but this was overwhelming. It turned her body into a giant pulse. She thought fleetingly of Mickey, whose arms she had enjoyed, but his kisses had never been so compelling. She'd never felt that she could not push him away if called elsewhere—to take a whistling tea kettle off the stove, to answer the door.

Connor, continuing the kiss, had turned her on her back so that she sank into his feather mattress under the solid weight of his body. Tingling, her breasts flattened against his chest, she slipped her arms around his neck to pull him closer, wishing that her nightgown were not between them, wishing she could feel his curling hair against her skin.

RELUCTANT LOVERS

ELIZABETH CHADWICK

LEISURE BOOKS NEW YORK CITY

For Billy and Anne,
who shared the Breckenridge adventure

A LEISURE BOOK®

December 1993

Published by

Dorchester Publishing Co., Inc.
276 Fifth Avenue
New York, NY 10001

Special thanks to my reading and writing friends, Joan Coleman, Terry Irvin, and Jean Miculka; to Val and Andy Bernat, who made their railroading library available to me; to Julie Commons, the Breckenridge librarian; to Rebecca Waugh of the Summit County Historical Society; and particularly to Marta Wallace, who took me on two wonderful tours of the historic district.

RELUCTANT LOVERS

Chapter One

"You'd make me the happiest man on the whole Denver, South Park, an' Pacific line, ma'am, if you'd agree to become Mrs. Patrick Feeney," said the railroad man, who had bounded after her when she left the dining room of the Pacific Hotel.

Not another one, thought Kathleen Fitzgerald, buttoning her heavy wool coat as she stepped out under the first-floor roof, whose ornate supports reached almost to the train tracks. "You'll catch your death of cold, Mr. Feeney," she advised, "coming out here in your shirt-sleeves." The wide, snow-covered valley of the South Park stretched away in every direction from Como, Colorado, where she had stopped to change trains.

"That's all right, ma'am. Cold don't bother me," Mr. Feeney assured her, although she could see the goose bumps rising on his arms where they emerged from the rolled-up sleeves of his flannel shirt.

"Not but what I don't appreciate your thinkin' of my

health," he added, a flush highlighting a face whose rough, unfinished quality needed toning down, not accenting.

Poor Mr. Feeney, thought Kat. He was a homely man, if the truth be told.

"But if you'd agree to be my wife, hell I'd—oh, excuse me, ma'am." He flushed a deeper red, having already been reprimanded for using bad language. "Heck, I'll ride with you all the way to Breckenridge in my shirt-sleeves. To ask your brother's permission, you understand. Don't need a ticket, so it won't cost me no money. Bein' as I'm an employee of the railroad, I got a pass."

Kat sighed. Mr. Feeney was a nice enough fellow once you got past his ugliness and his dreadful checked suspenders, which clashed with his plaid shirt. He had a fine head of black hair, not that she held a brief for hair like that. From the back, he looked enough like Mickey Fitzgerald, her late husband, to send a shudder of remembrance up her spine. And she certainly didn't want to marry Mr. Feeney, which meant that another ladylike refusal was in order. "As touched as I am by your kind proposal—" she began, trying to put a little feeling into the standard rejection speech.

"Excuse me." The gentleman who had occupied the far end of their table in the dining room brushed by, looking amused.

"—I fear that I must decline," Kat continued. "With thanks, of course, for the honor you do me." This was the seventh proposal she'd refused while en route from Chicago, via Denver, to Breckenridge, where her brother Sean lived. For some reason, half the male population of Colorado seemed to have decided that 1887 would be a good year to get married, only to discover that there were not enough females to meet the demand. Virtual strangers, like Mr. Feeney, approached her at every opportunity with matrimonial intent. *I must write Mother*, she thought. *Perhaps some of her boarders would like husbands*. Kat herself knew better than to fall victim again to romantic impulse.

"I got a fine job with the railroad," said Patrick Feeney, following her down the platform that led to the depot next door. "Boss of the roundhouse. Fine stone roundhouse. Be glad to show it to you."

"That's very kind of you," Kat murmured, "but I have a train to catch."

"Make more than enough money to support a wife an' any young uns God might see fit to bless us with." He had circled and was now walking backward, impeding her progress.

Kat scowled. She did not consider it proper for a man, seeking a lady's hand in marriage, to mention procreation.

"It's 'cause I used bad language, ain't it?" he asked, looking hangdog. "But it's what folks call the D.S.P. & P., ma'am. I just thought you'd be interested. I sure didn't mean to offend you."

Mr. Feeney had explained, as he and five other men shared her table during the midday meal, that D.S.P. & P. Railroad stood for "damn slow pulling and pretty rough riding." The male diners were vastly amused by the joke; Kat wasn't. "Most ladies are offended by swearing, Mr. Feeney," said Kat, wishing that she had followed her mother's advice and worn a wool scarf instead of a pretty hat. The wind, whistling across the treeless valley, was turning her poor ears and nose to ice while Mr. Feeney slowed her path toward a seat in the warm railway car. Why couldn't the man just accept her refusal as politely as she'd given it and be on his way?

"I own my own horse, an' I got a dog can tree a bear. I'd make you a real good husband."

"I have been married," she responded, "and I did not like it!" Plain-speaking was the only way with some men.

Mr. Feeney stopped backing and gaped at her.

"And now if you will be so kind as to step aside, I will bid you good day."

Since he did not step aside, she had to circle him and, in doing so, bumped into the gentleman who had interrupted

Elizabeth Chadwick

her initial response to Mr. Feeney's proposal.

"Poor Feeney," he said to Kat. "Looks like you disappointed him." He had been standing at the steps to the chair car with the conductor, both of them amused at Mr. Feeney's matrimonial pursuit and Kat's less than friendly response.

"I don't even *know* him," Kat replied, embarrassed to find that there had been witnesses to her departure from genteel conduct.

"Maybe I could just ride on over Boreas with you," said Mr. Feeney, having recovered from his shock. "You might get to like me better if—"

"Go *away!*" she snapped. It wasn't as if his heart were broken. He hadn't known her above an hour. In fact, he probably proposed to every female who came through town.

Mr. Feeney slunk off, and Kat, greatly relieved to be rid of her latest suitor, turned to examine the train that was to carry her on the High Line Spur to the Colorado she had read about—soaring, snow-covered peaks, outlaws, blizzards, fabulous gold mines. She could hardly wait to get there, she realized with a burst of optimism, then noticed that the actual machinery looked rather unimpressive. The train consisted of a freight car, a chair car, a tender, and an engine with a fat balloon stack—gaily painted, to be sure, but so *small*. Could that engine actually get over the towering mountains that ringed the valley?

The gentleman, having recovered from his fit of humor, took her valise and handed her up the stairs. *Good grief,* she thought, *I hope this one isn't planning to propose too.* He wasn't. When she had chosen the only empty double seat in the crowded car and taken out the long-sought-after book she had purchased in Denver, he swung her bag onto the overhead luggage rack. Then he helped her to remove and stow her coat, for the car was well heated by two pot-bellied stoves. Finally he said, "Ma'am," and, tipping his hat politely, continued down the aisle.

10

Now *he* was a fine-looking man, she decided, unlike Mr. Feeney. Enough gold and red gleamed in his brown hair that he evoked no unhappy memories of Mickey. Kat so admired the gentleman's circumspection in not forcing himself upon her attention that she wouldn't have minded making his acquaintance. The little engine released a whistling head of steam, belched black smoke that streamed by her window, then slowly rattled and bumped out of town on the narrow gauge tracks of the D.S.P. & P. Kat resolutely put the circumspect gentleman from her mind, settled into her seat, and opened her copy of Isabella L. Bird's book, *A Lady's Life in the Rocky Mountains*.

How she envied Miss Bird such a venturesome trip. So far Kat's adventures had involved touring Denver with a respectable Catholic family, fending off friendly male Coloradans, and wishing the Damn Slow Pulling and Pretty Rough Riding Railroad weren't so hard on a lady's bottom.

When the train stopped at Tarryall, a new passenger, obviously under the influence of spirits, lurched into the seat across the aisle. At the risk of being joined by some bachelor in search of a wife, Kat moved from the aisle to the window seat in order to get away from the drunk, who was, fortunately, too inebriated to make overtures.

Having lost to alcohol both her father and her husband, she disliked even the smell of spirits. Happily, Miss Bird provided distraction from the incoherent mumbling of the new passenger. The authoress wrote that she was living on a ranch, helping out not only in the kitchen but with the cattle and riding horseback as many as five times a day. The kitchen work sounded dull, but Kat thought that driving cattle might be exciting. Of course, being a Chicago girl, she'd never ridden a horse. The nuns at St. Scholastica hadn't included riding in their curriculum.

At Halfway near Halfway Gulch, where there were several buildings and a water tank and where two passengers got on, Kat was reading breathlessly about Miss Bird's ride to the top of the Continental Divide, almost eight thousand feet above sea level. The description included a frozen lake, a temperature well below zero, frightening solitude and hooting owls as the sun set behind a snow-covered mountain summit. Seeing it all in her mind's eye, Kat shivered in sympathetic awe.

"Miss!"

She glanced up to find a nervous-looking young man pointing a large pistol at her. What in the world did he think he was doing? she wondered. During her few days in Colorado, she'd had men display for her admiration everything from their gold nuggets to photographs of their mothers. Bishop Machebeuf, to whom she had carried a letter of introduction from Reverend Mother Luitgard Huber, had shown her the crucifix which he had carried all over the mining country in the days when he held mass from the back of a wagon, but no one had offered to show her a gun, and Kat thought it a rather ill-mannered method of attracting her attention. "Very nice," she said, her voice polite but distant. She quickly unpinned her hat and placed it on the red plush seat beside her so he couldn't sit down. Then she returned to the plight of Isabella Bird, whose foot was frozen to a stirrup.

"Miss!"

Again Kat marked her place and looked up. "What *is* it?" She now recognized him as one of two passengers who had boarded at Halfway. Good grief. She supposed that as soon as she got rid of this one, the other would begin to pester her.

"I'm holdin' you up, miss," said the young man, looking embarrassed.

"You certainly are." Here was Isabella Bird, freezing and alone on a mountain top, and this young man wanted to get acquainted.

After a moment of confused hesitation, he restated his announcement. "I'm robbin' the train, miss."

Wide-eyed, she forgot the plight of the adventurous Englishwoman. A train robbery? This was indeed the *real* Colorado—as opposed to four days in Denver under the wing of a wizened little French bishop. Still, she couldn't imagine why the train robber was calling his enterprise to her attention. Perhaps he didn't want her to miss the excitement.

"We didn't find the mine payroll what we expected to find," the young man stammered under Kat's interested gaze, "so we're holdin' up the passengers."

She glanced around and saw that her fellow travelers were eyeing her nervously, while at the end of the car near the pot-bellied stove, a burly, ill-kempt fellow, the second Halfway boarder, pointed a larger firearm with *two* barrels at the company in general. "Stop shinin' up to that girl, Kenny, and git on with it," the man shouted.

"By all means," said Kat. "Don't let me detain you, Mr.—ah, Kenny." Because she had to raise her voice over the sounds made by the drunken person across the aisle, who had awakened and begun to sing, she leaned forward so that she could address him. "Do hush, sir," she said. "You're interrupting a robbery and making an unseemly spectacle of yourself."

"Ma'am," said the gunman beseechingly.

"Just a minute." Kat addressed herself a second time to the drunk, who had ignored her and resumed his song. "Have you any idea what happens to those who drown their wits and poison their bodies with alcohol?"

"What?" he asked, halted in mid-chorus.

"You turn yellow, swell up, putrefy, and die," said Kat, who had seen it happen to her own father.

"Putrefy?" The drunk looked puzzled.

"Putrefy," Kat assured him, wondering if she should define the word.

"Look, miss, if you'd just hand over your jewelry an' your money—"

13

Kat turned to the young gunman, astonished. "You mean to rob *me?*"

"I mean to rob ever'one, miss, not just you," he replied apologetically.

"Are you a Westerner?" she asked, dismayed at this unexpected development.

"Yes, ma'am."

"Kenny!" The burly man with the shotgun was working his way down the aisle, relieving other passengers of their valuables.

"Well, I must tell you," said Kat, "that Westerners do not rob ladies. If you'll wait just a minute, I'll prove it to you." She thumbed quickly through her book and placed her finger on a relevant passage.

The young robber, who had been staring while she searched for an apt quotation, said, "You're sure pretty."

"Thank you," said Kat. "Now, pay attention. Isabella Bird says that Westerners *always* treat women with respectful courtesy. Would you care to read the passage?" She held the book out to him, adding, "Surely you do not consider robbing me an example of respectful courtesy?" The young fellow turned bright red and backed into the seat opposite, almost falling into the lap of the singing drunk.

"Shut up an' give the kid your ring an' that brooch," said the burly man, who had reached the middle of the car in time to overhear the conversation.

Kat's lips compressed. "And here. Listen to this," she persevered, addressing herself now to the second train robber. "On the next page, Miss Bird asks a gentleman whether she can expect to ride safely after dark, and the gentleman replies that even the *worst* ruffian in the area would do her no harm." Kat read the passage aloud and concluded, "There, you see!" She glanced triumphantly at the burly, unshaven outlaw. "If you'll pardon me for saying so, you're certainly a ruffian, but even a man like yourself—" She stopped abruptly because the ruffian had

14

raised his weapon and cocked it with an audible click.

"Badger," cried the younger man, "you wouldn't shoot her? Look at how pretty she is."

After that Kat was never quite sure of the exact sequence of events in the flurry of activity that followed. The outcome, however, was that the drunk fell into the young gunman and knocked him over while the circumspect gentleman— who, until the robbery commenced, had been reading his newspaper several seats forward—rose, wrapped his forearm around the ruffian's throat, and placed a pistol against his ear. "You're not going to shoot the lady," he said calmly, "unless you want me to blow your head off."

How courageous and resourceful! Kat thought. The incident reminded her of those schoolgirl romances she used to read before she discovered that real-life romance was highly overrated. Mickey, her late husband, had certainly never rescued her from anything. When he met his untimely death under the wheels of a beer wagon, *she* had tried to rescue *him*.

With much ado the train robbers were dragged off to the freight car by the conductor and various volunteer jailers. Kat nodded a polite smile of thanks at the circumspect gentleman and immediately regretted it because, unsmiling, he picked up her hat and sat down. As wary as she was of romantic entanglements, she didn't want to become acquainted with a man she found attractive. "I am most grateful, sir, for your intervention on my behalf," said Kat, snatching her hat away from him. "However, I did not invite you to—" She got no further.

"Madam," he interrupted. "I have never seen a greater exhibition of foolishness than I just witnessed. No one but a simpleton would deliver a lecture on chivalry to a man holding a gun."

Kat's mouth dropped open. "Well, I—"

"If you don't care about your own safety, you might consider the danger into which you put the rest of us."

Had she really endangered her fellow passengers? Admittedly, they seemed to be in a state of high excitement, but Kat could hardly believe that either bandit would have shot her, and she would have been desolated to lose to thieves the brooch that had belonged to her grandmother in Ireland. "Well, I'm sorry to have caused you unease," she said stiffly.

"Unease!" he exclaimed. "You could have got us all killed. I, for one, have two children dependent on me."

She nodded, thinking, *The attractive ones are always married.* Not that *she* cared one way or another, and certainly not in reference to a man who had just been unnecessarily rude to her. Why, if he thought her such a simpleton, had he bothered to intercede on her behalf?

"I sincerely hope that you are traveling to meet your husband," he continued. "I intend to get off the train and tell him what a foolish woman—"

"I am a widow," said Kat with dignity.

"Well, in that case, you should have accepted Patrick Feeney. Then you could have stopped doling out all those soft glances and sweet smiles. Even that young train robber was smitten after—"

"Soft glances!" she exclaimed indignantly. "Sweet smiles!"

"Unmarried women don't come to Colorado unless they're looking for husbands."

"Well, *I'm* not!" said Kat. "Romantic love and marriage are highly overrated, as I know from experience." She gave him a cool look and turned away as the train continued its noisy, laborious progress into the mountains.

James Connor Macleod sat transfixed. Good lord, she was a beauty! No wonder strangers proposed to her. He'd noticed the rounded figure and tiny waist back at the Pacific Hotel. How could he help it? The vest of her green dress with its gold buttons and black velvet trim fit her like a glove, and the gold tassels ending in little pompoms drew a man's eye straight to her breasts. What he hadn't noticed particularly, being at the opposite end of the table, was the rest—the sweet, rosy mouth; the rounded face; the determined little chin; and the curling black hair styled in a fringe on her forehead and knotted in a luxurious chignon at her neck, all under that black plush flowerpot hat with its jaunty red bird's wing, which she'd just repinned indignantly. And the eyes. A man could drown in those eyes, which were as clear and green as a mountain lake and fringed with long black lashes. Not that he could see her eyes any longer. He was now staring at the back of her head.

How many years had it been, Connor wondered, since he'd seen a woman who made his heart speed up? If he had an ounce of sense, he'd head straight back to his seat and his newspaper. Unfortunately, the drunk across the aisle, once awakened by the robber, had shown every intention of joining her before Connor pushed him aside. Then he recalled the girl's vehement denunciation of romantic love and marriage, which, in his opinion, showed an intelligence he wouldn't have expected in such a pretty young thing. He'd have to revise his opinion; maybe she *wasn't* a simpleton.

"Aren't you a little young to have abjured the joys of wedded bliss?" he asked, having always assumed that women wanted, above all things, to be married. "Not that I don't agree," he added hastily. He needn't have bothered, for she hadn't turned to listen. "I've no intention of ever marrying again myself," he added lamely. He felt a little foolish talking to the back of a woman's head.

Marrying again? That caught Kat's attention. Was he a widower? she wondered. She squelched a brief flare of interest but couldn't resist a reply. "One is never too young for sensible resolutions about the avoidance of matrimony." He too must have suffered through an

17

unsatisfactory marriage. She could sympathize with that. And he seemed a sober and sensible man, if somewhat irascible. At least, he was no wildly handsome ne'er-do-well like Mickey.

Kat folded her hands over the closed copy of her book and stared down at them, thinking of Mickey, with whom she'd fallen madly in love just out of convent school. She'd expected that life with such a charmer would be one long, romantic idyll. Ha! What an addle-brained notion that had been! Mickey, so handsome a bridegroom, got falling-down drunk on her father's fine whiskey at the wedding feast and countless nights thereafter. In fact, Kat had often wondered bitterly during their years together whether Mickey hadn't been attracted by Liam Fitzpatrick's tavern rather than his daughter. At any rate, losing one's heart to a handsome face was a fool's game.

She glanced surreptitiously at the man beside her, who was being congratulated by the conductor on foiling the robbery.

"You shoved that gun right in his ear," exclaimed the conductor. "Did my heart good to see it. Damned train robbers! Pardon my French, ma'am."

Kat turned away hastily when her seat partner glanced at her. For all his appealing gray eyes and sober expression, he had probably been a wife beater before his spouse's demise, she decided. That fitted with his bad-tempered treatment of her. Or perhaps he'd deserted the poor woman—or she him. Mickey had tried wife-beating, but Kat wasn't one to put up with that sort of thing—or to run. A cold night locked out of the house had cured Mickey of raising his hand to Kat when the drink was on him. Remembering that night in Chicago reminded her that she was beginning to feel shivery herself as the window and the train wall on her right became progressively colder.

Again she glanced at the well-dressed stranger, whose muscular arm radiated heat beside hers. If he were a

18

gentleman, he'd give her the warm seat. But she wouldn't suggest it. She wouldn't speak to him at all. Imagine! Berating her in a public place. She ought to ask him to move away. But if she did, that drunk might join her. This fellow was at least sober. Rude, but sober.

"Quiet in there," shouted the conductor. "You're embarrassin' the lady." The robbers were shouting obscenities in the freight car, and some of the remarks could be heard over the clatter of the train. Connor glanced at the girl to see how she was taking it. Her stiff silence made him uncomfortably aware that she probably considered him another ruffian of the same cut as the fellow he'd overpowered on her behalf. Still, she hadn't demanded that he leave, but then she might find him marginally preferable to the drunk across the aisle. And perhaps he *had* been a bit hard on her.

Rose Laurel, his late wife, had told him often enough that he was insensitive. Connor sighed. It was hard to believe that two people as much in love as he and Rose Laurel could have made one another so thoroughly miserable. He'd married a pampered beauty, who evidently expected their union to provide romance and adventure of a civilized nature. Instead she discovered that mining camps were primitive and uncomfortable, that if she was to eat, she had to cook and, worst of all, that lovemaking resulted in children, which she had to bear and tend herself.

His promise that they'd be rich some day hadn't been enough; Rose Laurel had been rich all her life—at least until she went vacationing in Colorado with her parents and met Connor. Well, now he was rich, but his disenchanted wife hadn't lived long enough to see it, just long enough to leave him with a load of guilt and two children to raise.

The girl at his side was right; romance and marriage were best avoided. He'd done so for eight years and intended to continue a widower. But Lord, she smelled good—like flowers. He gritted his teeth against the impulse to venture into conversation. Instead he stared out the window as the train wound its way into the mountains, where the trees thickened, the snow deepened, and the track zigzagged in an endless series of switchbacks. He was more aware of her pretty face than the passing view.

When the conductor came through to light the oil lamps in their ornate brass holders, the increasingly gloomy scene outside finally impinged on Connor's thoughts. "I don't like the looks of that sky," he muttered, forgetting that his seatmate wasn't an ordinary passenger to whom a comment on the weather would be welcome. "We'll be lucky to make it over Boreas Pass before the storm." His voice trailed off as he noted the heavy combs of snow overhanging the high peaks. Bad news, those, if they started to slide.

The girl looked startled, then said wistfully, "I should like to see a real Colorado snow."

Connor's brows shot up, both because her remark was foolish and because she'd spoken to him. She'd even looked at him when she spoke, bemusing him with those wide green eyes. He knew he was staring at her like some callow youth and scrambled mentally for the thread of the conversation. Snow—that was it.

"Don't wish yourself in a mountain storm," he warned. "A January blizzard in the pass can be too fierce for a man to stand up in and the snow so thick he can't tell which way to crawl."

She nodded and replied, "In that case, perhaps I should say a prayer to St. Christopher," and with Connor staring in astonishment, she bowed her head. "There," she said when she had finished, "that should bring us safely over the mountain." She gave him a smile that caused an unusual sensation in the middle of his chest.

Good thing the two of them were uninterested in romance, he thought uneasily. She was an appealing girl, if somewhat naive. Too young for him, of course. Did she really think her little prayer would protect the train if those black clouds engulfed them before they'd crossed the pass?

He cursed himself for a fool to be traveling this time of year, but he'd a mine on Gibson Hill that promised to be as profitable as the rich Jumbo or the diggings owned by the God-damned Trenton Consolidated Mining Company. Connor and his partner needed financing to develop the new claim and fend off a lawsuit; *he* had reason to be making this trip, but why had the girl's family let her travel in January—and by herself? He leaned his head against the back of the seat and closed his eyes, trying to ignore her enticing fragrance.

They sat in silence for another fifteen minutes while Connor considered returning to his previous seat. The drunk had fallen asleep, and he doubted that she would be accosted by any more outlaws. He had just about decided to excuse himself when she exclaimed, "Did you hear that?"

He had.

"It never thunders and snows at the same time in Chicago," she added, eyes wide and puzzled.

Connor, heart pounding, reacted to the ominous boom by jerking the girl from her seat.

"What are you doing?" she cried.

Before he could answer, a great force slammed into the train, and they were hurled into the aisle. He had only a second to realize how alluring that small, soft body felt against his before the peril of their situation commanded all his attention. Should the car, avalanche-tossed, tumble further down the mountain, he knew they'd die. Even if it stayed put, they could be buried under tons of snow.

Chapter Two

When faced with the choice of leaving the wrecked train or staying behind with less adventurous passengers, Kat asked her former seatmate straight out, "Are you a widower?"

"Yes, and I intend to stay that way," he replied, looking surprised.

"My sentiments exactly," she agreed.

"I'm glad to hear it, but why the devil would you ask just *now?*"

By *now* he meant their perilous situation. The avalanche had torn away the engine and hurled it down the mountain. The coal car lay within sight but almost buried. Only the passenger and freight cars, although derailed, had not disappeared in the thundering tide of snow. Those who were uninjured by the accident, Kat and the widower among them, were able to scramble out. "Because I don't want to go off into the storm with a man whose wife had to run away from him," she replied.

"She didn't, and you're not going," said the widower.

"No woman could get through this storm to the section and telegraph station at the top of Boreas Pass."

"You're still holding it against me because I argued with the robbers," she said accusingly, having definitely decided to go with him. He denied the accusation and finally gave in, but perhaps he'd been right, thought Kat minutes later as she reeled against him, knocked sideways by the force of the wind. Kat had not realized how exposed they'd be. The wreck had occurred after the track left the tree line. Because the area offered no protection, the wind bent them double and sometimes forced them to their knees. She now knew why Sean had told her to remain in Chicago until spring and why her mother, when Kat insisted on this winter trip, had been adamant on the subject of clothing, inner and outer.

"Wear your long woolen coat with the tight sleeves," Maeve had insisted when Kat preferred a more stylish short mantle with quilted lining and cape sleeves. "What if you encounter a blizzard, my girl? How will you manage with nothing to warm your limbs and the snow blowing up those foolish wide sleeves?"

Nothing to warm her limbs? Kat had grinned. Beneath her woolen dress, she'd have on her chemise, her woolen combinations, which stretched from shoulder to knee, her drawers, her corset and corset cover, and two flannel petticoats under the good silk one—so many undergarments that she had feared the snug line of her pretty traveling dress might be ruined. Kat had felt that she was quite prepared for any blizzard the state of Colorado threw her way. Now, even with the winter undergarments, the heavy, full-length wool coat, the lined winter boots and gloves, and the voluminous muffler lent her by a passenger who stayed behind, Kat felt ill protected against the howling storm through which they struggled.

Still, when he asked if she was all right, she replied, "Yes," shouting above the roar of wind, blinded by driving snow, and able to tell whom she had collided with only because he had kept close to her throughout this nightmare trek.

Minutes later, they were forced again to their knees, and Kat reflected morosely that skirts were inconvenient for crawling. As was a tightly laced corset. The combination of cold, tight lacing, and exertion left her breathless.

"Don't fall behind," shouted the widower.

Kat crawled faster but with greater difficulty because her clothes were wet; she could tell by the weight, although the dampness had not yet reached her skin. And the snow was getting deeper. If they didn't manage to rise from their knees soon, they'd suffocate. Only the muffler shielding her nose kept her from breathing in the fine, cold granules.

Then the widower dragged Kat to her feet, and they staggered forward as the wind veered and pushed them into a stumbling run. His hand kept her from falling, and her own determination kept her from giving up. Thought she was a simpleton, did he? Well, she'd show him! She'd demanded to come along, and she'd not complain now, although her limbs felt like lead, and her hands and feet had lost all feeling.

"You sure we ain't missed the track?" shouted one of the other men.

"No," came the reply, borne on the wind to Kat's ears.

She began to shiver. People froze to death in storms like this. What if—

"Snow shed," shouted the widower, and then they were out of the wind, staggering through a wooden tunnel.

She couldn't see it, although she brushed against its walls and blessed the shelter it gave them from the storm.

"Only six hundred feet to go," he told her.

"You've got courage; I'll give you that. And stamina."

Well, well. A compliment from the man who'd called her a simpleton. Or maybe he meant she was too foolish to realize the danger of what they'd just been through. Kat scowled and tried to blink, but her eyelashes were heavy with snow. She'd been guided blind through the snow shed which connected to the station. "Miss Bird says Western ruffians appreciate courage in a woman," she mumbled and forced her arm up to brush the snow away. When she could see once more, she realized that he was frowning at her. "Folk," she amended. "She said Western *folk* admire . . ." Her voice trailed off. He'd thought she meant *he* was a ruffian. And he had been—a bit. Now that they were safe in the log section house, tears of relief welled in her eyes, and she turned quickly away so that he wouldn't see them and think her a greater ninny than before.

"Better git her over to the stove," said the man named Charlie, who had admitted them to the Boreas station. Charlie caught her arm when she swayed with exhaustion and helped her over to the pot-bellied stove. As she stood shivering in front of it, he dragged up a stool for her. "Bad afternoon to be hikin' over the mountain," said Charlie. "Specially with a woman. I'm surprised at you, Connor. Takin' a lady sightseein' in January."

Western humor, she decided. Surely Charlie didn't think they were voluntarily crossing the pass afoot.

"Avalanche hit the train from Denver," said the widower, taking off his coat.

Huddled on her stool, Kat wished that he'd offer to help with her wrappings. She was still shivering so violently that she didn't think she could handle the coat buttons. The other two men were divesting themselves of wet clothes as well, standing behind her, holding their hands out over her shoulders toward the warmth.

"Figgered as much," said Charlie. "I'll get right to sendin' a message. That is if the wires are still up."

"You want me to find out for you?" asked the widower impatiently. "Those folks down the mountain need help."

"Someone hurt?" Charlie acted as if the possibility hadn't occurred to him.

"Your engine and crew are gone, and there are broken heads and bones among the passengers," said the widower.

"Well, why didn't you say so?" Sounding aggrieved, Charlie turned to the telegraph equipment. "Durn fools—travelin' this time a year." He sat down and began to operate the key. "No luck," he said after a few minutes.

"Then we'll have to go after the others," said the widower.

Kat's irritation vanished as she now looked at him with alarm. How could he face going out again into that storm? Yet, before she could speak, the four men, Charlie included, were preparing to leave, discussing who would drive the sled and mule team to carry the injured. Within minutes, Kat found herself alone in the station, thinking wistfully that she should have asked them to bring her hat, which she'd had to leave behind along with her baggage. It was the hat, with its pretty red bird's wing, that she regretted. *Oh stop it,* she admonished herself. Wouldn't that have been silly, suggesting to men who were risking their lives in a storm that they rescue her hat?

What if they never came back? she then asked herself in a rush of panic, but quickly decided that she was being foolish again. Of course, they'd get back. They were all natives and used to avalanches and howling snowstorms on wind-scoured mountain tops. Shivering, she bestirred herself. Before they returned, she wanted to find and use the facilities, hang her wet clothes by the stove, and see if she could locate dry ones. Charlie wasn't as big as the others—a lot bigger than she, to be sure, but beggars couldn't be choosers. If he had any clean clothes, she'd borrow them. But God save them all, how were they to get off this mountain if they couldn't send for help?

Well, sufficient unto the day the evil thereof; Mama always said that. She'd said it until the very day Papa died, always thinking maybe he'd rally. But he never did, and long before he died, the saloon became Kat's staggering responsibility. Obviously, a decent woman couldn't go in and break up the fights. She'd had to make decisions about problems she never saw with her own eyes, relying on O'Malley, her father's bartender.

And Kat hated alcohol, hated drunkenness, hated the memory of those heavy wheels rolling over Mickey and the surprised look on his drink-flushed face, then the agony that followed in the few minutes he lived. She hated the way her father had died, his liver like a boulder in his swollen belly. Well, she'd think no more of that.

Embarrassed at such an unsanitary action, she forced open the back door and, hanging onto the jamb, dumped the chamber pot she had used into the snow. Then she went to investigate Charlie's wardrobe. Her own outer clothes were already steaming by the stove, and her dress and silk petticoat, draped over a chair, weren't too wet. Maybe they would dry before the men returned. If not, when the other passengers arrived—all of them men—it would be hard to find a private spot to change from the overalls and flannel shirt she found and donned. There hadn't been another woman on the train, she realized belatedly. For a moment, she felt a dark fear close over her. She'd already discovered that Miss Bird was wrong about all Westerners, especially ruffians, treating women with respect. How many of those passengers were ruffians beside the two train robbers?

"I got one more pair of snow-shoes," said Charlie, gesturing to the Norwegian skis leaning against the wall. "Anyone else willin' to try for Breckenridge with Connor?"

As the men muttered indecisively among themselves, Kat went into a panic-stricken internal debate. If she volunteered, she'd have to place her fate in the hands of a stranger, one who had not been friendly to her, and make a dangerous trip on snow-shoes, about which she knew very little. Worse yet, no one was volunteering. She might be alone with him. On the other hand, if she stayed behind, a lone woman among many men, her prospects were even more terrifying. Better to depend on one rude man than a crowd of drunken, lascivious ones. "I'll go," she said.

"You!" The widower looked taken aback. "You don't know anything about snow-shoeing."

"Of course, I do," she retorted. "From Father John Dyer's book, *Snow-Shoe Itinerant*. Perhaps you've read it." She tried to look nonchalant and knowledgeable.

"I don't need to read it. I know John Dyer. Damn near everyone in these parts does."

Mr. Connor must be very upset, she decided. He'd sworn in her presence.

"And reading a book about snow-shoeing doesn't qualify you to shove off the top of a mountain in foul weather."

Kat had the terrifying conviction that he was right. Still . . . "I can ice-skate and sled," she declared with feigned confidence. "How hard can snow-shoeing be? You attach them to your feet and slide downhill." She had moved closer to him and said urgently, "I don't want to stay here with all these strangers. It wouldn't be—proper."

"Better to risk the impropriety," he muttered, "when the alternative is breaking every bone in your body."

"You think I'd be safe here?" she challenged, willing him to understand her fear without further explanation. If he left her behind, she didn't want these men to know that she was afraid of them.

Connor glanced at his fellow passengers. "It's crazy to even think of your going."

"I need to get to Breckenridge. If I didn't think every day counted, I'd never have come in this season."

"Most women want to *leave* Breckenridge in the winter. Half the female population's in Denver. Why do you—"

"My brother Sean's in Breckenridge. He's sick, and—"

"Sean?" His face changed.

"Sean Fitzpatrick. He's—"

28

"I know him." Connor couldn't believe his ill luck. "We're business partners," he admitted, "so I guess that makes you Kathleen."

"Yes, yes," she said eagerly, her relief so intense that she felt dizzy with it. "Are you Connor Macleod? Why, Sean's written of you. How could I not have—"

"It's a hard trip," he interrupted. "We'd have to leave in the middle of the night." Kat's eyes widened. "When the cold has put a good crust on the snow so we won't sink through. Sean's so sick he sent for you?" Connor's heart sank. He knew Sean's cough had worsened. They both feared miner's lung, although neither mentioned it.

But why the devil should Sean have got the disease when Connor hadn't? Maybe because, when Connor's wife died and he moved his children to Breckenridge, he'd stopped doing any mining himself. But Sean, after they became partners, hadn't. He'd managed the Too Late mine near Montezuma and the three mines up Ten Mile Canyon for another year and continued to go down every day. Connor loved the excitement of prospecting and the financial complications of making the claims pay, but Sean loved the mining itself. Still, Connor's conscience hurt him. In leaving the operations to Sean, he'd exposed his friend to another year of dust from the hydraulic drills—widow-makers, folks called them.

Then he looked at the girl, who was gazing at him anxiously. He didn't even like her. And she, after that lecture he'd given her, probably hated him. Still, she was Sean's sister. How could he leave her behind with this lot, a slip of a girl draped in those ridiculous overalls of Charlie's? And she was a beauty, a temptation to any man, especially a bunch of men isolated on a mountain top who, thinking they might never get off, thinking they had nothing to lose, thinking . . .

"I can make it," she said. "I got up the mountain, didn't I?"

29

She had, but that had been a half-mile walking—and crawling—then an easy trek through the shed. She had no idea what the trip down on snow-shoes would involve, the bitter cold they'd face, the lack of control and terrifying speeds, the terrible weight of a Norwegian ski, especially when the snow built up on top of it.

"Please."

And she was such a little thing. But could he leave her behind? The men were already drinking. Some had carried bottles up the mountain, and they'd found Charlie's supply. "Do you know how fast we'll go? Faster than a fast horse. If you hit a tree, you're dead." She nodded. Perhaps she *had* read the book and taken Father Dyer's trials to heart. "You'll have to do what I tell you." Again she nodded. "If it's too much for you, I'll have to leave you in a cabin partway down. I'll come back, but you'd be by yourself for a time. Could you do that?" Her head bobbed. "Without argument? I want your word."

"Whadda ya sayin', Connor?" called one of the men. "Leave the little lady here. We'll take care of her."

Over the laughter, keeping her eyes averted from the others, Kat said, "I'll do whatever you say." It irked her to agree so unconditionally. How could Sean have chosen as his friend and partner such a rude and arrogant man? No gentleman called a lady a simpleton. Well, the thing was to ignore that—for now.

"It's less than ten miles," Connor had told her, "but it's going to seem like a hundred." He said that men had been known to travel by snow-shoe from Breckenridge to Como in eleven hours. Of course, those snowshoers had not been attired, as she was, in long skirts and all the other female paraphernalia she had donned for warmth before leaving the Boreas Pass section house.

Thank God the snow had stopped falling and she could see Connor ahead on the moonlit trail, if there *was* a trail under the snow. The cold felt like nothing she'd ever known—a knife in her lungs—and the pole with which she was supposed to brake, steer, and knock the snow off her snow-shoes, not to mention fend off on-rushing trees and rocks, weighed enough that her arms had begun to ache within minutes, but she kept her lips firmly closed—both on the desire to groan and on the temptation to pant. Connor had warned her to breathe through her nose so that the air would be warmed before it reached her lungs—as if she, a Chicago girl, born and bred, didn't know *that*.

Why did they call them snow-shoes? she wondered. The boards under her feet were twelve feet long with blocks set in the center for her heels and straps over her toes. Six feet in front of her toes, the ends turned up like wooden dwarf's slippers in a fairy tale—but the boards were nothing like shoes. Thank the Lord, there were fewer trees than she'd expected on this side of the mountains, fewer things to run into and knock herself unconscious. Once they were on the trail, her velocity had become terrifying. Connor seemed to be able to control his, but she couldn't.

"Pray and keep your snow-shoes straight," she kept telling herself. The praying was easy, but keeping the snow-shoes straight was something else. Once already the boards had slid farther and farther apart until she'd thought her body might split in two. She was sure that the skirt of her dress had ripped at the hem before she fell. And Connor, coming back to drag her up, had glared in the moonlight.

Kat swallowed hard, because even now she was gaining on him and didn't know how to stop. If she tried to steer out of his path, something he'd warned her against, she might slide right off a cliff as Reverend John Dyer had. And what would she do then? She couldn't remember how the stalwart Methodist preacher had saved himself. And if she slid into Connor, she might kill him or herself or both of them.

At just that moment he glanced back and shouted, "Slow down."

31

How? the terrified voice in her head shrieked. Desperate, she threw herself over, and then the fine snow was exploding around her. Kat had expected bruises, if not broken bones, from falling on the hard crust. Instead she was enveloped in a cloud of swirling powder, lying on a soft pillow of snow, laughing and weak with relief.

"By God, Kathleen Fitzpatrick—" he shouted.

"Fitzgerald," she corrected. "And my friends call me Kat." She was too giddy to ask herself why she said that— as if inviting him to be a friend.

"Why Kat? Because you've got nine lives? You could have killed yourself with a trick like that. If you hadn't fallen onto a drift, I'd have had to deliver you to your brother in pieces."

Kat couldn't stop giggling. If her left foot hadn't remained attached to its board, she'd have made angels in the snow for the sheer fun of it.

"Well, get up," said Connor grudgingly and reached a hand to yank her out of the drift once he'd removed her remaining board. "God knows where your other snow-shoe is."

"It was poking me in the—ah—" Kat started to giggle again, and Connor, sighing, used his pole to dig around in the snow until he'd located the board. He brushed her off, got her back on her snow-shoes, and they set out once more, Connor marveling at her resilience. His wife had once cried for thirty minutes over a splinter in her finger. Kathleen Fitzgerald could still laugh after a fall like that and all the aches and pains he knew she was experiencing. He remembered his first hours on snow-shoes—his legs had throbbed miserably, and he wasn't a little bit of a girl.

Kat's legs did ache. Her arms ached. Her back ached. Her ribs hurt from trying to breathe against the wretched corset she'd had to wear so that she could fit into her dress, and her lungs burned with the cold, but she kept her eye on Connor, her snow-shoes straight, and her Hail Marys rolling. No one was leaving *her* in a cabin. Not if they sped through the night for the rest of their lives. Well, it wouldn't be night for the rest of their lives, she told herself fuzzily. Morning would come, and then they'd speed through the daylight. "Hail Mary, full of grace . . ."

She noticed that the slopes were not as steep and the speed not as terrifying, but it meant little to her at that point. She looked at nothing but the solid reassurance of Connor Macleod's back. What did he have in his pack? she wondered and fantasized hot coffee, or oatmeal, blessedly warm and laced with cream and brown sugar, or a good Irish stew such as Mama made for the poor, skinny Chicago working women she took in to house, feed, and mother. "Hail Mary, full of grace, be with us . . ."

Kat was jolted out of dazed concentration when she found herself caught around the waist. Her skis fell off, and her nose poked into the rough woolen coat that covered Connor Macleod's chest. "Didn't you hear me call to stop?" he asked. "Turn your head, and look below." Kat moved her face reluctantly away from his coat buttons, hoping that he wouldn't remove the arms that encircled her waist. "See," he said. "That's Breckenridge."

"It is?" She gazed down into the valley of the Blue, aches, pains, bone-deep weariness forgotten. It wasn't a big town. It certainly didn't look very grand—just a cluster of snow-covered roof peaks—but it offered shelter, rest, and warmth, and she could hardly wait to get there.

"We'll arrive within the hour if you can keep from falling asleep on your feet again."

She looked up to protest that she hadn't been asleep and saw that he was smiling at her. And what a fine, fair smile he had. Surprised out of her pique, Kat smiled back.

"I guess I should have known Sean's sister wouldn't be a quitter," he admitted, and he set her back on her

33

snow-shoes. "Think you have another half hour in you?"

"Of course," said Kat, although she wasn't that sure. And she soon discovered that the last lap was the worst. Now the snow built up on her snow-shoes with a vengeance, and she had to scoot the unwieldy boards along when there was no hill down which to skim. Now she'd have given her crystal rosary for a good steep hill, but she said nothing, not wanting Connor to reconsider his warmly given approval.

"That's Lincoln Avenue," he called as they approached the town. "Watch out for people and sleds, and don't let yourself get going too fast."

"How?" she muttered, but he, yards ahead, didn't hear. Kat saw no people. By the light, she judged that it was early morning, although who could tell? Clouds obliterated the mountain. And her skis were gathering snow again. Wearily, she tried to knock the snow off with her pole, which was a hard, slow process.

"Kat!"

The alarm in his voice penetrated her exhausted efforts. She looked up to find herself sliding straight toward a house—a small log structure on rollers. Kat blinked. Connor was to the side of her now, reaching out. She threw herself toward him, and they both tumbled over.

When she struggled into a sitting position, his breath came out in a great whoosh because she had landed on his chest. He pushed her off, gasping, "Couldn't you have fallen somewhere but on me?"

"You pulled me over," she retorted.

"Only to keep you from running into the house."

"Well, what's it doing in the middle of the street?"

Connor levered himself up, groaning. "I suppose they're moving it."

"In the middle of winter? And why did they leave it *here?*"

He shrugged and rose. "Over at Dillon, they moved

the whole town—twice. It's easier and cheaper to move a building than to build one, but it takes time."

Kat shook her head in amazement and allowed herself to be helped up. "We'll walk from here," said Connor, shouldering both sets of snow-shoes.

"How far is it?" she asked. Her voice quivered embarrassingly as exhaustion overwhelmed her.

"Just around this house and two lots down," he said kindly and put his arm around her shoulders. "Don't give up now. You're only minutes away from seeing your brother."

Sean. She'd almost forgotten her reason for going through all this. Obediently she trudged along beside Connor, sometimes wading in snow to the knee, gritting her teeth as she forced her weary muscles to carry her forward. And then they were on the porch of a small frame house, Connor pounding on the door, which was opened at length by her brother—Sean, in a nightshirt with a blanket over his shoulders, black hair tumbling into his eyes as it always had. Grumbling and looking so thin it broke her heart. Coughing that hacking cough she remembered from the last year before he left Chicago.

"I've a surprise for you, partner," said Connor and stepped aside. Sean gaped, then swept Kat into his arms.

"Mother of God," he cried. "I told you to wait for spring, little sister."

"Well, if I'm unwelcome, I can go back. Do you think we can make it up to Boreas Pass again, Mr. Macleod?" she asked.

"Absolutely not," said Connor. "You're stuck with her, my friend."

As the two men grinned at one another, Kat spotted the woman behind her brother. Sweet Jesus! If that was his wife, Ingrid, Sean had married an Amazon. Kat's nose didn't come as high as her sister-in-law's throat when she reached up for a hug after the introductions.

"Didn't I tell you she was a beauty?" Sean demanded.

"Yes," both Kat and Connor agreed, Kat having thought her brother meant Ingrid, Connor evidently having thought his partner meant Kat. She glanced with shy surprise at Connor Macleod. He thought her beautiful? But then what else could he have said? "Your sister's as ugly as a cart horse, and a simpleton besides?" And why should she care what he thought? She'd just thank him for his assistance— but then it was too late even for that. He was leaving.

"You haven't said how you came to be traveling with Kat," Sean called after him. "And on snow-shoes at that."

"She'll tell you," Connor called back. "But don't let her claim it was my idea."

"Well, come in, little sister," said Sean, "and tell us what tricks you've been playing on poor Connor."

"I don't know what you mean," said Kat indignantly.

"Oh yes, you do. We both know you could talk the Bishop of Chicago into turning Methodist."

"Sean Fitzpatrick, I wouldn't think of such a thing!"

Chapter Three

On her third day in Breckenridge, Kat reviewed the puzzling conversation she'd had with her brother, who claimed that Connor Macleod held her in great admiration.

"Admiration?" she'd exclaimed. "He called me a simpleton."

"Well, Kat, the man was terrified that you were going to get yourself killed by those train robbers. You can't blame him for overreacting."

"Oh." At the time, it had seemed to Kat that Connor was afraid she'd get *him* killed. "You're not matchmaking, are you?" she asked suspiciously.

Sean had laughed. "Would I do that? With two people as dead set against marriage as you two? Poor Connor fell madly in love when he was just a kid, eloped with this rich girl from the East, and then she put him through years of misery because she didn't like roughing it in the mining camps, although she knew when she married him that mining was the only chance he had of becoming rich.

I wouldn't be surprised if she died just to spite him, but he's been a good father to his children. If it were me, I'd be proud to have won the admiration of a man who usually runs the other way when he sees a marriageable woman."

"Well . . ." Maybe she'd misjudged Connor Macleod. The man had, after all, saved her life. And he was her brother's friend and partner. It wouldn't hurt to treat him with friendly courtesy.

"You know, Kat," said her brother seriously, "someday *you* might change your mind about remarrying." He put a silencing finger against her lips when she started to protest. "Not for love. I know, after Mickey, that you're through with love, but what about children—and companionship in your old age?"

She scowled at him.

"But if you don't change your mind, so be it." He grinned at her. "You'll always have a home with me. Why, my kids already adore you."

That wasn't surprising, thought Kat. Their mother hardly noticed them. "Oh, Sean," she sighed, "if I could find a man as good as you, I might indeed remarry." But she wouldn't, and her brother needed her. Even now he'd started to cough again, although she'd fixed him one of her mother's elixirs and forced him to drink it not a half hour since.

Dreading what Sean was about to say, Connor waited while a violent spasm of coughing racked his long-time friend and business associate.

"The doctor's suggested that I go to Denver. Thinks maybe the lower altitude and milder climate may help."

"Staying out of the mines would help," said Connor.

"That too." Sean grinned. "No mines in Denver. And there is a doctor who's had some luck with miner's lung."

Connor had never heard of anyone who could cure it.

"Kat probably thinks I got her out here to nurse me."

"Where is she?" asked Connor, who hadn't seen her in

the week since they'd snow-shoed into town together.

Sean grinned at him, as if the question signified something other than ordinary politeness. "My devout sister's off visiting the priests."

"She'll never make it all the way up the hill to that church," Connor predicted, uneasy with Sean's grin.

"Where religion's concerned, Kat has the stamina of an ox." Sean pocketed his handkerchief. "How'd you like her?"

"Well, she's a beauty," said Connor grudgingly, "and, as you always said, a wonder for energy and courage."

"She liked you too," said Sean, perhaps stretching the truth a little. He did think she liked Connor, but she hadn't admitted it. "I hope you realize she's not just a pretty face. I'm leaving my business affairs in her hands."

Connor frowned. He didn't relish the idea of being, in essence, partners with a pretty girl, no matter how smart.

"Well, don't look like that, my friend. You can't expect me to leave Ingrid in charge. Give her a dollar; she spends it." Sean grinned tolerantly. "No, it has to be Kat, and being as you like her, I think maybe you two ought to get married."

"*What?*"

"Sure, why not? If I die, Kat will get half my holdings and the running of the rest for Ingrid and the children. Given how intertwined our interests are, yours and mine, it makes good sense for you and Kat to wed."

"Sean, that's crazy. I hardly know her." Connor couldn't believe his partner had made such a suggestion.

"She improves on longer acquaintance," Sean assured him.

The most alarming aspect of Sean's idea was that for a minute, Connor's heartbeat had accelerated at the thought of having Kat Fitzgerald in his bed. He buried that thought and said with determination, "I'm too old for her."

"Kat's twenty-five. You're thirty-four."

Connor was surprised. Still, if Kathleen Fitzgerald had been exactly his age, it wouldn't have mattered. "To be perfectly frank, Sean, I don't want to remarry. Neither does your sister."

Sean sighed. Connor and Kat were made for each other; he'd been plotting their union for several years, and now he had to contend with their pigheaded objections. Kat, he knew, was intrigued with Connor even if she didn't like him, and Connor—well, Sean couldn't think of a man who'd ever met Kathleen and failed to fall in love. Young and old, married or single, they all fell at Kat's feet, usually unnoticed. Sooner or later Connor would too, all the faster if Sean could get them married before he went off to Denver.

"I'm not suggesting a love match, Connor. Poor Kat married for love, and the bastard made her absolutely miserable. He was a drunk and a philanderer, although I'm not sure she knew about the other women. And you didn't do so well in the love stakes yourself. I'm thinking along the lines of a nice, companionable, mutually profitable—"

"No," said Connor.

Well, hell! thought Sean. When his partner took that tone, it was time to back off and settle for plan two. Looking just a bit insulted, he murmured, "I'd never try to force my sister on you, but I do hope you'll look out for her. And Ingrid. They'll need all the help they can get while I'm away in Denver." He faked a cough to remind his partner of the ailment that necessitated his plea for Connor's assistance.

"I can do that," said Connor, his relief mixed with suspicion; Sean rarely gave up one of his crazy ideas so easily. "Business advice, that sort of thing."

"Absolutely. Kat knows nothing about apex litigation. She won't be able to handle my side of the lawsuit without help."

Connor nodded.

"Nor do I like the idea of my wife and sister living by

themselves. I think you'd better form one household."

"You can't be serious. That—"

"—would simplify the business problems, offer the women some protection, and the children—"

"Look, Sean—"

"Your Jeannie, for instance, is of an age to need a woman around, and my little ones will need a man in the house while I'm gone."

Connor was appalled. He didn't want to live with Sean's sister, who was too damned tempting at a distance much less across his table, and he certainly didn't want to share a house with Ingrid. "My house isn't big enough to—"

"You're right," Sean agreed.

Connor had to swallow an audible sigh of relief.

"We'll move the two houses together. There's a vacant lot by your place that I can buy."

"Look, Sean, I don't think—"

"And then there's Eyeless—he's getting old. The man would probably welcome some help around the house." Sean paused as if considering the many infirmities of Eyeless Ben Waterson, Connor's one-legged, one-eyed, irascible housekeeper and child minder, who had lived with Connor since shortly after Rose Laurel's death. "And Jeannie will be attracting beaus. How are you going to handle that?"

Connor went pale at the thought of his daughter becoming the target of lovesick swains.

"But not to worry, my friend. Kat's a good, sensible woman. She won't let any young buck seduce your daughter."

Connor tried to imagine Kat Fitzgerald as a chaperone for Jeannie—Kat, who didn't look much older than his sixteen-year-old daughter. He knew in his bones that this was a bad idea, but he didn't know how to combat it. How could he refuse a friend who might be dying?

*   *   *

"If I can walk up a mountain to Boreas Pass in a blizzard, dear brother, I can certainly walk up a hill to church," Kat had said tartly when Sean warned her that the Catholic church was difficult to get to. First, however, she walked a block and a half downhill to the corner of Lincoln and French and the remodeled frame structure that Reverend Mother Luitgard Huber, before she returned to St. Scholastica in Chicago, had purchased to house St. Gertrude's school.

"We couldn't hold school in the church any longer," the new prioress, Hilda Walzen, explained to Kat. "The children were freezing—when they could get to school at all. The church is most unfortunately situated."

"So the bishop told me," Kat replied and volunteered her services to the sisters of St. Gertrude's.

"That's very good of you, my dear, but don't think I've forgotten what an unruly schoolgirl you were," said Reverend Mother Hilda. "I'll have no pranks."

Kat grinned. Hilda Walzen had always been the strictest of the sisters in matters of discipline. Then, having hugged Sister Anastasia, who taught the lower school, and Sister Pauline, the music teacher, Kat said good-bye and set out into bright sunshine and deep snow to find St. Joseph's Hospital, which was, according to the sisters, one block uphill and one block south.

Kat was a bit out of breath by the time she forged a path through the drifts to the one-ward, one-private-room structure with its hall-laundry connecting it to the sisters' quarters.

"What would you do, child?" asked Sister Adelaide Stuerzel when Kat offered her services to St. Joseph's. "You wouldn't care much for the amputations and the poor miners coughing themselves to death with pneumonia."

Kat turned pale, and Sister Adelaide hastened to say, "Ah, poor child, I did hear of your brother's illness. We'll pray for him, and you'd best devote yourself to Sean. The Blessed Virgin knows his wife's an indolent woman."

Kat couldn't disagree with that. Before leaving the house, she'd had to wake Ingrid up to look after the children. "Perhaps I could help Sister Angela with the cooking from time to time." She did so want to aid the sisters, who had bravely journeyed to this outpost of Catholicism. Just trying to walk around town here in Breckenridge required a major expenditure of energy.

Sister Angela Quinlan burst into laughter and said, "We're here to save lives, not send our patients on to the life hereafter."

"Well, my cooking's not that bad," Kat protested, remembering that Mickey had excused his frequent absences by saying he'd rather eat the free lunch at the saloon than risk indigestion at her table. But Kat knew he'd been drinking his lunch and didn't return for meals because she allowed no spirits in her house.

"Now Kathleen, my girl," Sister Angela was saying, "your cooking mishaps are famous at St. Scholastica. They do say you filled the convent infirmary with patients who ate your—what was it, Sister Adelaide? You were there."

"Indeed," said Sister Adelaide. "I was never so sick in my life, and the cause was—hmm—a pudding."

"The eggs must have been bad," said Kat defensively.

"Most women check the eggs before they make a pudding. Of course, you were just a student. Still, Kathleen, we won't trouble you with cooking duties. If you'd care to volunteer for the laundry, the whole convent gathers to wash hospital linens at two a.m. Mondays."

"Two in the *morning?*" gasped Kat.

"Feel free to join us any Monday."

Kat nodded and, asking her way to the church, was told to head straight up the hill on Washington Avenue. As she waded, panting, through deep, untouched snow, Kat thought of her puzzling sister-in-law, Ingrid, who didn't seem to do anything but sleep—by day, at any rate. Surely Sean didn't expect Kat to do all the cooking and cleaning for his wife

43

while Ingrid took naps. And who watched Phoebe, who was only four, and Sean Michael, who was five, while Ingrid napped and Sean was out of the house? Kat shook her head and, distracted, floundered into snow to her waist. Ahead of her, on the near right corner of High Street, stood an undistinguished little frame building, isolated on the hill with nothing to recommend it but spectacular mountain scenery in the background. Gritting her teeth, she extracted herself from the drift.

What did Sean see in Ingrid—aside from the fact that she was handsome in an enormous way? Well, that wasn't fair. Ingrid was just tall. And she did have that silver-blond hair. Kat wrapped her wool scarf more closely around her neck. If she'd known what to expect of this trip, she'd have brought a snow shovel. One obvious thing Sean saw in Ingrid, Kat decided, was the lovemaking. Sharing a bedroom with the children, she could hear her brother and his wife in the night. Kat herself had been in a fair way to like that part of marriage. However, Mickey had gradually become less and less able to, well—it was the drink, of course. And in the end he'd come home too drunk to do anything but stumble into bed and snore.

But Sean and Ingrid obviously enjoyed their marital obligations, although the coughing fit into which Sean had fallen afterward terrified Kat, who heard it from the other side of the wall. At the church door, Kat realized belatedly that she was unlikely to find the fathers here. Had she been paying attention to the untouched snow, instead of thinking about Ingrid, she'd have saved herself wet boots and skirts.

Still, as she'd made the trip, she'd step in to look around and say a prayer for her brother's health. She pushed the door open and found herself in a room as cold as the air outdoors, a room with rough plank pews and sheet muslin on the altar. *It's the mass that counts*, she admonished herself as an antidote to shock and disappointment, *not the church.* Kat said her prayer for Sean and added one for herself, asking that she prove efficient in the handling of his affairs. Then she left the pathetic little church. A block away, she stopped a stranger and asked if he knew where the Catholic rectory might be.

"You mean where them papist priests live?" asked the man. He was on snow-shoes and planted his pole to keep himself from sliding away. "Thataway, but I wouldn't be goin' there if'n I was you, little lady. No tellin' what them ferriners be up to."

Kat surmised from his remark that people of her faith were viewed with suspicion here as elsewhere, but she'd never let that bother her before and didn't intend to now. She plowed determinedly toward the rectory to call on her parish priests, whom she found in what they, at least, considered dire straits. Both were ill, the eldest, Father Rhabanus Gutmann, being wrapped in blankets, lying on a settle while he bemoaned the miseries of life in Breckenridge. The young priest, Father Eusebius Geiger, accepted her message from the bishop and bumbled about trying to brew tea. After tasting it, Kat suggested that they hire a housekeeper.

"I doubt there's an unmarried woman between here and Denver," said Father Eusebius, "and if there were, the church could hardly afford to hire her."

"Don't the sisters—"

"They can't get to us through the snow," said Father Rhabanus, shivering in his cocoon of blankets. "We can't even get to the church through the snow."

"Nonsense," said Kat cheerfully. "I've just come from the church." Both priests gaped at her.

"There's been nothing but snow since we arrived in December by train—three hours late and stepping off into six feet of it," said Father Eusebius gloomily.

"Be glad you weren't derailed by an avalanche," said Kat. "I had to hike up to the section house at the top of Boreas Pass and then snow-shoe down. And that's the solution to your problem. You must learn to use snow-shoes," she advised enthusiastically as she thought of the man who had given her directions and how easily he had then set off for town.

"Us?" Father Eusebius looked dubious.

"Certainly. That way you can go wherever you want. I intend to have a pair made as soon as possible—probably by a man named Eli Fletcher, who's reputed to produce the best snow-shoes on this side of the Continental Divide."

"I think he's a Protestant," said Father Eusebius.

"And how would it look for a priest to be sliding about town with boards on his feet?" said Father Rhabanus, coughing, "even if we were well enough for such activities."

"Now, Father, you'll soon recover your health."

He glowered at her and replied, "We're freezing to death in this house. How Father Chapuis survived four years in Breckenridge I can't imagine. And the church is colder than the rectory."

"Well, when the congregation has gathered—"

"A pack of loose women and rowdy men," muttered Father Rhabanus.

"What?" asked Kat, astonished.

"You must excuse Father Rhabanus," the younger priest interjected hastily. "He's really quite ill."

"Yes, well, as I was saying, the presence of the congregation will warm up the church during mass, and as for your house, you must insulate it. I recommend that you tack up newspapers, flattened tin cans, whatever you can find, and then put wallpaper over it. That's what my brother's done, and his house is noticeably warmer than yours." Kat smiled encouragingly at them, but neither priest seemed much cheered by her suggestions. "Shall I bring you a nice pot of soup, Father Rhabanus?" Kat offered.

"Are you the Kathleen Fitzpatrick that poisoned the sisters of St. Scholastica in Chicago with a pudding?" he asked suspiciously.

My goodness, thought Kat. *Some people just don't want*

to be helped. Nonetheless, she'd see to the soup. The two helpless priests obviously couldn't be left to their own devices. That made six people she felt responsible for.

As Kat dragged her snow-laden skirts back home, she wondered where Connor Macleod lived. To please her brother, she could call on Mr. Macleod, perhaps meet his children, poor dears. How long had they been motherless?

"You find them papists?" asked the man of whom she had inquired earlier. She met him the second time in front of Sean's house. He now had his snow-shoes balanced on one shoulder while he carried a plucked chicken in the other hand.

"Indeed I did," said Kat. "Under the weather, both of them. That's a fine chicken you have there. Could you say where in town I might buy one? What the priests need is a good pot of chicken soup."

"Try Christ Kaiser's," said the man, shifting the snow-shoes to a more comfortable position and peering at her. "I'm putting my chicken in the snow bank back of my house," he offered by way of conversation. "Keeps it fresh till I'm ready to eat it."

"What a clever idea!" exclaimed Kat and smiled at him. "I'll have to remember that."

The man gave her a friendly smile in return and tipped his hat, causing the chicken to thump against his nose.

There! thought Kat as she climbed the steps to her brother's porch. And that man thought he didn't like Roman Catholics! People just needed to get acquainted.

When Sean announced that they were all invited for a social evening at Connor Macleod's house, Kat had been amenable, but it wasn't turning out to be a very pleasant occasion. Connor looked uncomfortable, and his daughter, a pretty sixteen-year-old with gold-red hair, was watching Kat as if she expected her to make off with the silver, although they probably had no silver. Connor had looked quite prosperous on the train, but his house was built of logs with clapboards nailed on the front for show.

No matter what her brother said, the child-rearing in the family had evidently been done by a miner-housekeeper, Mr. Eyeless, who sat spitting into a brass cuspidor that he kept on the floor by his rocking chair, while Connor's twelve-year-old son Jamie yawned every thirty seconds; obviously no one had taught the lad any manners.

And the parlor was a caution, just what one might expect of a group of males living together. It contained four rocking chairs, padded with wildly mismatched cushions, and an unpadded, straight-backed wooden seat Kat shared with her brother. The room also boasted a rag rug that had seen better days, a rolltop desk stuffed with papers, two tables, each topped by a lamp but otherwise unadorned, and no decorative touches whatever, unless you counted Mr. Eyeless's cuspidor. Pretty young Jeannie had made no feminine impression on the household, but then maybe she wasn't interested; her dress was unbecoming and ill-fitted, poor child, and she appeared to be wearing miner's boots.

"Carl Bostich said they're hoping to finish that Ware-Carpenter Concentrator by summer's end," said Connor.

Sean thumped the palm of his hand against his forehead and exclaimed, "By God, Kat, I forgot to tell you. Carl has made an offer for your hand." Sean roared with laughter, which brought on a spasm of coughing.

"Oh, you're such a tease," said Kat, trying to look cheerful, although that cough frightened her half to death.

"No such thing," said Sean. "Carl stopped me in front of the Engle brothers' saloon and said he'd be willing to marry you. The sooner, the better. His very words."

"Well, I don't know any Carl—Carl—"

"Bostich," supplied her brother helpfully. "Carl said you complimented his chicken."

Kat stopped blushing and frowned. "Why, I know who

48

you mean. He doesn't even like Roman Catholics."

"Nobody does," said Jeannie Macleod and received an admonitory scowl from her father.

"Guess with Carl it depends on how pretty the Roman Catholic is. As for you, Jeannie girl, I thought you were in love with me," continued Sean, "and I'm Roman Catholic."

"Oh, Uncle Sean," Jeannie stammered, "you never go to church."

"Do I take it you want me to refuse Carl's offer, little sister?" Sean asked Kat.

"Well, of course," said Kat, who had noticed that Connor was scowling at her. And why, for heaven sake? It was none of his business who proposed to her. "You know I've no intention of remarrying," she reminded Sean.

Jeannie suddenly looked more cheerful until Sean announced his joint-family plan. "Connor will take over as head of both families while I'm away in Denver. That suit you, sweetheart?" Sean asked his little daughter, Phoebe.

"Yes, Papa," she replied promptly and scrambled out of his lap to give Connor a wet kiss which landed at the edge of his eyebrow.

"Kat's going to watch out not only for my business interests, but for all you children. That'll be nice for you, Jeannie, sweetheart."

"I don't need a mother," said Jeannie sullenly. "Eyeless does just fine."

"I ain't nobody's mother," snapped Eyeless and spat into his cuspidor. "An' it's about time I got to retire from keepin' house."

Kat was horrified. What did her brother mean—announcing such an outrageous plan without even consulting her? Did he really think she'd agree to a combination of households in which she'd have to cook and clean for everyone? She glanced, scowling, at Ingrid, who wouldn't be any help at all. And what was Ingrid's role to be? Would she go to Denver with Sean?

But no, Ingrid was eyeing Connor Macleod like a hungry cat. Yes, that was Ingrid, all right—a big, blond, sleepy, night-prowling feline wearing half a bottle of perfume. Kat had to admit that she herself had had a furtive surge of interest in the idea as it applied to sharing a house with Connor—but not as his maid! In fact, not at all. What was she thinking of? She'd let her brother's talk of Connor's admiration soften her up.

Jeannie's face was noticeably flushed. "I certainly don't want—"

"It's already decided," Connor snapped, cutting his daughter off before she could voice further objections.

"This house will never hold eight people," Kat pointed out, beginning her argument with the most obvious and practical deterrent to her brother's hare-brained scheme.

"We'll just move my place downhill and find a carpenter to join the two houses up. You can take care of the details, Kat," said Sean.

Joining two houses? She'd never done anything like that. Her only previous real estate transaction had been the sale of the saloon, which her mother had agreed to instantly, planning to use the proceeds to buy more houses and board more working women in need of homelike protection from the dangers of life in Chicago. Because the two-house logistics were so intriguing, Kat was momentarily distracted from her objection. "I guess I'd have to make an architectural study of the town," she said thoughtfully, "if we really were to—"

"Good idea," said Sean as Connor was saying, "What the hell for?"

I'll have to speak to Connor about swearing in front of the children, thought Kat. *Not that I'd ever agree to any such plan.*

Chapter Four

Kat had spent hours crisscrossing the town looking at houses, finding at last the house she liked best on Washington Avenue just off Main. It had a steeply peaked roof, very practical during heavy snow, and a lovely boxed window in front. Best of all, the scrollwork was enchanting. She stood on the street gazing in appreciation, then mounted the two steps and knocked at the door. A Negro man answered.

"I'm Kathleen Fitzgerald," she stammered. He was the first person of color she'd seen in Colorado. "I like your house."

"Who is it, Barney?" called a woman's voice.

"A young lady who likes our house," the man replied. He stared at Kat for a moment, then said, "I'm Barney Ford."

"How do you do." Kat shook his hand, embarrassed at having been tongue-tied. A Negro woman appeared behind him, and Kat introduced herself to Julia Ford as well. "I admire your house so much, and I—ah—wondered who built it—so I could get him to work on my brother's place."

The couple exchanged glances, then invited Kat in for a tour of their home, which, they said, had been built by Elias Nashold. The place had no kitchen. "Does Mr. Nashold always leave out the kitchen?" Kat asked.

"Only for restaurant owners," replied Mr. Ford, "which I am. The Chop House. Perhaps you've eaten there?"

"Oh, I haven't eaten anywhere—except at Sean's, of course, and my sister-in-law isn't a very reliable cook. I mean sometimes she doesn't cook at all." Chop House? Kat thought of juicy chops, perhaps with potatoes and gravy. "Would I be welcome?" she asked wistfully, not sure that white people ate at Negro restaurants.

"Certainly," said Barney Ford. "You wouldn't be related to Sean Fitzpatrick, would you?"

"Why, yes," Kat replied eagerly. "Do you know him?"

"Indeed, we do," said Julia Ford. "Phoebe ate so much popcorn at our children's party last year that she threw up on the carpet."

"Oh, I'm so sorry." Would they refuse to tell her Mr. Elias Nashold's whereabouts because of damage to their carpet? It looked all right to her when, seated in the parlor, she had a chance to inspect it. Kat's sympathies went out to little Phoebe. Who wouldn't turn gluttonous if offered hot popcorn? She could almost taste the salt and rich, melted butter. Shaking off her popcorn fantasy, she asked herself why she was thinking so much about food lately. Probably because the breakfast served that morning by Ingrid had been woefully inadequate. With a surge of gloom, Kat reflected that *she* might be reduced to cooking.

"So you're marrying Connor?" asked Julia Ford after Kat had explained her need for a carpenter to join the houses.

"No, I'm not," Kat replied. "It's just a convenience." Mrs. Ford looked shocked. "For business reasons and for the children's sake." Mr. Ford didn't look very encouraging either. "Well, goodness," said Kat, "it's not as if we won't be well chaperoned. There's Ingrid."

"Oh yes, Ingrid," said Mrs. Ford.

"And the children. Besides, Connor and I hardly know one another. We couldn't very well get married—even if we wanted to." What *was* the problem? Kat wondered. Mrs. Ford obviously saw one. "The arrangement was Sean's idea."

"Wouldn't you know," said Julia Ford.

"That boy always was a scamp," Barney Ford agreed.

"Those two houses can't be combined," said Elias Nashold. "Not under my name."

"But Mr. Nashold, your scrollwork is so lovely that I thought—"

"—you could cover up an architectural abomination with gingerbread? Hard to believe Connor agreed to that."

"Well, he did," said Kat defensively.

"Try Otto Diederick. He's long on scrollwork and short on sense."

Chastened, Kat trudged off to find Otto Diederick, a hulking young German, but good looking in a blonde way—except for his eyes, which were as pale as new slush on a Chicago street. He took one look at Kat and said, "You vant to start today, Missus?"

Startled, Kat replied, "Tomorrow would do. Actually, we have to get my brother's house moved before—"

"I'll move it," said Otto Diederick. "Vere you vant it moved to?"

"Next to Mr. Connor Macleod's house on French Street between Lincoln and Washington. It has a big pine tree in front and six more in back where the outbuildings—"

"I know de vun. I come tomorrow morning at sunup if you be there."

What a strange young man. He hadn't asked what he'd be paid. And a good thing too, since Kat had no idea what carpenters were paid in Breckenridge. She'd have to find out before he arrived to move the house.

* * *

Connor had had doubts about trying to do business with a female associate, but so far the talks with Sean and his sister had been reassuring. Kat Fitzgerald seemed to understand what they told her, asked intelligent questions when she didn't, and wasn't given to giggling and disclaiming any interest in or ability to learn about mining. His doubts were now of another nature. First, there was that carpenter she'd hired, Otto Diederick. The young fool neglected his work to hang around Kat whenever she was at home. Worse, if Connor gave him instructions, he invariably said, "I'll have to check dat mit Missus Fitzgerald," as if Connor's house weren't involved in this brainstorm of Sean's. He only had to look out his window to see Sean's house, now perched next door, a half-witted German carpenter assaulting his ears with the sound of hammering as the corridor between the two houses went up.

"Well, I think that's outrageous," said Kat, calling his attention back to the meeting. Charlie Maxell, their lawyer, had been explaining apex law as it applied to the lawsuit in which Connor and Sean were involved. "How can this Mr. Fleming claim he owns the vein on land he sold to you himself?"

"Oh, Fleming's offered to pay back the money," said Connor.

"But he hasn't apologized for having the claim salted before he offered it to us," said Sean dryly.

Connor watched the little pleat of concentration between her eyebrows as she tried to puzzle out what salting meant. She wasn't a woman to bother you with questions she could answer herself. Finally she said, "I don't see what difference salt would make—unless it corrodes the ore."

"He salted it *with* ore," said Sean, "so we'd think it was worth a lot when he himself figured that it fell between the lode on our land and another vein they own." Kat still looked puzzled. "He thought he was selling us a worthless

54

piece of ground, honey. Connor, on the other hand, couldn't believe our luck and snapped it right up. And he was right; we weren't down twenty feet before we hit a pocket of rich galena ore—much better than the stuff Fleming had salted the claim with originally."

"So now he wants it back?"

"He says the apex is on their claim," said Charlie Maxell, "and as I was telling you, Miss Kathleen, the people who have the apex can follow and mine the vein no matter whose claim it's on or when the claim was filed."

"But he's wrong," said Connor. "The apex is on the section we bought from him, so we control his vein as well as the lode on our original claim. We're countersuing."

"Well, good," said Kat and smiled at Charlie Maxell, who blushed with pleasure. "I'm sure you'll win for us, Mr. Maxell. Your explanation was perfectly clear."

"Except that Sean and I could run out of money before it ever gets to a jury," said Connor. When she turned a puzzled frown in his direction, he explained that Trenton was a rich eastern outfit. "We're local, with limited resources. They'll just keep us in court until the legal fees eat up everything we own or borrow."

"Surely, you're overly pessimistic," Kat protested.

"If that wasn't what they were planning, they'd have accepted when we tried to negotiate a compromise. They can outspend—even outgun us. We're probably looking at another Farncomb Hill War."

"Let's hope it's not that bad," muttered Sean and described for Kat a litigation over gold claims that had gone from the courts to a pitched gun battle involving forty men and resulting in three deaths.

"But that's terrible," Kat gasped.

"Now don't you worry, Miss Kathleen," said Charlie Maxell. "It won't come to that. I'll keep it in court."

"Until we can't pay your fees any longer," said Connor.

"And in the meantime Fleming will be mining a vein that should be ours, trying to cover up for the fact that it was his miscalculation—and probably a desire to put one over on me—that let the apex get away from him in the first place."

"Oh dear," said Kat.

"No fear, ma'am. I'm not gonna drop out of this case because of money," said the lawyer, tucking a thumb into the pocket of his brown tweed vest.

Both Sean and Connor looked at him in astonishment.

"Well, that's very kind of you, Mr. Maxell, but we couldn't let you work free. Why don't we—let's see." She tapped her chin thoughtfully. "Couldn't we give Mr. Maxell a percentage of the profits on the disputed claim?"

"Sure, but he won't get paid unless we win the suit, and even if we do, that could be years. Charlie has to make a living too," said Connor.

"Not to worry, Connor. I think Miss Kathleen's suggestion is perfectly fair." Charlie Maxell beamed at her from beneath a bush of light brown hair that had fallen into his eyes as he became more enthusiastic about the case. "I'd be glad to continue on that basis."

Shortly thereafter, an agreement having been struck, Kat left to check on her building project, Charlie Maxell left to insure her safety at the dangerous building site, and Connor asked, "What the hell came over Charlie?"

"Oh, he fell in love," said Sean. "Happens all the time. So'd that carpenter. Haven't you noticed?"

"No," said Connor. "I just thought the German was simple, but I know Charlie isn't. Are you saying your sister deliberately set out to—"

"—to get us free legal services? Of course not. She didn't even notice what was happening with Charlie, and she won't notice until he proposes. Then she'll be taken completely by surprise and wonder whatever gave him the idea she'd be interested. It's been happening since she was thirteen, and the only suitor she ever noticed was the one she married, which was a disaster." If the expression of chagrin on Connor's face was any indication, Sean noted with satisfaction, Connor didn't like the idea that half the town would be proposing to Kat.

Of course, Connor was a stubborn man, and he thought he didn't want to marry again. It might take a half dozen proposals to build a fire under him, but that was all right. Sean was sure the suitors would be forthcoming. Kat had already acquired two in less than a week. And the gossip caused by their living arrangements might convince Kat that she wanted to remarry. Sean rubbed his hands together and grinned; he couldn't think of anyone he'd rather have as a brother-in-law than Connor Macleod, who had provided Sean with his first grubstake and thus his avenue to wealth and who had been a good friend and reliable partner these many years. And then there was the miner's lung. *If it gets me*, Sean thought, *I can always rely on Connor to look after Kat, Ingrid, and the children.*

"Is that song about beer?" Kat asked, remembering with a shudder the drunken singing at her father's saloon. Otto Diederick, who had been pounding on the framework for the corridor room and singing lustily in German, dropped his hammer and teetered precariously on his ladder.

"Ist ein German trinking song," said Otto, clutching the ladder.

"Have you been drinking?" Kat asked suspiciously. He'd knocked the porch off Sean's house getting it down the hill, and now he was swaying on that ladder as if he were in his cups. The last thing she needed was a drunken carpenter—goodness, the new room might fall down and kill someone.

"No, Missus," said Otto, his pale eyes anxious.

"Drinking is bad for your health," Kat murmured, the memory of her father's terrible death flashing through her mind as she fastened her mantle. "And for other people's health," she added. She'd nearly been killed trying to rescue Mickey. What if Diederick had dropped that hammer on her head? From the doorway, she stared at the yard, three feet below. Getting in and out of the house was difficult without a porch or steps.

Otto scrambled down his ladder, crying, "I help you Missus," and swung her to the ground, where the snow was churned and muddy because he'd been tramping through it.

"Thank you," said Kat.

Otto beamed.

"But I have to get in and out at other times too."

"Zo-o-o. I stay here to lift you." Kat frowned at him. "Zo I built you ein nice porch. All der vay across der front."

"Won't a porch take a long time?" asked Kat. "The Ladies' Altar Cloth Society is coming next week."

"I too," exclaimed Diederick, his face lighting up.

"What?" Had he thought she was inviting him? "It's only for ladies."

"Roman Catholic. I too. From Bavaria. I built nice stairs before ladies come."

Kat nodded and trudged off toward the grocery store. Ingrid was, as usual, napping in her room; Phoebe and Sean Michael were spending the afternoon with friends, meaning Kat would have to fetch them unless Ingrid woke up. Given the low, gray sky and dropping temperature, Kat felt she'd be lucky to get back from her shopping expedition before snow began to fall again. When she turned downhill onto Washington Avenue, she couldn't see the mountains that rose across the Blue beyond West Breckenridge; clouds had obscured them. Because of the need for haste, she denied herself the pleasure of admiring the Ford house, Elias Nashold's work of art, but she did so wish that he'd accepted her commission. No doubt Mr. Deiderick was doing his best, but he worked so slowly, and he was very uncooperative when Connor gave him orders.

The wind picked up, creeping into the cape sleeves of her mantle. She could almost hear her mother tut-tutting over Kat's foolish decision to wear something that was pretty rather than practical. She glanced again at the gloomy sky and hurried toward Main. With the best intentions, Mr. Deiderick might not be able to put steps back on the house in time for the ladies' meeting. The impending snow would certainly deter him.

She sighed at the many difficulties of life in winter Breckenridge. No wonder so many ladies went to Denver for the season, leaving their husbands here to drink themselves into a state of advanced foolishness. As she crossed Main Street and climbed up onto the wooden sidewalk, two such men reeled out of the Miner's Home Saloon, shouting at one another. Then to her astonishment, they drew guns. A man who was watching from the saloon door grabbed Kat and hauled her inside. As she righted herself, gasping indignantly, he said, "Sorry for the inconvenience, ma'am, but I couldn't let them shoot you."

"Surely, they weren't shooting at me."

"No ma'am, but bullets do go astray and hit bystanders." He stuck his head outside, then popped back in and announced, "Will Iliff's hauling them off. You're safe to continue on your way, ma'am."

Well, he was a polite saloonkeeper. Before leaving, she peeked at his establishment, finding it tidy and well appointed, with a long bar and a fine mirror behind it. However, the Miner's Home was not nearly as nice as Papa's saloon had been, and Papa had never allowed people with guns to enter. Kat edged back into the street. As she had expected, the first snowflakes were drifting down.

She hastened into the grocery store where the owner, excited because several of the bullets fired by the saloon patrons had entered his establishment, cried, "They missed me by that much," measuring the distance out at two inches between his fingers. Kat nodded and inspected his sparsely stocked shelves, finding that many of the items on her list were not available. The grocer explained that shipments were slow arriving because of the weather. "Got a supply of beer in, though," he added.

"They're shipping beer when people need food?"

"You can always sell beer," said the grocer. "How about potatoes? I can give you a fifty-pound bag of potatoes. Deliver it tomorrow."

She decided she'd better take the potatoes. What if the snow continued for weeks? Potatoes might be all they had. And Sean, whose cough got worse and worse, might not be able to leave for Denver and the doctor whose cures were reputed to be nothing short of miraculous.

When Kat stepped back onto Main Street, the snow was falling so heavily she couldn't see to the false fronts on the other side. Shivering, she crossed. The silence was eerie. Here in the middle of the business district she saw only two people, who loomed up out of the white curtain and then disappeared before she could ask how far she was from Lincoln Avenue. Putting out her gloved hand, she felt for a door, assuring herself that it was silly to be afraid. All she had to do was go in somewhere and ask. But when she did find a door, it was locked. They'd closed. Had everyone closed and gone home?

At that point, hoping to feel her way to Finding's Hardware, the only stone building in town, Kat stumbled off into a cross street and knew she had to turn uphill and hope to make her way to Sean's house—two blocks up and half a block over. St. Gertrude's was even closer. Trudging blindly through the storm, she told herself again and again that she could hardly fail to negotiate such a short distance. People didn't freeze to death just a few blocks from their own houses. If nothing else, she'd hear Deiderick hammering and follow the sound.

But no, Deiderick, in this weather, would have quit for

the day. Kat was on the verge of panic when she heard a voice calling her name and cried hopefully, "Here. I'm here." A horse appeared out of the snow, almost brushing against her as the rider bent and lifted her up. "Who—"

"Connor," he said in her ear, and she collapsed against his chest.

"H-h-how did you know?" she quavered.

"Well, it wasn't because that damn Ingrid could say."

He sounded furious. Had he been so worried? As cold as she was, the thought warmed her. "The children—"

"Mine are in. Sean's are safe at Hildreth's. Myrna wouldn't send them home in snow like this." He shifted her to a more comfortable position and slapped the reins against his horse's neck. "You were the only one we couldn't account for, and fortunately that carpenter knew where you'd gone, but why the hell you'd walk to town when the sky—"

Kat burst into tears.

"Well, Kat." He tightened his arm around her. "Here now. Were you that scared?" When she failed to answer, he said consolingly, "We're almost home, girl. Stop crying."

Feeling the brief pressure of his face against the top of her head, she snuggled against him, so grateful that she was safe. Her sobs tapered off to sniffles before he reined in and slid her down—into a drift. Wondering if she'd be able to haul herself up the three feet to the door, Kat floundered toward the light of a coal-oil lamp shining behind her brother's window. Then Connor was behind her, pounding on the door, lifting her up when Sean opened it.

"Stupid German," Connor muttered. "The first thing he should have done was replace the stuff he knocked off."

"Thank God, you found her," said Sean, whisking her into the room.

Kat decided that this might be the only time Ingrid's parlor would ever look good to her. She glanced at it as she took off her mantle. It was the reddest room she'd ever seen—maroon wallpaper cluttered with tiny blue and white roses, a red and gold carpet, stiff red velvet and mahogany sofa and chairs, a piano and little tables draped with fringed red scarves, and lamps with blush silk shades. Sometimes Kat thought hell must look like Ingrid's parlor. But it was, at least, warm.

She smiled at Connor, who had climbed into the room behind her after putting up his horse. The room's lurid gloom turned his ginger hair as red as Jeannie's, and his face seemed flushed. Maybe it was. The lady of the house had just given him one of those slow, hot looks of hers. Kat scowled at her sister-in-law. Sean, who didn't seem to notice his wife's strange behavior, was tossing wood into the stove, which had a handsome winged knight's helmet decorating the top. Kat sighed and set herself to claim Connor's attention before Ingrid did something outrageous, like sitting on his lap.

"You can't move into a house with a man to whom you're not married," said Father Rhabanus.

"Now, Father," Kat murmured, feeling his hot forehead, "we'll soon have you on the train to Denver, where the bishop can see you to a comfortable, warm hospital bed."

"It's scandalous to even think of such a living arrangement," he replied stubbornly.

"Nonsense," said Kat. "Mr. Macleod is a fine man. Why, he's saved my life twice now."

"With evil intent, no doubt," said the priest. "Of what faith is he?"

"Actually, I'm not sure. I don't think he goes to church. Maybe I can convert him."

"He'll seduce you," muttered Father Rhabanus. "Mark my words."

"And his children. I'll certainly have to see that they're put in school with the sisters at St. Gertrude's."

"Roustabouts and adulterers," muttered Father Rhabanus.

"What?"

"He's talking about the congregation," said Father Eusebius hastily. "And it's most kind of you to bring us the chicken soup."

"Fornication," mumbled the older priest.

"I know how hard chickens are to get this time of year," said Father Eusebius.

" . . . even the appearance of sin . . ."

"Yes, it's easier to get beer than chicken," said Kat. "You must preach a sermon on the evils of drinking, Father."

"Well, we mustn't forget the miracle at Cana," said Father Eusebius.

"I'm sure if our Lord had thought about it, he'd have changed the water into chicken soup instead of wine," said Kat.

Father Eusebius stammered, "That's a—that's a peculiar idea, my daughter."

"Heresy," said Father Rhabanus clearly.

"I beg your pardon?" Kat frowned at him.

"Only a full confession and penance. Loose women and rowdies—all of them."

"Well, Father, Mr. Macleod will protect all of us in Sean's family from the rowdies, and as for heresy, I don't doubt that the Holy Mother would recommend chicken soup over wine. You obviously haven't seen anyone who died of drink. No one dies of chicken soup." Then she turned to the younger priest. "The sooner we get Father Rhabanus into a hospital, the better."

"Don't do it, child," said Father Rhabanus. "Chastity is the most godly of states."

"Saints preserve us," said Kat, now thoroughly peeved. "We're sharing a house, not a bed."

"What in the world is that carpenter doing?" asked a member of the Ladies' Altar Cloth Society.

"Building a corridor between the two houses," said Kat as

she passed the coffee cups. The three women were looking at Ingrid from the corners of their eyes, and not because Ingrid had said anything. She rarely did. Perhaps it was the perfume. Or Ingrid's garish taste in clothes and home decoration. "After Sean leaves, Mr. Macleod is going to look after us."

"You mean you'll be living together in the same house?" asked Mrs. Bent. "Unmarried?"

"Ingrid is married," said Kat impatiently, "and the rest of us are too young or disinclined." The ladies gasped. "Father Eusebius didn't object," Kat pointed out, neglecting to mention Father Rhabanus's tirade. "And speaking of Father Eusebius, we must all keep an eye on the poor man. He looked very sickly the day we sent Father Rhabanus off to Denver, and as you know, the sisters have their hands full."

Kat would probably have wept when she put Sean on the train to Denver if it hadn't been for Bridget. They'd hardly set foot in the depot when a young woman cried, "Oh, you must be Miss Kat. Oh, thank Jesus, Mary an' all the Saints," and she threw herself into Kat's arms. "I thought I'd got meself off at the wrong station for sure, an' me without a penny to me name an' waitin' here in this cold station, afeared to step outside into the snow." The girl was about Kat's height and weeping copiously on her shoulder.

"I'm Bridget," cried the girl when she noticed Kat's astonished face. "Bridget what your good mother sent all the way from Chicago for a husband that your letter said was ever so easy to find out here in the Wild West. I come because I'd as soon have a husband of me own as work at dustin' someone's fine furniture an' gittin' meself pinched by the master, as happened at least twice a week an' even on Sundays, the saints preserve us, so I had to quit me job, an' yer good mother found me wanderin' the streets, ever so cold an'—"

"Stop for breath, Bridget," said Sean, laughing so hard he brought on a coughing spell.

"You'd best see to that cough, sir," said Bridget. "Be you one of the bachelor men as Mrs. Fitzpatrick—"

"Not me," said Sean. "I'm her stepson."

"Well, faith, 'tis Mr. Sean then, bless you. You needna worry I'll not work me passage off afore I marry."

"We're supposed to pay for your ticket?" asked Kat.

"Your mother said jus' send her the money, so she kin send another poor workin' girl as needs a husband, an' I'm to help out until I get mine."

Thinking of how little Ingrid could be counted upon to do, if it didn't involve sleeping in the daytime and making love at night, Kat welcomed Bridget with enthusiasm, causing the girl to burst into tears once more.

"Well, sister," said Sean, "I doubt you counted on running a matrimonial service as well as my house and business, but you'll have no trouble finding her a husband. Ninety percent of the population is on the lookout for wives."

"Including me," muttered Kat, who envied men having wives to do the housework and cooking for them and to take care of the children. However, when Sean asked what she meant, she just smiled and kissed him good-bye, waved as the train to Denver pulled away, and then walked Bridget back to the house, getting the news of her mother and Chicago and all the other working girls who boarded with Maeve.

"Quite a parade we made goin' off to mass of a Sunday," said Bridget as they passed Bradley's Saloon on the corner of Main and Lincoln and then Engle Brothers' Saloon at the corner of Ridge and Lincoln. The town wouldn't make a very good impression on devout young Bridget, not with a saloon on every corner. Kat decided to point out St. Gertrude's as an antidote to Breckenridge's wilder side, but Bridget hadn't noticed any of it. She was still talking.

"Filled up three rows at mass, we did," she exclaimed.

"Yer mother's a saint. The Blessed Virgin alone knows what would have become of me, wanderin' the streets among all them seducers an' such, as yer good mother says."

"Yes indeed," said Kat, wondering how many Chicago girls her mother intended to ship west. "Do you cook, Bridget?"

Chapter Five

Kat dropped into the rocking chair beside the stove and closed her eyes, unable to think when she'd had a more trying day. The night before, she had joined the sisters at the hospital laundry for the first time and found it exhausting. How could they stand rising at two every Monday to wash hospital linen until dawn? Then, as she was about to stagger home at sunrise, Sister Adelaide asked her to check on Father Eusebius, who hadn't arrived the day before to conduct early mass at the sisters' chapel. As it was the third Sunday of the month, he should have been there—first and third Sundays were devoted to Breckenridge. Other Sundays he spent in other towns, weather permitting.

Kat found him shivering and wheezing in his bed with no idea what to do for himself, poor thing. On the chance that he had pneumonia, she used the beer-bottle treatment recommended by the ladies of the Altar Cloth Society. Although she was successful in breaking his fever by dint of outlining his body with hot beer bottles, her only thanks had been the priest's distress when she poured out his beer so she could fill the bottles with hot water. Father Eusebius wanted to drink the beer first, and Kat had been sadly disappointed in him for suggesting such a thing.

When she finally got home, it was to find that Ingrid had disappeared, leaving the children to Bridget. Kat sighed. What an afternoon it had been—Bridget talking without pause as always, the children clamoring for attention, the carpenter pounding nails into the door frame between the new corridor room and Sean's house—that and coming into the parlor every five minutes to stare at Kat. He said he had to keep track of her comings and goings lest she be lost in another storm.

And now that quiet had finally descended on the house, Ingrid was still away. Kat wondered if she should wade through the snow to Connor's door and ask that he find her sister-in-law. Before she could decide, he came in, demanding to know when the carpenter would finish.

"Tomorrow," said Kat.

"Well, thank God for that." He looked at her closely. "You all right?"

"Of course. Well, no," and she told him about her day.

"Two in the morning?" he exclaimed. "And you walked over to St. Joseph's by yourself at that hour?"

"Would you have wanted to escort me?" she retorted.

"No, I'd rather you stayed home like a sensible woman. Why the devil would they do their washing then?"

"I don't know. Maybe it's a penance. And I'm worried about Father Eusebius. I hope he was joking about the beer."

"Perhaps you should have let him drink it. It might have done him some good."

"My onion poultices did him good," said Kat with a frown. "And where's Ingrid? Should we go looking for her?"

Connor grunted and rose from the uncomfortable red

68

velvet chair in which he had sprawled. Kat's rocker, newly purchased, was the only sensible piece of furniture in the overcrowded room. "When Ingrid wants to come back, she'll come," said Connor.

"Well, that's a strange thing to say."

"Go to bed, little one. Your eyes are closing."

"Going to bed's no use," muttered Kat. "I'm sharing with Bridget, and she talks in her sleep." Kat had originally suggested that she and Ingrid share the bed, but Ingrid, looking huffy, had moved into the children's room.

Connor grinned. "It's not humanly possible to talk night and day for long. Bridget's bound to lose her voice."

Connor went off to bed, but Kat had one last chore, a letter to her mother.

"Breckenridge, February, 1887," she began and told of Bridget's safe arrival, Sean's departure for the sanatorium in Denver, the fifty-five dollar bank draft she was enclosing to pay for Bridget's fare from Chicago, which would be repaid at three dollars a day, the usual rate for working women in Colorado, and finally of Father Rhabanus's peculiar reaction to the household-sharing plan. "One would think Sean meant for Mr. Macleod and me to live in sin," Kat wrote, smiling. "Father Rhabanus must have been quite delirious from his fever."

Kat and Bridget had planned a celebration for the breaking through to Connor's house—a festive dinner in the corridor room, food to be cooked by Bridget and a delicious temperance beer purchased by Kat from Mr. Dave Braddock, who bottled it in a nearby town of the same name. Ingrid was to play the piano, which seemed to be her only talent, and Kat hoped that the party would meld the two families into one happy, if temporary unit. The sight of Jeannie Macleod scowling from the other side when the carpenter knocked out the last log pieces boded ill for Kat's plans.

Still, Kat nodded to Ingrid who, sporting a low-cut, bright blue gown and goose bumps, broke into a lively tune that Kat recognized from her evenings as an invisible saloonkeeper. No one else seemed to realize the inappropriate nature of Ingrid's choice. Maybe they didn't know the words. Before Kat could stop them, Phoebe and Sean Michael fell upon the feast without waiting for their elders. Sighing, Kat asked Connor and Mr. Eyeless if she could help them to refreshments.

"I ain't *Mr.* Eyeless," said the old miner. "I'm Eyeless Ben Waterson. See." He pointed to the black patch over his eye, and while Connor's children snickered, Eyeless Ben Waterson insisted on telling her, in minute and gory detail, how he had lost that eye to an angry bear while he was placer mining on the Blue in '59. Kat stood in spellbound horror through the whole shocking recitation.

Over by the door to Connor's side, the master of the house was struggling into a heavy coat and arguing with Otto Diederick, who responded stoically to everything Connor said, "I talk mit Missus about dat." Connor wanted to pay him for the last of his work, and Kat didn't see what the problem was; however, before she could find out, the man she had met on the street carrying a chicken poked his head in Sean's side of the corridor and said loudly, "No one answered my knock."

"Ya," said Diederick, "der needs ein door in here."

"Mr.—ah—" Kat searched her memory for the newcomer's name. "Mr. Bostich, won't you help yourself to some refreshment?" She waved hospitably toward the table that had been carried in from Sean's kitchen and covered with a linen tablecloth that had belonged to Connor's late wife.

Ingrid turned from the piano, which had been moved in from her dreadful parlor, and called, "Hello, Carl."

Her greeting displayed the most vivacity Kat had seen out of Ingrid in their whole acquaintance.

"I come to see if you changed your mind, ma'am," said Carl Bostich to Kat.

"About what?" asked Kat.

"About my offer. It's still open." He looked around at the bare wooden walls of the corridor room. "You ought to tack up some paper and cans on them walls. Why, you ain't even got a stove in here." He rebuttoned his jacket. "Well, as I was sayin', I'm foreman at the smelter. Maybe you didn't know that when you said no, Miz Fitzgerald. The job pays good money, and I wouldn't beat you."

"How very—ah—" Kat remembered now that he had offered for her hand. "But no, I'm afraid I really couldn't—"

"Won't ask a third time," warned Mr. Bostich.

"Have you met Bridget? Come and meet Mr. Bostich, Bridget."

Carl Bostich studied young Bridget with her turned-up, freckled nose and curly red hair. "I suppose you be Roman Catholic?" he muttered. Bridget nodded with a merry smile, and those were the last words Carl Bostich got in for the rest of the evening.

"Missus," said Otto Diederick, "you need ein door from dis room to der porch."

Kat thought about it.

"Maybe mit sidelights," he continued.

She nodded eagerly. "Stained glass sidelights," she suggested, hugging her cashmere shawl around her shoulders, for the corridor room *was* cold.

"Ya. I send for der glass unt, vaiting, maken ein fancy door."

"What's this?" Connor demanded. "He hasn't even insulated this room, and now he wants to cut a door and let in more cold air?" Connor buttoned his coat and pulled a muffler from his pocket. "And a door to what? There isn't any porch because he knocked it off."

"Now Connor, be fair. He knocked the porch off Sean's house. This room hadn't even been built when Mr. Diederick

71

was knocking off porches." Kat pictured the beauty of the stained glass sidelights. "Maybe we could have a fanlight *over* the door as well."

"What's all this going to cost?" Connor asked.

"Goodness, I don't know, but I can ask." Diederick had already moved back to the refreshment table. "Think of how beautiful it will be, Connor. Every time we look at the door, we'll see the glass, glowing like a cathedral window."

"I haven't said yes," Connor muttered, but he knew he couldn't refuse, not when her eyes were alight with wonder at the thought of the door.

"Daddy, can I leave now?" Jeannie asked. "I'm freezing."

"Put on a coat. Diederick just wants more money," Connor warned, turning back to Kat.

"Nonsense," said Kat. "Breckenridge could use a little fancying up. Some beautiful stained glass is just the thing." Then her conscience nudged her as she remembered the pitiful little church up the hill, and she added reluctantly, "Although if I'm going to spend Sean's money on stained glass, the church should have first call."

"Nothing could improve that church," said Connor.

"Dad-dy!"

Ingrid at the piano broke into a dance tune. Carl Bostich, possibly to keep warm, asked Bridget to dance, although Kat hoped the reason might be romantic.

"Daddy, I'm going to catch cold."

"Why don't you ask Jeannie to dance, Connor?" Kat suggested, smiling at father and daughter.

"I don't know how to dance," said Jeannie.

"No? Well, it's easy enough. I'll teach you."

Jeannie immediately began to scowl. *Dear me*, thought Kat. *She's going to be a hard one to win over.* "Well, if you don't want to dance with your father, Jeannie, I will."

"I don't dance anymore," Connor protested, but that night

72

he did, for the first time in years, while Otto Diederick and Jeannie scowled at them both.

"I don't like that carpenter," he muttered in Kat's ear.

"Why?" asked Kat, surprised. In Connor's arms she hardly noticed the cold.

Kat felt frazzled. Reliable Bridget was no longer available after dinner, and Ingrid was always asleep during the day, her children tagging after Aunt Kat, demanding stories and games, making messes that had to be cleaned up, giving Kat sticky kisses and hugs, which were lovely but interfered with the endless round of work that needed to be done for a household of nine people—along with Diederick, who often took his midday meal with the family, and Carl Bostich, who showed up every evening and hung around until invited to dinner, then whisked Bridget away before the dishes had been washed and dried.

Eyeless was in full retirement. He did nothing but sit in front of the kitchen fire telling stories of the old days to anyone who would listen, a pastime for which Kat never had the time. Bridget, on the other hand, was always willing to listen but insisted on telling a story of her own in return. The girl had more to say about her childhood in Ireland than Kat's mother, also an Irishwoman, had said in Kat's whole lifetime. Connor's children, no matter how hard Kat tried to make friends of them, hovered scowling and unhelpful on the fringes of the endless household activity, and Connor seemed to feel that he need not consult Kat about mining business now that she was busy in his house. The last straw came when Eyeless invited all his friends for a dinner party, and while preparations were afoot, Bridget announced her impending marriage.

"You can't," Kat wailed, for she hadn't got the hang of cooking here in Breckenridge. Things just never turned out right, although she couldn't understand why.

"Ah," said Bridget, "but Mister Bostich, me fiance, he

do plan to pay you every cent I owe for me tickets."

"It's not the money, Bridget," Kat groaned.

"Now, Miss Kathleen, you'll get along just fine, you will. Jeannie, she's a big girl and can help you, and I'm for marriage. 'Tis true love indeed I feel for Mr. Bostich."

Kat could have told Bridget a thing or two about true love but hadn't the heart. After all, her mother's purpose in sending Bridget to Colorado had been to find her a husband. So Eyeless's dinner party was postponed until after Bridget's wedding feast. Then the Bostiches departed for Dillon, the next major stop on the Denver, South Park & Pacific, for a two-day honeymoon, leaving Kat to endure Connor's teasing about her success as a matchmaker and Eyeless's endless changes of mind about the menu for his dinner party.

"Never had a dinner I didn't have to cook for myself," said Eyeless. "This here's gonna be a real pleasure. Now let's see. Maybe we oughta have beans insteada potatoes."

"Why not have both?" asked Kat dryly.

"Good idee. Beans, potatoes, venison—"

"I don't know how to cook venison," Kat objected.

"Ever'one knows how to cook venison."

"How many deer do you think were running around a city the size of Chicago?"

"Hundreds?" asked Eyeless.

"None," said Kat. "How about Irish stew?"

Eyeless glared at her. "No stew. But I want a big cake. Yep. An' then . . ."

Kat groaned, added cake ingredients to her list, and went off to the grocer's before Eyeless thought of anything else he wanted.

Kat would never have believed a group of men could make such a fuss about being served temperance beer. What had they expected? To get drunk in the parlor while she cooked for them? Now they were sitting around the scarred oak table, knives and forks in their fists, drinking Eyeless's whiskey and swapping yarns. Kat checked the potatoes in the oven, thinking it was lucky she had bought that fifty-pound bag the day of the gunfight and blizzard. Once again her grocer had plenty of beer to offer, but little food.

"Then the dang rat fuse hung fire," came Eyeless's voice from the table, "so I went back to see what happened, an' the dang giant powder blew up dang near under me."

Kat shuddered and turned the meat on the spit.

"Doctor didn't even have to amputate, just sewed up what was left of my leg."

Eyeless was telling another of those horrible stories about mining disasters. She checked the beans and found them bubbling satisfactorily.

"You'd probably be callin' me Pegleg if the grizzly hadn't got my eye."

"Twarn't a grizzly," said another of the old miners.

Kat glanced at the cake, which would go into the oven after the potatoes came out. She had forgotten the cake earlier because of an argument with Eyeless, who refused to hold his dinner party in the corridor room. "Our old bones cain't stand the cold in there," he'd said of his guests.

"I shot me a grizzly up on Indiana Creek," said another voice. Kat took it to belong to Brady Markham, a man who had made his living for years as a professional hunter. "Sold the meat for three cents a pound to that feller run the tavern up at Angel's Rest. They had 'em a grizzly barbecue. Course ever'one was so drunk afore the bar got cooked that Jerry, he coulda fed 'em buzzard an' they wouldna known the difference. Jerry Krigum was his name—somethin' like that. Always a party goin' at Angel's Rest."

Kat shook her head as the men guffawed. As far as she could see, the whole of Summit County had a drinking problem. She opened the oven door and poked a fork into one of the potatoes. Done, she decided, removing the potatoes and popping in her cake.

Kat served them a dinner that was truly a disaster. The beans were like stones, and Eyeless claimed to have broken a tooth on them. Then Brady Markham did break a tooth while chewing a bite of potato. He grunted, spat out the mouthful, and something pinged ominously on his plate. With his fork he poked, first the tooth fragment, then the other object. "You been shootin' at your potatoes, ma'am?" he asked.

Kat scowled at him, suspecting some joke she didn't understand. The object was passed from hand to hand. All the male guests agreed that she had served Brady the load from a cartridge, although there was lively dispute as to what type of gun the lead had come from.

"What say we take bets," said Brady. "I'll hold the money and take ten percent to pay the dentist."

"Ain't no way to settle it and find out who wins the bet," Eyeless objected.

"Why, Miz Kat only has to tell us what kinda gun she used to shoot the potato."

All the guests howled with laughter, slapping their knees. Kat, her chin raised defiantly, said, "I can't settle the matter, but you might ask the drunks from the Miner's Home Saloon who were shooting into the grocery store the day I bought these potatoes."

Connor shook his head. "I swear, Kat, I can think of no other woman who attracts odd happenings as you do."

"It's all the fault of drinking," said Kat resentfully. "If the saloons were closed—"

The horrified guests broke into a babble of protest, forgetting entirely the bullet-riddled potato and Brady Markham's tooth. Close the saloons? They'd never heard such an anti-social idea.

The last culinary disaster was the cake. Kat could have wept because her cake bubbled, filled the air during dinner with a delicious aroma, and then fell. All through dinner the guests reminisced about the old days and the superior cooking of Mrs. Silverthorne at the Silverthorne Hotel. The vinegar pies—what was a vinegar pie? Kat wondered resentfully; it sounded awful—the tasty biscuits . . . they went on and on, and at the same time that they praised Mrs. Silverthorne, they laughed about Kat's dinner.

"Easy to see you don't know nothin' about mountain cookin'," said Eyeless. "Didn't make a single adjustment for altitude, did you? Why even Jeannie here knows you gotta cook the beans longer—lots longer."

If they all knew, why hadn't they said anything? Kat managed to take the teasing calmly, but her temper flared when Connor mentioned a fine he'd had to pay for missing a meeting of the volunteer fire department. "All they did was finish a keg of beer and quarrel about Father Dyer using the fire bell," said Connor. "It's not as if I missed much."

"They drink beer in the firehouse?" asked Kat, appalled. "How can we expect protection if the firemen are drunk?" Kat remembered the terrible conflagration in Chicago in '71 when she was nine years old. "Something should be done to stop it."

"Well, Father Dyer would agree," said Connor. "Nothing he hates worse than drinking, unless its dancing, which we also do at the firehouse." He grinned. "And I know you approve of dancing, Kat."

"I like a drink now and then," said Ingrid.

"Me too, sweetheart," said Brady, the hunter, at whom Ingrid had been casting sloe-eyed glances. Ingrid's conduct made Kat very uneasy; her sister-in-law didn't act like a respectable married woman.

Connor, laughing, said, "I suppose you might make cause with John Dyer, Kat, but you'd have to give up dancing."

"It's not funny," said Kat. "Drinking is a great social evil."

"Well, don't tell me," Connor replied. "Your brother was more given to imbibing at the fire station than I."

Through the rest of dinner and the cake debacle, Kat worried about Sean. Could he have fallen into their father's dangerous ways? Was Sean's wife a drinker as well? And why was Ingrid rubbing her finger up and down that hunter's hand?

"Pity you're married, Ingrid," said Brady. "I could use me a pretty wife to keep me warm in my declinin' years."

Ingrid gave him a look that Kat found shockingly provocative.

"How about you, Miss Kat?"

Kat glanced with surprise at the hunter.

"Feel like marryin' the best shot 'tween here an' Denver? You'd never lack for game on your table, even now when what woods we got left are just about hunted out."

Since the men were all laughing, Kat took the proposal as another of their tasteless jokes.

"Give it some thought, Miss Kat," Eyeless advised. "Not many men Brady's age got a head of hair like his."

Brady Markham did indeed have a full head of long, flowing silvery hair and a handsome, weathered face, but his next remark didn't incline Kat to view him with any favor.

"'Sides bein' a handsome fella, I can cook. Be glad to teach you if you'll marry me," he offered. "An' I'll promise never to shoot up your potatoes."

"No, thank you," said Kat and rose, amid the guffaws, to collect the cake plates and coffee cups.

Several hours later, Connor found her in his kitchen surrounded by dirty dishes and pans. "Ingrid and Jeannie are already in bed," he remarked.

"Now, why doesn't that surprise me?" Kat kept her back turned so he wouldn't see her tears.

"And the guests have all gone."

"Still talking wistfully about the wonderful meals they

had at Mrs. Silverthorne's table and what a terrible one I subjected them to?"

Connor laughed. "Well, it wasn't really a wild success, but—Kat?" He turned her away from the sink. "Kat, it's nothing to cry about." He sounded surprised.

"You're right," she agreed, sniffing. "In fact, it would be funny—the bullet in the potato, the beans no one could chew—except that most of it need not have happened. Ingrid, Eyeless, Jeannie—any one of them could have warned me about the pitfalls of high-altitude cooking, but all they did was laugh."

Connor shifted uneasily. "Well, they didn't mean to be cruel. It was just—miner's humor, I guess. Nothing to cry about. Why don't you leave this mess and go to bed?"

Kat's lips tightened. She could imagine what her mother would say to leaving the kitchen in such a state. "Go to bed so I can clean it up tomorrow?" she asked bitterly. "Along with all the other chores I'll have?"

"Well, I'm sure the others will offer to—"

"No, they won't. Since Bridget left, nobody moves a finger around here but me—and I didn't come to Colorado to be anyone's maidservant." When he started to protest, Kat cut him off. "You're as bad as the rest, Connor. You're quite content to assign me your housework while you take over Sean's business."

"Well look, I thought—"

"And that's not what Sean meant to happen."

"Nobody's stopping you—"

"You haven't said one thing to me about business since the houses were connected and I got stuck with all the housework."

Kat watched the expressions flit across his face, waiting for him to explode with resentment because she wanted to intrude on territory he considered his own. Then to her surprise, he rested his hands lightly on her upper arms and said, "You're right. Starting tomorrow, I'll be keeping you abreast of Sean's interests. As for the house—"

"I'll take care of that," said Kat, feeling much more cheerful. "I find that I make a poor martyr, so tomorrow I'll get after the slackers."

"And tonight you'll get some sleep. You've three pairs of hands to command in the morning." He steered her firmly toward the parlor door that led to her side of the house. "I'd not want your brother to think I let my family make you miserable, Kat," he said, and he gazed at her so intently that Kat thought for a minute that he meant to kiss her. His hands on her arms tightened just a fraction before he turned away.

As she prepared for bed, she chided herself for such a foolish thought. Why would Connor Macleod be kissing her? Still, she dreamed of him that night.

The next morning Kat dragged her sister-in-law out of bed and, having made sure that the whole household was assembled at Connor's table, served the worst breakfast she could devise.

"This is disgusting," cried Jeannie, pushing away a bowl of lumpy, lukewarm oatmeal.

"You're quite right," said Kat. "I really am a dreadful cook, especially in Colorado, but isn't it fortunate that you and Eyeless and Ingrid all do know how to cook at these altitudes." Jeannie gave her a suspicious look. "Since Sean expects me to see to business, not spend my time cooking, you, Jeannie, can make breakfast from now on."

"I will not."

"Eyeless can do the midday meal and Ingrid the evening. Any future complaints should go to the cooks, not to me." Kat rose and dumped the detestable oatmeal from her bowl into Sean Michael's. He had been scooping it up and dropping it with an intriguing splat. Then she snatched up Phoebe's bowl as well and left the room.

Behind her there was a hubbub of protest.

"I won't," Jeannie repeated.

"Yes, you will," said Connor. "And there's a pile of dirty dishes from last night awaiting you and Ingrid." Ingrid, who had been half asleep, woke up. "Since neither of you lifted a hand on that dinner, it's only fair."

"Daddy," wailed Jeannie but subsided at the look she got from her father. "What about Jamie?" she mumbled.

"Jamie's going to chop wood, since the pile's low."

"Oh boy!" said Jamie. "Can I use the big axe?"

"Only on the woodpile," said his father dryly.

"Well, bein' as I taught Jeannie to cook, we'll be gettin' one decent meal a day," said Eyeless, smirking. "As for me, I'm retired. She'll have to find someone else for—"

"Remember the old cattle-camp rule, Eyeless?" Connor interrupted. "If you complain about the food, you have to do the cooking yourself. Well, you've been complaining."

"I haven't complained," said Ingrid, smiling at Connor.

"Those who don't help don't eat," said Kat, returning for more plates. She piled the rest in a tilting stack and headed back to the kitchen, saying, "I'm through for the day. You dishwashers better get busy, or there won't be any dishes to put Eyeless's noon meal on." She glanced over her shoulder in time to see Ingrid rise and head toward the door to Sean's house. "Ingrid," Kat said softly. "Remember, Sean left me in charge of the money."

Ingrid paused.

Chapter Six

"The door's going to be beautiful, Diederick," said Kat, standing back to admire the carved paneling as he hung the new door in the frame. "When will the glass arrive?"

"Soon," said the carpenter. He had built the frames for the side and fanlights, but without glass, the corridor room, which Kat had planned as a family gathering place, was too cold to use. "Now you need a porch, Missus."

"A porch?" With snow piled in six-foot drifts around the house, Kat couldn't work up any enthusiasm for a porch.

"Ya, along der whole front a der house. Long porch mit just vun steps in der center. I knock der stair off his place first." He gestured toward Connor's front door.

"Well, I don't know," said Kat dubiously.

"Forgot it, Diederick," said Connor, who had just drawn rein in front of the house. "I don't want a porch on my side."

"Von't look gut—half a porch," warned Diederick.

"Why don't you put up some—some barge boards," Kat

suggested. She remembered the beautiful scrollwork barge boards decorating the eaves of the Pacific Hotel in Como. "We can talk about a porch after the stained glass comes." Then, following Connor into his parlor, she called, "You haven't forgotten the sleigh ride?"

Kat felt she was making progress with Jeannie. First, she had talked the girl into a new dress. Then, insisting that a new dress deserved to be worn somewhere, Kat had nagged the whole family into attending afternoon Sunday school, Benediction, and a covered dish supper that followed. Ingrid had caused a minor scandal by flirting outrageously with someone's husband, but Jeannie had attracted the son of one of the Catholic families, who invited her to a sleigh ride. Kat remembered with amusement the argument that followed.

"She's too young," said Connor.

"I am not," said Jeannie, who hadn't been enthusiastic about the invitation until opposed.

"Nonsense," said Kat. "Jeannie's sixteen."

"But I don't care if I go or not," said Jeannie perversely.

"And she's the prettiest girl in town," Kat continued, noting Jeannie's startled surprise. "What are you going to do, Connor? Hide her in a wardrobe for the rest of her life?"

"She's too young to be walking out with boys. How do we know there'll be chaperones?"

"We'll chaperone the young people ourselves," said Kat with smiling enthusiasm. No amount of grumbling on Connor's part overcame her insistence that he had a fatherly duty to his pretty daughter. "And she'll need a new dress," said Kat when she had won.

"She can wear the new dress she just got. No one saw it because the church was so cold she couldn't take her coat off."

Kat glared at him.

"What's the matter? Are you going to tell me you'll need a new dress too?"

"Goodness no," said Kat. "Why would I? I'll just be with you, Connor. Unless you'd rather take Ingrid."

"God forbid."

Kat had been very pleased at that response. "We have to be at the church at six," she reminded him now.

"I haven't forgotten."

"No one's going to see my new dress *again*," Jeannie complained as she came into the parlor wearing the gown in question, a peacock blue wool with embroidered lace panels at the hem and an ivory lace collar and sash. "I have to wear my coat on the sleigh ride, and then these what-do-you-call-'ums will get crushed."

Kat eyed the overskirt, which draped from the waist in panniers over Jeannie's slender hips. "Turn around," she said, frowning. Jeannie had a point. The back, cascading over its bustle, would be even more vulnerable, given Jeannie's heavy wool, princess-line coat. "We'll have to see about a new coat," Kat decided. "Maybe a mantle that—"

"For goodness sake," snapped Connor. "The girl's sixteen. She doesn't need—"

"That's just when a girl does need a pretty wardrobe, Connor," said Kat, remembering that she herself had spent her girlhood wearing the prim uniforms of St. Scholastica. Couldn't Connor see that his daughter looked absolutely lovely? He should be proud. "And Jeannie, the dress looks wonderful on you. It brings out your eyes." Young Jeannie wasn't going to fall in love with the first handsome fellow who paid her attention. She'd have a chance to meet lots of boys and then make a *sensible* choice, some nice young teetotaler, thought Kat, nodding to herself. "And young Sam will see your dress when—"

"I don't care about him," Jeannie interrupted disdainfully, having turned pink at the mention of her eyes.

"—when we stop at St. Gertrude's for hot chocolate," finished Kat.

"We're going to a *nunnery* after the sleigh ride?" asked

Jeannie, horrified. "You didn't tell me that."

"Oh, you'll love the sisters," said Kat and fled through the corridor room before Jeannie could refuse to go. Kat herself would have been very disappointed to miss the sleigh ride and party. It was going to be such fun.

Connor, who had thought he'd feel like a fool, was enjoying himself. The night air was crisp and cold with the tang of wood smoke and pine sharp in his nose and a winter moon above him playing coy among silvered clouds. Snuggled at his side in the sleigh, Kat laughed and traded banter with the young folk.

When the other parental couple had remarked that they'd need to chaperone Kat and Connor, he had been offended. Now, with her soft body in the curve of his arm—for warmth's sake, of course—he wasn't so sure he didn't need a chaperone himself. On the other hand, Kat didn't seem to be overcome by his nearness. She'd just produced a snowball and thrown it at young Sam, Jeannie's beau, resulting in a tussle with much laughter and young men leaping from the sleigh to get their own snowballs, and Mr. Bagbaugh shouting, "Now children. Children, stop that." To no avail. The driver lost control of the horses, tipping the occupants of the sleigh into a snow bank.

"I take it that you're all right," said Connor, for his fellow chaperone was giggling like a schoolgirl. He raised himself on one elbow and looked down at her. "Kat, you are all right?"

Kat nodded, and in trying to pull herself to a sitting position, pulled him down instead. She felt, first, warm breath against her face and the brush of his cheek, then the warmth of his mouth. She hadn't been looking to be kissed and was taken by surprise—both by the kiss itself and by its nature—lovely, light, warm. His arm, which was beneath her, tightened as he pulled her against his chest. Even through their thick layers of winter clothing, his body felt good to her, solid and exciting, and the pressure of his lips spread heat through her veins. She had imagined being kissed by Connor and dismissed the idea, never having expected to feel this wonder, this amazing delight in his touch.

"Kat, I—" He'd taken his lips from hers and seemed as surprised as she that they should be lying in the snow kissing. "I don't know why I—"

"It's all right, Connor," she assured him, bemused. "I didn't mind, but with all the young people, perhaps we—"

"Oh, my god. Jeannie!" He struggled to his feet, horrified at the thought that if he, a sensible man of thirty-four, long widowed, should be making a fool of himself, God knew what his young daughter might be doing. However, before his imagination got further than the first spurt of fatherly panic, he found Jeannie helping the driver to calm the frightened horses.

"Don't look so worried, Daddy," she said. "I wasn't hurt."

"Good. Good," Connor mumbled, embarrassed at having suspected Jeannie of the very behavior for which he himself was guilty.

"Look, Kat, I—er—"

Connor didn't know what to say. It had been an unsettling evening. First, the kiss. Then after the sleigh ride, he'd been introduced to a gaggle of nuns, many of whom seemed to be personages from Kat's childhood, the kind of women who might accuse him of attempted seduction if they knew about that kiss. He'd been fed hot chocolate by the sisters and queried about his religious affiliation, something he never gave much thought to. Were they judging his suitability as a prospective husband for Kat? Surely she hadn't—but no, Kat wouldn't have mentioned the kiss to that formidable prioress, Hilda Walzen.

And once home, his daughter had given him a good-night

hug and said disdainfully, "That Sam's really *dumb!* He
didn't know *what* to do when the sleigh tipped over. *I* had
to help the driver," making Connor even more embarrassed
about his suspicions. And now a smiling Kat offered him a
cup of coffee as if she'd entirely forgotten that he'd kissed
her.

Well, the problem had to be addressed. "Kat, I don't
know how I could have—"

"Don't worry about it, Connor," she said gently, but her
smile had faded. "It was just a—a sort of—accident, don't
you think?"

"I guess so," Connor mumbled, a little hurt that she
considered it no more than an *accident*. The sleigh tipping
over had been an *accident*. The kiss, on the other hand—
well, what *had* it been? Dissatisfied with her easy dismissal
of his kiss, he watched her tripping off to her side of the
house.

But it had been a *nice* accident, Kat reflected as she let
herself into her icy bedroom. A pleasant accident. Although,
of course, they'd have to be careful that it didn't happen
again.

"He's stealing our workers," said Connor. "I'm not sure
how, but in the last six weeks at least ten men, good ones,
have moved from our mines to Trenton's."

"But why would Fleming do that?" asked Kat.

Connor shrugged. "The fewer people we have working,
the less ore we bring up, the less money we make, the less
we're able to sustain a protracted lawsuit. Labor trouble can
kill a mine."

"I don't suppose we can afford to pay more?"

"If we did, we'd cut into our profits, not to mention
bringing the other mine owners down on our backs."

"Don't our miners have any loyalty to us?"

"What miners have these days is resentment. Ten, twenty

87

years ago, a man had a chance to make his fortune mining. It didn't take a big investment to work a placer claim, but the surface stuff and the free gold are pretty much gone. Lode mining takes a considerable investment in equipment and payroll. It's corporations that are making the money, and the miners—they're just wage earners in a hard, dangerous business. They resent management."

"What if our living conditions in the dormitories were better?" asked Kat. "What if the food were better, if our mines were safer—"

"They are safer," said Connor, "safer than anything Fleming runs. As for the rest, I guess it's something we could try without starting a wage war."

"We should visit every mine. I'll investigate conditions and find ways to make their lives better."

Connor grinned. "Just having a pretty woman show up would improve their lives, but I don't think you know what you're volunteering for. The weather's bad. The mines are—"

"As Sean's representative, it's my duty to go." She put down a sock she had been knitting and rose to poke the fire. "Of course, Ingrid will have to take over the housework," she added.

"Ah. That's why you're so eager to leave town." Kat's startled look made Connor chuckle.

"Mother?" Kat had come out, bundled in an old paisley shawl, to give the new stained glass a quick cleaning. "Mother, is that you?" The sight of the little figure in black standing at the foot of the stair took her completely by surprise.

"Have you forgotten what your own mother looks like?" asked Maeve Fitzpatrick briskly.

"But what are you doing here?"

"Coming to rescue my daughter's reputation. What else would I be doing, Kathleen, when you write me that you're ignoring your priest and living, unmarried, with some stranger, endangering your good name and—"

"Mother, for heaven sake, Sean—"

"Your brother should be ashamed of himself for suggesting such an arrangement. Faith, I could hardly believe that my own stepson and the blood offspring of a fine woman like Kathleen Fitzpatrick, your father's sainted first wife, would suggest that you live in sin."

She paused to take an indignant breath, and Kat managed to protest that she wasn't living in sin.

Maeve sniffed. "I'm here to see that this situation comes to a stop immediately."

"Well, I don't see how the living arrangements can be mended now. As you can see, the houses have been joined."

"Then we'll just unjoin them."

"Say, Missus," called Diederick, his face appearing over the porch roof where he had been installing intricately scrolled barge boards along the eaves. "Say, Missus, I vas puttin' up dis porch, unt no one ist takin' it down."

"Who's that?" demanded Maeve.

"The carpenter," Kat replied, noting for the first time that two other women stood at the foot of the steps. "Can I help you?" she snapped. Whoever they were, they'd be spreading the word all over town that Kathleen Fitzgerald's own mother thought she was living in sin.

"They're here to help *you,* Kathleen—and to find husbands," added Maeve. "Hortense Kruger." She indicated a stocky woman in her forties. "And Mattie Law." The second was a young Negro woman. "Girls, this is my misguided daughter, Kathleen."

"I ain't a girl, an' I ain't here to marry," said Hortense.

"Mother," whispered Kat, "where am I supposed to put two women—three, counting you?"

"Well, I won't be staying long."

"Still—"

"You have a carpenter. Tell him to stop nailing up that

silly wooden filigree and build another room."

Diederick's head appeared upside down again. "I ain't got time now for another room."

"Don't argue with me, young man," snapped Maeve. Then sailing through the new door, she called over her shoulder to Kat, "I visited your brother, Kathleen. He seems to be improved. Now where are Phoebe and Sean Michael? I've a mind to see my dear departed Liam's grandchildren."

Kat was at her wit's end. Connor's house had a living room, a dining room, and a kitchen in front and three bedrooms off a hall that ran from the kitchen, but even with that bounty of rooms, Jamie and Eyeless shared the room next to the kitchen. Sean's house, however, was a square four-room structure with only two bedrooms. Ingrid already shared the room behind their kitchen with Phoebe and Sean Michael, and she didn't like the arrangement. Kat was now sharing the bedroom behind the red parlor, not to mention the bed, with her mother, which left no place for Hortense Kruger and Mattie Law. One couldn't, after all, stash them in one of the various barns and sheds out back.

With no easy solution in view, Kat had been tempted to run an ad in the *Leader* or the Summit County *Journal* for a bride auction. Unfortunately, there weren't, as far as Kat knew, any unmarried Catholic Negroes to bid on Mattie, and Hortense, a widow, insisted that she never wanted to marry again, a sentiment Kat could appreciate. The temporary solution was that Mattie slept on a pallet in Sean's crowded parlor, her head under the piano and her feet under the red velvet sofa. Hortense, to whom Eyeless had taken a surprising fancy, was sharing Jeannie's tiny room next to Connor's larger end room. Eyeless had gallantly insisted.

Jeannie complained bitterly, which didn't seem to bother Hortense, who was a gruff and hardy soul, but it bothered

Kat, who'd thought she was beginning to win Jeannie's friendship. No one could sleep in the corridor room. It was unheated, and the roof leaked. Seemingly determined to ignore Maeve's insistence that he build a new room, Diederick was fixing the leaky roof as Kat left in search of a partial solution to their housing problems.

Ten minutes later she was marching up to the door of the Barney Ford home. "Good morning, Mrs. Ford."

"And what can I do for you, Mrs. Fitzgerald?" asked Julia Ford after greeting Kat.

"Well." Kat shifted from one cold foot to the other. "I was wondering if you knew any eligible Negro men." Mrs. Ford looked so nonplussed that Kat stammered, "It's my mother, you see."

"Is your mother a Negro?" asked Julia Ford cautiously.

"No, Irish. She's—er, a rescuer of women in peril, and she rescued a young woman named Mattie Law, a Negro. From the railroad station in Chicago. Where she was being—er—beguiled by a man of—of dubious reputation."

"I see." Mrs. Ford didn't look as if she saw at all. Kat could only assume that Mrs. Ford had never been a young woman alone in the Chicago railroad station—or the Denver railroad station or possibly any railroad station.

"So Mother expects me to find Mattie a husband, and I don't know any eligible Negro men, so I thought maybe you—"

"There aren't that many in Breckenridge," said Mrs. Ford. "I'm always on the lookout for my own daughters. We've even had to entertain white suitors."

"Really." Kate found that interesting and wondered if white and colored people ever married one another. She sighed. "I don't even have a bed for Mattie, and goodness knows where I'd put one. Still, I can't have her sleeping on the floor while she works off her railroad passage doing housework."

"She's a maid?" Mrs. Ford's eyes lit up.

"Yes, and Mother brought Hortense too. Hortense is white, and Eyeless insisted—"

"I'll take the colored one," interrupted Mrs. Ford. "How much do I owe you for the railroad tickets?"

Goodness, thought Kat, *if people are that anxious for domestic help, I could probably get a finder's fee for*—but of course, Mother would be horrified at the idea of profiting off her working girls. Maeve only charged enough in the boarding houses to cover costs and her own living expenses. After thanking Mrs. Ford, Kat set out for home, wondering how long her mother planned to stay. Maeve Fitzpatrick had absolutely forbidden Kat to travel around the county visiting mines with Connor. They'd end up with no mine workers at all if her mother stayed long.

Connor had returned to the house for his daily business discussion with Kat, an occasion he had come to look forward to. Instead, he found Maeve Fitzpatrick awaiting him. How much like her daughter she looked—another tiny woman but without Kat's rounded curves. She had the same black hair, although Maeve's was straight and tinged with gray, and the same large eyes fringed with black lashes— but Maeve's were gray, not the clear, sweet green of Kat's. Still, their faces were so alike that they might be sisters. He doubted that Kat's mother was much over forty, and she looked younger if you discounted that glint of mature determination in her eyes.

"Where's Kat?" he asked uneasily.

"She's off to find a husband for Mattie," Maeve replied.

"What, the Negro girl? Well, we'd best not wait dinner on Kat's return. Colored are as scarce in Breckenridge as roses in a snow bank. She may have to go all the way to Denver for a black bachelor."

"I'm very glad of this opportunity to talk to you alone, Mr. Macleod," said Maeve, ignoring what she took to be facetious remarks.

92

"Oh?" Having already had Sean suggest that he marry Kat, he hoped he wasn't about to receive another such offer.

"My Kathleen, as I'm sure you've noticed, is a flighty girl. Cheerful, hard working, but . . ."

Except for her verbal attack on the train robbers, Connor wouldn't have labeled Kat flighty.

"She has failed to realize the social consequences of the situation in which she finds herself."

"What social consequences?"

"Scandal. What do you think people are saying about the two of you living together?"

Connor looked astonished. "There's nothing between your daughter and me." He felt a slight twinge of conscience. There had been that kiss, but as Kat had said, it was just an accident, not a harbinger of unbridled lust. "What the devil could they say? There are eleven people living here. How many chaperones could anyone ask for?"

"I didn't say *I* thought anything was amiss," said Maeve Fitzpatrick stiffly, "but tongues will wag, Mr. Macleod, and I do not want my daughter's precious good name—"

"She's sleeping with you, madam, not me," said Connor, "and she's living in my house because her brother thought she'd be safer if she had a man's protection. Breckenridge isn't some staid New England village, you know. It's a rough mining town, so until Sean changes his mind, I intend to honor my promise." Connor stalked out.

A strong man, Maeve murmured to herself approvingly. Perhaps he wasn't like the majority of the male sex, most of whom were vile seducers of innocent women. Still, she'd keep a sharp eye on the two of them. She well remembered Kat's sudden and inexplicable passion for Mickey Fitzgerald, God rot his soul. And Liam—welcoming Mickey into the family because of his surname.

"A good Norman-Irish name is Fitzgerald," Liam had

said with satisfaction. "Just like me own. The boyo's none of your potato-eating bog Irish."

And what had Liam thought *she* was? Maeve had wondered at the time. O'Fallon, *her* name, wasn't one of your fine Norman Fitz-thises or Fitz-thats. But, God rest their souls, they were dead and gone, both Liam and Mickey. She shouldn't be thinking ill of the dead.

Maeve tramped outside and instructed that foolish carpenter to stop tacking up useless decorations on the porch and get started on a new room. *Germans!* she thought as she went back inside to check on Hortense, another one who was always so sure she knew what was best. A stubborn lot, they were, Germans. And blond. Maeve had always been suspicious of blonds. Ingrid was a case in point. If ever a woman had the makings of a harlot—well, Sean had made a poor choice there.

Having changed Hortense's dinner menu, Maeve routed Ingrid out of bed and set her to mending the babies' clothes. What sort of mother let four- and five-year-olds traipse about a cold house with holes in the elbows of their blouses? It was a wonder the little ones didn't have pneumonia. "Come, Sean Michael. Sit on Grandma's lap. I've a fine prayer to teach you."

"What's a prayer, Grandma?" asked Phoebe.

"A heathen as well as a harlot," Maeve muttered. And what would herself among the saints in heaven be thinking now that her only son has married himself such a woman? Maeve always thought of Liam's first wife as a saint, for Kathleen Fitzpatrick, before the onset of her fatal illness, had taken Maeve in when she was a frightened fourteen-year-old, alone in a strange country.

"If Mattie can sleep on a pallet, I don't see why Hortense can't," said Jeannie.

"Mattie's gone to live with the Fords." Kat watched

Connor's mouth quirk and slanted him a questioning look.

"Has Julia found her a husband?" he murmured.

"Julia has found herself a maid."

"Better than marryin'," muttered Hortense, thumping a large bowl of stew and dumplings down on the table.

"As fine a cook as you are, Hortense," said Eyeless, "I hope you never leave us."

"Well, I for one hope Hortense gets married tomorrow," said Jeannie, "since no one seems to care whether I ever get my bedroom back."

Eyeless glared at Jeannie. Hortense muttered, "Don't hold your breath for my marriage, missy." Maeve said, "Oh, you'll change your mind, Hortense, when we've found you a good, steady man." And Kat said, "Diederick's going to build another room, Jeannie."

"Another room?" Connor scowled. "How long am I supposed to support him?"

"I'm paying for the room," said Kat.

"Working girls should have their own rooms," said Maeve. "It's only charitable."

"What about daughters?" asked Jeannie as Hortense brought in a plate of biscuits and announced, "I'm no charity case, and I'm no girl neither."

"But you're a fine figger of a woman," said Eyeless.

"Daughters should make themselves more useful and complain less," said Maeve to Jeannie. "Sean Michael, did I just see you throw a biscuit at your sister?"

"It slipped, Grandma," said Sean Michael.

"The road to hell is paved with slips, my boy," said Maeve. "Now Kathleen, by way of making yourself useful, I hope you realize that your duty to these young women extends beyond finding them suitable husbands." She ignored Hortense's angry banging in the kitchen. "You must also see that they are properly fed and clothed, properly chaperoned in their courtships, and that they go to mass regularly."

"Yes, Mother," said Kat, stifling a giggle because she had caught the look of suppressed laughter on Connor's face.

"You did see that Bridget went to church?" asked Maeve.

"Yes, Mother. We went the one Sunday we could wade there through the snow."

"One!" cried Maeve. "You've only been to mass once?"

"The priests can't always get there either, Mother, and they only offer masses in Breckenridge on first and third Sundays because they've other towns to visit. Besides that, the church is unheated and the rectory almost as bad, so they're often sick. Father Rhabanus is still in Denver in the hospital, and Father Eusebius had pneumonia."

"One mass?" Maeve shook her head. "What kind of heathen place is this?"

"A right snowy one, ma'am," said Eyeless, "and if you papists wanted folk to come to church, you shouldn't a put your church up the hill where no one can get to it."

"Well then, Kathleen, you must hold prayers for the girls here at home. Now about Bridget. I hope there was no scandal attached to her courtship and marriage. I was most unhappy to hear she had married out of the faith. You'll simply have to do better for Hortense and Coleen."

"Who's Coleen?" demanded Jeannie. "And whoever she is, she's not sleeping in my room."

"And I'm not marrying anyone, in or out of the faith," said Hortense, who had finally taken her own chair.

Maeve leaned across the table and slapped Jamie's hand when he reached for the dumplings with his fingers. "Use the ladle, young man," she said, "and wait for grace." Jamie scowled. Kat's mother then said grace and launched into a discussion of the discrimination suffered by older working women in Chicago.

"Although they are more experienced and better workers, older women either lose their jobs because of their age, or they're paid less," said Maeve disapprovingly.

"Same with us old miners," said Eyeless. "Not that anyone could say *you're* old, Miz Hortense."

"If all old miners are missing eyes and limbs, Mr. Waterson," said Maeve, "it's not surprising you lose your jobs. My advice to miners would be to find another line of work before your profession maims you."

"Have you been talking to my employees?" asked Connor.

"I do not want to hear another word about your labor troubles, Mr. Macleod," said Maeve. "My daughter is not going off with you on an unchaperoned trip to various rowdy mining camps. The late Mr. Fitzpatrick would turn over in his grave if he knew what you were proposing."

Connor wondered whether the late Mr. Fitzpatrick might have died, not of a liver complaint, but from the strain of living with such a strong-minded wife. On the other hand, Sean had said his father was the world's most hard-headed man. What a marriage that must have been!

"You still haven't said who Coleen is, Mother."

"Or where she's going to sleep," added Jeannie.

"Coleen is a fine, devout girl who'll be coming to Colorado as soon as she finishes a religious retreat with the sisters of St. Scholastica."

"You mean she's a *nun?*" asked Jeannie, horrified. "We're going to have a *nun* for a maid?"

"Well, Kat, for a woman opposed to love and marriage, don't you find your new role as matchmaker to half the female population of Chicago somewhat ironic?" murmured Connor during the one interval after dinner when Maeve didn't have her sharp eye on them.

Kat grinned. "I don't know about ironic, but I'm certainly uncomfortable with Mother's expectations. How am I supposed to marry off Hortense? She doesn't even want to find a husband."

"I wouldn't work too hard at it," Connor advised. "If

you find her a husband, you'll be back to parceling out the household chores to Jeannie, Eyeless, and Ingrid."

"Where *was* Ingrid tonight? We have so many people at the table these days that I didn't notice she was missing."

Chapter Seven

"Charlie, what the hell are you doing here in the middle of the afternoon?" Connor demanded.

"Well—ah—I was explaining new developments in the case to Miss Kathleen."

"What new developments? Fleming's stalling."

"And apex law. I was explaining about—"

"You've already done that."

"Goodness, Connor, don't be so inhospitable. It's not as if we're alone in the house conducting some—some rendezvous." Kat giggled at the idea. "The house is full of people."

"I don't see any."

"Well, just check the rooms. Mother and the children are taking naps. Hortense and Eyeless are in your kitchen swapping recipes. Jeannie's sulking in her room. Jamie—goodness, I don't know why I have to defend myself to you. Mr. Maxell comes at least once a week to keep me abreast of developments in the case."

"He *what?*"

"Well, I guess I'll be going," said Charlie Maxell. "Miss Kathleen can tell you—ah—"

"About apex law?" suggested Connor sarcastically as Charlie grabbed his coat and fled.

"Well, of all the rude—"

"Now you listen to me, Kat. I don't want you having private afternoon *tête-à-tête*'s with Charlie. It's bad enough he's forgoing his fee because he's smitten with you."

"He's no such thing. Whatever gave you that idea?"

"Any idiot can see—"

"Then any idiot would be wrong, and it's no business of yours anyway."

"Sean would expect me to protect your reputation."

"Nonsense! If you're worried about my reputation, you wouldn't have invited me to live in your house."

"I didn't. Sean invited you. I just said yes because he's my friend." Then Connor felt terrible because she looked so stricken. "Listen, Kat, I didn't mean—"

"What in the world are you two children quarreling about?" asked Maeve, who had been awakened by their argument.

"Nothing," said Connor and stalked out.

"Of all the dreadful men," Kat muttered, unwilling to admit, even to herself, how much he'd hurt her feelings.

"Why Kathleen, Connor's a fine man. I hope you haven't been sharpening that quick tongue of yours on him."

"Since when are you so concerned about Connor Macleod, Mother? I thought you took him for a seducer of helpless widows."

"Well, I believe I misjudged Connor. I find him, on further acquaintance, to be a solid, sensible man, the kind to keep food on the table."

"What he is is rude and bad tempered."

"He's just jealous, Kathleen."

"Of what? Charlie Maxell's my lawyer, not my suitor,

and why would Connor be jealous? That would imply
that he has some—some romantic interest in me, and you
can just stop smiling like that, Mother, because Connor
Macleod is not in love with me." *Is he? Of course, he
isn't,* she told herself hastily. "And if you've any idea of
my remarrying, you're wasting your time."

"Now Kathleen, a woman needs a husband. Your mistake
was in marrying for love. Marriage is not about love; it's
about security. Take your father—"

"My father was a drinker!" exclaimed Kat.

"That may be," said Maeve, "but we never went hungry,
and he left us well provided for. Could I be carrying on my
good work if it weren't for your father's money? Maybe you
think I was mad in love when I married Liam Fitzpatrick
after Sean's sainted mother died, God rest her soul. She
told me on her deathbed, 'Take Mr. Fitzpatrick, Maeve,
and you'll never go hungry,' and I never did. Nor did you.
I always tell my girls, look for a man who'll keep food on
the table; love is for ninnies and rich folk."

"Well, neither Connor nor I have a mind to marry, so
you may as well give it up, Mother."

"Ah, well," said Maeve, "who knows what's in Connor's
mind, fine man that he is. I doubt not he'll come to have a
care for your reputation, my girl, even if you don't. Now
who have you found for Hortense?"

"Hortense doesn't want to marry either."

"I guess I'll just have to look out a husband for her
myself. You'd best give a party, Kathleen. We can say
it's to introduce your mother to the good Catholics of the
town."

Remembering Father Rhabanus muttering about his
congregation of roustabouts and loose women, Kat had
to stifle a giggle. Mother would be fair shocked to meet
the unsifted Catholic population of the area. Still, there
were fifteen Catholic families Kat could invite and a few
respectable bachelors.

*   *   *

"Yer mother, Missus, ist eine devil voman," said Diederick. "She don't let me eat mit der family no more." He looked as if he might cry. "Unt yesterday she say I better builden dat room or . . ."

Kat closed her ears to Diederick's complaints. Maeve might be hard on him, but he hadn't started on the extra room he'd been told to build. "Never mind about that, Diederick," Kat broke in. "I want you to install a flue through the ceiling of the corridor."

"Dat room ain't finished. Vould taken me days to make it so der kalt don't come trew der valls."

"Well . . ." Kat thought about it. "Well, we'll have a party, and everyone can tack up newspapers and tin cans, and then we'll put up wallpaper and dance."

"I ain't never heard of a vallpaper party."

"There are quilting parties and barn-raising parties," said Kat, "so why not a wallpaper party? Anyway, my mother's set on it, Diederick. I promise she won't come around and scare you if you'll just put in the flue." What a big blond booby he was—afraid of a woman half his size and twice his age.

"Vell, I don't know—"

"Of course, I could get another carpenter."

Diederick, looking hurt, agreed, much to Kat's relief. She wasn't sure she could find another carpenter who would work in this weather.

"That young fool still hasn't started on the new room," fumed Maeve.

"I know, Mother, but he's putting a flue in the corridor room so we can have the party. Now you and I must pick out wallpaper and a new stove."

"What's Connor going to think of your spendthrift ways, Kathleen? You'll never win him if—"

"I'm not looking to win him, Mother, and Sean can afford

a stove and wallpaper. I saw some fine-looking stoves down at Finding's Hardware. They're black with handsome brass fittings. Do come and help me choose."

Grudgingly, Maeve put on her coat and bonnet, but she shouted, "Get to work, you," at Diederick when she caught him peeking out as she and Kat left the house. "Trust a German to be standing about gaping when he's supposed to be putting in your flue," she muttered.

"He's terrified of you, Mother."

"Good thing. The boy's slower than a spavined nag."

"If you wanted to lose a leg, son," said Eyeless, "I coulda got you a rat-tailed fuse an' some giant powder. Do a lot better job of blowin' it off than a gun." He and Kat were attempting to stem the flow of blood from Jamie's thigh while Jeannie ran for the doctor and her father.

"Did someone shoot you, Jamie?" asked Kat, dropping a kiss on his sweaty forehead. "If some drunken saloon patron shot you, I'll have Sheriff Iliff arrest him."

"I shot myself," admitted Jamie, flushing.

"And maybe you'd like to explain where you got the gun." Connor loomed in the doorway, scowling at his son while Jeannie rushed to her brother's bedside.

"Connor," Kat protested, "the poor child's—" Connor's angry look silenced her.

"It was your gun, Papa," Jamie mumbled.

"And what were you doing with it?"

"Playing gunfighter."

Connor stared at his son until the boy turned bright red. "Of all the jackass tricks, that has to be the stupidest. Obviously, I need to find something to keep you busy, boy, or you'll not live the year out."

"Why isn't he in school?" asked Maeve, who had just come in, cheeks pink with the cold. "Why aren't any of these children in school? Do you and Kat aim to raise a gaggle of illiterates?"

"No school during the heavy snow months," said Connor brusquely. "It's too hard for the children to get there."

"Nonsense," said Maeve. "The sisters are holding school at St. Gertrude's. I've just come from there."

"You want us to go to school with nuns?" gasped Jamie.

"What a good idea," said Kat, who'd been too busy to implement her own plans for enrolling the children at St. Gertrude's. "They might even take the little ones."

"I'm not going to St. Gertrude's," said Jeannie, who, glancing nervously at Maeve, tried to edge toward the door. However, with six people in the tiny bedroom as well as two beds, a scarred, straight-backed chair from some long-defunct dining room set, and wall shelves that held the clothing and possessions of Jamie and Eyeless, she couldn't escape.

"We've had fifteen party acceptances so far, Kathleen, not counting the sisters and Father Eusebius," said Maeve, "and no doubt there'll be many more."

"And I've found a fiddler," Kat replied, neglecting to tell her mother that the rest of the Catholic residents might not know how to behave themselves and, therefore, hadn't been invited. A change in the direction of the conversation was in order. "What a shame you shot yourself and won't be able to dance, Jamie. The little McNaught girl will be devastated."

"She will?" asked Jamie eagerly, then amended his enthusiasm to say, "Well, I don't care."

"Here's the doctor. What'da ya think, Doc?" asked Eyeless. "Think we'll have to amputate?"

The doctor squeezed between Maeve and Connor, skirted Jeannie and boomed cheerfully, "Could be. Could be. Best get hold of that carpenter. He's handy with a saw."

Jamie went pale, and Kat said quickly, "Don't you worry, dear. No one's going to cut off your leg." Jamie gave her a look of such gratitude that she glared at the doctor and Eyeless. *Western humor, indeed!* she thought and patted

Jamie's shoulder. "But if I ever catch you with a gun again, I'll fix all your meals myself for the next four years. Did I ever tell you about the time I poisoned all the sisters at St. Scholastica with a pudding?"

Jamie grinned weakly. "Gee, Kat, if I promise to give up fast-draw practice, will you promise to give up cooking?"

Diederick had at last finished installing the flue, and the new stove made it possible for Kat to pull her rocking chair into the corridor room and spend a quiet moment knitting and admiring the stained-glass windows. Sean's children had followed her and were improvising a game with pebbles and pine cones. Kat sighed and rocked and thought of the three additional people now living in the house. Long expected, Coleen O'Shaunnessy had arrived, fresh from her retreat at St. Scholastica, a pale girl—pale skin, pale hair, pale, timid eyes. She'd been fired from her job as a maid in Chicago because she spent too much time praying. Unheralded, Jilly Nevin arrived with her, a young woman as vivid and giggling as Coleen was pale and quiet. And hot on their heels, Connor's father came to town.

Kat shook her head in amazement, unable to believe that the two were father and son, for James Connor Macleod, Senior, was a will o' the wisp, an itinerant photographer, smaller and slighter of build than Connor with the same thick hair, but James's was red with strands of gray. The children all adored him, for he was a teller of tales, a singer of merry songs. Sean Michael and Phoebe would have been tagging at his heels this moment if he weren't out of the house. Even Kat's mother seemed to like James, who had blown into their lives like a traveling show, exclaiming within minutes of arrival, "And who, my boy, is this beautiful young lady?"

"This is Maeve Fitzpatrick, Kat's mother," said Connor dryly. "Maeve, my father, James."

"Mother of a grown daughter? Surely not." And James

105

had kissed Maeve's hand, causing her to blush, something Kat had never seen her mother do. They were off this moment exchanging the sedate wallpaper Kat and her mother had chosen several days earlier. The invited guests had been surprised enough at the idea of a wallpaper party—although reassured when they heard about the fiddler and the feast and dancing to follow. The blessed saints knew what they would think when they saw the wallpaper James picked out. Kat expected minstrel figures or Arabs riding camels across the walls around her prized stained-glass windows.

And Jeannie was still sulking because she couldn't invite her Protestant friends. "We'll have lots of parties when you *can* invite your friends," Kat had promised, "and you'll get to wear your beautiful new dress again." Kat herself intended to have a gown made up for the party. "But, Jeannie, Mother would never forgive me if one of the girls fell in love with a Protestant." Kat shuddered at the thought. She got a lecture every night as they retired about her lax supervision, which had allowed Bridget to be plucked off the Fitzpatrick matrimonial vine by Mr. Bostich.

Problems seemed to multiply. Jeannie hadn't understood at all about the dangers inherent in disappointing Maeve, and poor Jamie got out of bed much sooner than he should have—all because he wanted to dance with the little McNaught girl, not that he'd admit it. He said he didn't want to miss the fun of flattening tin cans and nailing them to the walls of the room-between.

"Oh, Miss Kat." Jilly came running in and hid playfully behind Kat's chair while a gangling boy, carrying a box of groceries, stopped bashfully in the doorway when he saw Kat. "This is Jimmy Don. He's delivering your order, Miss Kat." Jilly sprang from behind the rocking chair and disappeared into Connor's parlor with Jimmy Don in hot pursuit, but not before, giggling, she said, "I invited him to the wallpaper party."

"Jilly," Kat shouted, frightening the two children at her feet.

Chastened, Jilly reappeared. "Yes, mum?"

Kat beckoned her over and whispered, "Is he Catholic?"

"Oh yes, mum. Would I be so foolish as to offend Mrs. Fitzpatrick?"

"No, I don't suppose so," Kat muttered. Just seconds later, she could hear Jilly and the grocery boy giggling as they put away Kat's order. Kat supposed her mother would expect her to hop up and chaperone them, but with any luck Hortense was in Connor's kitchen to look unfavorably upon young romance. Kat's kitchen—she no longer thought of it as Ingrid's—had been fitted out with two beds and a small tin bathing tub and converted into a room for Jilly and Coleen and a place for everyone to wash. The men and boys got it for one hour each day, females the rest of the time when its occupants weren't sleeping. And Diederick was still managing to avoid building an extra bedroom. He insisted that they needed a second outhouse, a point of view with which everyone but Maeve agreed.

Kat heard the door open and close and looked up as her mother said, "Get on with you, James Macleod. You've a wicked tongue. And you've still not said what your faith might be."

"Dearest Maeve, my faith is in the beauty of God's creation, of which the most beautiful part is a pretty woman like yourself."

Kat rolled her eyes and rose as Phoebe and Sean Michael went tumbling over to beg for a story from their surrogate grandfather. She put away her knitting, eager to see what wallpaper had been chosen by Connor's father. Connor himself was out of town. He'd left to make a mine tour only two days after James began sharing his room and bed, and now Kat was beginning to wonder if he'd be back in time for the wallpaper party. Somehow the festivities didn't promise as much fun if Connor wasn't in attendance—

although he claimed not to like dancing, so why should she care?

"Do look at the paper we've chosen, Kathleen," said Maeve.

No camels, thought Kat with relief. In fact, it was quite pretty, dark green with white dots and a tracery of vines. Not a speck of red in it.

"Come lass, did you think I'd bring home something terrible?" asked James, his eyes twinkling.

Kat glanced at him warily. How had he known that? Then she began to laugh. Connor's father really was a dear, even if he didn't seem the kind of man Maeve would recommend. Kat knew that James had been off on one photographic expedition or another all during Connor's childhood, leaving Connor in New York with his mother. When the mother died, Connor's education ended because James had returned and whisked him off to Colorado. What a strange, unsettled childhood to have produced such a steady man as Connor.

"I think it's a fine-looking paper," Maeve was saying with satisfaction.

"How could it be otherwise with two such artistic folk as us choosing it," James replied.

"Oh, get on with you. Me? Artistic?"

Kat stared at her mother. There seemed to be a different soul inhabiting that little body, but just as Kat had the thought, Maeve caught sight of the grocery boy and asked suspiciously, "Who's that? Is he Catholic?"

"So Jilly says," Kat replied.

"And who's been chaperoning them?"

James roared with laughter. "Who's been chaperoning us, Maeve?"

Maeve looked at him with blank astonishment. "I don't need a chaperone," she replied. "I *am* a chaperone. I've twenty-three girls back in Chicago who can tell you so."

* * *

Kat's party was a great success. Not only did everyone she invited arrive, but dozens of people she hadn't came as well, some claiming to be Roman Catholics, some who just assumed they'd be welcome because the party was at Connor's house. Maeve soon recovered from the shock of having to entertain Protestants; she was so busy plying Father Eusebius and the Benedictine sisters with refreshment during the brief time they stayed, giving orders to the insulators and wallpapers in the corridor, introducing her three chicks to every eligible Roman Catholic, keeping Ingrid busy at the piano, and later dancing with James and other admirers that she didn't have time to complain about the presence of non-Catholics.

The finishing of the room-between turned into a contest. All the guests brought tin cans and newspaper for the job. Boys amused themselves stomping on the cans; men competed to see who could nail up the most cans and tack up the most newspaper. The layer of makeshift insulation grew so thick that the room actually felt comfortable for the first time, and Kat anticipated that the two families would gather there if for no other reason than that it was the warmest place in Breckenridge. Then, while the ladies gossiped in the parlors to either side, the male guests put up the wallpaper and moved in Ingrid's piano, after which the ladies returned to admire the effect and exclaim over James's inspired good taste. They even asked Kat who her carpenter was, having admired her barge boards as they came in.

The women also brought enough food to cover Connor's dining-room table and crowd his kitchen, although Kate had not asked them to. Still, she was touched and relieved. Maybe they'd known how many uninvited guests would turn up—most of them male. Kat herself had so many dancing partners she hardly had time to check on the food and Ingrid. Maeve's protégés were in great demand as well, although Coleen responded to friendly gentlemen by fleeing as if they had sprouted horns, tails, and cloven hooves. Hortense thawed enough to accept invitations to dance, but she didn't put up with marriage proposals. Dark-haired Jilly danced at least twice with every man under thirty, giggling continuously. Kat caught her hugging and kissing some fellow, not the grocery boy, by the sink and said repressively, "I believe my mother is on the way in, Jilly." Jilly looked understandably terrified.

The young man, Kestrel McHale of a million freckles, mumbled, "My intentions are honorable, ma'am."

"I believe it," Kat replied, having received several marriage proposals herself that night. "But you and Jilly will have to talk to my mother."

"I never said yes," protested Jilly.

"Then don't be kissing him," said Kat. Lord, but she hated her responsibilities as a chaperone!

Still, it would have been a wonderful party if Connor had come. If she were honest about it, she'd commissioned the new slate-blue dress with its jet buttons and graceful waterfall draperies so she'd look pretty for him—and because she hoped the subdued color would placate Maeve, who thought Kat should still wear mourning for Liam and even Mickey, who had died four years ago. Kat hated black. She liked colors that were bright and gay and wished Connor could see her in a rich green or—but why was she thinking of him? He hadn't even returned for the party and didn't deserve the least consideration.

Later in the evening she stopped dancing, having discovered that all her partners compared unfavorably with Connor; they weren't as smart, or as interesting to talk to, or as attractive—actually, Kat thought Connor was handsome. Her mother didn't agree. Maeve declared that James was much the better looking of the two, but Kat couldn't see that at all. Connor had that lovely hair with only a hint of red in it, while James—but goodness, why was she still thinking of Connor, who couldn't be bothered to get back for her party. She dumped another pile of dishes into hot water, having taken on kitchen duty because there was still food and guests were still eating.

"Where's Ingrid?" Maeve demanded from the door.

"I don't know, Mother. Isn't she playing the piano?"

"She disappeared while I was saying good-bye to the McNaughts."

"Well, Jamie will be sad to see their little girl go home."

"No, I won't." Jamie had limped in to help himself to a piece from a cake that had not yet been served. "Just 'cause I danced with her doesn't mean I *like* her."

"Of course, you don't," Kat agreed. He had danced every other dance with the girl once there were no more tin cans to stomp. "Is your sister having a good time?"

"Course. She's got three boys from Braddock dogging her every step."

"Braddock?" Kat hadn't realized she had guests from other towns, although she'd purchased a lot of temperance beer from Dave Braddock. She felt quite smug about that. The men had complained early in the afternoon, but she hadn't heard a grumble in hours, which just went to show that men didn't need alcohol to have fun. She'd like to have pointed that out, but she thought it better not to remind them. Besides, Maeve frowned on objections to alcohol; she felt Kat's temperance sentiments were disloyal to the memory of Liam Fitzpatrick.

By midnight, the party was over, not because the guests wanted to leave but because Maeve shooed them out. Kat then sent the family to bed and set about picking up. She didn't feel tired, just dispirited. Until the last guest left, she'd thought Connor might arrive for at least some of the party, but that had been a vain hope. Kat swept rubbish into a corner with her broom—let someone else gather it up and take it outside, she thought—dried the last of the dishes, and trudged into the room-between to extinguish all the lamps but one. Then she dragged her rocking chair in

111

beside the stove and sat down with her knitting.

She liked a quiet time to herself before she went to bed, a time to think over the day just past and to plan her projects for the next day. And she liked to knit. It was soothing— one of the few domestic chores, beside taking care of the children, that she enjoyed. She was knitting a muffler for Connor—who certainly didn't deserve it. Maybe she'd send it to Sean instead.

What would her life have been like, she wondered, had she and Mickey had children? Well, she wouldn't be here in Colorado, and she did like the West, so regretting what would never be was foolish. After all, she had Sean's children. Ingrid hardly seemed to notice them. And good grief, where *was* Ingrid? Had Maeve ever found her?

Kat had jumped up with the idea of checking her sister-in-law's room when the front door opened, frightening her half to death. Trembling, she clasped her hands at her breast, then saw that it was Connor. "I'm having locks put on the doors," she declared.

Connor, who had been trying unsuccessfully all day to get home, was taken aback. "Well, thanks," he said. "That's a fine greeting. Are the locks meant to keep me out?"

"You didn't come to my party."

"Well, Kat—" He took a step toward her, noticing with dismay that tears welled suddenly in her eyes, blurring their sparkling green color. "Did it go badly? The men didn't get rowdy, did they?"

"No."

He glanced at the walls. "The room looks real fine. Warm too." Kat said nothing, and Connor approached her warily. "I did try to get back."

"You couldn't have tried very hard."

"I'm sure you had plenty of dancing partners without me," he said, giving her a smile that wasn't returned. "I got caught in a snowslide in Ten-Mile Canyon."

Kat's eyes widened. "An avalanche, you mean? Were you hurt?"

"No."

"Then why didn't you come home for the party?"

"I tried," said Connor, frustrated.

"You just didn't want to dance."

"It wasn't that." He put his hand tentatively on her shoulder, although his fingers longed to encircle that tiny waist. Lord, but she looked pretty. "I was looking forward to a dance or two with you," he confessed.

"Truly?"

"Truly."

Kat's smile flashed at last. "There's a dance next week at Broncho Dave's hall in Braddock. Temperance beer and a three-piece band. We'll all go."

In the face of her excitement, Connor hadn't the heart to refuse, but he did wonder if he'd been suckered. Much to his surprise, Kat went on tiptoe and kissed his cheek. Then she tripped off to bed, leaving Connor with his fingers touching the kissed spot and his body remembering a kiss in a snow bank. He shook his head. Turning off the last lamp, he headed for his own section of the house. *Must be getting foolish*, he thought, *remembering an accidental little kiss as if it were an event.*

Chapter Eight

"Well, I suppose I could stay a while longer," said Maeve, who had originally insisted that she'd only be in Breckenridge a few days. "Genevieve writes that all is well at home; she's looking after the girls. And I do want to see Coleen, Hortense, and Jilly married before I go." There was an ominous rumble from Hortense as the three women sat sewing around the stove in the room-between. Maeve ignored Hortense's wordless protest. "Where's Coleen?"

"Still up at St. Joseph's," said Kat. "She went last night to help with the hospital laundry."

"You, Jamie," called Maeve. "Run over to St. Joseph's and escort Coleen home."

"I've been injured, Mrs. Fitzpatrick. Had you forgotten?" said Jamie.

"Injured!" exclaimed Maeve. "The boy who danced all evening? Be off with you, lad, unless you're planning to stay home from the festivities in Braddock."

Jamie gave up and put on his coat.

"Coleen is more with the sisters than with us," Kat remarked to her mother.

"Better that she's giving her time to the church than just disappearing," said Maeve.

At the Braddock ball, Connor found himself un-accountably irritated with Kat. She'd been talking to Dave Braddock for a half hour now, listening to tales of how his bottling plant had been destroyed by wind and fire in '83, complimenting him on his temperance beer and the fine dancing floor of his two-story hall, and fascinated by his experiments with growing vegetables at high altitudes.

"They say our growing season in Summit County is two weeks or less," said Dave. "Frost just about every night—that's the problem, but I cover the plants at sundown."

"Fresh vegetables are very healthful," said Kat.

How would she know? Connor wondered. If ever a woman couldn't cook, Kat was the woman.

"You'll see some fine specimens coming into Breckenridge from my fields next summer."

"And you won't find a better customer than us, Dave."

Why was she calling the man Dave? She hardly knew him. And he was married. Good lord, his daughter Mattie had been delivering the mail to Preston since '84.

"I'll have my boy Frank drive the vegetable wagon by your house for sure," said Dave.

"Did you want to dance or not?" Connor demanded and then felt embarrassed at his ill humor because Kat's face lit up and she rose immediately.

"You only had to ask," she said over her shoulder as she headed for the dance floor to take her place in a set beside Jeannie who, wearing a new ruffled dress, had been felling all the boys from Braddock.

Kat, Connor noticed with admiration, had taken that slate-blue gown she'd worn to the wallpaper party and added lace frills at the throat and wrists and a vest of a different blue. As he swung her through the set, his hand rested at her waist just above the bustle. Why did women wear those things? he wondered, remembering the first one he'd ever seen—on a rich lady who'd come from Denver to summer in Breckenridge. He'd thought the poor woman was deformed and turned his eyes politely away. Females were certainly an enigmatic species. He'd never understood Rose Laurel, and he supposed that was why he'd raised his daughter as if she were a boy. But Kat had changed all that, he reflected wryly as Jeannie whirled in and out of his arms, laughing and saying, "You might at least smile, Daddy."

Connor realized abruptly that he probably wasn't much fun anymore. It was a wonder Kat wanted to dance with him, yet she did seem to. She was smiling when the set brought her back into his arms, and he smiled back. *We must be friends, Kat and I,* he decided, feeling a little surprised at the thought—and pleased. She was like a ray of spring sunshine and he like a man who'd been snowbound in his cabin all winter and suddenly found that someone had brought a festive party to his doorstep.

"It's a hard world for a working woman in Chicago. The employers, hypocrites that they are, excuse themselves from paying a living wage by pretending the girls are being supported by their fathers," said Maeve. "Yet if the girl admits she's alone, they won't hire her." Their party was seated at a big table for the midnight supper.

"Oysters," continued Maeve, sniffing as she looked at the splendid repast furnished by Broncho Dave Braddock. "A working girl can't afford oysters. Why, Jilly was sewing for piece rates. She'd be lucky to earn five dollars in two weeks, and her room and board was two-twenty-five a week before I took her in. Sixteen and going hungry, she was."

"Miz Fitzpatrick saved my life," said Jilly, who was

eating oysters as if they were ambrosia and holding hands under the table with some young fellow she'd just met.

Kat noticed but hated to call Jilly's penchant for indiscretion to Maeve's attention.

"And Hortense," continued Maeve. "Lost her job entirely. I took her in for free and a bit of housekeeping until she got new work."

"Aye. I was the best cook and waitress they ever had," said Hortense bitterly, "and they fired me because I was too old. Said the customers didn't like my looks."

"Men of no taste," declared Eyeless.

Kat and Connor exchanged amused glances.

"Only work I could get was laundressing," Hortense grumbled, "and I do hate laundressing."

"And that little Mattie that went to Fords'," said Maeve. "I snatched her from the hands of a fancy man at the railroad station. A railroad station is a dangerous place for women, a haunt of vile seducers."

"The lord smiles on your good works, my dear," said James. "Beautiful and an angel of charity as well."

"Oh, get on with you, James," protested Maeve.

Connor choked as he witnessed Kat's look of bemusement at the byplay between his father and her mother.

"I'm no charity case," snapped Hortense.

"No. Go away," cried Coleen, who had just been asked to dance by another young man.

"Why don't you ever dance, Coleen?" asked Jeannie. "It's fun."

Kat gave Connor an I-told-you-so look across the table. He had intimated that this expedition was to satisfy Kat's love of dancing, not Jeannie's. But Connor liked it too, Kat thought with satisfaction, no matter what he said. He'd led her to the floor twice, hadn't he? And her mother once, and Ingrid not at all. Kat felt a bit smug about that.

*   *   *

"Much help you were, my lad," said James. "I never had an assistant worth less." Over coffee and cake, Connor and James had been telling stories about their adventures photographing the West. "Always off quizzing geologists."

"They were questions well asked," said Connor. "If you'd come prospecting with me, Dad, you'd be a richer man."

James laughed. "Nothing worth photographing in a mine and no light to do it by. And you, you're lucky you didn't starve, eloping at seventeen with that spoiled miss. Not an ounce of sense between the two of you."

"Well, I'm not the man who let the pack mules eat the photographic chemicals while he was trying to get a perfect picture."

"That was a misfortune," James agreed. "One of the best pictures I ever took, and I lost it for lack of developing chemicals."

"Not to mention the fact that the mules died, and we had to lug all your equipment back ourselves—on foot."

"That picture would have rivaled anything William Jackson ever took, even that poor excuse for a photograph of the mountain with the cross of snow."

"I've seen that picture," said Kat.

"And if I let the mules eat the chemicals," said James good humoredly, "you were always off flirting."

Connor shrugged. "So I was young and romantic. I've learned better in my old age."

Kat found she didn't like that comment much—even though she might have made it herself.

"A man's never too old for romance," said James.

"Where's Mother?" asked Kat. They had already traveled a mile of the four from the Braddock station to Breckenridge when she realized that her mother was not on the train.

Connor, tired from a night of dancing, rose wearily to count heads. Maeve Fitzpatrick was indeed missing. So was his father, which Connor pointed out to Kat. "Don't worry. Dad will see no harm comes to her."

"I suppose," said Kat, "but how did they manage to miss the train? Now, unless they rent a buggy, they won't be able to get back until tomorrow." She shifted Phoebe, who was asleep in her lap, and peered out the window. "Look at the sky. What if they're snowbound in Braddock?"

"They'll just put up with Dave," said Connor. "Folks are hospitable. Our parents won't be left out in the cold."

It did snow, and Kat couldn't sleep that night for worrying about her mother. Finally she threw a shawl over her nightdress and, carrying a candle in a holder, went to wake Connor. "What if they didn't just miss the train? What if they were attacked by robbers? They could be lying unconscious in an alley, covered up by snow."

"Robbers?" Having been awakened from a deep sleep by a beautiful young woman in her nightdress, Connor was having some trouble focusing on Kat's anxiety. The candle highlighted the rounded curves of her face and the curling hair that had escaped her long braid.

"Yes, robbers. We were robbed. Ruffians might have accosted my mother as well."

Connor wondered how her hair would look hanging free. "You're right, of course. If she gave a robber the same sort of lecture you did, he might well have knocked her unconscious." Kat turned pale, and he was sorry he'd joked about her fears. She had him at a disadvantage because he couldn't sit up for a normal conversation; he was naked under his blankets. And she was naked under that nightdress. Connor dragged his eyes away from the little hand that clutched a shawl against her breast. "Ah—Kat, this is my bedroom," he reminded her. "It wouldn't look good if anyone found you here."

"Oh." Her mouth rounded in surprise. "Of course, you're right." She turned toward the door, mumbling, "I just know something terrible has happened."

"Maeve will be all right," he called after her. "She and Dad'll be in on the train tomorrow morning."

Connor fell back on his pillow as the door closed silently behind her, knowing that he was in for a sleepless night, not because of Maeve's disappearance, but because he couldn't erase from his mind the picture of Kat in her nightgown.

Trudging along in the snow toward the Lincoln Avenue bridge and the railroad station on the other side of the Blue, Kat worried about what her mother would say if Connor mentioned that visit to his bedroom. How embarrassing to have done such a thoughtless thing and then have it pointed out to her by a man—as if it were his reputation at stake. But she had been worried! So Maeve had better not say anything about that few minutes in Connor's room. After all, Kat wasn't the one who had stayed behind in a strange town with a strange man.

"Oh, my goodness!" She had just caught sight of an old man with a ruggedly uncompromising face. "You're Father Dyer!"

"I am." He peered at her. "Do I know you?"

"No. No, you don't, but I've seen your picture—in *Snow-Shoe Itinerant*. I own a copy. Oh, I'd so like to have you sign it for me. If I ran home and got it—"

She looked at him hopefully, and he in return looked quite surprised to be accosted by a pretty young woman requesting his autograph. It wasn't something that happened everyday to Methodist ministers with unpopular convictions.

"I do so admire your stand on temperance," said Kat. "If only more people would campaign against the evils of drink, think how many ruined lives could be redeemed."

"Well." Father Dyer looked quite pleased. "I'm on my way to the church. If you'd care to bring your book by, I'll be there for an hour or so."

"I'll run right home," said Kat and turned to do so,

realizing only when she was half a block away that she'd forgotten about meeting her mother. *Well, goodness,* she assured herself, *James can see Mother home. It's not every day I get to meet Father Dyer.*

"Jilly, where's Miss Kathleen?" Connor was ready to leave for the station but couldn't find Kat.

"She's gone to meet the train, Mr. Connor."

Connor felt a stab of conscience. Because he'd taken so long to fall asleep last night, he'd overslept this morning. Kat must have thought he didn't mean to pick up Maeve and James, and now she was trudging across town by herself to meet them. And, good lord, she didn't even know that ladies never went to West Breckenridge, which housed two red-light districts. Or did she know? Maybe she'd gone to the stop at the edge of town.

On the other hand, she'd probably realize that James and Maeve—oh hell, he didn't know which way she might have gone, but he decided to check the depot first. Even if she knew that area was forbidden to respectable women, she might have gone there to spite him for having stayed abed. He hastened to follow her. As he'd surmised, Maeve and James were on the train and got off at the depot. However, Kat was not there. Nor had the station master seen her. "She wouldn't come here," the man declared, glaring at Maeve, who had unwittingly flouted Breckenridge custom.

Connor then drove by the ladies' stop at the edge of town, but Kat wasn't there either—or anywhere on his route. When he deposited his father and her mother at home, no one at the house had seen Kat.

As worried as she'd been about her mother, she wouldn't have decided not to meet them, Connor reasoned. Could some ruffian, taking her for a soiled dove because she was on the wrong side of the river—well, it didn't bear thinking on. "We'll have to go looking for her. Jamie, bundle up. Dad?"

"Of course," said James. "Now, don't you worry, Maeve. We'll find your chick."

"I'm not worried," said Maeve, taking off her gloves and cloak. "You might try St. Gertrude's or St. Joseph's."

"Or St. Mary's or St. Scholastica's," Jeannie murmured to her brother.

"St. Scholastica is in Chicago, child," said Maeve, "and the church here is not fit to be called by the name of the Blessed Virgin. Mayhap Kathleen is off seeing to your education with the sisters."

Jeannie groaned and fled. Connor left, having given instructions to his father and son for the search. Jamie was assigned the respectable side of town, much to his disappointment. Connor and James crossed the river.

Kat tripped across Lincoln Avenue clutching her signed copy of *Snow-Shoe Itinerant,* having had a most satisfying chat with Father Dyer about temperance. She wished her priests were as interested in the cause, but one had to take support where one found it. She had promised Father Dyer to give a temperance lecture on the sad fates of her father and husband, which she'd do was soon as Maeve returned to Chicago. The thought reminded her of her mother's disappearance. Had she got home? Kat increased her pace toward the house.

"Kathleen Margaret Fitzgerald, where have you been?"

Kat breathed a sigh of relief; her mother was safe. "I'm so sorry I didn't meet your train. I'm afraid I got sidetracked with Father Dyer."

"That's just what I told them," said Maeve. "I said to check with the sisters, and if I didn't mention the priests, I'm sure they thought to check the church and the rectory."

"Who?" asked Kat, not bothering to correct her mother's assumption that Father Dyer was a Catholic priest.

"Connor's got James and Jamie out looking for you.

I don't know what he thought might have happened. In a town this size, we'd have heard if anything had gone amiss."

Kat remembered all her midnight fears for her mother and wondered how Maeve could so casually dismiss the seeming disappearance of a daughter.

"Ah, James dear, there you are," cried Maeve.

James dear? Since when was her mother calling him *James dear?* And fussing about whether he'd caught a cold while he was out looking for the errant daughter. Her usually sensible parent seemed to be entirely dazzled by James Macleod, which made no sense. An itinerant photographer was hardly Maeve Fitzpatrick's type of man.

Kat was touched by Connor's obvious relief when he returned to the house a half hour later and found her safe. "I am sorry to have caused you worry," she said, "but I was perfectly safe and visiting with Father Dyer at his church."

She seemed to know *why* he had been worried, he thought, which meant he didn't have to explain why ladies never went to West Breckenridge. Good lord, how could he have mentioned prostitutes to Kat? And all the time he'd thought she might have been abducted, she'd been talking temperance with John Dyer. "Does your mother realize that you've been consorting with Methodists?" he asked, grinning.

"No, she doesn't, and don't you tell her," said Kat, her green eyes twinkling.

"I ought to tattle just to get even for all the trouble you caused."

"And very sweet it was for you to take my disappearance so to heart." Mother certainly hadn't, thought Kat and impulsively squeezed his hand. Mickey would probably have treated himself to a celebratory drink if she'd disappeared, but then Mickey found endless causes to drink while Connor—well, she never smelled alcohol on him. There weren't too many men of his high principles, she thought approvingly.

"I should warn you," said Connor, resisting the impulse to keep her hand in his. "Father Dyer's a menace. We've been feuding with him because he insists on using the firehouse bell to call people to church—even when we told him not to."

"And why shouldn't he? He has no bell on his own church, although it's a sight better than ours," added Kat. "Ours has no bell, no insulation, no decent pews, no sacristy, no—"

"He shouldn't because the volunteer fire companies can't tell whether to turn out for a fire on Sunday morning or turn over and go back to sleep."

"The volunteer firemen should be in church."

"We'll probably end up having to move the firehouse to keep the bell out of his hands."

"Well, I just hope I don't snow-shoe into it while it's in the middle of the street," said Kat wryly, "which reminds me, Connor, Eli Fletcher has finished my snow-shoes, so we can have a snow-shoeing party this weekend."

Seeing in his mind's eye Kat in her nightdress with the long braid hanging down her back, feeling again that little squeeze she'd given his hand, Connor said, "All right."

She was astonished at his easy acquiescence. He must like snow-shoeing better than dancing, but she wasn't about to comment. She had snow-shoes to borrow for those who had none. Would Mother want to try it? she wondered.

In the week that followed, she found her mother hard to catch. Maeve was always away from the house, ostensibly to interview potential husbands for the Chicago girls, and she took James with her, although Kat couldn't imagine why. James hardly seemed the type to offer an informed opinion on what man would or wouldn't prove to be a responsible husband. And then there was the problem of Hortense and Coleen, neither of whom wanted to marry, and Jilly, who seemed more interested in suitors than a husband. Kat had caught her kissing one of the McNaught boys in the pantry and dutifully scolded her, but she doubted that the scolding would have much effect.

"What's this I hear about your giving a lecture at Fireman's Hall next Sunday, Kat?"

They were all having hot chocolate at home after the snow-shoeing party when Connor posed the question. *Duplicity will out,* thought Kat gloomily. On the one hand, she couldn't refuse Father Dyer when he asked her to speak as part of a two-person temperance program, the other speaker an out-of-towner. On the other hand, she'd rather have put her appearance off until Maeve went home. Even when that option was lost to her, Kat had hoped that Maeve might not hear about the program or notice her daughter's absence on Sunday afternoon. It wasn't, fortunately, one of the Sundays when the church would be open for services.

"Father Dyer asked me," Kat mumbled.

"Then I heartily approve," said Maeve.

"That's mighty tolerant of you," said Connor.

"Why should you be surprised? I'm a tolerant woman. On what subject are you speaking, Kathleen?"

"Temperance," mumbled Kat.

Her mother glared, then added grudgingly, "If the good father asked you to, I suppose you must. We'll all go."

Kat groaned silently. Jeannie groaned aloud.

Trying to make the most of a situation that might cause trouble, Kat asked Father Dyer and his wife to dinner. At least then, when Maeve discovered that he was Methodist, she'd also discover that he was a fine man, and Lucinda Dyer might keep him from saying anything dreadful about Catholics when he discovered that not only his speaker, but her whole family were papists. Kat knew from his book that he did not approve of her church but assured herself that it was only because he had first been exposed to Catholicism among the Mexicans, who were doubtless very different from Catholics in Chicago.

Although Lucinda Dyer fell ill and couldn't come to dinner, the temperance lecture was a startling success in terms of attendance, the hall mobbed with people, mostly miners. Afterwards, seven men signed the pledge, two proposed marriage to Kat and, when she refused, asked to be included on her list of possible suitors for the marriageable girls she imported from Chicago. Jilly immediately introduced herself to one of them and invited him home to dinner.

Maeve said, "How could you be so disloyal to your father's memory?"

Connor said, "When our miners hear about this, we could lose the whole work force."

"I don't see why," Kat retorted as they walked home on a path worn through the snow.

"Because you advocated closing the saloons on Sunday. That's what they look forward to all week—drinking on Sunday."

"Abomination," cried Father Dyer, who had been walking ahead with Hortense, a temperance advocate herself. "Were you one of those who tried to take my church organ for sinful dancing at the Fireman's Hall?"

"Kat's the dancer, not me," Connor replied and grinned when she scowled at him.

"I wasn't even here then, Father Dyer," said Kat.

"I didn't know the church had an organ," chimed in Maeve.

"Well, here we are," said Kat quickly. "Hortense, shall we put dinner on the table?"

"Since when did you help serve?" asked Hortense.

At dinner Maeve stated suspiciously, "I didn't know the church had taken up temperance, Father."

"Well, where have you been, woman? I've been preaching

the evils of drink up and down the state for years now."

Maeve frowned. "Even so, do you think, Father, that the Blessed Virgin would approve of a daughter who spoke ill of—"

"Blessed Virgin?" Father Dyer looked horrified. "You're not a papist, are you?"

Maeve bristled. "I am a member of the true church, the Holy Roman—" She stopped. "What are you, then?"

"Methodist," said Father Dyer.

Maeve crossed herself. Then, looking at Hortense, who had just brought in two apple pies, she murmured, "But Hortense was once a Methodist, and you do have temperance in common. Have you considered marrying, Father? I believe Methodists are allowed to."

"I am married," said Father Dyer.

"I like a drink now and then," said Ingrid. "What's all the fuss about drinking?"

"A Methodist," whispered Coleen. She stood up, dropping her napkin on the floor. "I must get to St. Joseph's."

Father Dyer looked astonished. "She's taking the veil because she met a Methodist?"

"No, no. She's going over to help with the hospital laundry," Kat assured him. Her hope that actually meeting Catholics might ameliorate his prejudice was fast disappearing. He must think them all strange, very strange.

"And to think that you, my daughter, would speak ill of the dead, and at the behest of a Methodist," said Maeve as they made ready for bed.

"Don't talk to me about Methodists, Mother," Kat replied. "You were ready to marry him off to Hortense."

"'Twas only a fleeting impulse," said Maeve defensively. "They're both temperance."

"Speaking of which, I thought my talk went quite well. Seven converts."

"They'll be back in the saloons before the week's out," Maeve predicted. "Men will drink."

"Not if I can help it," murmured Kat, but she did worry about Connor's objections. Perhaps he was wrong about the miners taking her sentiments amiss. After all, most of the audience had been miners, and the linchpin of American liberty was freedom of speech. They'd not deny her her right to speak out, especially when it was their own welfare that concerned her. Mickey had got only himself killed, reeling off the curb in Chicago. A drunken miner might kill himself and everyone else on his shift. As her brother's representative, she had a duty to see to the safety of their employees.

Chapter Nine

"Mother, are you sick?"

"No," said Maeve.

"But you were throwing up." Kat wiped her mother's forehead. "It's probably the influenza. I'd best get the doctor."

"I am not sick," said Maeve, falling back on her pillow. "I'm with child."

"What?" Kat looked at her in horrified astonishment. "You can't be with child. Papa's dead."

"Marriage is not the only way to make a child," said Maeve. "Sins of the flesh will accomplish the same thing."

"Sins of the flesh," Kat whispered. "But who—"

"James, of course."

"But Mother, you haven't known James long enough. I mean even if you'd—done anything—"

"We did."

"You did?" Kat didn't believe that. Women, later in life, sometimes got strange notions. Maeve must be imagining the whole thing. "Even if you had," said Kat in a reasonable, soothing tone, "it's too soon—I mean you couldn't tell so fast."

"Kathleen, I know how babies are made, and I remember quite clearly the early months when I was carrying you," said Maeve. "I knew within days of your conception."

Kat gulped, then shook off the idea that Maeve might actually be with child. Poor Mother, thinking she was pregnant. At her age. And if Maeve was imagining the pregnancy, maybe she was imagining the intimacy with James—who was a grandfather, for goodness sake.

"Mother, this is Connor's father you're talking about. And you're my mother. I'm sure you don't mean to say—"

"Go away, Kathleen. Give a temperance lecture or something. I shall seek out a priest and make my confession this afternoon when I'm feeling better."

"But Mother—" Suddenly Kat knew it was true. Maeve would never make a false confession. "Confession won't help!" she cried. "You'll still be with child!"

"Concerns of the soul take precedence over concerns of the body." Maeve turned over and closed her eyes.

After staring at her mother for a moment more, Kat raced to the other side of the house. Maeve might be concerned about her soul, but Kat intended to look out for her mother's body, as well as her mother's reputation. "Connor," she said, catching him as he was about to leave the house. "I must talk to you."

"Talk away," he replied amiably.

"Alone."

"That's impossible in this house. We've got thirteen people living here."

"I'll meet you outside as soon as I get my coat."

"We lost three more miners last week," said Connor as she caught up with him on the porch. "They quit because—"

"Your father has seduced my mother," said Kat.

He turned on the step and stared at her. "Where did you get that crazy idea?"

"He not only seduced her. She's with child."

"Come on, Kat."

"With our—our brother or sister."

"She's too old to have children."

"I quite agree. It will probably kill her." Kat blinked back tears at the thought of her mother's peril. Childbirth was dangerous enough for young women. "And I won't have her die bearing an illegitimate child. He'll have to marry her." Connor opened his mouth, but she cut him off. "Don't think I haven't noticed that you said she was too old, not that he was too fine a person to have done it. He must have tricked her into staying with him in Braddock and then seduced her."

"Well, Braddock had to be the site," Connor agreed. "If it had been here, there'd have been at least eleven—"

"Connor, this is no joking matter. I never thought I'd be in the position of trying to see that my own mother was made an honest woman of."

"Does she want to marry him?"

"She's just worried about her soul, so we'll have to take care of the rest."

"We've been waiting for you, Mother," said Kat. Connor and James were sitting in the room-between as well, all others having been chased away. James, looking distastefully cheerful, was fiddling with some photographic equipment. Kat felt like snatching the camera and hitting him with it.

Maeve eyed them warily as she unwrapped a heavy knitted shawl from her head. "That Father Eusebius is the sickliest young man," said Maeve, taking a seat. "I had to put him to bed with mustard plasters and a honey-and-whiskey cough syrup."

Kat felt a hysterical desire to giggle at the idea of her mother seeking out a priest to confess her sins of the flesh and staying to provide mustard plasters. "Connor, I think you should handle this."

"Well—ah, Dad, Maeve, it's come to our attention that you two are—um, going to be parents."

"I've been your parent for thirty-four years, lad," said James. "If you've just noticed—"

"Of a new child," Connor interrupted before Kat could fly into a rage. "Yours and Maeve's." James looked startled. "That being the case, Kat and I think you should marry."

"Marry?" James' mouth dropped open.

Kat could see that Irish Catholic pride stiffening her mother's spine as Maeve said, "What would I be needing with a Protestant husband?"

"Mother," cried Kat, "this is no time for religious quibbling."

"I'm no Protestant," protested James. Having recovered his equilibrium, he was now beaming at Maeve. "We Macleods are good Scotch Catholics, whose ancestors fought in the '45 with Bonnie Prince Charlie."

"We did? That's the first I've heard of it," said Connor, looking suspicious.

"If you're a good Scotch Catholic, why aren't you in church on Sunday?" Maeve demanded.

"Well, back-slidden a bit," James confessed.

"A profession of faith is good enough for me," said Kat. "I'll see to the wedding immediately. Saturday would be a good day, don't you think?"

"The priest is sick," said Maeve.

"He'll get well," Kat retorted. "If we have to, we can hold the wedding at his bedside."

"I'm not so hard up for a husband that I need marry one—"

"You are too, Mother!"

James interrupted the argument by sweeping Maeve out of her chair. "Did you think I'd not want to marry you, my love? I'll admit I might have been too young for marriage and fatherhood when I married Connor's mother—"

"Did you get *her* with child before the wedding too?" Kat demanded angrily.

"Old history," said James.

"I never knew that," said Connor.

"But now I'm ready and willing, my love," James said to Maeve. "James Connor Macleod at your service."

He gave Maeve a long, enthusiastic kiss with Kat looking on, feeling embarrassed and just a bit envious. Her mother broke free and cried, "James, get on with you, you devil. Kissing me in front of the children."

"Well, Kat did insist that this was the best weekend for the wedding," Maeve was saying to Mrs. McNaught. "I, for one, wanted to wait so the bishop could marry us." She looked quite beautiful in a dress of charcoal gray, which satisfied her notions of proper attire for a widow. However, to satisfy James, the dressmaker had added red velvet at the high collar, the jacket lapels and the cuffs.

"Mother!" Kat was still aghast that her mother had wanted to put off the wedding until Bishop Machebeuf arrived to officiate at a veiling ceremony. Even with this quick wedding, the child would be born a month early and cause a scandal. Kat knew she must be the only twenty-five-old daughter in the world who had had to suffer the embarrassment of arranging the wedding of her unmarried, pregnant, forty-one-year-old mother.

"Well, Kathleen," said Mrs. McNaught, "I can certainly see your mother's point. I'd like to have been married by a bishop. I'm sure every girl would."

"Mother's not a girl," Kat muttered.

"She's as pretty as one," said James, bending to kiss his bride, who blushed like a girl. "I'm a lucky man to have won myself such a beautiful wife. Now maybe God will bless us with a second family."

Kat stared at him with amazement. Was he so tipsy he was going to reveal why they'd married in haste?

"Do you realize that we've made you and Connor brother and sister? Both of you only children, and now we've given you families." James beamed sentimentally.

"I have a brother already," snapped Kat. *And Connor is not my brother,* she added to herself, hating the idea with an inexplicable passion. Probably his stupid Western sense of humor. Even now he was grinning and suggesting that his new sister might like to dance. However, before she could accept and get away from James and his indiscreet babble about starting second families, Jilly came scampering up with Jimmy Don, the grocery boy.

"We're getting married too, Miss Kathleen," she announced.

"Ah, returning to your first love, are you?" asked Kat.

Maeve bent a sharp eye on Jilly. "Is he Catholic?"

"Are you sure James is?" Kat murmured.

"If he isn't, he soon will be," Maeve murmured back. "Well, you and Coleen are next, Hortense."

Coleen burst into tears, and Hortense said, "That's it. I'm quitting." She took off her apron, dropped it on the floor, and stamped out of the room with Kat in pursuit.

Behind her, Kat could hear James talking about the photography studio he planned to establish in Denver in competition with his famous rival, William Jackson. "How exciting, James," Maeve was saying. Kat shook her head. Did her mother really think a photography shop was going to put food on the table?

In her panic-stricken drive to see her mother married, Kat hadn't stopped to think how much misery this union might cause. Not that there'd been any choice, not with a child coming, but Maeve had flouted her own tenets and fallen in love. The price might be as heavy as the one Kat had paid for that mistake. With a gloomy heart, she stopped Hortense in the dining room.

"You can't change my mind, Miss Kat," said Hortense. "I'm not staying to be married off."

"I know, but I wondered if I could offer you another job."

Hortense eyed her suspiciously. "I'm sure not going to Denver with your mother."

"No, no. I wouldn't ask it. We're having labor troubles at several of the mines, and I thought if you were to cook at one of the camps, the men would be happier. It pays well, but on the other hand, the camps can be rowdy— at least, so Connor says. Consequently, I'd understand if—"

"What's it pay?"

"Three-fifty a day."

"I accept."

"Did you talk her out of leavin'?" asked Eyeless anxiously when Kat returned to the reception.

Kat shook her head and explained the agreement she'd reached with Hortense.

"Well, that was a stupid idea," Eyeless snapped. "Who's goin' to do the cookin' here? Jilly's leavin', Coleen's never around, Ingrid's always asleep, an' you're—"

"Don't give it a thought," Maeve interrupted. "I'll have Genevieve send out a few more girls from Chicago."

A cheer rose from the single-male contingent, and then someone called that Father Eusebius was ready to toast the newlyweds. The priest fell into a coughing fit.

"Give the father a drop of that whiskey, James," said Maeve.

"Give us all one," called several other male guests.

Kat muttered to herself as she watched the bottle being passed. What would Father Dyer think if he knew? And Father Eusebius had just tossed back a half tumbler. It was worse than a wake.

"I'll have a shot," said Ingrid.

*   *   *

Coleen was the only one in the family to accompany Kat when two novices took the veil at St. Gertrude's, and Coleen, embarrassingly, sobbed loudly as the bishop transformed Katie Rupp and Philomena Leib into Sisters Hedwig and Ehrentrude. "Sh-sh-sh," hissed Kat. Coleen subsided. Kat had thought Jeannie might like to attend, but she'd disappeared at the last moment, she and Ingrid. Connor was escorting Hortense to the Ingrid's Ring mine on Gibson Hill, where their labor troubles were most acute. He had pronounced Kat's offer to Hortense "brilliant." Kat still felt a little curl of warmth when she thought of his praise.

On the other hand, he had joined the others in telling her that she could not invite Bishop Machebeuf to stay with them. Kat supposed she couldn't. There still wasn't a spare room, but they certainly could have invited him to dinner! Kat was sure she could have fixed a meal good enough for a bishop, although no one else thought so. "An' I'm not cookin' for no Eye-talian feller," Eyeless insisted.

"He's French," Kat had said.

"Thought they all come from Rome."

"Only the Pope," Kat retorted, "and he won't be here."

So the bishop would sleep at the Denver Hotel, have dinner at McNaught's, and then come to Kat's for coffee and cake. Coleen had asked for the honor of baking the cake, and Connor should be home in time for the party. Kat wondered if he'd like the bishop.

Whether or not he did, the next time Bishop Machebeuf came to Breckenridge, Kat would be able to offer him hospitality. As soon as Connor left town, she contracted with Diederick to build a second story on her side of the house. They were discussing the plans while he painted both sides a lovely blue-green. At first, Kat had thought it a strange color for a house, but Diederick explained that paint was scarce and you used what was available and hoped you had enough to cover the whole house. Which explained the bold colors on other homes in Breckenridge—yellow ochre, barn red, dark green—and the many houses with no paint whatever.

The veiling ceremony concluded, and Kat rose to offer hugs and congratulations to the new sisters and the other nuns of St. Gertrude's. "Well, Kathleen," said Reverend Mother, "I hope you've been behaving yourself." The bishop, who was standing beside the prioress, raised his eyebrows.

"I was a pupil at St. Scholastica," Kat explained, flushing.

"You're not the girl who made the infamous pudding, are you?" asked the bishop merrily.

"She is," said Reverend Mother Hilda. The bishop looked alarmed.

"But I won't be cooking when you come tonight," said Kat.

"Kathleen, I don't believe you've met our newest arrival from the mother house, Sister Fredericka."

"Freddie!" cried Kat joyously and threw her arms around the young nun.

"Oh dear," said Mother Hilda. "You two went to school together. How could I have forgotten? Sister Fredericka, I'll have none of those madcap antics in my convent."

The bishop was looking at his cake as if its major ingredient might be hemlock.

"Coleen made it." Kat wondered how many times she'd have to disclaim any personal efforts to feed him. Out of the corner of her eye, she could see Connor trying not to laugh. Too bad he got back in time for the party, she thought sourly. Coleen was blushing and curtseying like a ninny. The bishop patted her on the head.

"Now Kathleen," he said, "I had a long talk with your good mother before I came to Breckenridge."

Oh no, she didn't tell him about the baby, Kat thought despairingly.

137

"She's very worried about your association with Methodists and their causes."

"Well goodness, I'm just trying to save people from the evils of drinking and to get the saloons closed on Sundays."

"Indeed," said the bishop. "I find that a curiously *Protestant* point of view."

The guest of honor had gone back to his hotel, the guests to their homes, the members of the family to their beds, and Kat, having cleaned up after the party, was in her room, taking down her hair for night braiding and thinking that Jeannie and Ingrid might have offered to help with the dishes now that the household was servantless again, except for Coleen who had gone home with the sisters. Then suddenly Kat realized that Jeannie had not been at the party. She ticked off the members of the household, dredging up bits of conversation to assure herself of their presence. Everyone, even Ingrid, had been there—except Jeannie, whom Kat had not seen since her departure with Coleen for the veiling ceremony.

Alarmed, Kat dropped her brush and sped across the house to Jeannie's room. It was empty, the narrow bed unslept in, the hour late. Where was she? And how could Kat have failed to notice her absence all this time? She stood undecided in the girl's little room, knowing that this was not something she could put off until morning. She had to awaken Connor and admit that she had lost his daughter.

Squaring her shoulders, she marched to his door and knocked softly. What if he didn't answer? He must be tired, having come back from visiting the mines here and in Ten-Mile Canyon. He was probably too deeply asleep to hear her knock, yet she didn't want to invade his room as she had that other time, the time he'd reminded her that she shouldn't be there.

Even while she was hesitating, he whipped the door open and demanded, "What the hell is it this time, Eyeless?" then paused. "Kat?"

Kat wanted to flee. He was wearing only the bottoms of his long underwear, confronting her with a broad, bare chest. She swallowed hard.

"What is it, Kat?" He drew her into the room and closed the door. "You look scared to death."

"It's Jeannie," she stammered, telling herself she was being silly. It wasn't as if she'd never confronted a male chest—she's seen Mickey's, even her father's when she'd had to help Maeve during his last days. "Jeannie's gone." She forced herself to look up at him—away from that intriguing field of curly, ginger-colored body hair. "I can't find her anywhere."

Connor was staring intensely. "My lord, your hair's beautiful!" He touched it with the tips of his fingers. "I've wondered about it."

"What?" she asked, glancing to the side as he ran his palm over the sweep of black waves. Kat felt short of breath and fluttery.

"Your hair. Ever since you came to my room that time, I've wondered what it would look like down."

"Connor." She put her hand over his to push his away, but then of their own accord, her fingers closed. "Jeannie," she reminded him in a weak voice.

"She's at Finding's house." He turned his hand and clasped hers, raised it to his mouth. "You shouldn't have come here," he murmured and bent forward, encircling her waist and lifting her against him.

Kat's heart was beating so hard she felt smothered as his lips closed over hers. She hardly noticed when they moved to his bed, so bemused was she by his kiss. The first one, the accidental one, had been pleasant, but this was overwhelming. It turned her body into a giant pulse. She thought fleetingly of Mickey, whose arms she had enjoyed, but his kisses had never been so compelling. She'd never felt that she could not push him away if called elsewhere—to take a whistling tea kettle off the stove, to answer the door.

Connor, continuing the kiss, had turned her on her back so that she sank into his feather mattress under the solid weight of his body. Tingling, her breasts flattened against his chest, she slipped her arms around his neck to pull him closer, wishing that her nightgown were not between them, wishing she could feel his curling hair against her skin.

"Ah God, Kat," he groaned, lips against her neck.

Kat strained up to him as he slipped his arms under her. The air of his room was cold, but she could feel the heat of his skin even through her nightdress, and then he was inching it up, and she felt a moment of panic before the sensation of his knee rubbing against the inside of hers turned her body liquid with heat. She gasped as the nightdress continued to travel up her legs. His thighs rubbed against hers, and she responded helplessly, never in her life having been so dazed with passion.

"Sweetheart," he whispered, and then there was nothing between their bodies, for he had raised the fabric above her waist and lifted her arms so that he could pull the gown, with its demure tucks and ruffles, over her head. Kat twisted beneath him, feeling what she had desired before, the sweet abrasion of that curling hair against her nipples. He groaned and, having dropped the nightdress beside the bed, slipped his hands beneath her hips. His fingers were rough from years of mining as they rubbed against her tender skin, squeezed gently, caressed until tremors rocked her body, and she tipped herself up to him in blind yearning.

A deep sigh escaped from her lips to his when she felt the first nudge, then the penetration, and finally the deep possession. He paused, imbedded and hot inside her, before beginning to move, leisurely, so that she could savor it as the tremors and then the ache built. And built. When it all exploded, he was ready and closed his lips over hers so that others in the house would not hear her outcry. She realized what he had done later, but not then. Then she felt only the wonder of sensation so intense she thought it some kind of miracle, like a vision of light that enveloped her whole being, at the center of which was Connor, shuddering inside her as their mouths and arms clung.

When it was over, Connor fell back beside her. Kat was pleasantly dazed for a time, but then the heat and languor of slaked passion seeped away, and, naked, she became aware of the sharp cold on her cooling skin. His room had no stove and was farthest from the warmth of the kitchen. Wondering how one minute she could have been totally concerned about Jeannie and the next overcome with lust for Jeannie's father, she began to shiver.

"Here, love." Connor put his arms around her, then reached to the bottom of the bed for a quilt. "Are you all right?"

Kat nodded automatically. She was all right, she supposed, in the sense that she wasn't dead. She hadn't been struck down by a bolt from heaven—but merciful God, she had a sin to atone for. She blinked back tears.

"Don't cry, sweetheart," he begged. "So help me, I don't know how that happened. It's just that you looked so beautiful in your nightdress, and your hair—dear God, that's no excuse, is it?"

"For me either," said Kat sadly, thinking of how beautiful he had looked to her. It would have been nice if he could have offered some better explanation than confusion and fleeting attraction. She wouldn't even have minded if he'd said he'd been struck by love, but then Connor was an honest man. He didn't know how it had happened, so he'd said so. Kat sighed. "It's going to be embarrassing," she admitted. "Having to go to confession."

Connor pulled back and stared at her.

"Well, I have to do it," she said defensively. "There's my immortal soul to consider." *I'm just like my mother,* she realized, *although not pregnant, pray God.*

Now Connor realized how sorry he was for what had happened. He knew he should have felt remorse before—for her sake—but the prospect of that coughing pip-squeak, Father Eusebius, looking at him askance, was appalling. And just because Kat was such a damned devout woman. And because he hadn't been able to keep his hands off her. How *had* that happened?

"I guess I'd better get back to my room," said Kat.

Connor had an immediate and overpowering desire to keep her with him. "I guess," he said. He'd have to reaccustom himself to the idea that Kat Fitzgerald was off limits.

Chapter Ten

Connor had left town again, the coward, and Kat was plowing up the hill to find Father Eusebius. Fortunately, Father Rhabanus was still in Denver. Having warned her not to move into Connor's house, there was no telling what he'd have said to her now. She knocked at the younger priest's door and was admitted by a red-nosed, sniffling Eusebius Geiger. "Father, I'd like to make confession."

"Couldn't it wait?" he groaned, then turned away to sneeze as he shivered in the open door.

Kat frowned at him. "No, it couldn't."

"Oh, all right. Come in, and I'll get my vestments."

"Aren't we going to the church?" Kat didn't want to make her confession in the priest's *house*.

"Do I look in any condition to walk up there?"

"But what about the confessional?"

"We don't have one. You can sit in here, and I'll sit in the kitchen—near the stove."

"I'll have to shout," Kat protested.

"My hearing's very good," he mumbled and blew his nose.

"Forgive me, Father, for I have sinned," she began, once they were seated on their respective sides of the wall. "I haven't been to confession since I left Chicago." And whose fault was that? she thought. The priests were always sick or out of town. And they didn't even have a proper confessional. She heard a muted response from Father Eusebius.

"Father, I have—" Kat gulped. This was really awful. "I have committed the sin of fornication." There was another mumble and some sneezing. She supposed he'd asked for details. "With Connor Macleod. You know, my mother's husband's son. Oh lord, was it incest?" She hadn't considered that aspect of her dilemma.

"Mumble, mumble, my daughter," said Father Eusebius and fell to coughing.

"What did you say?"

"I said, 'Have you anything else to confess?'"

"Good heavens, isn't that enough?"

"Certainly, my daughter. Now you must make a sincere act of contrition."

"Oh, I will, Father."

More coughing. "Say five Hail Marys," he gasped at the end of it.

"Five?"

"Oh well, three should be enough."

"Three Hail Marys?" Kat echoed weakly. She could hear him blowing his nose.

Then he granted her absolution and came in from the kitchen. "I could use another pot of your chicken soup."

"Is that part of my atonement?" she asked, feeling somewhat the way St. George would have felt had he entered a cave expecting to face a huge dragon and found instead a spindly hermit. Kat had been a great reader of saints' lives as a child and had thought St. George very romantic.

"No, of course, soup isn't be part of your atonement," said Father Eusebius. "You're under no obligation—"

"I'll bring it tomorrow," offered Kat and escaped before he had time to reconsider his view of her sin.

Could he have misunderstood? she wondered as she walked home. Or had she misunderstood the seriousness of her fall from grace? Surely not, but he had said three Hail Marys ought to be enough. That was hardly a slap on the wrist. Maybe younger priests viewed sins of the flesh more tolerantly than older priests. But what if he'd been blowing his nose when she mentioned fornication? Did that mean that she wasn't absolved? Kat shook her head. She'd never had a problem so puzzling. Of course, she'd never before committed any serious sins. But he hadn't even given her a lecture on the glories of chastity.

Kat had heard that Father Rhabanus would be back in time for Easter, which was April tenth this year. *I sinned not a minute too soon,* she thought wryly as she walked toward Main Street.

"Would you care to buy a picture of Father Dyer?" asked a young lady carrying a box labeled Methodist Ladies' Aid Society. "They're only twenty-five cents, and the money will go to supplement his salary and buy him a new suit."

"I'll take two," said Kat promptly.

"Really?" The young woman looked delighted. "I'm Gertrude Briggle, a school teacher here in Breckenridge."

"And I'm Kat Fitzgerald."

"You must be Methodist if you want two. Would you like to join the Ladies' Aid Society?"

"Actually, I'm Catholic." Gertrude Briggle looked stunned, but Kat continued bravely into what might well be a prickly field of intolerance. There seemed to be a lot of it in Colorado. "I am very interested in the temperance movement, however. In fact, I gave a temperance lecture for Father Dyer."

145

"Oh, my goodness, I should have recognized your name. I was out of town but heard you were very moving. How terrible to lose a father *and* a husband to drink."

"Yes," said Kat, feeling more cheerful. "Maybe we can get together and close down a saloon some Sunday."

"Why, I'd love to," said Gertrude. "Did you have any particular Sunday in mind?"

"One a little warmer," suggested Kat, glancing at the lowering sky. April didn't seem to promise spring, only more snow. Kat bade her new acquaintance good-bye and went on to visit several business establishments in town, where she ordered mine supplies. Then she stopped at St. Gertrude's to arrange for the education of the four children. If she enrolled them, they'd have to go, she reasoned. After all, who would dare disappoint Reverend Mother?

"Good for you," said Hilda Walzen. "St. Gertrude's will do them a world of good, poor things, growing up heathen. What was your brother thinking of?"

"You might ask the same of Connor Macleod," said Kat. "His father says they're Catholic as well, although the daughter, Jeannie, not only didn't know it, she seems to dislike the church. She may be a problem to you."

"I relish the challenge," said Reverend Mother Hilda.

Kat nodded and excused herself, a new thought having popped up in her head: what she needed was one of those wonderful, reassuring, heart-to-heart talks with her childhood friend, Sister Freddie.

"Well, if he said you're absolved, I guess you are," said Sister Fredericka, a tall and imposing figure in her habit.

"I'm so glad you think so, Freddie. I really didn't want to confess all over again."

"I'm sure," said Sister Fredericka drily. "Well, Kat, I have several things to say since you've asked for my advice. First, I'm astonished; I'd never have taken you for a fornicator. Second, stay away from Connor Macleod.

146

You're obviously in a fair way to fall in love again as you did with Mickey."

"I am not."

"And you know how badly Mickey turned out. Third, stop calling me Freddie. It's undignified."

"I'll try," said Kat.

"And fourth, please don't ask me for any more advice about sins of the flesh."

"Freddie, who else would I talk to? You're my best friend."

"I'm a nun."

"Well, yes." When she thought about it, Kat didn't suppose many nuns were asked to discuss fornication. She sighed. In the old days there hadn't been anything she and Freddie couldn't discuss. "Well, there's something else I wanted to talk to you about." Freddie looked at her inquiringly. "Temperance," said Kat. "I want to close down a saloon some Sunday. And don't tell me that's a *curiously Protestant point of view,* as some would say." Kat didn't mention that it was the bishop who'd said that. "Just look at it from the church's point of view, Freddie. If the saloons are closed on Sunday, the miners won't have anything to do when they come to town. So they'll go to church."

"Close down a saloon?" Sister Fredericka mused. "I'd love to."

Kat waited until the whole family had assembled at the dinner table before announcing the enrollment of the children at St. Gertrude's.

"I am not going to school with a bunch of nuns," said Jeannie. "Tell her, Daddy."

"Me either," Jamie agreed. "My friends would make fun of me."

"The friends who encouraged you to shoot yourself in the leg?" asked Connor. "The sisters may be just what you need."

"Well, I don't need them," Jeannie declared.

"Women should be educated," said Kat. "Look at me. I've had to take over my brother's business, and before that my father's business. What if your father needs you? Are you going to say, 'Sorry Daddy, but I don't know anything except the recipes Eyeless taught me.' "

Connor started to protest, then changed his mind and muttered, "She's got a point, Jeannie." Kat wondered whether he had supported her because his conscience hurt where she was concerned or because he agreed.

"I don't see why everything has to be *her* way," complained Jeannie. "She's not your wife." Connor shifted uneasily on his seat. "Why should I have to get stuck in the sisters' school just because *she* did when she was young? And why is it *she* gets a new room on her side of the house when mine's hardly big enough to hold my bed?"

"We'll compromise," said Kat, bidding a temporary farewell to her second story, which hadn't materialized because Diederick was still painting. He'd decided to paint the trim and scrollwork a different color, an innovation hardly seen in a town where many houses displayed bare wood or logs. "You start back to school, and I'll have Diederick build the next room on your side." Education was more important than space or architectural beauty, Kat told herself. Besides, with all the children out of the house, there'd be less housework to force on the often-missing Coleen, the never-willing Jeannie, and the absolutely unhelpful Ingrid.

"My God, you want to keep that carpenter on?" Connor exclaimed. "I don't like him."

"His work is perfectly acceptable," said Kat.

"Maybe on your side. On mine he'll probably cut a hole in the wall and then leave it."

Kat felt a little stab of conscience. She was using their mutual fall from grace to get Connor's agreement to things he wouldn't have supported otherwise. Ten minutes later, when she came out of the kitchen to collect the last of the plates, which Coleen was washing, Kat found Ingrid practically sitting in Connor's lap, on the pretext of discussing whether she should allow her children to attend St. Gertrude's. And she was smiling at him. Ingrid wasn't much of a smiler.

"Ingrid, it's your turn to dry," Kat snapped.

Ingrid, who never argued, wandered off, and Kat asked with impulsive resentment, "Are you sleeping with her?"

"Sh-sh," he hissed, glancing around. Then coming close, he said in a bare whisper, "I'm not sleeping with anyone, Kat, certainly not Ingrid."

Kat scowled. He'd slept with her. And why, if he didn't love her? But that wasn't fair. As well ask why she had slept with him. Oh, she couldn't believe she'd got herself into this fix. Was there something in the Colorado air that undermined the rectitude of formerly virtuous women like her mother and herself?

"Do you really think I'd be interested in a woman that stupid?" Connor was saying, still on the subject of Ingrid.

"Maybe you like stupid women," Kat retorted. "Maybe you think all women are stupid."

"You aren't," said Connor. "Except about temperance. Gertrude Briggle's telling people that you and she and Father Dyer are going to start closing down saloons."

And Sister Freddie, thought Kat with satisfaction. *Just you wait.* What she said to him was, "My religious life is none of your concern. You've made it difficult enough without—"

"Oh, Kat." His face softened into lines of regret. "I guess it must have been pretty bad, talking to Father Eusebius. Every time I see him, he scowls." Connor rubbed the back of his neck. "I am sorry. I hope you know that, but if you go closing down saloons, it's going to hurt us—hurt Sean, and you promised to look out for his interests."

"I *have* been neglecting Sean's interests," Kat agreed. "We'd better make that tour of the mines."

"We can't," he protested, looking alarmed. "Not after—well, it—it just wouldn't be a good idea."

"Perhaps you're right," said Kat craftily. "And if I stay home, there'll be time to launch the first Sunday saloon-closing campaign."

"Damn it, Kat. I'm not going to let you blackmail me."

"You're going to be mad when you hear this, Daddy," said Jeannie, her mouth set in lines of smug satisfaction.

"What's that, honey? Oh, say Kat, Sean sends love." Connor had just returned from Denver. "He's a lot better. And where's Ingrid? I've got a message for her."

"I have no idea," said Kat absently. She was so glad to hear of her brother's improved health that for once she didn't care about Ingrid's unexplained absences.

"Listen to me, Daddy," said Jeannie impatiently.

Kat looked down at her plate, hiding a smile. She had a good idea what Jeannie was about to say.

"Kat did just what you told her not to. She and Sister Fredericka and Father Dyer and Miss Briggle, the public school teacher—the rest of the Methodist Ladies' Aid Society wouldn't go because they said it was too dangerous and unladylike—"

"Will you get to the point?" grumbled Connor.

"They went into the Engle Brothers' saloon and wouldn't leave."

"Women aren't allowed inside saloons." Connor's gray eyes turned dark with anger. "It's against the law. Did you realize you could be arrested?" he asked Kat.

Kat shrugged.

"They told all the miners how they shouldn't be drinking, especially on Sunday, so the miners got mad and left, and then the Engles got mad and told Kat she ought not to come to their saloon, especially bringing a nun."

"How'd you manage that?" Connor demanded.

"And that's not all, Daddy. This gambler named Cameron

Powell said to the Engle brothers, how could they take issue with a beautiful lady, and he kissed Kat's hand." Jeannie smirked triumphantly.

"That's it!" rumbled Connor. "You are not going back to any more saloons, Kathleen Fitzgerald."

"Oh, but I am. We're meeting next Sunday afternoon—"

"Next Sunday afternoon, you'll be in Montezuma on your way to the Too Late Mine."

Kat gave him a sweet smile. "Well, of course, if I'm needed on a matter of business—"

"I've just been suckered, haven't I?" Connor muttered.

"You're going to take *her* with you?" cried Jeannie. "After what she did? You never take me."

Kat had been highly suspicious when Connor told her at the last minute that they would have to postpone their mining tour in order to attend a meeting about the Ingrid's Ring litigation. She nodded her thanks when he held the door for her as they entered the building that housed the court and county offices. Had he known about this meeting earlier in the week and waited until it was too late for her to organize another attack on the saloons of Breckenridge? Now it would be at least two weeks before she could return to her temperance campaign, unless she refused to go on the postponed mine tour, but when he saw her wavering, Connor had mentioned that there was to be a fancy dress ball in Montezuma the weekend of their visit, "And you know what a fool for dancing you are, Kat," he added.

"Lover of dancing, yes," she had replied tartly, "fool, no." Yet here she was entering the judge's chambers with no plans for a temperance effort on the weekend, and next week she'd be in Montezuma at the ball. It was too tempting to miss; her ball gown was already taking shape at the dressmaker's. Besides, she owed it to her brother to keep an eye on his holdings, and there was Dixie, whom she'd heard about each time Connor went to Montezuma.

"Guess you'll be goin' to see Dixie," Eyeless would say with a cackle. Who was Dixie? That was what Kat wanted to know.

Connor introduced her to the judge, then to Medford Fleming, the rival who ran the Trenton Consolidated interests in Colorado—a handsome, middle-aged man and a snappy dresser, but he had evil eyes—and last to Harrison Ponder, Fleming's lawyer.

"What a pleasure to have such a pretty lady attending our negotiations," said Ponder gallantly. He had the most aristocratic nose Kat had ever seen.

"Thank you," she replied with a gracious smile, wondering if Connor too thought she looked pretty. Had he noticed the outfit she'd resurrected from her pre-mourning wardrobe? She herself thought the dress very becoming. It had a cream silk pleated shirt front under dark green velvet lapels, the fitted bodice and horizontally draped skirt being made of striped cream and moss-green moire. She had noted happily, as she looked at herself in Ingrid's mirror before leaving for court, that the skirt style made her waist look satisfyingly tiny.

"Pretty ladies," snapped the judge, lending a sarcastic emphasis to Ponder's compliment, "ought to stay home where they belong."

Connor probably hadn't noticed her dress, she decided. If she'd worn a burlap bag, he wouldn't have noticed because he never looked at her anymore. Well, just wait until he saw her ball gown. Then he'd look. And how dare the judge say she didn't belong in court to support her own brother's interests?

"Women don't vote; they oughten to mess in the law," said the judge.

"They *ought* to vote," Kat retorted.

Connor gave her a warning nudge as if to say, "Don't offend the judge." Fleming smiled condescendingly. Charlie

Maxell, their lawyer, said, "Colorado is actually very liberal, Miss Kathleen. Women here vote in the school board elections."

Connor frowned at Charlie as the judge said, "Fool idea. Women's schools teach 'em sewing an' such. Don't need to vote on sewing lessons."

Sewing lessons? Well, that was just the sort of misguided remark one might expect of a judge who wore plaid suspenders, Kat decided. She'd like to have told the old fool a thing or two but realized that one had to be circumspect when dealing with the judge who would be presiding over one's financial well-being. Harrison Ponder, however, proved himself to be a man of principle, she noted with approval.

"Not all of us take so narrow a view of women's education, Miss Kathleen," said the opposition lawyer. "I hope I may call you Miss Kathleen."

"Oh, certainly," Kat agreed, thinking it couldn't hurt to be polite to him. He might take a fairer view of the litigation if treated courteously.

Fleming was glaring at him, as was the judge, but Ponder added, "Not only can women vote in school board elections, but ladies can *run* for the local school boards."

"Really?"

"Yes indeed. My esteemed colleague didn't mention that."

"I was coming to it," said Charlie Maxell.

"That's what we get for having a woman in chambers," said the judge disgustedly, "chit-chat! Now I want no more of it. I've called the parties in because I won't have this case in court for years. Nothing bores a jury more than apex litigation. Hard on the judge too, so let's hear some serious bargaining from you people."

Connor discussed the origins of the case, which he said were firmly rooted in Fleming's original dishonesty. Charlie Maxell discussed the legalities, showing off a bit,

Kat thought; then he went on to what sort of settlement would satisfy his clients. Harrison Ponder, with frequent courteous nods and bows in her direction, discussed the Trenton claim to apex rights. The judge fidgeted and finally snarled that he'd heard the same accusations and arguments before. "I want to hear something new."

"Good," said Fleming. "We have an offer to make."

Kat noted the well-manicured state of his hands, the distinguished touch of gray at the sides of his dark hair. It pleased her to see that that oh-so-carefully groomed hair had receded on both sides of his forehead. She wouldn't trust the man an inch.

"We're listening," Connor replied brusquely.

Kat smiled at the opposition lawyer and murmured that she hoped the proposal would be a serious attempt to settle the case amicably.

Ponder looked distressed. Fleming snapped, "Fifteen thousand."

"Fifteen thousand!" Connor stood up. "That's lower than your original offer, which was an insult."

"Take it or leave it," said Fleming.

"I'm sure you can do better than that," said Kat, slanting a cold look at Medford Fleming, then a smile at his lawyer.

"I wish we could, Miss Kathleen," said Ponder.

Connor was already leaving, which Kat considered quite rude. Charlie Maxell offered her his arm, and the other men were on their feet when Harrison Ponder murmured to her, "May I call on you, Miss Kathleen?"

Did he plan to offer his good offices to negotiate between the parties? "Yes," she murmured, "please do."

"Your honor, at this time I wish to withdraw from the case," said Mr. Ponder.

"What's this? Your withdrawing will set us back months," cried the judge.

"Nonetheless, I must withdraw due to"—He smiled at Kat.—"conflict of interest."

154

"The woman's seduced my lawyer!" exclaimed Fleming.

"I beg your pardon," Kat gasped. "I never saw Mr. Ponder before in my life."

"I must protest this insult to my client," cried Charlie Maxell. "She has no interest whatever in the opponent's lawyer."

Ponder gave him a smug look and excused himself.

Fleming snarled, "I'll sue you for this."

"You already are," Connor muttered.

"Comes of letting women mess in the law," said the judge.

Kat allowed herself to be helped into her coat by Charlie Maxell. She and Connor were exchanging glares. Surely he didn't think she *had* encouraged that silly lawyer. She tipped her chin up and sailed by him with Charlie hurrying behind her, offering to see her home.

"She doesn't need to be seen home," Connor shouted. "She's with me."

"Just two minutes ago," said Kat, glancing back at him, "you were in the process of leaving without me."

"You realize that this will set us back months in getting the case to court?" Connor said to her after dinner.

"Well, it's none of my doing."

"Of course, we can afford to wait now that you've charmed poor Charlie into offering free legal services."

"I did not; he's getting a percentage."

"Did you or did you not say Ponder could call on you?"

"Well, of course. I thought he wanted to talk about the case."

"You thought that about Charlie."

"He does talk to me about the case."

"Why do I get into these idiotic arguments with you?"

"Make an idiotic accusation, get into an idiotic argument," said Kat with a bland smile.

Connor burst out laughing, and Kat joined him. It was

155

the first time she had felt comfortable with Connor since—well, that didn't bear thinking on. But sin was a great destroyer of friendships: she'd best keep that in mind when they embarked on their trip.

Chapter Eleven

"I don't understand why Jeannie dislikes me," said Kat as she and Connor left town in the buggy, headed for French Gulch and Sean's First Strike silver mine.

Connor shrugged. "She's probably afraid we mean to marry." He glanced at Kat out of the corner of his eye, but she'd turned her head away, so he couldn't see her expression. "Once she realizes we've no such intention, she'll settle down." Still no comment from Kat. She seemed more interested in a rickety wooden structure that snaked down the gulch on V legs. "That's a flume," he said. "It carried in water for hydraulicking."

Kat stared unseeing at the flume, thinking, *He needn't seem so positive. What would he have done if he'd gotten me with child?* Still, Kat knew she wasn't with child, and there'd be no reason in the future to worry about *that*.

"What are these piles of rocks?" she asked, surprised to note, now that the snow was melting, a landscape littered with unsightly debris, as if God had swept up dull little

157

rocks and bits of gravel from all over the world and dumped them in this river valley between towering peaks.

"What's left from the placer mining days and hydraulic operations," Connor replied. "Looks like hell, doesn't it?"

"You really should watch your language," Kat warned. "You set a bad example for the children."

"Comes of spending so many years with miners," he replied. "And the kids are used to it. They've never lived anywhere but mining camps." He went on to explain placer mining, which involved washing sand and gravel in pans and sluice boxes to sift out the heavier gold, and hydraulicking, which was even more destructive to the landscape because jets of water were directed against the walls of the gulches for the same purpose.

"Couldn't they clean it up when they're through?"

"When they're through, they move on," said Connor. "In the '60s, Summit County yielded millions in gold to men with the patience and luck to take it. You didn't need any investment, just greed and a willingness to spend a lot of time cold, damp, and aching." He pulled up the buggy and pointed to a mine entrance, a square wooden frame where the tunnel into the hillside began. The few buildings outside were primitive and unpainted. "That's the First Strike. Sean developed it on his own in the early '80s, about the time he met Ingrid."

"He wasn't writing to me much then," said Kat. "He came out here for his health and to work on the Alpine Tunnel, but he never said why he quit."

"Lots of men came for the tunnel in 1880. They got their fare paid, but not many stayed with the job. It was miserable work—hard, high altitude, terrible winter storms." Connor helped her down. "The First Strike's a silver producer. He ships the ore down to the smelter in Cucumber Gulch." As they watched, mules pulled a loaded cart from the tunnel entrance, and men transferred the ore into wagons. After an inspection of the mine, Connor was satisfied with the work, if not with the output.

As they drove on to the Rose Laurel on Farncomb Hill, Kat asked hesitantly, "If—if anything should happen to Sean, what would the legal status be on ownership of his claims?"

"You mean if he dies?" Connor asked bluntly. "Like he said, you'll inherit half in your own name and control of Ingrid's half. Anyone but a child can own a claim in Colorado. Now we're coming up on the Rose Laurel." He pointed. "Gold," he told her. "I heard about the strike down here not too long after I quit my job as foreman in Sts. John in '78 and started prospecting the Montezuma area. My wife was fit to be tied when I moved her and the kids into a cabin outside Montezuma, although it wasn't much different—same twelve-foot drifts as in Sts. John."

"Women like a man they know is going to put food on the table," Kat murmured, quoting her mother.

Connor scowled at her. "I kept them fed, but Rose was always after me about something. When we first got married, she wanted to live in Colorado Springs with the rich folks—as if I had that kind of money. As if I had any money." He reached out to hold Kat's arm when the buggy jolted on the rough road, and Kat, reacting to his touch, inhaled sharply.

"I had to take the job at Sts. John because Jeannie was on the way. Then we had a baby die between Jeannie and Jamie, and Rose Laurel was with child again when I came here—not that close to her time," he added defensively, "and I had a feeling about Farncomb Hill."

"Did it work out?" she asked.

"Well, I was right about the mine, but not about her. Our cabin was isolated by a late blizzard while I was away, and the baby came early. Rose bled to death before the neighbors got to her." His face was pale and grim. "She was buried, she and the baby, by the time I got back to tell her we were going to be rich."

159

Kat shivered, thinking what a terrible time it must have been for all of them. "Were Jeannie and Jamie there when she—when Rose—"

"Jeannie went out to get help. She's lucky she lived through the storm," he replied. "Both kids had nightmares for months, though I don't think Jamie remembers it now. I moved them to Breckenridge after that."

They inspected the Rose Laurel and headed back to Gibson Hill. "I prospected the Ingrid's Ring," said Connor. "You can see the Jumbo mine over there. They've got a ball mill, jawbreaker, shaker table, and tram. Now see the next tram? That's ours. I brought the mine in just after the Jumbo in the summer of '84. Then Sean put up half the development money. His share came from the First Strike, and we named it Ingrid's Ring because she wanted a wedding ring made from the gold."

"Hadn't Sean already given Ingrid a ring?" asked Kat curiously. "Goodness, Phoebe and Sean Michael would have been born by then."

"It's a good vein. We're making a lot of money here. Hey, Hortense!" He reined in the horse and jumped down, leaving Kat with her question about Ingrid unanswered as she surveyed the cluster of steep-roofed, unpainted buildings.

Hortense barreled down the hill from the mine dormitory and kitchen shouting, "I either get paid, or I quit. You got that, Macleod?"

Before the day was over, they'd fired the Ingrid's Ring superintendent, Bod Jenkins, and put the mine foreman in his place. "Why the hell would Bod do that?" Connor grumbled over dinner at a boarding house in Preston operated by John Shock, the postmaster. "We'd damn near stopped having trouble at the Ingrid's Ring once we hired Hortense. Kat, are you paying attention?"

She was inspecting a hat—rough straw with a wide green ribbon around the crown and a bow in back, which she had bought from Mrs. Hattie Shock shortly after they arrived in town. Kat dragged her attention away from the new purchase. "That's the lawsuit mine, isn't it?" she asked thoughtfully. "Do you think Fleming could have been paying Mr. Jenkins to make trouble?"

Connor rested his fork in a puddle of gravy and stared. "I'll see if I can find out where Jenkins turns up next."

The boarding house was noisy, and Kat found bugs in her bedding. She slept badly and rose with alacrity the next morning for their train trip to Dillon and transfer to the spur that went up Ten Mile Canyon.

"That's Red Peak," said Connor, pointing to one of the sights near Dillon.

Kat found herself inordinately sensitive to the brush of his arm across her shoulder and had to force herself to concentrate on his words rather than the proximity of his face and body.

"In '82, there were twenty-four mines operating up there, not a one of them owned by me, though I'd hate to think of how many holes I put down on that mountain—on my own or grubstaking someone else. I saw a lot of color, but I never found a single vein."

"Color?" Kat asked faintly.

He leaned back, relieving her of the tension generated by his closeness. "You see a change in soil or rock color, maybe you've got ore." Until they left the train at a siding that served the Dead Wife Mine, he gave her a lesson in mine geology while she craned her neck, peering up at the precipitous rock walls that edged the canyon and down at the rush and plunge of Ten Mile Creek.

"Dead Wife?" Kat couldn't believe he'd named it that.

"I was pretty unhappy at the time," Connor confessed.

As far as Kat could see, he still was.

"I met Eyeless in a saloon right after I'd moved to Breckenridge with the kids, and he told me about some silver lodes in Upper Ten Mile Canyon. Our deal was, he'd look after the children while I prospected Elk Mountain. I figured I'd never have got up there if she hadn't died, so I named it the Dead Wife. Reckon I'm a hell of a lot luckier mining than I was marrying.

"I used profits from the Rose Laurel to develop the Dead Wife after the Denver and Rio Grande laid track into Leadville and made the mine profitable. Then I grubstaked your brother, who was working for two-fifty a day drilling and blasting, and he found the Sister Katie and the Silver Cigar. We're partners on those."

"He named a mine after me?"

Connor grinned at her. "I reckon, unless you two have a sister named Katie."

"He used to call me that when I was a little girl."

"The Silver Cigar—he found that lode stubbing out a cigar on an outcropping." Connor laughed at the memory.

"Sean had no business smoking!" exclaimed Kat. "He came out here because of bronchitis."

In Ten Mile Canyon she saw mine buildings clinging to the high ledges, their roofs slanting away from the very rock of the mountain so that avalanches would pass over rather than sweep the buildings away. She saw great mills, ugly and monstrous, bigger than factories in Chicago. She saw mine tailings like bastard offspring of the mountains themselves, but barren and ugly, as if the mating of man and mountain had produced a nature that would never know springtime and new life.

Insisting that she see it all—not just the safer outside trappings, Kat rode hoists down the vertical shafts that took them deep into the stone ramparts. Wearing a miner's hat and carrying a candle spiked on a rough holder, she plodded through tunnels and cavernous rooms, shiveringly aware that only the frail wooden cribbing kept her from being buried under tons of rock.

Why had Sean liked this life? she wondered. Why had he come into the mines willingly when he could have stayed above ground, safe and healthy? Down here, the men coughed as her brother did. Kat herself felt that she couldn't get enough of the dust-laden air into her lungs to sustain life. And through it all, she was aware of Connor's eyes on her.

They inspected miner's dormitories crowded with cots and men's belongings and reeking of men's sweat. They ate with the miners at the Silver Cigar on Sheep Mountain, a huge meal of stew with dumplings, soda biscuits, cake and pudding. When Kat commented on the amount of food, Connor replied that the men worked ten hours a day, six days a week. "If you think this is a lot, you should see the breakfasts."

She got some idea going over the books with their lists of food purchases—ham, bacon, sausage, eggs, dried fruit, fixings for pancakes and oatmeal, coffee—anything people ate for breakfast was served here. And she was glad of it, thinking their lives miserable. At least they ate well.

"Hear you fired Brett Conklin," Connor remarked to the superintendent at the Sister Katie while Kat was checking purchase lists.

"Yep, caught him highgradin' again. Runnin' nuggets out in his boots, for God's sake."

"Anyone else take him on?"

"The Wheel of Fortune did, but he's dead. Giant powder hung fire on him. His tombstone reads, 'Here lies Brett Conklin, Blown to Bits, Good Riddance." When Kat looked horrified, the superintendent said, "He was stealin' from them too."

"What do the men do in their off hours?" Kat asked as they headed back toward Frisco.

"Gamble, drink, and sleep," Connor replied.

"Drink?"

"Don't even think about it," he warned. "We can't afford a strike."

Kat subsided, but she didn't like the idea of those men up there on Sean's mountain drinking their nights away. If they really understood what they were doing to themselves—she was distracted by the view coming into Frisco. "I don't understand why there aren't more trees."

"Charcoal kilns are big business around here. So's lumbering. They cut the big trees for timber, a lot of it bought by the mines. The small stuff they use for charcoal."

"But it's the same around Breckenridge."

"Fires have destroyed the forests over the years. The Utes used to set them for spite or to drive game or make things tough when the plains tribes came into the mountains to hunt and cut lodge poles. Then lightning starts forest fires. So do white men."

"I wonder what it was like in the old days," Kat mused.

"Beautiful," said Connor. "I traveled here with Dad before so much damage had been done. It was God's own country. I still love it."

Kat nodded. "I guess I do too. Did you see those yellow violets by the snow bank? I couldn't believe it."

"You'll see more flowers than you ever imagined through the late spring and summer—columbine, larkspur, I don't know all the names."

The main street of Frisco was wide, deep in spring mud, and crowded with horses, buggies, pack trains and ore wagons. Its most welcome sight—to a weary Kat—was the Leyner Hotel, a two-story clapboard structure with eight long, narrow windows marching across each of its two floors and eight slender supports holding up a first floor roof that jutted out over the raised wooden sidewalk. When she retired that night to her lumpy bed, Kat sighed with happiness, thinking that the last two days had been the most interesting of her life and Connor Macleod the most interesting man she'd ever met.

The next day the traveling conditions, which hadn't been ideal, deteriorated. They took the spur from Dillon to Keystone, then a jouncing freight wagon to Montezuma, where various men hailed Connor on the street.

"Come for the game?" asked one.

"Nope," Connor replied.

"What game?" asked Kat.

"They've had a round-the-clock poker game going here as long as I can remember—even after the town passed an anti-gambling law back in—oh, '82 or so."

"Why doesn't the sheriff stop it?" asked Kat, shifting miserably for the hundredth time on the hard wagon seat, where she was wedged between the driver and Connor.

"What'd the sheriff wanna do that fer?" asked the driver. "No one gonna git no votes around here if he shuts down the town poker game."

"Come to see Dixie, Connor?" called another man from the door of a saloon.

"Who's Dixie?" asked Kat. Eyeless was always talking about Dixie. She turned to Connor and noticed the high color washing across his cheekbones.

"I don't visit Dixie," he mumbled, and Kat's lips tightened as she realized what kind of woman Dixie must be.

"Here you are," said the driver, hauling his team to a stop in front of a boarding house. Connor hopped down and unloaded their luggage before he bothered to lift Kat from the high seat.

"We'll be heading straight out," he said, making it clear that he didn't intend to discuss Dixie, "but we'll have to ride from here."

"Ride?" Kat had thought her aching bones would find relief once they abandoned the freight wagon.

"Horses."

She remembered thinking, on the train to Breckenridge, how much fun it would be to ride and herd cattle as Isabella Bird had done. Now, faced with the prospect of actually seating herself on a horse, she was tempted to tell Connor that she'd just stay at the boarding house and visit with the landlady, who had boarded Gertrude Briggle when Gertrude taught school in Montezuma.

"So how's Gertrude doing in the big city?" boomed the landlady, showing them to their rooms so they could change from train clothes to riding clothes.

"The big city?"

"Breckenridge. Got a railroad there, don't they? That's what I call the big city. Now you two just take notice. My sheets are clean, and they stay that way. Anyone gets drunk and throws up on them, out they go. And I don't like to be woke up in the night, so if you're going to the fancy-dress ball, keep quiet when you come back. Wake me up, and out you go."

"Yes, ma'am," said Kat, wondering how many boarders were ejected for throwing up on the clean sheets. It was a daunting thought, but not as daunting as that immense horse whose reins Connor held when she arrived downstairs. How did one get on a horse? She wasn't going to admit that she didn't know.

"Well, come on. I'll give you a leg up."

Gingerly, Kat put her foot onto his laced hands, and he tossed her into the saddle, frightening her half to death.

"Damned nuisance you forgot a split skirt," he muttered as he mounted. "There aren't that many women in Montezuma, much less sidesaddles."

Without any coaching from her, Kat's horse trotted after Connor's. She noted unhappily that, with no riding habit, her ankles were displayed. When they were halfway to the Too Late Mine, he said, "Let me guess. You've never ridden a horse before."

Kat remained stubbornly silent. If she'd ached from the wagon, now she felt close to tears.

"Why didn't you say? Sean doesn't own any part of the Too Late. You didn't have to come."

"Why did you name it the Too Late?" she asked to divert his attention from her ineptitude.

"I knew about this one before I ever went to Farncomb Hill. If I'd filed and worked here instead of chasing after Farncomb gold, Rose might not have died."

"And then again, she might," said Kat. His life seemed to be overshadowed by that guilt. "Many women die in childbed."

He sighed. "You're right." Then he changed the subject. "This is a rich mine, but getting the ore out's expensive. And even when we've brought it down, there's a long freight to the railhead at Keystone."

As they climbed a steep, narrow path, Kat was terrified the horse would misstep, but Connor didn't seem to notice the danger. He stared up at the mine, still far above them. "What I need is a tram like the one I've got near home. They do say now they've got electricity in Aspen, they'll be electrifying the trams."

"Electricity?" Kat laughed. "It doesn't work. I was taken to see an electric trolley at the Colorado Seminary in Denver, and after all the fuss, it rained and the trolley wouldn't run. What good is that?"

Connor looked amused. "You don't put much faith in modern science, do you? Well, I'd settle for the old fashioned kind of tram where the weight of the ore bucket going down full pulls the empty buckets up. Works well enough for me."

At the mine, Kat received several proposals of marriage, much to Connor's disgust.

"Well, it's not my fault," said Kat testily as the horses picked their way down a trail where spring snow slides had washed out sections and the animals slipped precariously on loose earth and rocks. "I didn't ask them to propose."

"I hate to think how many more offers you'll get tonight. Especially if you wear that dress."

"You said it was a fancy-dress ball, so I had a fancy ball dress made up," retorted Kat, closing her eyes and murmuring a quick prayer as they crossed another terrifying section of the trail. She'd be lucky to survive until ball time. As an antidote to terror, she concentrated on her gown. If Connor worried about the dress now, wait until he saw it on her. The green silk brought out the color of her eyes, while the silver-gray gloves and panels added a certain demure accent belied by the triple ruching that left most of her shoulders bare and then plunged in a deep V over her breasts.

Connor had no idea how fetching a lady he'd be escorting. Her new corset minimized her waist while lifting her breasts to maximize her cleavage, and the skirt draped in loose diagonal folds of green tulle with ruffled edges, highlighted by a scattering of moondrops that she had sewed on herself. It had been a *very* extravagant purchase, she admitted, trying—and failing—to feel guilty about the extravagance. After all, if Connor got a shock when he saw her, he might reconsider his plots against the fledgling temperance movement in Breckenridge. He might be glad to keep her home and less daringly dressed. Kat smiled to herself.

"What's the smile for?" asked Connor, for they had just negotiated a particularly difficult slide area.

"Why, I was thinking about the dance," said Kat.

"Goodnight," Connor whispered, mindful of the dangers of awakening the landlady.

"Goodnight," Kat whispered back, and bouncing up on tiptoe, she kissed his cheek in sheer exuberance. "I had a wonderful time."

"I noticed," said Connor dryly.

Pleased at having taken him off guard with the kiss, Kat giggled. Then she danced into her room, closing the door with exaggerated care. What a wonderful evening it had been—wonderful music, friendly people, and she had danced every dance, often changing partners in mid-tune to satisfy the demand. Everyone had commented on how beautiful she looked, how lovely her dress was, and although

Mother always said that beauty was only skin-deep, the compliments were nice to hear. Even Connor had said she looked beautiful and failed to criticize the low neckline. In fact, she'd caught him staring. Kat had felt deliciously brazen. Then she stopped her happy reminiscences to sniff the air of her room. Strange. What was that odor?

And of course, there had been the usual proposals of marriage. Following each, she had invited the suitor to visit the house in Breckenridge, should he happen to be in town, and meet whatever young lady or ladies from Chicago were in residence, since Kat herself was not looking for a husband. Connor had been rather difficult about those invitations, several of which he overheard. Well, he shouldn't have been eavesdropping, and Mother did expect her to marry off the Chicago girls.

Kat sniffed again. The odor smelled like alcohol, but given the upright character of the landlady, it must be some sort of cleaning solution. How nice of her to clean this evening. There'd be no bugs tonight, Kat was sure. Now where was the lamp? Having been lost in her thoughts, she hadn't paid much attention to her whereabouts in the dark room. She put her hands out and walked into a wall. The next try did not produce a lamp or a candle.

Oh well, thought Kat, *if I can find the bed, there's a chair beside it. I'll just undress in the dark and lay my clothes on the chair.* She yawned, thinking yearningly of the landlady's clean sheets, and fumbled forward again, bumping at last into the bed. She reached out to fold back the covers and went still with shock. Then she turned and ran, blundering into a wall, then through the door into the hallway, bursting—panic-stricken—into Connor's room.

"There's—there's someone in my bed," she stammered, falling into his arms.

Connor looked down at her quizzically, disentangled himself, and, picking up his lamp, went into her room to investigate. Kat followed but no further than her door. "See,

I told you," she whispered as he inspected the large body under the blankets. Connor shook the sleeper's shoulder, but with no result.

After several more tries, he said, "My guess is he's dead drunk and not likely to wake until morning."

"Well, can't we drag him out into the hall?" Kat was still trembling, appalled at the idea that she might have climbed into bed with that huge man.

Connor studied the sleeping mound, which rose and fell majestically under the blankets. "He weighs three hundred pounds," was the gloomy report. Then Connor turned and noticed her trembling. "Go back to my room and wrap up in a blanket. You look like you're half frozen."

She didn't tell him it was fear. She did obey, and Connor joined her a few minutes later. "Nothing I can do about him." He closed the door and sat down on the one chair. Kat sat shivering on his bed. "We've got a problem," he remarked. "One room, two people, and a landlady who'll toss us out if we wake her up."

"But surely when we tell her—"

"Take my word for it, she won't be sympathetic." He eyed Kat warily. "I guess I'm expected to give up my bed."

"Then you'd freeze." Kat blinked back tears. She was so tired and so cold. Montezuma wasn't Breckenridge; here it was still winter.

"You ever heard of bundling?"

Kat shook her head, but it didn't sound good to her, not like something that should be considered by two people who'd already given in to sins of the flesh.

"Old-time custom. Engaged couples shared a bed with a board between them."

"We don't have a board, and we're not engaged." Could he be considering a proposal of marriage? Her heart gave a little skip.

"So we put the pillows between us, get some sleep, and

leave in the morning before anyone discovers we spent the night in the same room," said Connor pragmatically, as if he were suggesting that they buy a new mule team or have Diederick build another shed in back of the house.

"Oh." Kat bit her lip. "Well, I really don't think—"

"I've learned my lesson, Kat," said Connor, his face very serious. "You'll be perfectly safe."

What did that mean? That he no longer found her attractive? He hadn't acted at the ball as if he were immune to her charms. Or was it the dress? Show a little cleavage and any man—even one who didn't like you—would look. All at once she felt very sad, as well as tired and cold. She wished she'd worn a dress that covered her to the chin. "My clothes are in the other room," she mumbled. How embarrassing that she should think sleeping beside him a great danger, while he saw none at all in the situation.

In minutes he was back with her belongings. "I'll step out in the hall if you want to put on a nightgown. I don't reckon you'd get much sleep wearing a bustle and corsets."

Kat nodded, changed hurriedly once he disappeared, and slipped into his bed, placing the pillows in the middle. *I shouldn't be doing this,* she told herself, heart speeding up when she thought of Connor lying just beyond those pillows. *Just because he says he's learned a lesson—what lesson? God will never forgive me if I—*

Connor reentered the room and blew out the lamp, saying not a word to her. As if she weren't even there. How could she voice her objections when he was ignoring her? Was he really that indifferent, or was he waiting to pounce? Shivering with nerves and cold, she listened to him moving around the room, then felt the bed sag as he got in, pushing the pillows right up against her as he tried to make room for himself. Still he said nothing.

This is terrible, thought Kat. *Sinful. Nothing between us but a few feathers. And everyone knows men are creatures of lust. That's what Mother always says, and she certainly proved herself right. Pregnant at her age. That could happen to me too. That dress probably convinced him I wouldn't mind if he—*

She frowned, listening. Connor was breathing like someone asleep. Was he pretending in order to catch her off guard? Was he—Kat herself yawned as the warmth of the bed, now holding two bodies, seeped through her. *Connor is, after all, a nice man in most ways....* Her trembling had stopped. *... but sinful. He might be a nice man, but men ...* She yawned again *... have to keep alert ... keep eyes open ...*

Kat stirred once in the night when Connor shifted his position. They were back to back, the pillows having migrated to the bottom of the bed. She thought sleepily of trying to reestablish the barrier, but the warmth of his body was so cozy and she so sleepy that she ducked her nose back under the covers and drifted off.

Kat opened her eyes to find the lamp lit and Connor dressed. "Have you changed your mind?" she asked, confused, wondering if he'd found himself less indifferent to her than he thought. Was he avoiding temptation? Or maybe it was her he distrusted. Kat scowled.

"It's almost morning. Get your clothes on, and we'll leave," he whispered, interrupting her disturbed thoughts.

Almost morning? They'd slept together without—"We did it!" she exclaimed.

"What do you mean?" he asked, frowning. "We didn't do anything."

"I know. That's what I meant."

Kat gave him such a beautiful smile that Connor was swamped with regret for having been such a gentleman.

Chapter Twelve

They were taking the train home from Keystone. In contrast to Kat's exuberant happiness, Connor felt grumpy. He knew why she was so pleased; they hadn't committed any "sins of the flesh," as she'd put it the one time they had. But good lord, what had she expected? That he'd toss the protective pillows on the floor and rape her? Personally, he thought his plan had worked out very well, but she didn't have to be so damned happy about it. Did she find him unattractive now? She hadn't when they'd fallen into bed together at the house. Then he had another thought. Maybe she found him too attractive. Maybe she was pleased that *she* had been able to resist temptation. Connor smiled for the first time during the trip home.

"You're going to say yes, aren't you?" she exclaimed.

"What?"

"Oh, thank you, Connor. It's going to be such fun."

He searched his mind desperately for the lost thread of their conversation.

"If we find a new mine, will we be joint owners, or third owners with Sean?"

Prospecting—she wanted him to take her prospecting.

"Where shall we look first?"

"Nigger Hill," he said quickly.

Kat frowned. "Why would anyone name a place that? Especially with Mr. Ford such a prominent citizen in Breckenridge. He must feel very hurt when he hears that name."

"It's named after him," said Connor. "In the early days, he and several other Negro prospectors had claims stolen from them on that hill. Some lawyer in Denver was able to cheat Barney because coloreds weren't allowed to file mining claims. In fact, people still think he's got gold buried up there. Barney says every time he leaves town, people follow him hoping to find where he's hidden it. Irritates the hell out of him."

"Watch your language," she said absently. "Is that why you want to prospect—well, I'm not going to call it Nigger Hill. Are you looking for Mr. Ford's gold?"

"The prospecting's your idea. I chose Nigger Hill because it's close."

"Oh, I see. You don't really expect me to find anything, so you don't want to waste your time going very far afield. Well, all right."

Connor studied her as she turned back to the train window. She didn't act like a woman who was smitten with his charms. Good thing too.

Connor's temper didn't improve when they arrived in Breckenridge to discover that there had been a fire which destroyed, among other buildings, some property of his and Barney Ford's Chop House. Kat was all sympathy for Barney, who said phlegmatically, "Just have to rebuild," but she didn't say a word about Connor's losses.

Then they continued on to the house and discovered

174

Jeannie in a twit because Diederick had abandoned her new room to build a fancy trellis for Kat's end of the porch.

"Well, it *is* beautiful," Kat exclaimed, studying the intricate trellis. "Jeannie, would you like to share my room while Diederick—"

"I'd rather die," said Jeannie.

Kat sighed. "Perhaps I'll grow sweet peas on my new trellis," she said sadly. "Someone told me how beautiful they are in Aspen."

"You gonna cover up der trellis mit flowers?" Diederick demanded. "Mein trellis ist ein vork of art."

"Forget about the damn trellis, and wall up the damn hole in my daughter's room," shouted Connor.

"Der hole's in your room," said Diederick, "unt I vork for—"

"You won't work for anyone around here if you don't do what you're told. Kat, I'm sorry about Jeannie. She's—I don't know what her problem is."

Because Coleen crossed the street every time they saw more than two males congregated, Kat feared they'd never reach the railroad depot in time to pick up her mother's latest protégée, Mary Beth Halloran. How in the world was she ever to find a husband for a girl who couldn't walk past a person in pants without trembling? "Come *on*, Coleen. Look at that mud. Do you really want to wade through it?"

"Yes," said Coleen, who had spotted a group in front of the barber shop under the sign that advertised hot baths.

Kat grabbed her arm and dragged her forward. Then she stopped because she recognized a face. "Jamie Macleod, what are you doing here?" Kat brushed by several of the lounging boys and snatched a bent cigarette with tobacco dribbling out both ends from the hand of Connor's twelve-year-old son. "Why aren't you in school?"

"Yes, Jamie," mimicked one of the boys, "why aren't you in school?"

Kat whirled and pushed the surprised youth off the sidewalk into the mud. "Coleen, don't you run off," she ordered, perceiving that Coleen was about to flee. "You'll have to see that Jamie goes straight back to St. Gertrude's. No, don't say a word," she snarled at a boy who had just opened his mouth. He closed it and slunk away with his companions, leaving Jamie red-faced. "Imagine. Skipping school," she said to Jamie. "It's your Christian duty, Coleen, to see that he gets to St. Gertrude's."

"Can I stay there too?" asked Coleen.

"Oh, I suppose so. I'll stop for you on my way back." Kat then continued to the station. With the advent of spring, Breckenridge had become frenetically busy. Men, animals, and wagons thronged the muddy streets. And it was noisy—teamsters shouting, animals braying, bells and whistles sounding. Kat found it quite exhilarating. She crossed the bridge to West Breckenridge, taking in all the sights, and barely made it to the station in time to meet the train.

Once she arrived, the stationmaster tried to send her away. "Ladies don't take the train here," he snapped.

"I'm meeting it, not taking it."

"Ladies don't meet the train here. They don't get off the train here."

"You're wrong," said Kat, pointing to the young woman disembarking. "Yoo–hoo! Are you Mary Beth Halloran?"

"What a strange man," Kat murmured once she'd arranged to have Mary Beth's trunk delivered to the house. The stationmaster bade them good-bye by insisting that they *couldn't* think of walking back, not from *here*. "It's not that far," Kat assured him. Was he some sort of woman-hater, she wondered, refusing to allow females in his railroad station?

She liked Mary Beth Halloran at once. The girl didn't bat

an eye when called to by various men as they walked home. "Friendly town," Mary Beth remarked. "Catch anyone in Chicago saying hello to a stranger."

She looked quite surprised when they picked up Coleen, who assured her that, although the town was a terrifying place, it did have two priests, a church, a house of Benedictine sisters, a convent school, a hospital, a—

Mary Beth interrupted to say that Coleen had mentioned more than enough religious institutions to satisfy the most ardent Catholic.

"I don't want to go to school with nuns," Jamie complained when Connor had been apprised of his misdeeds.

Connor earned Kat's disapproval by laughing and saying, "Watch it, boy. I'll take you out back and make you smoke until you throw up. As for school, I've paid your tuition, so you'll go."

"Yes sir," grumbled Jamie.

"Aunt Kat," cried Phoebe, "you promised us a story."

Pleased that Connor had taken care of the problem with Jamie, Kat lifted Phoebe into her lap and tucked Sean Michael beside her in her big rocking chair. "Did I ever tell you the story of St. George and the dragon?" she asked. The saints' lives she'd read as a child were coming in handy.

A female shriek brought Kat tumbling out of bed. In the corridor room she found Coleen, nightgown-clad, cowering by the stove while Connor swore at her.

"What happened?" Kat demanded.

"I just fell over another damned Chicago girl," he shouted and stamped off. Coleen burst into tears.

"What were you doing here?" Kat asked as she escorted Coleen back to bed.

"Praying," sniffed Coleen. "Mary Beth—" She burst into tears again.

"Mary Beth what?"

177

"Mary Beth said I was keeping her awake."

Kat threw up her hands. "Couldn't you pray silently?"

"The Blessed Mother might not hear me. How do I know—"

"What's all the noise?" asked Mary Beth, popping out from under her covers in the bed by the sink, her head encased in a huge nightcap. "I can't do a good day's work without a good night's sleep."

"I quite agree," said Kat. "Now go to sleep, Coleen."

Then she went to get a robe and recrossed the house to knock on Connor's door. "Not a word," he admonished, scowling at her through the three-inch opening. "I'm up to my ass in Chicago girls and—"

"Well, really!" Kat whirled around and left. Such language! It wasn't her fault Coleen was a silly twit.

The next morning, Coleen was gone, and Mary Beth hadn't heard her leave. "I'm a heavy sleeper," she replied to queries and went back to sweeping the porch, having already served breakfast and scrubbed the kitchen.

When asked if he knew Coleen's whereabouts, Connor replied, "Chicago, let's hope." Kat didn't speak another word to him during the twelve hours the sheriff spent searching the town. Coleen was finally located at St. Gertrude's.

"She didn't say that she hadn't told you where she'd be," explained Sister Freddie.

"I think the child has a real vocation," added Reverend Mother Hilda.

"You mean she's joining St. Gertrude's?" Kat didn't know what to make of it. "What will my mother say? She expected me to marry them all off."

"And so you are," said Sister Anastasia. "Becoming a bride of Christ is a fine calling."

"Just consider Coleen a contribution to the church," Sister Freddie advised.

Kat told Connor when she next saw him, "You've driven the poor girl into a nunnery with your terrible language."

178

"At least *you're* talking to me now."

"No, I'm not." And she ignored him for several more days while the children giggled about the thunderstorm atmosphere pervading the adult world, Eyeless taking Connor's side, Mary Beth Kat's, and Ingrid, as always, asleep or out.

Connor found that he missed Kat's conversation and her ready smile. He missed their business discussions at day's end and her quick laughter, but he had no idea how to make up. Did she really think it was his fault that Coleen had run away to the sisters? The girl had spent all her time there anyway, the only difference now being that she slept at St. Gertrude's instead of taking up space in his already crowded house.

Mary Beth was worth four of Coleen. Surely, Kat saw that. Maybe she was still angry about his language, but he couldn't take it back now, so how was he to restore their friendship? Maybe a gift—but what would be appropriate for a woman who was a friend rather than—

"Stop that damn hammering!" he shouted at the carpenter and then looked around nervously to see if Kat had heard him swearing again.

"Can't build a room vitout hammering," Diederick shouted back and resumed his racket.

Connor's eyes narrowed. He didn't like Diederick, which gave him a good idea. Smiling wickedly, he went off to see Mrs. McNaught.

"Peace?" Connor held out a wooden box.

"What's that?" asked Kat. The box was filled with little mud balls, bits of green sticking out here and there.

"Sweet peas," said Connor.

"Oh!" A delighted smile lit her face. "Oh, wherever did you get them?"

"Dug 'em up."

Kat clapped her hands as Diederick came around the house to peer into the box. "You're not going to cover up mein trellis mit dose—"

"Of course, I am," said Kat. "Aren't you supposed to be building a room?"

Diederick skulked away. Connor grinned smugly and asked, "Am I forgiven?"

"Well—" She paused. "Are you going to take me prospecting?"

"When?" he asked cautiously.

"Now! I'll just get my bonnet."

"Bring a warm coat," he warned.

"In May? Oh, you're teasing."

"I never tease about the weather."

"If it weren't so cold, I'd be the most excited person in the world," said Kat, snuggling against Connor on the wagon seat.

If it weren't so cold, you and I would probably be up on that hill getting ourselves into trouble, Connor thought, tightening his arm around her. It had been a prospecting trip like none he'd ever made, with Kat flitting around, scrambling over rocks and through bushes asking, "How's that? That's a different color, isn't it? Look at this rock! The soil here is yellow. It must be gold, don't you think?" And the crazy thing was, he thought they'd actually found a prospect worth staking a claim to.

"I've a friend at the smelter who can run an assay for us on the quiet. We don't want people hearing and filing claims ahead of us."

"Oh, goodness, could they do that?"

"First come, first served."

She glanced around as if she thought someone might be eavesdropping on their conversation. "What shall we call it?" she whispered.

"If the assay looks good, we could call it—" He thought

a minute. "How about Chicago Girl?"

Kat beamed at him and, bouncing on the seat, brushed a kiss on his cheek, which, through quick reflexes and lack of common sense, he managed to catch briefly against his lips. Lord, but she had a soft, sweet mouth. And an utterly surprised look on her face. He turned his head quickly and vowed to watch that sort of thing in the future.

"And, oh Sean, it was so exciting! I understand completely why you love the business." Her brother had come home for a visit, saying he was much improved and had obtained financing in Denver about which he wanted to talk to Connor. "You won't believe how good the assay results are. You're going to be ever so much richer."

"No sweetheart, you're going to be rich. You and Connor found the claim."

"But I was acting for you."

Sean laughed. "You just look after what I've already got and keep my wife from spending it. Where is she, anyway?"

"Well—" Kat had no idea. She never knew where Ingrid was. Did Sean expect her to follow his wife around? Did he know Ingrid was given to disappearing?

"No matter," said Sean easily.

"You really are better, aren't you? You haven't coughed once. What did your doctor say? Can you stay?" And did that mean the houses would be separated again? Maybe Sean wouldn't need her any more. Of course, now that she and Connor were partners in a claim, she'd have reason to stay here in Breckenridge and to see him, but—

"My doctor expects me back, love; I haven't been well for that long, but with any luck I can come home for good in a few months. How are you and Connor getting on?"

"Oh—fine." How *were* she and Connor getting along? "Look, here's Ingrid."

Kat thought Ingrid took Sean's return very casually. She

neither explained her absence nor expressed any surprise at his unheralded return. The only change was an increase in Ingrid's already liberal application of perfume and the resumption of lovemaking noises in the night. Kat was again sleeping with the children, while Mary Beth and a new young woman brought by Sean, Noleen Pratt, shared the kitchen-bedroom.

In less than three days, Sean began to cough again and returned to Denver. What could it be? Kat wondered, her euphoria dampened. He'd arrived feeling so well, and he hadn't gone down any mines. If Sean had to spend the rest of his life in Denver to stay healthy, he and Mother might expect her to move too. She found that prospect depressing.

"It's damned irritating," said Connor, "that I have to sit on a jury when I can't get my own case into court."

Kat forbore to complain about his language, realizing that he blamed her for the delay in their case, even though she hadn't seen Harrison Ponder since he claimed conflict of interest and deserted his clients, Medford Fleming and the Trenton Consolidated Mining Company.

"Oh, don't look so conscience-stricken, Kat. I realize you can't help all these men falling at your feet."

"No one's falling at my feet," she muttered.

"No? How many men have proposed this week?"

"Only two," she replied, "and they're from Montezuma."

"Some of those you invited to call, by any chance?"

"I introduced them to Noleen and Mary Beth," said Kat.

"Which means we'll soon be without household help again, and those two seem to be fairly sensible girls."

"If I don't keep marrying them off, the house will get crowded." But Kat was beginning to find it depressing to be exposed to all these courtships, to be arranging marriages and acting as chaperone to people gazing soulfully into one another's eyes, even kissing in hallways and corners.

It made her feel old and unwanted—not that she herself coveted any of her housemaids' suitors.

"I think I'll buy myself a rocking chair to take to court," said Connor thoughtfully. "Might as well be comfortable while I'm being bored. In fact, maybe I'll buy rocking chairs for the whole jury. Someone did that—where was it? Silver Plume or Georgetown."

"Wouldn't that be expensive?" Kat asked.

"Not if it influenced the jury in our favor when our case comes to court."

Kat laughed. "Why, that's worse than trying to influence the lawyers."

"So you did that on purpose, did you?"

"I did not. Does Diederick seem bad-tempered to you lately?"

"Who cares?"

"I guess he's still sulking about the sweet peas, although I don't know why. They all died."

"He probably killed them."

Chapter Thirteen

The sign "Clothing and Gents Furnishings" caught her eye, and she entered Watson's on impulse, thinking that Jamie, although he didn't want one, needed a suit for Sunday and for school programs at St. Gertrude's. The store was a curiosity, long-antlered animal heads decorating the walls, waist-high stacks of miner's overalls piled on the floor. Did they have anything suitable for a twelve-year-old?

"What a tragedy," Kat overheard a woman customer saying to the proprietor. Kat studied a wall of boxes, wondering what they contained.

"And it just happened?" Mr. Watson shook his head. "It's always a terrible thing when a child dies."

"I heard it was two children, and no one watching them, poor things, or they wouldn't have been down by Blue in May when the snow runoff's high." The woman, who was flipping through the overalls, sounded very self-righteous, as if she'd never let a child in her care wander off.

Kat had left Phoebe and Sean Michael with Ingrid.

184

Whirling, she ran out the door and up the hill toward home.

"Where are they?" she screamed at Ingrid, shaking her awake. Kat burst into tears at the thought of Phoebe and Sean Michael struggling in the cold water, being sucked under, their lifeless little bodies washing ashore. "You're the most irresponsible woman I've ever met." Ingrid just sat there staring at her with big, blank eyes. "You can't be trusted to do anything you're asked."

"What was I supposed to be doing?" asked Ingrid.

"Watching your children! They're—"

"Mary Beth was watching them."

"I asked you."

"Well, I asked her."

"Then where are they?"

Ingrid shrugged. "Ask her."

Kat wanted to strangle her sister-in-law. "Two children just drowned in the Blue."

Ingrid stretched, thinking. "It wouldn't be Phoebe; she's afraid of water. I suppose Sean Michael—"

"Shut up! Shut up! Shut up!" Kat ran out of the house to look elsewhere for the children. She ascertained within a half hour that Sean's son and daughter hadn't drowned. After another hour of frantic searching, she found them at St. Gertrude's, tossing a ball with Mary Beth and Sister Freddie. They'd been visiting the school in which they were to enroll shortly.

"Oh, Freddie," Kat wailed and fell into her friend's arms.

"Goodness, Kat, we'd have asked you to play if we'd known how much you wanted to," said the young nun, smiling whimsically.

Kat's sobs tapered off to sniffles. "I thought they were dead."

"Why in the world would you think that?"

"What you need is a nice cup of tea, Miss Kat," said Mary Beth.

"Or a different sister-in-law," Kat muttered. Now she'd have to apologize to Ingrid. No, on second thought, she wouldn't. Just because they weren't dead, didn't make Ingrid a good mother. Undecided, Kat explained the whole situation to Sister Freddie. "So what do you think, Freddie?" she finished.

"I think if Reverend Mother hears you calling me Freddie, she's going to rap your knuckles with a ruler. As for Ingrid, she doesn't sound too bright. Maybe by now she's forgotten that you yelled at her."

"But that means she will have forgotten that she's supposed to be a responsible mother," said Kat glumly.

"Well, madam," said the older gentleman who had invited her to dance, "you have my congratulations. You've almost made a public eyesore look presentable."

Kat glanced around Fireman's Hall. The second-floor ballroom, she was told, had once been very fine with its wainscotting and its columns dividing sections of elaborate wallpaper. Now, however, the wainscotting and dance floor were scuffed and the wallpaper faded and stained. Kat had accepted with reservations the request to decorate for the dance, which was being held to raise money for the refurbishing of the interior. The exterior would be ignored for the time being since a debate was in progress over whether to move the hall away from Father Dyer, who not only fulminated against dancing but continued to insist that he be allowed to use the firehouse bell on Sundays. Kat had looked over the hall, then sent teams of young people out to denude the area of flowers, which were then used in ingenious ways to disguise the flaws.

"However, a few flowers will not cover up what is a disgrace to the city. Nor will your efforts convince me that the place should not be renovated or, better yet, sold to someone who will take care of it."

"You can't sell the town firehouse!" exclaimed Kat,

resenting his backhanded compliment—as if she were responsible for the deterioration of the building.

"Well, that's enough dancing for these old joints. A pleasure to have met you, madam."

Kat stared after him in astonishment as he left her in the middle of the dance floor with the music still playing. How could he say they had met? He hadn't introduced himself.

"Surprised you'd dance with that old coot," said a bewhiskered gentleman carrying a cane. "Charles E. Hardy." He bowed with a flourish, hooked his cane over his arm, and said, "May I claim the rest of the dance my colleague was too decrepit to finish?"

Bemused, Kat nodded and allowed herself to be jogged away. Hardy? Wasn't he the editor of the *Leader?* "Does that man work for you?" she asked.

"Bless you, no, my dear. That was Jonathan Cooper Fincher of the Summit County *Journal,* my arch rival. And you are the young lady who gave him his comeuppance." Kat gasped in indignant remembrance of her written altercation with the man who called himself "Ye Editor."

Colonel Fincher, on the occasion of her visit to the Engle Brothers' saloon, had written an editorial saying, "Female busybodies should be kept out of saloons lest they interfere with the accustomed social life of the mining population on whom our Summit County economy depends."

Kat had shot back a letter saying, "Male imbibers should be kept out of saloons lest they interfere with the health and safety of innocent females on their way to the grocery store," after which she had related her first introduction to Breckenridge drunkenness, the gunfight that had resulted in a tooth injury to her guest, Brady Markham.

"Mrs. Fitzgerald, in a town little given to temperance sentiments, your bullet-in-the-potato story bids fair to become a classic. You may indeed have curbed the consumption of alcohol. Men in our saloons laugh so hard over the tale of Brady's tooth that they're unable to continue drinking. Pray do send your stories to me in the future. I'll always be glad to tell your side of any controversy."

"Why, thank you, Mr. Hardy," said Kat.

"Ah, my dear Kathleen, at last we meet again."

Kat stared at the gentleman who had just called her so familiarly by her given name. "Mr.—Ponder?" She recognized him now as the one-time lawyer for Trenton Consolidating Mining.

"And so coy withal." He chuckled. "As if there were no understanding between us."

"What understanding?"

Mr. Ponder swept her onto the dance floor, seemingly intent upon apologizing for his prolonged absence, as if she had noticed. While he went on and on about some presumed pique on her part, Kat lost interest and scanned the crowd for her charges. Mary Beth was dancing with a nice-looking young man, but unless Kat was mistaken, he worked at the undertaking establishment. Did Mary Beth know that? And there was Noleen, chatting with the fellow who had done the Chicago Girl assay for Connor. He had made a nuisance of himself after he met Kat, and she had had to excuse herself from the parlor repeatedly, leaving him in Noleen's company. Ingrid was in the corner, staring into the eyes of some fellow Kat had never seen before. Why couldn't Ingrid just dance like a normal woman?

Now where was . . . Kat spotted Jeannie, looking absolutely charming in a pale blue frock. Connor had said no to the original pattern, which had a low, square neckline. He objected to the exposure of his daughter's chest, so Kat had filled in Jeannie's neckline with lace, then used the unaltered, low-necked pattern for herself in an emerald-green and white print. When Jeannie saw Kat's dress, she raised objections to her own version, yet she had received a raft of compliments from her friends, from goggle-eyed boys her age, and from several gentlemen whom Kat considered too old for a girl of sixteen. Then, of all the nerve, Connor had tried to object to Kat's neckline too, but she'd paid him no mind. "Well, did you have a nice trip then?" she cut in on Mr. Ponder.

"Dear Kathleen, you haven't yet said you forgive me," he responded with a melting look.

The man was drunk, she decided. She could smell alcohol on his breath. "I haven't yet given you permission to call me by my given name either," she said tartly.

"Well, I hardly think I need permission for that."

"Really?" Kat stopped dancing. "You are presumptuous, sir."

Mr. Ponder's eyes narrowed. "I gave up a lucrative case for you when you said I might call." He was beginning to look quite mean.

"I said you might call to discuss the case," she stammered.

"I was offering my heart. Why else would I have forgone a huge fee?" Harrison Ponder clamped his fingers over her arm and squeezed.

"You're crazy," she gasped. "You don't even know me."

"Why, you little—"

"My dance, I believe."

Kat had never been so glad to see anyone in her life as she was to see Connor Macleod at that moment.

"You'll excuse us, Harrison." Connor removed the hand from her arm and whirled her away.

"He's drunk," Kat gasped.

"Possibly," Connor agreed. "Harrison's a very able lawyer, but he has been known to show up in court— as well as elsewhere—drunk."

"He seems to—to think, because he saw me once in a judge's office, that he has—he has some claim to me."

"I'll set him straight," said Connor quietly.

"He grabbed my arm."

"It's all right, Kat. Ponder won't bother you again."

"I can see why Sean wanted you to take care of us all," she mumbled. Then mulling over the situation, she exclaimed, "But you shouldn't have to! I didn't do anything to make him think whatever he thought. I was just being polite."

Connor thought wryly that with Kat, politeness was all it took. As Sean said, they all fell at her feet, unnoticed.

"Have we met before?" Kat was trying not to stare at her newest partner. Not only were his clothes astonishingly splendid—he made her feel like a humble sparrow partnered with a strutting peacock—but he was wearing expensive jewelry.

"Cameron Powell. I'm desolate you don't remember me."

Kat smiled weakly. She didn't remember him. "Your stick pin is very handsome," she remarked. Since it was at eye level, she couldn't help noticing it. Its centerpiece was a large, possibly genuine diamond set in gold with red stones around it. Rubies? And it was stuck into a satin ascot which was in turn tucked into a brocade waistcoat.

"Collateral," said Mr. Powell.

What did that mean?

"If I'm in need of money, I can sell or pawn the stick pin. I'm a walking bank," he said with evident self-satisfaction.

"Are you?" What a strange man. Most people put their money in a real bank or invested it in buildings or businesses. This man walked around with his assets on his person, ready to sell them off in case of need. Or perhaps he was a jeweler. She opened her mouth to ask, but then the dance ended.

"Mr.—ah, Powell, may I introduce Mr. and Mrs. McNaught—" The McNaughts eyed him warily. "My sister-in-law, Ingrid Fitzpatrick—" Ingrid gave him that strange look, as if she had just awoken from a deep sleep to find that she had influenza. "Mr. Connor Macleod, who is—"

"May I have another dance?" Mr. Powell interrupted.

"I believe I've been promised this dance," said Connor and whisked Kat away.

She was surprised. Connor didn't usually seek out her company at balls. He escorted her, danced with her once or twice, and then talked to other men while keeping an eye on her. Doing his duty, she had always surmised. Well, she wasn't going to complain. She'd rather dance with Connor than, say, Mr. Powell, who was rather peculiar. She still couldn't place him. "I wonder if he's a fancy man?" she mused aloud.

Connor's mouth dropped open.

"I remember Mother talking about fancy men. She must have meant someone who dresses like that. Did you see that stick pin? He said he sells them."

Connor recovered his equilibrium with difficulty. Kat evidently had no idea that the term "fancy man" referred to a procurer. "Powell's a gambler, Kat. I thought you'd met him the day you invaded the Engle Brothers' place."

"Well, for goodness sake." Her eyes followed Mr. Powell, who was now dancing with Ingrid.

Connor grinned. "What a hard-hearted woman you are. I remember quite distinctly that Jeannie said the man fell in love with you, and here you don't even remember him."

"Oh, what nonsense," said Kat. "Do all gamblers dress like fancy men?"

"Kat, maybe you shouldn't use that term."

"Why not? Look at his clothes."

"Yes, but—" What was he supposed to say? He couldn't explain that fancy men sold women for purposes of sin. She didn't know anything about—he felt a sharp pang, remembering that he'd taught her something about sin that night in his room. Connor glanced down at her curly hair, at the long black lashes and clear green eyes, and felt a

191

great desire to protect her, yet as far as he knew, he was the only man in Breckenridge against whom she'd needed protection. With everyone else, she seemed quite competent to ward off unwelcome advances.

"Ingrid's disappeared," said Kat, frowning.

"She'll turn up. Would you like to dance again?"

"I'd love to." Three times. Connor had asked her to dance three times in one evening. She forgot about Ingrid.

"I can't find her. She didn't sleep in her bed." Kat had asked everyone in the house if they knew where Ingrid had gone. Then, desperate, she went to Connor.

"She'll probably turn up," he replied.

"I knew we should have investigated last night when she disappeared from the ball. What if she's been kidnapped?"

"Well, I doubt—"

"We must contact the sheriff."

"Let me ask around first," said Connor quickly. "We don't want to create a scandal."

"I suppose you're right. Oh dear. Would you? Look for her, I mean."

Connor did, but they still had no word of Ingrid by nightfall when Kat again insisted on contacting the sheriff.

"Kat," said Connor slowly, "did you notice who she was with the last time you saw her?"

Kat searched her mind. "The gambler," she decided. "Do you think we should ask him before we go to the sheriff?"

"He's gone too."

Kat's mouth rounded in an "oh" of surprise. "You think she's been kidnapped by a gambler?"

"Well, possibly," said Connor, "but—"

Kat was already throwing on a shawl in preparation for her visit to the sheriff, who, when she found him, didn't seem very upset about the disappearance of Ingrid.

"If she's comin' back—"

"What do you mean, *if?*"

"If she's comin' back, Miz Fitzgerald, she will. If she's not, no use my goin' after her. She's a grown woman."

"She's my brother's wife."

"Mayhap," said Sheriff Iliff. "Like I say—"

"What if she's come to no good?" gasped Kat.

"Wouldn't surprise me any to hear it," drawled the sheriff.

Kat fretted and fumed for two days, sure that Ingrid had been kidnapped. Then Charles Finding, coming in on the Denver and Rio Grande, reported seeing the gambler and a woman who looked, from the back, like Ingrid, staying at a fancy hotel in Leadville, "happy as bear cubs in a honey tree," as he put it.

"The Finding girls are my best friends," wailed Jeannie. "I'll be embarrassed forever. Daddy, we've got to split the houses before our reputations are ruined."

Kat had turned pale at the news and left the room. It occurred to her that Ingrid might have run away because Kat had screamed at her about the children. But to leave with a man! Kat was almost in tears by the time Connor arrived to discuss the problem. "What am I going to tell Sean?" Kat whispered.

"Tell him nothing for the time being. It might not have been Ingrid," Connor advised.

"First Coleen, then Ingrid," mumbled Kat.

"I hardly think the two disappearances are comparable."

"They both eloped. You drove Coleen away, and I drove Ingrid."

"*Coleen* didn't elope."

"Of course she did. She's going to become a bride of Christ, but Coleen, at least, isn't married already."

Connor had to stifle laughter. Kat had such a unique way of looking at things.

"Are you smiling?" she asked suspiciously.

*   *   *

"It's the fault of dancing," said Father Dyer when they met at the butcher shop and walked together uphill, he to his church, she to visit Sister Freddie. "Dancing is a great promoter of sin. Many a wife and mother has left her husband and children because of dancing."

"Or drinking," said Kat gloomily. "Ingrid always said she liked a drink. As for dancing, I enjoy it, and I never deserted my husband."

"Dancing is a great evil. Now that you must stand mother to your niece and nephew, you should give up your sinful ways."

Kat had no intention of staying home from the balls because Ingrid had deserted her children. "That gambler, if that's who she ran off with, spent all his time in saloons."

"Ha!" cried Reverend Dyer. "I'm not surprised to hear it. Drinking is as great an evil as dancing."

"Worse," said Kat. "I think we should devote our weekends to closing down the saloons."

"The sooner the better," Father Dyer agreed.

Having set a date for the first fusillade in their new attack on the town's saloons, Kat trudged home, thinking of how happy she had been at the fireman's ball, whirling in Connor's arms. She'd been in a fair way to developing a romantic interest in him, but the case of Ingrid was a good lesson, a reminder of the results of romantic love. Sean had obviously been wildly in love with his wife. When he'd returned from Denver, he and Ingrid had hardly left their bedroom for the first two days. It had been embarrassing. They'd probably still be there if Sean hadn't started to cough again. And just weeks later, Ingrid ran off with a gambler. So much for romantic love. Poor Sean. Poor Kat, who'd been wild about Mickey. Poor Connor, who'd fallen head over heels for Rose Laurel. They'd all best eschew romantic love in the future. Kat certainly intended to.

"Mrs. Fitzgerald!"

Kat was jolted out of her unhappy thoughts by the sharp

voice of Mrs. Brune, who sang soprano in the church choir.

"Something has to be done about Mr. Macleod's boy, Jamie. That young rascal and his friends threw mud all over my wash while it was hanging on the line. I had to redo every sheet, and some of those stains I'll never get out."

"Oh, my dear Mrs. Brune, I'm so sorry." Thinking of how hard the washing sessions at the hospital laundry were, she felt for Mrs. Brune, although she resented the fact that Mrs. Brune's cow habitually grazed in Kat's yard, leaving behind disgusting evidence of its visits. When she'd complained to Mr. Brune, he'd said, "Makes the grass grow, Miz Fitzgerald. Ought to charge you for her contributions," and he'd gone away laughing. "Are you sure it was Jamie?" Kat asked.

"Absolutely. No one has red hair like that boy's."

Kat promised that Jamie would never again attack Mrs. Brune's wash and continued home to take the matter up with Connor, realizing as she walked along that Jamie must be skipping school again. She'd have to alert Freddie, who could warn her when the boy went truant. However, when Connor heard, his solution to Jamie's bad conduct took care of the truancy problem.

"Don't like school, is that it?"

"I told you so," said Jamie apprehensively.

"And you're still running around with those young fools who got you in trouble before?"

Jamie thrust a lip out and remained silent.

"Fine," said Connor. "You can go to work in the mines. Tomorrow, six o'clock at the Ingrid's Ring. If you're late or miss work, you don't get paid, and being a working miner, you'll pay room and board here."

Jamie looked astounded.

Kat cried, "He's only twelve. He can't work in a mine."

"Of course, he can."

"There are laws about child labor."

"Repealed in '81," said Connor.

"Well, he's still too young to—"

"I am not," said Jamie. "I think it'll be fun—more fun than going to school with the nuns. And miners make $3.50 a day. I'll be rich."

His father gave him a wry look. "Beginners don't make $3.50, but that's what I like to hear—enthusiasm for hard work. And Jamie, you'll be paying Mrs. Brune for the damage to her sheets. Those payments, plus your room and board, ought to keep you poor for a month or so."

Jamie, at that news, looked a little less enthusiastic.

Chapter Fourteen

June did not start auspiciously. Fathers Rhabanus and Eusebius, both of whom required hospitalization during their first winter in Breckenridge, decided to follow Kat's advice about insulating their house. When she saw their lamentable efforts—papers and cans falling off the walls, blackened fingernails from misdirected hammer blows— Kat suggested that Connor and Jamie help the priests.

"I'm too busy," said Connor.

"I'm too tired," said Jamie. "After all, I'm only thirteen years old, and I'm putting in a full day at the mine." Although he tried to look pitiful, his exuberance shone through, and Kat was surprised that the novelty of mining had not yet worn off.

"Send Diederick," Connor suggested. "Once I forced him to close up the hole he started in my wall, the oaf stopped working on Jeannie's new room."

Kat knew why Diederick was ignoring Connor's side of the house. Unable to bear Ingrid's red parlor, she had decided to change the wallpaper, which was water-damaged anyway. Surely Ingrid—if she returned—wouldn't object. At this very minute Diederick was hanging the new paper— slowly.

Kat had estimated that the job would take only a day, and then he'd get back to work on Jeannie's new room without father or daughter noticing. No such luck, and the wallpaper project would certainly attract notice if left half done. Therefore, Kat told Diederick to hurry up with the parlor and trudged off herself to aid the priests, finding that she was quite handy with a hammer, although she was tempted to use it on Father Rhabanus. He not only chided her about her scandalous living situation but quibbled about the wallpaper she offered to bring over once she'd finished padding their walls with makeshift insulation.

"Did you buy it from a Protestant?" Father Rhabanus asked.

"There are no Catholic purveyors of wallpaper in Breckenridge," she pointed out. "But since you both visit other mining towns, perhaps you can find a parishioner who deals in *Catholic* wallpaper."

That Saturday, still irritated with Connor over his refusal to aid in the rectory insulation project, Kat collected Jeannie and took her along to a picnic in Dillon organized by Gertrude Briggle. For all her pre-picnic resistance, Jeannie met a young miner named Tom Weston and had a wonderful time. So did Kat. They took the train to Dillon, then wagons to the ranch of a young man named Harry Crandle, where they picnicked under cottonwood trees amid fields of wildflowers. Kat thought wistfully of Connor, who had told her there would be wildflowers come late spring. Indeed there were, but he wasn't here to enjoy them with her. Instead she was paid court by two lawyers in the party— Harrison Ponder, now sober, whom she ignored, and her own lawyer in the apex suit, Charlie Maxell, not to mention the rancher on whose property they had gathered.

Kat found Harry Crandle quite interesting with his tales of recent hard winters and drought in the cattle industry. He had turned his hand to raising milk cows near Dillon when his luck ran bad in beef cattle. "But I need to buy a good bull," he said morosely, "and haven't the money."

"Well, the milk business sounds promising to me," Kat declared. "I'll lend you the money." She had already seen profits from the Chicago Girl mine. Of course, Connor might not approve of her branching out into new endeavors, but Kat was excited at the prospect of business diversification. She imagined herself becoming a thriving Western entrepreneur, the Guggenheim of mines and milk.

Charlie Maxell, because he couldn't refuse her anything, drew up a contract, and laughing merrily, Kat became partners with Harry Crandle in a dairy ranch. It cost her remarkably little, and she went home with a lapful of flowers besides. She even tucked one into the green ribbon band on the sailor hat she'd purchased in Preston from Miss Hattie.

The only problem with the outing, which Gertrude and Kat had organized to enlist volunteers for their temperance campaign, was that none of the gentlemen and only two ladies would volunteer. In fact, Charlie Maxell tried to talk Kat out of it and even tattled her plans to Connor, who forbade her to have anything to do with Father Dyer and his saloon-closing crusade. Kat neglected to mention that she had suggested the crusade to Father Dyer, not the other way around, and that she had no intention of missing out on it.

Jeannie entertained everyone at Sunday supper the day after the picnic with tales of Kat's many admirers. "They were all in love with her," said Jeannie disdainfully.

Connor scowled and later told Kat privately that he thought she was setting a bad example for his daughter. Kat reminded him that Jeannie had followed her remarks on Kat's suitors with the comment, "Isn't that disgusting? I'm never going to get married." "So you see, Connor," said Kat, "you yourself, with your openly stated aversion to marriage, have ensured that your daughter will be an old maid. As for me, you've no reason to say that I'm setting a bad example. I did not encourage any of those men. In fact, I cut Harrison Ponder dead, although he was quite sober."

Just for spite, she moved the first temperance demonstration up a week. Six days later Kat, Father Dyer, his wife Lucinda, Sister Freddie, Gertrude Briggle, the two recruits from the picnic, and a couple who had grown up in the Greeley temperance colony in eastern Colorado marched into a saloon carrying signs that said, "Drink Kills." The event was marginally successful. Sister Freddie spotted the parent of one of her students and informed him that if his son ever chewed tobacco in her classroom again, she was going to break his nose. The father evidently mistook her words for a threat to his own nose and fled in terror, irritating the proprietor at the loss of a patron who was a prodigious drinker. Father Dyer climbed up on a table and harangued the crowd with descriptions of the hell-fire that awaited drinkers and dancers.

Kat could have done without the dancing content of the sermon. She spotted at least five customers with whom she had danced at various local balls, and they all stared at her mournfully as they leaned on the bar, a long counter held up by barrels—filled, no doubt, with beer or spirits. From a business point of view, Kat found the arrangement an interesting provision for storage of the establishment's product. From a moral point of view, she naturally disapproved of the whole place.

The two picnic volunteers were no good at all; they hung around on the outskirts of the action looking terrified until the father of one appeared and dragged her home, the other asking if she could go along. The temperance couple from Greeley got into an argument because the wife said the husband was making eyes at Kat, and no one in the saloon took the pledge, although many customers left, muttering that they liked to drink in peace and would find another place to do it.

When Kat complained to Father Dyer about their dubious success, he replied that moral reform took time and that if they cleared out enough saloons on Sunday, the owners might give up and close. Kat, however, wasn't sure how much time she could count on before she and Connor had a serious falling out over her activities. Then she thought of her father's horrible death and of her husband, cut almost in two by the wheels of that heavy beer wagon, and she vowed to persevere. As gruff as her father had been, she had loved him. And for a time, she had loved Mickey too.

There was no word from Ingrid. Didn't she realize that the gambler would desert her eventually? What would she do then? Her only talent seemed to be piano playing, and a woman couldn't get a job playing the piano—not in any respectable place. Every night before going to bed, Kat asked herself if she had made enough effort to befriend her sister-in-law. Yet how could you become friends with a woman who was always asleep, silent, or gone?

And Kat worried about her brother, who didn't yet know that Ingrid had decamped. He had left Kat to look after the interests of his wife and children, and now she'd lost his wife. He was bound to think she'd done her job poorly.

Most of all, however, she worried about the children. Poor dears, when they realized that their mother wasn't coming back—and Kat had stopped expecting her—they'd be devastated. Both mother and father gone from their lives in the same year. Kat talked the sisters into taking Phoebe and Sean Michael into St. Gertrude's as day students earlier than planned, hoping to distract them, although they didn't seem overly concerned—Ingrid hadn't been around that much, even when in residence. *I must begin to think of them as my own,* Kat told herself, *and spend more time with them.*

Accordingly, one sunny Sunday afternoon, she took them with her on that week's saloon venture, a hugely successful expedient. The sight of Kat with two children, a nun, and Father Dyer in tow, cleared out the first saloon they visited in just under three minutes.

Unfortunately, the second saloon contained many of the refugees from the first. This time they scowled at her. Father Dyer preached his usual sermon on the evils of drink, and then Kat announced, having taken his place on the table, that these two little children had lost both uncle and grandfather to drink. "Are you gentlemen planning to follow in the footsteps of my late father and husband?" she asked. "Will you too expose yourselves to terrible deaths, leaving your families bereaved?" Several men surreptitiously dabbed at tears. One, far gone in his cups, asked loudly when the pretty girl was going to stop talking and start singing.

The man next to him took offence at the insult to a lady and smashed a whiskey bottle on the offender's head, after which a wild fight broke out, and Kat had to flee with the children, both of whom thought Sunday with Aunt Kat was marvelously exciting—much better than Sunday School and Benediction, which took up their afternoons two Sundays a month, weather permitting. Freddie, her wimple askew, her eyes shining, asked Father Dyer, "Where shall we go next?" They stopped at one more saloon, where the entire clientele left as soon as they entered.

Connor, when he returned to town from a trip to Ten Mile Canyon and heard of her exploits, shouted at her, which hurt Kat's feelings. "At least, Ingrid didn't *do* anything," he roared. "You put those children in danger."

Kat had to agree and now regretted her actions, especially since she knew the children would make a fuss when they found themselves excluded from her next outing.

"I want you to promise you'll never do anything like that again," said Connor severely.

"I promise," said Kat.

"Well—" He looked surprised. "Well, good."

The next free Sunday, Kat, true to her promise, left the children with the McNaughts, taking Noleen and Mary Beth with her to swell the ranks of the Breckenridge Temperance League, as she and Father Dyer had christened their group. She had asked Freddie to see if any of the other sisters would like to join them, but Freddie refused, saying Reverend Mother would have her hide if and when she found out that Freddie was participating.

"She doesn't know?" gasped Kat, amazed at Freddie's daring.

Freddie waved the black winglike sleeve of her habit and said, "It's a good cause," and off they went to visit yet another of Breckenridge's nine saloons. This one promised to be their greatest challenge yet, for the owner had vowed publicly that he would not be closed down by a preacher and a gaggle of women. Gertrude had suggested that they go back to Engle Brothers, who had been more courteous. Kat rather suspected that Gertrude liked one of the brothers, although the schoolteacher would never admit it, being steadfast in her opposition to liquor.

Father Dyer, however, had his heart set on bearding a recalcitrant sinner in his den. The Greeley man had come along, but without his wife, which made Kat rather nervous. She certainly didn't want to be the cause of marital dissension. She kept herself solidly surrounded with her own Catholic contingent—Mary Beth Halloran, Noleen Pratt, and Sister Freddie. No man, even a Protestant, was going to make advances to a woman in the company of a nun.

As they entered the saloon, which had fine embossed parchment wallpaper and a beautiful stained-glass cigar advertisement, various miners called out, "Afternoon, Miz Kathleen." They were men she had met on the tour she made with Connor, and Kat was shocked that they would come so far to get a drink. She frowned at them.

Others called out, "Hey, Sister Freddie," making Kat very uneasy. Reverend Mother, if she heard about this, wouldn't like it at all. Freddie, smiling casually, strode over to a clutch of her admirers and told them straight out that they should put down their drinks and take themselves off to their families, their churches, or whatever proper companionship might be available to them.

One man said, with a lugubrious expression, "Ain't got nowhere but a saloon to go, Sister Freddie."

Kat, meanwhile, was besieged by miners who wanted introductions to Mary Beth and Noleen, who were smiling and peeking at their admirers as if they were at a church strawberry festival instead of a saloon. Father Dyer had just swept a three-card monte game off a table and was preparing to mount for his usual exhortation against the evils of drink when Sheriff Will Iliff arrived, summoned by the saloonkeeper, who demanded that the whole group of temperance crusaders be charged with disturbing the peace.

"Well now, Bartley," said Will Iliff, "I'm not gonna arrest Father Dyer. Like his ideas or not, he pretty much stands for Christianity here in Summit County."

As the sheriff was speaking, Kat noticed with contempt that the man from Greeley slipped out the swinging doors. She, however, stood her ground bravely. She had right on her side and was sure no sheriff would arrest her for attempting to do good.

"An' I sure couldn't arrest Miz Gertrude, bein' as we've not got so many schoolteachers we can afford to throw any in jail."

Gertrude winked at Kat, and the two of them grinned, both sure that the sheriff was working his way up to telling Bartley that no one could be arrested.

"So I reckon that leaves Miss Kathleen an' her two Chicago ladies, an' Sister Freddie—St. Gertrude's got plenty of teachers to take her place." He glanced slyly at Bartley as a loud argument broke out between those miners who had solicited and received introductions to Mary Beth and Noleen and didn't want to see eligible spinsters arrested and those miners who were more interested in uninterrupted Sunday tippling than women. "Course, Connor's not gonna be pleased to hear you made me arrest ladies from his household."

"Connor be damned," said the irate saloonkeeper. "I want 'em arrested."

Will Iliff scratched his head. "Well." He looked at Bartley sideways. "You sure about this?"

"It's against the law for women to be in a saloon."

"That's true," said Will Iliff. "An' that bein' the case, ma'am, maybe you oughta just leave." He was addressing Kat.

"No," said Kat.

"Well then, ma'am, you're under arrest for disturbin' the peace an' bein' a female in a saloon."

Kat couldn't believe it. He'd sent the Methodists home and arrested the Catholics—even a nun! It was a clear case of religious bigotry.

Reverend Mother Hilda Walzen was the first to arrive. A lesser man than Sheriff Iliff might have been intimidated when she said, "You have *arrested* one of the Sisters of St. Benedict?"

"Yes ma'am," said Will Iliff, "but I'm willing to drop the charges and release Sister Freddie—"

"Sister *Freddie!*"

"Yes, ma'am. She's the one of yours I arrested, and as I say, I'll release her in your custody—"

"What charges?" boomed Reverend Mother Hilda Walzen.

"Well, visitin' a saloon, ma'am."

Reverend Mother turned a stern eye on Sister Fredericka, then on Kat when the four young women were brought in. "This is worse than the pudding incident, Kathleen," she said. "Worse than the time you glued Marjorie Battenburg to her chair while the bishop was giving a talk on the Annunciation of the Virgin."

"Like I was sayin', ma'am," interrupted Sheriff Iliff, "I just need your word she won't go in any more saloons anywhere in my jurisdiction."

"You have my word, Sheriff." Reverend Mother grasped Sister Freddie by the arm and whisked her out the door, calling over her shoulder, "And she is Sister Fredericka— Fred-er-ick-a!"

Kat sighed. Mary Beth and Noleen giggled, sure that this was the most exciting day of their lives.

Connor arrived a few minutes later, looking thoroughly enraged, and Kat was relieved to see that he too thought the sheriff had acted unconscionably. However, when he had heard the story, Connor said, "I ought to leave you in jail."

"Oh, Mr. Macleod," cried Mary Beth, "you wouldn't."

"Not you, Mary Beth, nor you either, Noleen," Connor assured them. "I don't doubt Kat lured you into this as if it were some summer lark."

"I did no such thing," said Kat indignantly. "Temperance is not a lark. It's a sensible, moral—"

"I don't want to hear it," Connor shouted. "I told you—"

"Now, now, folks," the sheriff intervened. "No need to get all het up. Bartley may be fussed, but he'll simmer down long as he's sure it's not gonna happen again. You just give me your word, Connor, that she won't ever—"

"He can't speak for me," said Kat.

"You have my word, Will. If she ever goes into another saloon, I'll send her straight back to Chicago."

"You can't send me anywhere!"

"Just try me." Connor grabbed her arm, signaled the two young women to precede them from the sheriff's office, and dragged Kat out.

"You should have left her in jail," said Jeannie when they got home.

Kat was shocked at Jeannie's animosity.

A person who looked like a cowboy was sitting on the edge of a chair in the corridor parlor. "In jail?" he echoed.

"Who are you?" Connor demanded.

"I brung a letter for Miz Kathleen Fitzgerald." He fished it out of his vest and looked from woman to woman.

"I'm Kathleen Fitzgerald," said Kat.

"The one in *jail?*" gasped the amazed cowboy.

Connor snapped the letter out of his hand, tore it open, glanced at it, and said, "Someone named Harry Crandle wants to marry you."

"Why are you reading *my* mail?"

"That's the cattleman who fell in love with her at the picnic," said Jeannie. "I think we should send her right off to Dillon."

"In jail?" marveled the cowboy.

"We're just partners in his ranch," said Kat. "Nothing else."

"How'd you get to be partners in a ranch?" Connor demanded.

"I lent him money for a bull and other improvements. You see, it's been a bad year for cold and drought and—"

"I don't want to hear it," snapped Connor. "What's your answer?"

"Answer?"

"Do you want to marry him?"

"No, of course not." Kat felt hurt that he didn't seem to care one way or another what her response would be.

"She's not interested." Connor handed the letter back to the cowboy. "Show him out, Jeannie. You'll be wanting to get back to Dillon before dark," he added to the cowboy.

"Actually, I was thinkin' I might stop by one of the saloons an' have a drink."

"Mrs. Fitzgerald will have closed them all down from what I hear," said Connor.

"Closed 'em down?" echoed the cowboy. "But it's Sunday."

"Exactly," snapped Kat. "It's Sunday. People should be in church."

"In church?" echoed the cowboy. He left, shaking his head, still clutching the letter with its rejected proposal.

"I think you should have married him," said Jeannie. "They have saloons in Dillon you could close down."

"Enough, Jeannie," snapped her father. "Leave the room." When Jeannie, sulking, had done so, he turned to Kat. "Do you have any idea what you're doing? Do you know why I've been out of town so much lately? No, of course, you don't. I wasn't sure why myself. All I saw was labor unrest, grumbling miners not showing up for their shifts, making trouble. Everyone in the county must have known you'd be heading straight back to the saloons—except me. I, like a fool, believed your promise."

"I only promised to leave Phoebe and Sean Michael home."

"Of course. I should have realized that you'd be planning to break your word and excuse yourself with some sort of devious Jesuit reasoning."

Kat blinked back tears. That was the second time today she'd been attacked for being Roman Catholic, but she hadn't expected it of Connor.

"We won't have a mine open anywhere in the county if—"

"That's not true. The Breckenridge Temperance League has only been active in Breckenridge. We haven't had time to address ourselves to the drinking problems in places like Dillon and Montezuma."

"And you won't," said Connor. "I gave Will my word,

208

and by God, you're not going to make a liar of me. If I have to, I'll get hold of Sean and—"

"I really think you're overreacting," said Kat, worried at the idea that Connor might actually trouble her brother just because she'd been aiding Father Dyer in his good work. Poor Father Dyer—he'd so wanted to go to jail with them, but Will Iliff wouldn't have it. He said he'd be up for reelection in the fall and wasn't going to ruin his chances by arresting the most respected man of God on the Western Slope. Obviously he didn't anticipate that arresting Roman Catholics would hurt him with the voters, Kat realized bitterly. But in the meantime, there was Connor's threat. "You wouldn't tell Sean." She tried to sound confident.

"I would."

"Well, go ahead. See if I care." Sean would understand—wouldn't he? Unfortunately, Mother hadn't. Kat sighed. Nobody seemed to understand that she just didn't want others to suffer the tragedies that had befallen her own family. She didn't want to spoil anyone's fun. You didn't need to drink to have fun—not when there were picnics and strawberry festivals in fair weather and sleighing and snow-shoeing during the snow season and balls no matter what the weather was like. And none of *those* activities endangered your health or dignity. Kat herself was having a wonderful time in Colorado—well, except when Connor got mean—and she'd never taken a drink in her life.

Maybe she ought to suggest to Father Dyer that instead of invading saloons, they set up a series of lectures on how to have a good time without alcohol. Connor couldn't object to that. They could tour all over the county, visiting the halls and the miners' dormitories, espousing picnicking and dancing and—her heart sank. Father Dyer hated dancing. He'd never agree. And Connor would never agree to the temperance campaign. Fiddlesticks! Men were so difficult. And muddle-headed. And bossy. It was a wonder women ever agreed to marry them.

Chapter Fifteen

As they rode back from Harry Crandle's ranch, Connor named for her the peaks that surrounded Dillon—Red, Buffalo, and Tenderfoot. He pointed out the rivers that converged where the town stood in the valley—the Blue, Ten Mile, and Snake. "Used to be LaBonte's Hole in the old days," he explained, encouraged to continue because she was so fascinated with the history of the area. "The trappers and Indians met here to drink and trade. Eyeless remembers it from when he was a boy—or so he says. That would be forty or fifty years ago." He turned the buggy onto the main street of Dillon, heading for the Warren Hotel, which had been recommended to Kat by John Dyer. "In '82 a lot of houses were moved here from Frisco," he continued. "Then the whole town moved in '83 when the railroad came and again two years later to this area between the rivers."

"Well, I hope they haven't moved the hotel somewhere else," said Kat. "I'm tired." She had received a second note from Harry Crandle, saying he had decided to get out of the dairy business. He wanted her to buy his half of the ranch, and Connor had insisted on escorting her to Dillon while she looked into it, a ploy, she suspected, to keep her away from Father Dyer. They'd left on Saturday and would have to stay until Monday if a deed of sale was to be drawn up by a lawyer. Connor had already found her a family to run the ranch in return for a percentage of the profits.

"Still there," said Connor as they pulled up in front of the hotel, climbed down, and met their hosts, Chauncey and Mary Elizabeth Warren. Over dinner Connor told her about the Dillon picnic ground with its dance platform, horse racing, and popular Fourth of July celebration. Kat was just finishing her apple pie and suggesting that they take the children to the festivities when Harry Crandle appeared at their table, shifting from boot to boot, bending his hat out of shape with sweaty fingers and announcing that, since the ranch was sold, he'd decided to get a head start on prospecting and leave that very night.

"But the Landises have gone to Robinson to pack up their belongings," said Kat. "Can't you wait until they—"

"Ain't my ranch no more," said Crandle. "Why should I stay?"

"But don't the cows have to be milked every day?"

"Twice a day," said Crandle. "I'll shore be happy to quit that. Never did think it was real man's work."

"I've never milked a cow," she protested. Kat had the suspicion that he was pleased to be inconveniencing her.

"Reckon you an' your friend'll think of somethin' by milkin' time tomorrow. 'Less, a course, you changed your mind about my offer for your hand."

"You're trying to blackmail me," Kat gasped. "And after I lent you money."

"Yep. Well, I'll be goin'. 'Less, a course, you—"

"Absolutely not."

Crandle shrugged and left, spurs jingling. Kat turned helplessly to Connor. "Do you know how to milk a cow?"

"I've done it," he admitted reluctantly.

"He has twenty out there."

Connor nodded. "Reckon both us and the cows are going to be pretty unhappy till the Landises get in from Robinson. I'll send them word to hurry. Then we'd best pack up and head for the ranch."

"Tonight?"

"Cows wake up early."

Kat discovered that she hated cows. They acted as if they wanted to be milked, mooing pitifully if you didn't get to them fast enough, but then they wouldn't cooperate. They shifted around, slapping your face with their tails, kicking the milk pail over, knocking you off the stool. Connor milked seventeen to her three the first morning, and sixteen to her four that night, laughing at her infuriated attempts to master the process.

Her hands ached so badly after the first morning that she tried to hire the man who transported the milk to town as a substitute milker. He refused. That night she was so tired, she could hardly keep her eyes open over dinner. Then she faced sleeping again on gray sheets because Mr. Crandle had no clean bedding. *Gray sheets!* She felt like some workhouse orphan in a novel by Charles Dickens. Even the poverty-stricken working girls in the romances she read before she married Mickey hadn't slept on *gray* sheets while they waited to be rescued by a rich and handsome hero.

And Connor was no hero. The second morning he dragged her out of bed before sunrise. She milked four and a half cows and then staggered in to fix breakfast, thinking that she now understood why girls wanted to leave the farm, go to work in the big city, and live in her mother's boarding houses where they didn't have to cook their own breakfasts while their hands ached from milking wretched cows. And at Mother's, the sheets were *never* gray. Kat considered washing Crandle's sheets, but she was too tired. She took a nap so as to be ready for the evening session, when, invigorated by the extra sleep, she milked six cows and was still awake after washing the dishes.

"I think you're getting the hang of it," said Connor.

Kat appreciated his compliment, since Connor was still doing over two-thirds of the milking, in addition to tossing hay around with a giant fork and shoveling manure. She promised herself to wash the sheets the next day. He probably hated gray sheets too, and she did want to do her share. Goodness, this wasn't even his ranch!

"Have you written Sean yet about Ingrid?" he asked, breaking into her thoughts.

Kat sighed. "I keep hoping she'll come back."

"He has a right to know."

Kat nodded. "It's just that I feel so guilty. He's sick, and now I've added to his woes by driving his wife away," Kat said miserably. "Just before she left—you remember when that little boy drowned in the Blue?"

"Yes," Connor replied, puzzled.

"I heard in the gents furnishing store that two children had drowned, and I'd left Ingrid to look after Sean Michael and Phoebe. I thought—I thought they were the drowning victims. I ran home, terrified, and there she was—asleep— and the children gone." Kat pressed a fist against her mouth, face drawn in guilty remembrance. "Connor, I screamed at her. I can't even remember what I said, but it was awful, and all the time the children were at St. Gertrude's with Mary Beth and Sister Freddie. And I never apologized to Ingrid."

"And you think that's why she left?" Connor put his hands over hers on the table. "Kat, you can bet Ingrid's leaving had nothing to do with anything you said to her."

"Then why would she do it?"

"Because she was bored. She saw something that looked better to her and left."

"But she's Sean's wife, and—and a mother."

213

"Not so anyone ever noticed," said Connor dryly. "You're the closest thing to a mother those children ever had, and no one could blame you if you resent it. Should your brother die, you'll be—well, you'll find yourself saddled with two kids, not your own."

"Goodness, I don't mind *that*. They're lovely children. And they're the only ones I'm ever likely to have since—since Mickey and I never had any."

"Did you want children?" asked Connor, surprised. "Given what you've told me about your marriage—"

"Well, that doesn't mean I wouldn't have liked children. What woman doesn't want to be a mother?"

"Rose Laurel didn't seem to," said Connor.

"Oh." Had Connor's wife been like Ingrid—completely irresponsible? "Well, I'm not afraid of having to raise Phoebe and Sean Michael. I'm lucky to have them. I just feel bad about Sean losing his wife."

"Kat," said Connor seriously, "you do know, don't you, that your brother probably doesn't have many years to live? Maybe not even many months."

"I don't know any such thing."

Connor sighed and tightened his fingers over her hand.

Kat thought how pleasant it was to sit here talking to him at day's end and how comforting the weight and warmth of his hand felt on hers. What if they'd met each other first—before Rose Laurel and Mickey? Would they have—but that was silly. Connor must have been seventeen when he first saw Rose Laurel, which would have made Kat eight and not a likely target for romantic notions on his part.

And it was romantic notions that got you into trouble. If Harry Crandle hadn't had romantic notions, she wouldn't be sitting here with aching fingers and twenty milk cows who'd start bellowing tomorrow morning while Kat was still in bed and wishing she could stay there.

*   *   *

Fuming, Kat inspected the weapon. She didn't know if it was loaded. She didn't know how to shoot it. What gentleman would leave a lady alone with a firearm she didn't know how to use? Not that she expected anyone to come around. She hadn't seen a soul but Connor and the milk delivery man in the three days they'd been there. She peered at the exterior of the gun, lifted the heavy piece to her shoulder, putting her finger experimentally on the trigger, depressing just a—there was a sudden explosion, and one of the four mismatched chairs at the rough table fell over, mortally wounded. Dazed, Kat picked herself up. Now she knew that the gun was loaded, and she supposed that if she pulled the other trigger, she could kill another chair—or an intruder, if need be.

She laid the gun down carefully on the table, picked up a pot of water, now boiling, and dumped it into a shallow wooden tub. Stubborn as a mule, was she? He'd had no right to say that. She dumped the second pot in. Never thought of the consequences of her actions? What nonsense! The consequences, she hoped, were that people would stop killing themselves with alcohol—she worked the pump vigorously—stop taking the bread from the mouths of their helpless wives and children—she tossed the bucket of cold water in after the two pots of hot—stop endangering innocent bystanders on their way to the grocery store—she began to strip out of her clothes.

She and Connor had been arguing about temperance again, he saying she'd end up closing their mines. She tossed her last piece of clothing, a pair of pretty lace-edged drawers, onto a surviving chair, stepped into the water, and leapt out with scalded toes. She hadn't closed down any mines yet, she thought defensively as she worked the pump handle. A half bucket ought to do it. And her investment in this dairy ranch *hadn't* been stupid. How dare he call her stupid? She poured the last of the water into the tub and dipped her stinging toes in, more cautiously this time.

Of course, she shouldn't have shouted that if he thought

the transaction so stupid, he could just go home and she'd look after her own investment. *That* had been stupid. When she thought of those twenty cows, all of which she'd have to milk herself tomorrow morning, she didn't feel quite as angry as she had before. Sighing, standing in her wooden tub bath, she used a soup ladle to pour water over herself.

If she hadn't been so dirty and tired, she wouldn't have shouted at him. She picked up the only soap she'd been able to find—terrible stuff that made her skin turn pink, as if she were washing in sand. Kat scrubbed herself down briskly and retrieved the ladle to rinse off. And oh, it felt good to be clean. If she'd shooed Connor out of the house and had a bath instead of having a fight with him, she wouldn't be facing those twenty cows all by herself tomorrow. Kat dribbled water over her breasts, thinking that she'd have to hurry. The temperature dropped rapidly here in the mountains after the sun had set, and she couldn't afford to take a chill.

What happened to an unmilked cow? Did it explode? She bent over and splashed water on her face, deciding that she'd better wash her hair while she was at it. Sighing, she took out the pins, tossing them onto the table, and the hair tumbled in curling masses down her back. The water would be lukewarm to cold by the time she got to the rinsing, and—

The ranch house door flew open, and Kat, terrified, grabbed for her towel with one hand and the shotgun with the other. "Get out!" she shouted. "I'm armed."

"It's me," Connor stammered, immobilized in the doorway by the sight of Kat with a shotgun clutched awkwardly in one hand and a towel in the other, dangling from between her breasts, all those rosy curves exposed to either side. Connor was struck dumb.

He hadn't got five hundred yards from the ranch house before he'd begun to regret losing his temper and leaving her there alone. He'd slowed his horse from a canter to a trot, conscience-stricken at the thought of how frightened she must be by herself at night, so far from help. The image of a frightened Kat tightened his hands on the reins, and the horse slowed to a walk as Connor pictured her trying to manage those twenty accursed cows after a sleepless night.

Serves her right, he thought, but he didn't believe it. As much as her crack-brained temperance campaigns infuriated him, he didn't wish her ill. What if she were injured out there all by herself? Those beasts kicked; he had a bruise to remind him. He was picturing her unconscious, trampled by a recalcitrant cow, when he heard the shotgun blast. With a jolt of fear, he yanked the horse's head around and headed back toward the ranch at a hard gallop. Had she shot herself? Or shot someone trying to do her harm? Some hardcase stopping by the ranch for a meal and finding a woman alone and unprotected? She knew nothing about guns. Connor pulled up by the ranch house porch in a cloud of dust and flung himself at the door.

And there she was. Safe. And naked . . . and terrified. "It's me, Kat," he said again.

"Connor?" she stammered in a squeaky voice.

"Put the gun down, darlin'," he said soothingly. She was the prettiest thing he'd ever seen. Prettier than Rose Laurel when she was sixteen and he madly in love with her. Prettier than his newborn daughter, the sight of whom had turned his heart soft with love. Prettier than sunlight on the branches of an ice-covered tree, or a mountain meadow splashed with spring wildflowers, or the first silent fall of snow in a pine forest.

Connor found himself moving across the room toward her, drawn like gold dust to mercury, and she staring at him, lips slightly parted as the droplets of water trickled over the round curves of her breasts, skirting the rosy nipples. He could see her swallow, the slight up-and-down movement in her throat. He noticed how wide her eyes were, clear green in the lamplight, with the black lashes stuck together. Her hair fell below her waist, one strand clinging damply to her shoulder, another curling onto a hip as if pointing to the juncture of her thighs, which was covered by the towel.

Connor felt himself grow hard at the thought of her, beneath that towel, at the remembrance of how it had felt to lie between her thighs, embedded in her tight warmth.

"The water's getting cold," he said, reaching out to close his hand over hers. With the other hand he took the shotgun and laid it on the table, never taking his eyes away.

"I was going to wash my hair," she whispered.

"Another time."

"But—"

Connor lifted her out of the tub and into his arms.

"I'm all wet," she whispered.

"You're so beautiful." He carried her to the blankets by the hearth, where he had been sleeping so that she could have the one bedroom.

"I never did wash the sheets," she murmured regretfully, drawing up a gray, ragged sheet and a rough blanket as Connor began pull off his boots.

"I don't think we're going to care," he replied, his eyes warm as he leaned forward to kiss her.

"I was so proud of us," she murmured wistfully. "In Montezuma when we didn't . . ." Her voice trailed off.

Connor, having divested himself of the rest of his clothes, slid under the blankets and took her into his arms. "You don't want me to stop, do you, sweetheart?"

"No," she admitted. The sound of Connor calling her sweetheart sent a tremor of happiness through her, and she wrapped her arms around him, raising her mouth to his. Instead of kissing her, he ran the tip of his tongue across her lower lip, eliciting a little "oh" of pleased surprise. Raising himself on his elbows, his knees between hers, he plunged both hands into her hair and, holding her head, kissed her neck, then darted his tongue into her ear. She shivered and tried to lift herself so that her breasts, now aching with excitement, would touch his chest.

He moved his knees, forcing her legs further apart, so that she expected him to take her without further lovemaking. Instead he began to move his lips down her neck, onto her shoulder and upper chest, using his body to force her thighs wide, cupping her breasts with his hands, forcing them up to his mouth while his lips sought her nipples and fastened there. She was flooded with a hot delirium as he rubbed the rough surface of his tongue against the swollen tips. When her hips tipped up against him, he slid one hand under her, guiding her to rub back and forth against him. She whimpered, her body all mindless yearning, all empty, pulsing hunger. The shuddering release had already come to her once, and he hadn't even—"Connor," she gasped, digging her nails into his shoulders.

"H-m-m?"

"Connor!" She reached for his hips, for his buttocks, digging her fingers in, dragging him upward, willing him into the starved heart of her, feeling his mouth leave her breast, move up, cover her lips as he rocked into her and groaned.

It was a wild mating, punctuated by the harsh rasp of their breathing, the accelerating pace of their bodies coming together, a violent, shuddering climax at which Kat cried out in a high, keening sound that convulsed Connor into one last mindless plunge.

"Oh God, Kat," he gasped when he had come back to himself to find her lying beneath him, shaken by fine tremors, damp with sweat, that sound still in his ears, although she was now silent. She was such a little thing, and he'd gone after her like a stag in rut. "Sweetheart, I'm so sorry. Did I hurt you?"

"Oh, no," she whispered. At the end she had lost her grip on him, on everything. Now she wrapped her arms around his waist. "It felt wonderful."

There was a sound of awe in her voice that humbled him, made him feel more a man than he'd ever felt in his life. He snuggled her into the curve of his arms, wanting to say something to her, some words that would prolong the moment, somehow make it right although, as his passion receded, he knew it had been very wrong.

He looked down at her, her head resting on his shoulder, eyes closed, and Connor was flooded with tenderness for her, his friend's sister. Because neither of them wanted to marry, he had betrayed Sean. And Kat. Even as he thought it, she turned her face into his chest, kissed him, and sighed into sleep, her lips curved in contentment.

But tomorrow. Oh lord, he had a fair idea of how contented she'd be tomorrow. When she started thinking about "sins of the flesh" and going to confession and how he'd walked in on her bath without even knocking, without asking if she wanted to go to bed with him again.

Of course, she *had*. Maybe not the first few minutes, while she was in shock at being caught naked, but pretty damned quick. It wasn't all his fault.

There was no time to discuss what had happened because they overslept and were awakened, still in each other's arms, by the complaints of twenty unhappy cows. Without breakfast, both embarrassed, they staggered out to the barn. Kat was so upset that she punched a cow who tried to kick over the milk bucket. That morning she milked seven of the twenty—a record for her. They had just finished when the Landises, their three children, and their household goods arrived, explaining that they'd stayed the night in Dillon.

"If you were that close, you should have come straight out," said Kat irritably. Last night would never have happened if her new tenants hadn't been so dilatory, if Connor hadn't been so rude as to walk right in on her, if— She compressed her lips and threw clothes into her valise, anxious to get back to Breckenridge.

"You didn't have to take it out on them," said Connor as they drove the buggy back to Dillon. "It wasn't their fault we—"

"We what?" snapped Kat. "We fell into sin again? Now I'll have to go to confession. Father Eusebius will never believe that I made a sincere act of contrition the last time. And what if I get Father Rhabanus? He told me not to move in with you."

"So don't go to confession."

"What? And endanger my immortal soul?"

"Kat, I doubt that God cares one way or another what we did. He's got more important things to worry about."

"Are you a heathen?" Kat asked, shocked. "Good heavens, if I'm pregnant—"

"Pregnant?" Connor looked horrified.

"Yes, Connor, pregnant." It gave her a stab of spiteful pleasure to mention that possibility. "After all, look what happened to your father and my mother. You'd have to marry me. Then you wouldn't be so smug." He didn't look smug; he looked as if marrying her would be a fate worse than death. She turned her head and squeezed her eyes shut on a sudden mist of tears, no doubt from the dusty road.

"I can't imagine anything worse," she added, "than being forced to marry a heathen backslider. I'd almost rather marry a Protestant." She raised her chin defiantly, unable to bear the idea of Connor Macleod thinking she *wanted* to marry him.

"You're a religious bigot; do you know that?"

"I am not. I have lots of friends in other faiths."

"People in love don't run on and on about heathens and backsliders."

"Who said anything about love?" Kat retorted, her heart giving a little skip.

"No one," he snapped, but his heart told him that to feel what they'd felt, they had to be at least a little in love. Still, he shouldn't have said it.

221

*　　*　　*

"Mary Beth, what are you doing?" Kat demanded.

Mary Beth flushed. She had been kissing a young man in the parlor when Connor and Kat walked into the house. "His intentions are honorable, Miss Kat."

Kat burst into tears and ran out of the room.

"Is Miss Kat sick?" asked Mary Beth.

"She's just—ah, tired out," said Connor. "Three or four days of milking cows will do that to a city girl."

"My goodness, yes," Mary Beth agreed. "Farm life is hard. 'Specially when the land plays out and you can't grow enough to feed the family. That's why I had to leave home. Guess I'd still be in the Guardian Angel Day Nursery and Home for Working Girls if Mrs. Fitzpatrick hadn't taken me in. She and Miss Kat sure are fine women."

Connor felt like a villain. He'd just seduced a fine woman and then spent the train trip back working up his resentment against her because of her temperance campaign and all the trouble it was causing him. As irritating as Kat's crusades were, he could understand that she meant to do good, and in Mary Beth's case, at least, was a better guardian angel than that home for working girls.

If Kat had her own guardian angel, she wouldn't be crying in her room this very minute, dreading the prospect of visiting the priest and confessing her sin. Connor, too, hoped she didn't have to face Father Rhabanus. Kat had never said what penance the younger priest imposed on her. And what if she were pregnant? He'd find himself married to another resentful woman. Beautiful though. And passionate! He'd never bedded a woman so exciting. *Well, you'd better stop thinking that way,* he told himself. *She made it pretty clear she doesn't want to marry you.*

Chapter Sixteen

By the end of June, Breckenridge and the surrounding countryside were bright with aspen and cottonwoods in full leaf. The yellow and purple of wildflowers sparkled in alpine meadows; the streams, once locked in snow and ice, foamed white on blue; and the lakes, where mining hadn't clouded the waters, reflected downy clouds in a blue sky vivid with sunshine. Even the two priests became enthusiastic about the glories of summer in the high country, although their constant traveling told on the health of Father Rhabanus.

Because the priests were so often absent, Kat's conscience hardly bothered her for having failed to make her confession. As long as she didn't see her partner in sin, she managed to forget that she had once again fallen from grace. She left the housework to Mary Beth and Noleen and the business to Connor, trusted that Jeannie would keep out of trouble at St. Gertrude's and Jamie at the mine, and spent her days rambling the countryside with Sean's children.

Having written to her mother of Ingrid's disappearance,

she even put from her mind how Sean would react to his wife's defection, just as she had banished thoughts of the night she spent in Connor's arms. Nothing had come of it. She was not with child, and Connor obviously had no feelings for her beyond lust; if he had, he would have proposed marriage.

Sooner or later, she assured herself, Sean would return, health restored, and they would raise his children together. Since Connor complained about the configuration the house was taking on under Diederick's hammer, it would, no doubt, be better if Sean purchased Connor's half. Then Connor Macleod would be out of her life for good. So she reasoned as she and Sean Michael and Phoebe frolicked under the summer sun.

Then Maeve, her four months' pregnancy showing, arrived with James and destroyed Kat's plans for the future, for Maeve had come to take Sean's children to Denver with her. "Since their mother's seen fit to desert them," she said, "they'd best be close to their father."

"But I'm taking care of them," Kat protested.

"You consider dragging them into the midst of saloon brawls a responsible thing to do?"

Kat flushed. Who had told Maeve about the free-for-all that ensued the one time Phoebe and Sean Michael joined a Sunday afternoon excursion of the Breckenridge Temperance League? Surely, Connor, on one of his trips to Denver, wouldn't have betrayed her that way. "They're happy with me, Mother," said Kat defensively. "And Sean's sick; he can't look after two children."

"They'll live with James and me," said Maeve.

"But Mother, you're expecting a child of your own."

"So?"

"It will be too much for you."

"Nonsense. I've never felt better in my life."

"Nor looked more beautiful," said James.

Kat had to admit that her mother seemed in excellent

health and spirits, but that didn't mean Kat wanted to give the children up. "Mother, now Ingrid's gone, I thought Sean and I would raise them—as soon as he's well."

"If you want children so badly, Kathleen," said her mother, "you'd best marry and have some of your own. Don't set your heart on Sean's. He'll remarry and—"

"Ingrid isn't dead. He can't—"

"They were never wed in the church," said Maeve. "This time I'll see he takes a good Catholic girl to wife. Speaking of which, why haven't you found husbands for Mary Beth and Noleen?"

"It's not for lack of suitors," Kat muttered. Her parlor was full of lovesick miners every weekend.

"Well, as I was saying, it's time you remarried, Kathleen. I recommend that you consider Connor. He'd make you a fine husband."

Kat turned pale and changed the subject, but by July first her mother and James had left with the children. Although their departure broke her heart, there was nothing Kat could do to stop them because Sean had agreed to the plan. As for Phoebe and Sean Michael, they were so excited about the prospect of a train ride to Denver that they seemed quite cheerful during their final hugs and kisses. Connor was, as usual, out of town—avoiding her, Kat thought. Therefore, missing Phoebe and Sean Michael terribly, she threw herself into other projects.

First, she visited Sister Freddie, who commiserated with her over the loss of the children. "You ought to remarry, Kat," said Freddie, "and have your own children."

"You sound just like Mother," Kat muttered.

"How about Connor? You're living with him already and, from what you've told me, you're powerfully attracted to him."

Kat burst into tears.

"Well, goodness," said Sister Freddie, "I didn't mean to make you cry. I just thought because you two had—"

"I don't want to talk about it," sobbed Kat. "And he doesn't want to marry me. I think you and I should start up the temperance campaign again."

"But I promised Reverend Mother to stay out of saloons, and Connor promised the sheriff—"

"—that we wouldn't go *inside* any saloons. Who's to say we can't do whatever we want outside?"

"Mother Hilda won't like it," said Freddie.

"Why? We'll just stop people before they enter and urge them to go to church instead, or donate their time to St. Gertrude's or St. Joseph's. Think how happy Reverend Mother would be to have male help with repairs. Why, they could build another room on the hospital. Goodness knows, St. Joseph's is too small. The doctors perform amputations in the same room where the fever victims lie recuperating. How would you like to be lying in bed suffering from pneumonia while someone was having a leg cut off?"

"It's not likely to be a problem," said Sister Freddie dryly, "since St. Joseph's doesn't take women."

"Right. They need a room for women. It's not fair to have hospital facilities for men and none for ladies."

"That argument won't carry much weight with the miners who each pay a monthly subscription to support St. Joseph's."

"Freddie, are you coming next Sunday or not?"

"I'm coming."

Kat's second project was a scheme to distance herself from Connor even further, and she used Diederick as the means to accomplish it. The carpenter wanted to build a back porch, which Kat vetoed because the lot sloped up too sharply for as extensive a porch as he envisioned. Instead she told him she wanted an octagonal tower on her side of the house. "With leaded windows and a balcony," she added. She'd read about such a place in Aspen and reasoned that if she had her own tower room, she'd feel as if she were hardly in the same house as Connor.

Of course, now that the children had gone to Denver and Ingrid had run off, she could insist on having her own house, but somehow she couldn't face the idea of living by herself, just she and whatever girls Genevieve sent from Chicago. With Connor hiding out of town all the time, his children still needed someone to look after them. Eyeless had got out of the habit. He spent his days reminiscing with cronies at Barney Ford's new cafe, the Saddle Rock. So, Kat rationalized, she couldn't desert the Macleods entirely, and there was her brother's business to consider. If she weren't living in the house, Connor might try to exclude her from all business matters, and she wasn't having that. No indeed. "Can you build me a tower room, Diederick?"

"Sure, Missus. I build you ein castle if you vant vun."

"Oh, the tower will do. Why don't you start today."

"Hello!" Connor shouted as he entered the silent, empty room that connected his house to Sean's. Having become used to the continuous bustle that had overtaken him with Kat's advent in his household, the silence made him uneasy. He'd been away two weeks, first checking into operations at the Too Late in the Snake River country and then backtracking to Denver to finalize an arrangement Sean had made with English investors who were interested in the potential of the Chicago Girl on—well, he couldn't call it Nigger Hill; Kat would have his hide. He laughed at the thought and then wondered where she was. Two weeks away had made him a little more relaxed at the prospect of seeing her again.

"Good day, Mr. Macleod." Noleen Pratt bustled in, her blond hair frizzled around her flushed face, smudges of flour marking her cheeks, chin, and bosom. "I've been baking," she explained unnecessarily.

"Where is everyone?" he asked.

"Well, Mr. Eyeless is out with his pals, like usual, and

Jamie won't be home from the mine for two hours yet, and your daughter is in her room doing school work."

"That's a first," Connor muttered. "Where's Miss Kat?"

"Probably off bothering people about drinking," said Jeannie, who had put away her books and come to greet her father.

"Now, Miss Jeannie, you know that's not so," Noleen intervened quickly.

"Well, she was last Sunday. And the Sunday before. As soon as you leave town, Daddy, she's out there doing just what you made her promise not to. The miners have been grumbling like anything, and it's all her fault. And Reverend Mother Hilda was furious when she heard that Kat had recruited Sister Freddie again." Jeannie giggled at the scene that had provided entertainment for all the fascinated students at St. Gertrude's.

"Reverend Mother called Kat a naughty girl and said she'd take a ruler to her backside if she ever caught her leading Sister Freddie astray again. And then she said it was Kat's fault that everyone in town calls Sister Freddie Sister Freddie, which was undignified, instead of Sister Fredericka, as she should be called. And Kat said being called Sister Freddie was a mark of affection, and everyone loved Sister Freddie, which was an improvement in the church's relations with the town."

When Jeannie realized that her father had stopped looking angry about the temperance campaign and begun to laugh at her description of the scene between Reverend Mother and Kat, she said hastily, "You'd better talk to her, Daddy. She doesn't mind you any better than she minds Reverend Mother."

"I've noticed," Connor muttered, sobering. He couldn't believe Kat had been out preaching temperance again. She'd promised. And to do it behind his back! While he was out of town! "Where is she?" he demanded.

"Ten Mile Canyon," said Noleen. When Connor looked

astounded and perturbed, she added, "All three mines went out on strike."

"Probably because she's trying to see they can't get a drink on the weekends," said Jeannie.

"I don't know why you dislike Miss Kat so much," said Noleen. "If it weren't for her, you wouldn't have a wardrobe full of new clothes and every boy in town half in love with you."

Jeannie flushed.

"When did she leave?" asked Connor.

"Last Monday," said Noleen. "She took Mary Beth out to the Ingrid's Ring to replace Hortense so she could take Hortense up to Ten Mile Canyon to oversee the cooking and dormitories at the three mines there."

"Why the hell didn't she wait for me?"

"She didn't know where you were or when you were coming back, Mr. Macleod, so she went off to settle the strike herself."

"Fat chance of that," he snapped and picked his bag up again.

"Daddy, you're not leaving already?" exclaimed Jeannie.

"I am," he replied grimly.

Connor took the D.S.P. & P. to Dickey and from there begged a ride on an ore train that went into Ten Mile Canyon on the spur, after which he borrowed a horse and rode to the Sister Katie where the superintendent gave him a bed for the night and the information that Kat was farther down the canyon at the Silver Cigar or the Dead Wife.

"What about the strike?" Connor asked.

"Settled," said the superintendent. "They got some damned fool notion that the mine isn't safe, said we're buying rotted timberin' to save money. I dunno how she convinced 'em otherwise. Don't seem to me like she knows nuthin' 'bout cribbin', but they went back to work. Helped when they had their first meal cooked by that Hortense, who'll be cookin' here two days a week. Anyways Miss Kathleen moved on. Talked to ever'one, she did. Dunno about what, but I reckon jus' gittin' to talk to a pretty woman's enough to break a strike."

Timbering? Connor knew he never skimped where mine safety was concerned. "You see anything wrong with the wood we've been getting?" he asked.

"Nuthin' *was* wrong with it. Just rumors, I reckon. You know how miners are."

"Rumors like that could put us out of business," Connor replied uneasily. "You sure it didn't have anything to do with temperance?"

"Well, they all know she's temperance," said the superintendent. "Suppose it could."

"It had nothing to do with that," Kat insisted. Connor had caught up with her at the Dead Wife.

"I gave Will Iliff my word," he replied stubbornly. "And you—"

"—haven't been inside a tavern since. We stayed out on the street." Kat couldn't help but look a little smug. "You're not my keeper. I'm a free woman, and if I want to urge people not to drink—"

"If you get those saloons closed on Sunday, you'll close every mine we own right along with the saloons."

"Here in Ten Mile Canyon? They'd don't drink in Breckenridge. Neither does the Snake River country, and all our mines outside Breckenridge are running. If you'd just listen to me, I can prove to you this trouble has nothing to do with temperance. The fact that *I* settled the strikes should give you a hint."

"All right, I'll listen. The superintendent at the Sister Katie said something about timbering."

"Not just that. There are all sorts of rumors—about wood,

about the dynamite, the food, the hoist cables. Anything that can go wrong, someone's telling them it will. At the Silver Cigar, Hortense and I had to ride the lifts to prove they were safe." Connor turned pale. "After we'd been up and down five times, they felt like fools."

"I should think."

"And they went back to work."

"I don't understand why they'd suddenly decide I can't be trusted."

Kat sighed. "I've been talking to miners for days now. Tracking down the rumors. You remember Jenkins?"

"The superintendent we fired at Ingrid's Ring?"

Kat nodded. "He's drifting around, buying drinks and dropping hints that our mines are dangerous, that we're cutting corners because we don't have enough capital to do otherwise and that we fired him because he complained about our negligence."

"Fleming," Connor muttered.

"Probably," she agreed. "And it's not just Jenkins. In two cases men who hired on recently started the rumors. Jenkins disappeared as soon as I got here, but the other two I fired, and they've threatened to make trouble with the miner's association. I don't know, Connor. It seemed the right thing to do at the time, but—"

"I'll talk to Pat Morrisey. He's the head of the association."

"I spoke with him myself, but he doesn't much appreciate negotiating with a woman. Thinks it's improper or something. Still, I've made a few friends among the miners."

"Which means, I suppose, you've had a few more marriage proposals."

"What business is that of yours?" she snapped. When he looked surprised, she moderated her tone. "Anyway, I have people watching for rumor-mongers, so if there's more trouble, maybe we can head it off."

231

"You've done a good job," he admitted grudgingly, "but next time would you wait for me?"

"And let three mines lie idle for days?"

"What the devil is that?" Connor was staring, aghast, at the second story rising above Kat's side of the house, an unexpected addition that had appeared in the three days they had been gone.

"That's my octagonal tower," said Kat proudly. "It's going to be just beautiful."

Diederick climbed down the ladder and glared at Connor. "She says build. I build," he said challengingly.

"It's all right, Diederick," Kat murmured. "It's my tower, and I'm paying for it. You ought to be delighted," she said to Connor. "You'll have your house practically to yourself once I've moved upstairs."

He glanced at her ruefully. "I never said I wanted you out of the house."

"She vants *you* out. Dat's vy I build der octagonal tower room."

"Then you should have checked the meaning of octagonal," Connor retorted. "It means eight-sided, and you've only got five."

While Kat was circling the house to count the sides, Diederick, flushed and angry, started toward Connor with the hammer raised.

"Whatever are you doing, Otto?" cried Jeannie, who had been watching from the porch. "You look like you're about to hit Daddy." Diederick drew back, and Jeannie said triumphantly to her father, "Didn't I tell you the trouble was because of her temperance marches? Isn't that what you found out?"

"No, it isn't," said Kat. "You're right about the number of sides, Connor, but I suppose five will do."

"You'll freeze up there this winter," Connor predicted, "but then he'll never get it done that fast."

"For *Kat* he will," said Jeannie. "Oh, and a rider just came in with the news that there's trouble at the First Strike."

Connor swore.

"And this *is* about her. The miners think she's going to forbid drinking in the dormitory."

"They drink in the dormitory?" Kat asked.

Connor glared at her and climbed back into the buggy with Kat right behind him. "Maybe you'd better stay home," he snapped.

"It's Sean's mine, and I'm going," she snapped right back.

They found the night shift milling around at the shaft head. Connor, taking stock quickly, noted two new men, who seemed to be leading the grumbling, the gist of which was that they didn't like working for an owner who confronted them at the door to the saloon when they came into town for a drink, an owner who had threatened to fire them for having a beer on Sunday. Connor shot her a telling glance.

Kat, who had been listening from the buggy, stood up and said loudly, "Have I ever fired a man for entering a saloon?" After the muttered *no's,* she asked, "Have I ever kept anyone from entering a saloon if they wanted to?" More shuffling. "Maybe you delicate fellows are afraid to walk past a big, frightening woman like me. Or is it Sister Freddie who scares you off?" Grins and laughter were breaking out in the crowd at the idea that they might be afraid of little Miz Fitzgerald or of Sister Freddie. "So what is it?" she demanded. "Because you disagree with me, you don't think I have a right to express my opinions?"

"We heard you was goin' to lay off anyone as takes a drink," said one of the men.

"You mean someone who shows up at the hoist drunk?"

"No ma'am. Anyone goin' down the shaft likkered up deserves to git fired."

"I don't let people go except for incompetence. Same policy my brother followed. Who said I would?"

She could see the men glancing at the newcomers.

"Who are you working for?" Connor asked the strangers, his voice hard. "Us or Fleming?" Then Connor addressed the others. "Most of you know me. You have my word that your jobs are safe as long as you do your work. But you might think twice when some stranger tries to get you to strike over a pack of lies. You're the ones who'll be losing your wages, not the fellow who's being paid by Fleming to cause trouble."

"Well, I think we took care of that," said Kat with satisfaction as they drove back.

"And I don't want to take care of it again. You've got to quit the temperance campaigns—at least, until the lawsuit's over."

"That could be years."

"It won't be years if we go broke first."

Kat sighed. "Father Dyer's leaving town anyway," she said. "Some Methodist conference."

"Thank God for small favors."

They drove in silence for a time, Connor satisfied that he'd solved at least one problem, Kat resentful that he expected her to put business concerns before her principles. Her thoughts were interrupted when Connor exclaimed, "Will you look at that!" He pointed up the hill at a large construction project. "Someone's building another house on Nickel Hill."

Kat shrugged. "That's Medford Fleming's new mansion."

Connor started to laugh.

"I don't see anything funny about it."

"No? Well, up till now there's been nothing on Nickel Hill but houses of ill repute." She looked at him askance. "To put it bluntly, Nickel Hill is one of our three red-light districts." Connor could remember a time when he'd been embarrassed at the thought of having to mention to Kat the red-light districts in West Breckenridge. It was nice to have as a friend a woman you could be comfortable with.

"Oh, my goodness." Kat had started to giggle. "I wonder if the Flemings know about their neighbors."

"Evidently not, and I, for one, hope no one tells them, at least till the house is built."

Kat had bought a horse and tried to ride every day. Her usual practice route was two miles out of town and two miles back, accompanied if she could find someone to ride with her, alone if not. She had invited Jeannie to be her companion, but Jeannie refused. Connor's daughter spent her late afternoons with her school books, and Kat could hardly argue about such scholarly diligence even if she did suspect it to be an excuse used to foil overtures of friendship. She was convinced that Jeannie spent the time napping.

The only person who seemed to take much interest in Kat's desire to become an accomplished rider was Diederick, who had asked three times that afternoon if she wasn't going out on her horse. Finally, she'd saddled up just to please him. She supposed he was trying to make up for having got the wrong number of sides on her tower, which made her wonder uneasily if he knew how to build a tower. She wouldn't like to be sleeping there when the first storm of winter came along and blew it down.

Maybe she should get Mr. Elias Nashold to come over and inspect it for durability. He had, after all, only recommended Diederick as a purveyor of scrollwork, not as a builder of reliable structures. Much of Breckenridge contained what folks called balloon-frame buildings—projects put up so hastily that they sagged or tilted or bulged alarmingly, looking as if they might collapse on their occupants. Was Diederick that kind of builder? Well, not in the sense that he built in a hurry. So slowly was the tower room progressing that she suspected Connor might be correct when he said that it would not be in place by winter.

Her thoughts were thus engaged as she guided her horse up the hill and spotted the curl of smoke coming from Connor's side of the house. For a moment she wondered why they'd have a fire going on such a warm afternoon. Then she realized that the house was burning, shouted as much to the nearest passerby, and brought her heretofore unused whip down on her heretofore unwhipped horse. The startled animal bolted into one of many deep pits in the street and stumbled, dumping Kat into the dust. She staggered up, cast one guilty glance at the injured horse, and ran up the hill, shouting the names of those she feared might be trapped inside, for she could now see flames through the window of Connor's dining room. "Connor!" she called. "Jeannie? Noleen? Eyeless? Diederick?" No one answered as she sped around the side of the house, looking for a way in. Flames in the front had sent her to the back, where there was an outside door from the hall that led to Connor's bedroom.

Kat had been through the Chicago fire. She knew all the stories and harbored all the fears left over from that childhood experience, but she also knew Jeannie might be asleep in the middle bedroom, so she ripped her own skirt off and dunked it into the bucket of water they kept in back, wrapped it over her head, and stumbled into the smoke. Within seconds she was on her knees, coughing, seeking clearer air as she crawled to Jeannie's room and then to her bed, on which, as she had thought, the girl lay.

Kat shook her and got no response but a strangled cough. Glancing apprehensively over her shoulder, she could see that the hall was now black with smoke. Therefore, holding her breath, she slammed Jeannie's door and then flung up the sash of the one window, which seemed to be the only safe exit. Then she dragged Jeannie off the bed, across the little room, and thrust her upper body through the window. Kat's lungs burned from the smoke as, coughing and gasping, she pushed the girl's legs over the sill. Then she leaned weakly against the wall, knowing she had to get through that window herself, get them both away from the house, but she didn't seem to have that last ounce of strength left. She could see clear air ahead but was unable to drag herself up because whirling blackness filled her head.

"Connor, where the hell you goin'? Didn't you hear the fire bell?"

"I just got word that the Ingrid's Ring is—"

"Hell man, there's a house afire on French Street."

"French?" His house was on French. Connor turned back and minutes later saw Kat's horse thrashing in the street, its leg broken, then the flames in his parlor and dining room. He found his daughter unconscious in a heap by her window, which was open and pouring smoke.

By the time he had carried Jeannie away from the house, the first fireman arrived. Connor told him to see to Jeannie, and then he plunged into the window. Jeannie had been asleep when he left, which meant whoever saved her might still be in there. He found Kat unconscious in the smoke-dense room and dragged her out, calculating desperately. Jamie would be at the mine, Eyeless probably downtown. Diederick—where the hell was Diederick? And Noleen. Dear God, was she still inside?

Connor staggered into the back yard with Kat in his arms and ran into Diederick, who looked as if someone had shot him in the heart.

"Gut God," the carpenter cried. "She's dead! Missus ist dead."

"Where's Noleen?"

"Mit der nuns at St. Gertrude's, her unt your girl."

"My girl damned near died in the fire and Kat too, trying to save her."

Diederick, pale as whitewash, tried to take Kat's body from Connor.

"Get away," Connor snarled at him. "Where the hell were you when the fire started?"

Diederick burst into tears.

Chapter Seventeen

With a house half destroyed and a mine shutdown that he'd not yet found time to investigate, Connor was in no mood to talk to Otto Diederick the morning after the fire. "Start the repairs," he ordered abruptly when the young carpenter with his odd, pale eyes appeared on the doorstep.

"How ist Missus?" Diederick asked.

"Listen for yourself," snapped Connor, his face drawn with worry. "The doctor's ordered both of them to stay in bed." Coughing could be heard from Kat's room.

"Both?"

"I told you Jeannie was caught in the fire too. They're sharing Kat's room, Eyeless and I are in the children's room, Jamie on the floor in the parlor, and Noleen's sleeping and cooking in the old kitchen. So get busy repairing the other half of the house. We can't go on like this very long."

"Better I tear it down," said Diederick. "Missus' house still gut. You shoult move avay. Shoult send Noleen avay. Fire started in der kitchen."

"How do you know that?" Connor asked suspiciously.

Diederick's eyes darted from side to side. "Vere else?"

"You never said where you were that afternoon."

"Other vere," he replied evasively, shrugging as if it were a matter of no importance.

"Well, get to work."

"I got Missus' tower to built. Better I tear down your place."

"The hell you—"

"Take only two days," Diederick promised.

The sound of coughing cut into their argument. When they turned, it was to find Kat leaning weakly against the door frame.

"Kat, the doctor said for you to stay in bed." Connor started toward her, alarmed, but she waved him away.

"If you can't make the other side livable by week's end, Diederick," said Kat, "I'll hire someone else."

"He shoult move out," said carpenter, his mouth turned down like a sulky boy's.

"He'll do no such thing." Her voice rasped painfully, and Connor winced. "I'd be dead if it weren't for Connor," she finished, giving the carpenter a fierce look. She remembered bitterly that Diederick had urged her to go riding and then left the house, obviously thinking she'd never know she was paying him for work he hadn't done. Because of him, she'd had to overcome her childhood fear of fire in order to rescue Jeannie. Coughing racked Kat's body, and she wondered miserably if it would ever stop. She hated being sick, having to stay in bed. "Get to work, Diederick," she ordered in a hoarse voice as she allowed Connor to lead her away. Diederick, shoulders slumped, headed toward the damaged section of the house.

"Don't talk," Connor murmured and helped her into bed. "Noleen," he shouted, "bring Kat some more broth."

"I don't want more broth," Kat muttered.

240

"I'll have some, Daddy," Jeannie whispered from her side of the room.

"Connor, the mine—" Kat began to cough again.

"Don't talk, darlin'."

"You have to get out there."

Connor thought the fire had been set. Somehow Fleming had managed it, perhaps thinking to keep Connor away from his most profitable mine, and the scheme had succeeded admirably in that respect. The Ingrid's Ring was closed, and Connor afraid to leave his womenfolk. If that damned worthless carpenter hadn't snuck away—

"I can look after things here," said Eyeless. He had been to town and bought a double-barreled shotgun.

"Me too, Pa." Jamie came in behind Eyeless, armed with a rifle and a pistol, both new, Connor's weapons having been destroyed in the fire.

"Go," Kat whispered. "We can't let them beat us." Again the hacking cough shook her small frame. "Not now that we've got them on the run."

Connor stared at her in surprise. They'd almost burned down the house, damn near killed her and Jeannie, and she thought she had Fleming on the run?

"They wouldn't have gone this far if they thought they were winning." Kat gave him a weak smile.

What a woman she was! Connor leaned forward impulsively to drop a kiss on her forehead. Then, because his daughter was staring at him balefully, he kissed her as well and, taking the rifle Jamie handed him, strode out to see what he could do about the strike at Ingrid's Ring.

"All right, Pat, are you speaking for the men?" Connor asked. He'd had a hard time getting the work force together so that he could talk to them.

"They want more money. Fleming's raised wages."

Connor's eyes narrowed. "I can't afford more money, and you know it."

241

"Fleming's paying three-seventy-five a day."

"As of when?"

"Last week."

"Well, you're still better off working for me. Fleming charges for board and then feeds his men swill."

"You big corporations always got an answer, but we're the ones who pay for your greed," shouted one of the men.

"Right. The miner ain't got a chance no more," complained another.

"I'm no big corporation," Connor retorted, "and I came up from just where you are. I was a hard rock miner at Sts. John, prospecting on the side. I can drill and blast with the best of you. Can Fleming say that? Any of those eastern swells at Trenton Consolidated ever even been down a mine, much less swung a pick? I prospected this claim myself. My son was working down the shaft until today."

"What's he doin' now? Sittin' on his butt in your office?"

"He's sitting in my house with Eyeless, armed to the teeth because someone set fire to it yesterday."

Pat Morrisey said, "Look, Connor, if you think we—well, we don't operate that way."

"I know it, Pat. No one's accusing the association. But that is the way the big corporations operate. Fleming's filed suit to try to get this mine back; he's sending strangers around spreading rumors in all my mines and Sean Fitzpatrick's. When Sean's sister put a stop to that in Ten Mile Canyon—"

"Hey, Connor, whyn't you send Miss Kat out? We wouldn't mind seein' a pretty woman, even if she is one a them temperance types."

"That what this strike is about? You want to negotiate with Kat?" He grinned, then sobered as he remembered what had happened to her. "Kat won't be doing any negotiating. The fire damned near killed her and my daughter too. Set by Fleming's people—that's what I figure."

"You know that for a fact?" asked Morrisey.

"You mean, did I catch someone with the torch in his hand? No. I was on my way out here when I heard my house was on fire."

"Miss Kat all right?" asked one of the men.

"I don't know," said Connor morosely. "She wasn't burned, but she hasn't stopped coughing since she dragged Jeannie out of the house."

"Don't nuthin' scare Miss Kat," said one of the men admiringly, "not even Will Iliff haulin' her off to jail."

"Your daughter all right?" asked another.

"Same as Kat, coughing like she's got miner's lung."

Uneasy silence fell over the crowd. Miner's lung was something most owners never mentioned. Except Connor Macleod. He contributed to St. Joseph's for his men instead of making them pay their own dollar a month for care. He found work for the families of stricken miners. His own partner, Sean Fitzpatrick, had it. The men at Ingrid's Ring reconsidered and went back to work.

"Kat."

Kat looked up from her book. She was rereading the *Handbook to the Kansas Territory and the Rocky Mountains and Gold Region,* stifling laughter because laughing made her cough. "What is it, Jeannie?"

"You shouldn't laugh."

"I know."

"I never did say, but—but thank you for saving my life."

"You're welcome." Kat wondered if that might be the first small step to a better relationship with Jeannie. Probably not. She wouldn't get her hopes up.

"What were you laughing about?"

"Oh, I read this book before I came out here, and it said the only trunk sturdy enough for a trip to Colorado was one you could throw off a three-story building. So I found a three-story building, hired a man to haul the trunk up, and had him throw it out."

Jeannie's eyes rounded. "What happened?"

"The trunk survived, but it looked so terrible Mother wouldn't let me bring it with me."

Jeannie started to giggle. "You're making that up."

"Don't laugh," said Kat and started to laugh herself. "And I did do it."

They were both coughing when Connor walked in, a worried frown on his face.

Kat waved her hand reassuringly and gasped, between spasms of coughing, "Our own fault."

"Kat threw her trunk off a three-story building," said Jeannie and started laughing again.

"There are no three-story buildings in Breckenridge," Connor reminded them. "This will be one of the few two-story buildings if Diederick ever finishes it." He'd just had another argument with the carpenter, who had again insisted that Connor move out because the burned side of the house couldn't be renovated before Christmas.

"And leave the women unprotected?" Connor had snapped, all the angrier because he knew that their living together in such close quarters would cause gossip. "One week, Diederick. You get it renovated in one week, or I'll find someone else."

"Missus—"

"Damned near died in that fire."

Diederick turned pale. "Von't happen again."

"How do you know? Now get to work." The house wasn't that bad, he assured himself. Most of the destruction was in the kitchen, dining room, and parlor. The bedrooms just needed airing out and repapering because of smoke damage. A week wasn't too short a time. Or maybe he just wanted to get rid of Diederick.

"Big news in town," he said to Kat and Jeannie. "Tom Groves and Harry Lytton brought in a nugget from Farncomb

Hill that weighs over thirteen pounds." He slapped his hat against his thigh and added bitterly, "Other people are finding giant nuggets, and I can't even keep my mines open."

"What happened at Ingrid's Ring?" Kat asked.

"They're back at work—at least until the next time Fleming finds some way to turn them against us."

"I just returned from a conference, or I'd have come by to pray with you earlier," said Father Dyer. He had brought his wife Lucinda along, and Lucinda was fluffing Jeannie's pillow, having already fluffed Kat's.

Noleen, who had been serving a midday meal of soup when the Dyers arrived, looked at the Methodist preacher as if she expected him to attack Kat on her sickbed.

"I'll take that, dear," said Lucinda Dyer and immediately sat down with both bowls of soup and began to spoon them alternately into the mouths of the two patients.

"I can eat my own soup," said Jeannie and began to cough.

"Don't talk, dear," said Lucinda and popped another spoonful into Jeannie's mouth.

"This may be a punishment from God," Father Dyer pointed out.

Kat couldn't protest because the spoon was in her mouth.

"For dancing," the Methodist minister explained.

"We think Medford Fleming had the fire set," said Kat, once she'd swallowed her broth.

"An evil man," Father Dyer agreed. "He doesn't let me preach at his mines. And I'll have to admit that God does look favorably on your work for the cause. Do you think you'll be up and around by Sunday?"

Kat sighed. "Maybe, but Connor is adamant that I give up talking to miners outside the saloons. He says it's causing labor trouble."

"God has probably moved Macleod's miners to strike

because he opposes temperance," said Father Dyer, "and because he dances."

Jeannie was listening to this conversation, open-mouthed, which made it easier for Lucinda to spoon more soup into her. "Shut your mouth and swallow, dear," Lucinda advised.

"But I haven't given up on Sunday closing," said Kat and received another dose of soup.

"You're a Methodist at heart, my child," said Father Dyer. "You must free yourself from the evil toils of the Pope in Rome and—"

"Now, Father Dyer, we've had this conversation before," said Kat good-humoredly. "I've decided that woman's suffrage is the best hope for closing the saloons."

"God did not mean for women to vote," said Father Dyer.

"Why not?" asked Kat.

"Open your mouth, dear," said Lucinda.

Kat obeyed, swallowed, and continued, "If women get the vote, we'll have no trouble passing a Sunday closing law."

"A woman's place is in the home, not at the polling place."

"Who would you rather see voting, Father Dyer? Some drunken miner or Mrs. Dyer?" Kat could not pursue that line of argument because Mrs. Dyer, having fed more soup to a giggling Jeannie, then thrust another spoonful into Kat's mouth.

"Woman suffrage is not a Methodist idea," said Father Dyer.

"But I'm not a Methodist," said Kat.

"You should be."

"Indeed, my dear, you really should," said Lucinda.

How could you argue with a woman who kept your mouth full of soup? Kat wondered as she swallowed yet again. Nonetheless, Kat was convinced that giving women the vote would be a more successful method of gaining support for temperance than hanging around saloons on Sunday getting arrested and irritating Connor.

"The new school is opening today," said Jeannie wistfully on August first when she was still under doctor's orders to stay in bed.

"I know," said Kat. She too had wanted to attend the opening of St. Gertrude's boarding school.

"And I'd have been honored for my grades, but now I won't be there."

"You're on the honor roll? That's wonderful, Jeannie."

"If she can make the honor roll, I can," said Jamie, who was sitting in their room, importantly armed with a pistol.

"You can't be on the honor roll if you're not in school," Kat pointed out. She'd noticed how eager Jamie was to give up mining and assume guard duty.

"I could go back to school," said Jamie.

"I think that's a wonderful idea."

"And I could become a boarder," said Jeannie.

Kat sighed. If Jeannie wanted to become a boarder, it was because she wanted to get away from Kat. "You wouldn't like it," she warned. "They're very strict."

"Oh."

"Why don't we get up and go to the ceremony," Kat suggested. "It's silly for the doctor to keep us in bed. We've both stopped coughing." Jamie opened his mouth to protest. "Of course, we'd have to take Jamie for protection, and you could enroll while we're there, Jamie."

"Daddy'd scalp us," said Jeannie after considering the tempting suggestion.

"Oh, I hardly think your father knows how to scalp anyone."

"Of course, he does," said Jamie. "He was here when the Indians were still massacring people. Want me to tell you how it's done?"

"No, thanks," said Kat hastily.

247

* * *

"Kat, wake up!"

Kat stirred and yawned. "Jeannie, what are you doing out of bed?" she murmured groggily.

"You were having a bad dream." Jeannie turned and flopped down on the bed cross-legged, with her knees poking against the skirt of her nightgown. "What were you dreaming about? The fire?"

"My father," said Kat. "I was dreaming about the way he died." She shivered, although the August afternoon was actually rather warm.

"Did something awful happen to him?" asked Jeannie with the avid curiosity of the young for horror stories.

Kat thought about the slow, terrible deterioration of her father and, in recalling it, described it for Jeannie. "At first, he lost his appetite and got thin, although he'd always been a husky man. Mother thought maybe he had a cancer because his stomach hurt and he threw up and was weak. But it was his liver. The drink had done it. His doctor said he had to stop drinking entirely, but my father wouldn't; he didn't even stop going to the saloon. He owned a saloon in Chicago; I guess you didn't know that. And his nose would bleed, gushes of blood. It frightened the customers.

"By then he'd turned yellow and begun to swell up. And he was mean. He'd yell at my mother one minute, and the next he wouldn't remember who she was or what was happening. He started mistaking her for his first wife and asking her what she'd done with baby Sean. And his hands shook. He finally stopped drinking because he couldn't hold a glass or get out of bed, and Mother wouldn't give him whiskey. In the end he choked to death on his own blood, all swollen and rotting, blood everywhere." Kat shuddered.

Taken aback, Jeannie mumbled, "I guess that's why you're so against drinking."

"That and the fact that my husband would have died the

same way if he hadn't fallen, drunk, in front of a beer wagon."

"I'm glad Daddy doesn't drink."

Kat nodded. "Your father's a good man." Then she thought of that night on the ranch outside Dillon and added, "In his way."

"He's really mad at you," said Jeannie. "He came in fuming about an hour ago, but I wouldn't let him wake you up. Maybe you ought to tell him about your father's death."

"He knows. What did he say?"

"It's all over the mining country that you're going to get women the vote and then see that all the saloons are closed. He said the miners will shut down our mines with strikes before that happens."

"They give me too much credit," said Kat dryly and hopped out of bed.

"What are you doing?"

"Declaring myself well," she replied as she started to dress.

"But the doctor said two more days."

Kat was throwing on clothes, lacing on boots.

"Daddy will be furious."

"According to you, he already is," Kat replied.

"But where are you going?"

"Out to find how that rumor got started."

The investigation didn't begin very auspiciously. Because she'd been in bed so long, Kat was tired by the time she got to the livery stable to rent a horse, her own having been shot after breaking its leg in the rutted streets of Breckenridge just before the fire. Then her first attempt at riding since the fire landed her in the street again, this time at the very feet of the mayor. She rose wearily, inspected the rented horse, which had survived unhurt, and turned on the mayor to give him an angry lecture about his civic responsibility to maintain safe, level streets.

"Well now, Miz Fitzgerald, I reckon it isn't so much my streets as your riding," said the mayor complacently. "Ladies are mighty ornamental, but they're just not riders."

"Of all the stupid things to say! Just wait till you come up for reelection!"

The mayor laughed. "Gonna get ladies the vote and vote me out, are you?"

Kat scrambled astride the rented horse and rode off. She didn't have the time for retribution right now, nor, if the truth be told, the energy. She hoped to visit as many mines as she could in the immediate area today, and she started at the Ingrid's Ring. It didn't take long to ascertain that Fleming's agents had been spreading discontent in the saloons.

The men, even with their drinking threatened, were happy to talk to her, eager to hear about her rescue of Connor Macleod's daughter in the fire. "Fleming had that set, you know," she said to each man who asked. When they grumbled about the threat of women voting, she retorted, "How many saloons have I been able to close so far?"

None, they had to admit.

"And how long has woman suffrage been proposed and nothing done about it?"

Since territorial days, they admitted.

She hired a bug-infested bed in Preston that night, and Connor caught up with her before she could take the train to Dillon.

"Will you, for God's sake, stay home the way the doctor told you?"

"I'm fine."

"You look half dead."

"Thank you very much, Connor."

"Oh, all right, you look beautiful. But pale. Now please come back to Breckenridge. I know what you've been

250

saying to the men, and word will have spread up the Snake and over to Ten Mile Canyon by day's end."

Kat allowed herself to be escorted home. She needed the rest, not to mention time to work out an alternative plan that had come to her.

Kat didn't know how Medford Fleming had found out about her scheme to pursue temperance legislation through woman suffrage, but she had talked to enough miners to know that those rumors, like others that had caused labor problems, originated with Fleming's agents. Had Father Dyer mentioned their conversation to someone? Not with any favor; he didn't approve of the idea. Lucinda? Kat doubted it. Jeannie? Because they had shared the same room for several weeks as they recuperated from the fire, Jeannie hadn't seen anyone without Kat being present. Had Diederick, Noleen, or Jamie overheard and gossiped? She didn't think any of the three would be that interested. So who could have told Fleming? And how could she get information on Fleming and Trenton Consolidated with which to counterattack?

As soon as Connor calmed down and went back to work, Kat began a research project, remembering a chance remark of his that statistics gathered by the Colorado Bureau of Labor came from the mine owners. She began to ask questions about accidents at the mines of Trenton Consolidated. Then she compared her notes to the published record of the state bureau. Just as she had thought, Fleming was lying to them. His mines actually had a terrible safety record and a rapid turnover in the labor force, which kept miners from realizing how dangerous a situation they were signing up for. Now she had the proof and intended to confront him. Maybe she could force him to stop causing trouble by threatening to retaliate in kind if he didn't.

* * *

Fleming listened to everything she had to say, the evidence that he had been starting rumors among their workers, the fact that he was covering up his deplorable safety record while telling her employees that they were working under unsafe conditions. And all during the time she talked, he studied her with a supercilious smile.

"You're prettier than I remembered," he remarked when she stopped for breath.

"And you're uglier and more despicable," she snapped. Actually he was quite a handsome man, well dressed, urbane, and she could see that he didn't like being called ugly and despicable. His smile had disappeared. Good! He thought he was so safe behind his big desk, sitting in his expensive leather chair!

"Two can play the rumor game, Mr. Fleming—only my rumors will be true. I've met a lot of miners in the course of my research. Now I'll go back and tell them all about you. Maybe I'll call a town meeting and tell the citizens about you. I'm not sure people realize how many men in your employ have been killed. Or that the widows and children never receive a penny of help from you. Or what happens to your men who are disabled by accidents or miner's lung."

"And do you really think anyone will listen to a woman who runs around trying to close saloons in the company of a nun, a schoolteacher, several housemaids, and a crackpot Methodist preacher?"

Kat's eyes narrowed. "People will be interested to hear that you consider Father Dyer a crackpot. Especially since you're an outsider, and he's a respected citizen of long standing."

"Ah, but of course, I'll deny ever having said any such thing. Maybe I'll make a contribution to his church. And you might keep in mind that I'm a Protestant, while you are one of the detested papists—or hadn't you noticed that local prejudice against your kind?"

"No, I haven't. I've found *everyone* in Breckenridge very friendly—everyone who doesn't work for you."

"Why, I'm prepared to be friendly, Mrs. Fitzgerald." He gave her a nasty smile that sent a shiver down her spine.

"I'm going to insist that the sheriff investigate how that fire started in my house," she threatened. She hadn't an iota of evidence that he was responsible, directly or indirectly, but Noleen had sworn that she'd left nothing burning or even hot in the kitchen before she went off to St. Gertrude's, and no lamps had been lit.

"Maybe you should consider that I can sue you for slander if you start making wild accusations," he retorted and stared at her as if she were a purchase he might make should he decide she was of acceptable quality. "Why don't you give up these aggressive notions of yours, Mrs. Fitzgerald. They're hardly becoming in such a pretty woman. If you've so little to occupy your time, let me suggest that you and I get better acquainted. I like your spirit. In fact, I think you'd make me a excellent mistress."

Kat's mouth dropped open.

Fleming, an amused smile on his face, rose from his desk. "Such passion is wasted in front of saloons, waving signs and harassing dullards, or making threats against gentlemen who—"

"Gentlemen?" Kat gasped, refusing to back away as he circled his desk.

"Indeed," said Fleming. "I think you'll find me a gentleman of suitable generosity and a lover of some talent and expertise."

"I'd rather sleep with a pig," she gasped, snatching up a heavy gold-nugget paperweight and hurling it at him before he could get any closer.

As she fled, the trickle of blood issuing from his forehead gave her great satisfaction. But she heard him mutter, "Bitch. You'll regret that to your dying day."

Never, she thought. *If I'd had a shovel, I'd have knocked your head off*. Still, for all her brave thoughts, he'd frightened her badly.

Chapter Eighteen

Shaking with anger and close to tears, Kat left the offices of Trenton Consolidated. How dare he make such a proposal to a respectable woman? Did he think, because he was a wealthy Easterner, he could treat her with contempt? He was threatening her livelihood, he'd burned her house, and now he'd seen fit to treat her like a—like a hussy—and what could she do? What protection did women have against such men? Now she understood the dangers her mother had said women alone faced. Now she knew why Sean had insisted on leaving her under Connor's protection. But Connor was out of town, putting out more brush fires—started by Fleming, no doubt.

Kat wanted more than anything to cry on her mother's shoulder. Only another woman would understand the humiliation of being treated like that by a man she hated. *Another woman*—it was as if her mind lit up with an inspiration, a sun of an idea, banishing clouds of fear and futile anger. Women might lack the temporal power that men exercised, but one thing women did have; they were the arbiters of respectability. Here, in Chicago, all over the country—women brought civilization and decency with them and stood ready to defend their ground. Fleming had used rumor and gossip to further his ends, and she had threatened to do the same, although never meaning it quite this way. It would be a dangerous gambit, her own reputation the stake she risked, but still . . .

Kat changed her course. Instead of heading home, where she could bury her head under a pillow and weep, she headed for the Dyer cabin on the Blue, where this afternoon the Methodist Ladies' Aid Society would be meeting. Women needed to stick together, thought Kat, and she was about to give them the chance.

"Why, my dear Kathleen, what a surprise," said Lucinda Dyer.

"Oh dear, Mrs. Dyer," said Kat. "I've interrupted your—your—"

All the Methodist ladies were looking as surprised as Lucinda, except Gertrude Briggle, who said, "What's wrong, Kat? What's happened?"

Kat burst into tears. She'd been on the verge since leaving Fleming's office; it was a relief to let go.

"My dear child," cried Lucinda and took Kat into a motherly embrace.

Thinking of her own mother, Kat cried all the harder while the ladies gathered around offering tea, handkerchiefs, cookies, consoling pats—and questions.

Finally, hiccupping and sniffing, Kat said, "I went to see Medford Fleming." The ladies looked at each other in astonishment. "He's—he's turned our miners against us, and—and b-burned our house." The ladies all gasped. "I t-told him to st-stop. Jeannie—Jeannie would have died if—"

"You too," said Gertrude. "Kat nearly died rescuing Jeannie, but I didn't know the fire was set."

"Couldn't it have been the stove—or a lamp?" asked one of the ladies. Fire was a terrible danger in frontier towns. No one wanted to think that there were people who would use it as a weapon against women and children.

"The stove was c-cold. It was daytime, n-no lamps lit. N-no one has reason to wish us ill but him."

"What did he say to you, dear?" asked Lucinda.

"Oh, I can't tell you. It was so horrible. If only my mother were here."

The women all exchanged looks, and Lucinda said, "Would you like to talk to Father Dyer, Kathleen?"

Kat raised her tear-stained face and exclaimed, "I could never talk to a *man* about it, not even kind, good Father Dyer." She could see that half the ladies were desperate with curiosity and the other half overcome with horrified, if uninformed, sympathy.

"My dear Mrs. Fitzgerald," said a women known as the most avid gossip in town, "you must unburden your heart to us. We women have to stick together."

"You're right," Kat agreed, glad to find her very own sentiments in another's mouth. "If I don't tell someone, he might—he might insult and humiliate some other poor woman with his—his disgusting proposals." Eight shocked gasps greeted this statement. "These—these horrid, rich outsiders think they can say anything at all to respectable women just because we're—we're only local people."

"What did that scoundrel say to you?" asked Gertrude, who looked as if she might march off to attack Medford Fleming herself.

So Kat told them. Every insulting word. "He acted as if being temperance were akin to being a—a fallen woman."

Every lady in the room held temperance sentiments, and the response was everything Kat could have hoped for.

"My poor child," said Lucinda Dyer. "I think we should

all say a prayer of thanks that you escaped unscathed from that—that lecher's clutches."

"What is the world coming to when a woman can't defend her home and children without having her honor threatened by disgusting Easterners?" said the town's premier gossip when the prayer was concluded.

"That man needs to be taught a lesson," said Gertrude, her young face grim.

"You're all such dear, kind friends," said Kat and allowed herself to be plied with tea and escorted home by a cordon of militant ladies.

In the next three days, no less than eleven additional ladies called on Kat to express their sympathy for her terrible ordeal. Five of them assured her that if they ever had the opportunity, they would cut Medford Fleming dead. Kat was pleased to hear it and even more pleased to think that their husbands were going to encounter Fleming in the work place and make his life difficult.

"How come you're having all this company?" asked Jeannie, who arrived home from school every day to find some female visitor, often Protestant, having coffee and cake in her father's parlor, which still showed the effects of the fire. "And why don't you entertain them on your side of the house?"

"We're all sleeping over there," said Kat, who wanted the physical evidence of Fleming's arson to be seen by as many people as possible. She'd have invited the whole town in to view the damage but decided that might be too obvious. "And they're won't mind. Breckenridge is such a friendly town."

"It didn't used to be—not to Catholics."

Kat smiled to herself. How wrong Fleming had been when he suggested that her religion would deprive her of allies. Christian ladies, Catholic and Protestant, had flocked to her standard. On Friday, the Ladies' Altar Cloth Society

voted to attempt the withdrawal of Roman Catholic miners
from Trenton Consolidated. Kat made them a small speech
of thanks, saying ladies had to stick together if decency was
to be preserved in the face of evil outside elements.

Three local merchants stopped her on the street and
congratulated her on having put a well-deserved lump on
the head of Medford Fleming. Nothing was said by the
gentlemen about why she had done that, but they all assured
her that Fleming's head was still bandaged. They had taken
the trouble to check, while raising the prices on supplies he
bought from them. Kat was delighted to know that she had
sent his costs skyrocketing. His eastern colleagues wouldn't
like that.

On Sunday, Reverend John Dyer preached a sermon
on the unlikelihood of a rich man getting into heaven,
especially one given to despicable lusts. Everyone in the
congregation knew exactly what rich man Father Dyer was
referring to, and both newspapers mentioned the sermon.

The following Tuesday, a delegation of women called
on Sheriff Iliff to ask if there wasn't a law against gross
insults to ladies. Will Iliff said he wished there were, but
to his knowledge no such law appeared on the books. Kat,
during the growing furor, went about her business looking
pale and demure while people murmured about what a brave
little thing she was. Connor, fortunately, was in Denver.
She had no idea how he'd have reacted to the scandal, but
she was satisfied that the terrible chance she'd taken had
worked in her favor. Medford Fleming might not know it,
but his name was anathema in Breckenridge.

Sister Freddie, looking amused, said on Wednesday, "I'd
offer my sympathies, Kat, but from what I hear, Mr. Fleming
has come out the loser."

"People have been very kind and supportive," Kat
replied.

"About what?" asked Jeannie, who was sitting with them
in the parlor. No one had mentioned the matter to her,

since such shocking events were kept from innocent young girls.

"What I really came to talk to you about is Jamie," said Sister Freddie. "He said the most astonishing thing during religious instruction this afternoon. I asked the class what our Savior was doing on the Mount, and Jamie said, "He was probably prospecting." When Jeannie started to giggle, Sister Freddie gave her a quelling look and continued, "Perhaps you should tutor him in the New Testament, Kat. All the children laughed at him."

"Oh, he knows what Christ was doing on the Mount, Sister Freddie," said Jeannie. "That's an old Colorado joke. They were meant to laugh."

"Were they indeed?"

Freddie's expression reminded Kat of Hilda Walzen in the old days, and two things occurred to Kat. First, Jamie was in trouble, and second, Freddie, her old childhood friend, might one day become a Reverend Mother herself. Just the thought made Kat feel old.

The next day word came of an accident at the Too Late, and Kat set out for Montezuma by herself because Connor was still away. The message told of a misplaced explosive that had flooded the mine, drowning one man and injuring two. Kat went armed with Jamie's pistol. As she rode a rented horse up the dangerous trail, she submerged her anxiety by trying to remember what Jamie had told her about loading and shooting the weapon.

The men at the Too Late, having expected Connor, were shocked to see her. "He shouldn't have never given the mine such a bad luck name," said the superintendent.

"Nonsense," said Kat. "What happened?"

"New fella made a mistake—too much powder in the charges an' he placed 'em wrong. Blew the side wall, an' we got water—God, you wouldn't believe the water. He was lucky an' got out, but there was three fellas didn't.

259

We're blastin' an adit to drain it off, but till we finish, we won't be sendin' out no ore."

Kat thought of the salaries they'd have to pay with no profits coming in. If this continued, Fleming would win. "The man who blew the side wall—is he still here?"

"Shore."

"How long employed?"

"Month maybe. Come from Aspen."

"I'd like to talk to him."

The man, Pel Marcus, was brought into the office, a slouching, unshaven fellow whom Kat distrusted on sight. She pulled Jamie's pistol out of her reticule and leveled it carefully with both hands. "Now Mr. Marcus, you can tell me who put you up to flooding the mine."

Pel Marcus turned pale while the superintendent began to sputter a protest. "Just stay away from my line of fire, Mr. Ketchem," she said to the superintendent. "I wouldn't want to hurt an innocent bystander."

"But Miz Fitzgerald, what are you gonna do to Pel?"

"Nothing if he tells the truth. This isn't the first trouble caused by agents of Trenton Consolidated. I've had my house burned down—"

Ketchem's mouth dropped open.

"—with Jeannie Macleod in it."

"Connor's daughter's dead?"

"I dragged her out just in time." Kat waved the gun at Pel Marcus. "And then I was personally insulted by Mr. Fleming, who made lewd remarks to me, so be warned, Mr. Marcus—I knocked Mr. Fleming on the head with his own gold nugget, and I'm quite prepared to do you an injury as well. I have reached the end of my patience."

"But I ain't—I ain't done—"

"Now, if you admit that you were hired to flood our mine, I shall simply turn you over to the authorities. Otherwise— let's see. This is the trigger, I believe. I shall pull the trigger. If you are innocent, God will protect you."

"You're crazy!" Pel Marcus had turned gray with fright.

"Obviously you know nothing of church history, Mr. Marcus. Guilt or innocence has been left in God's hands for centuries, so you need not fear for your life if you are an innocent man. You will be protected."

"Fleming hired me," Marcus cried.

"You're not just saying that because you're a person of little faith?"

"He hired me," cried Marcus. "Paid me fifty dollars. Twenty-five to git a job here. Twenty-five when the mine was flooded."

"I don't know, Mr. Marcus. You could be lying," said Kat, steadying the pistol.

"The money's in my Sunday boots. I swear it."

"Very well, if you will swear on a Bible, I'll take your word for it. Call the men in, Mr. Ketchem. They should know what we're up against so they'll be vigilant in the future."

A blubbering Pel Marcus took his oath in front of the furious Too Late miners. "Please do him no injury, gentlemen," said Kat as she prepared to ride back to Montezuma for the sheriff. Ketchem escorted her.

"Fleming insulted you, ma'am?" he asked hesitantly.

"Yes, he did," said Kat. "The things he said to me— well, you'll understand, Mr. Ketchem, that I cannot repeat them. It would be too embarrassing for both of us, but he is a lewd man in whose company no respectable woman would wish to spend one single moment."

Mr. Ketchem's eyes were as round as buckets when Kat had finished being discreet on the subject of her confrontation with Fleming. She was sure that some miner from Montezuma would find his way to Breckenridge within the next week looking for more details and that those details would be available because so many ladies had whispered to their husbands the shocking story of Medford Fleming.

Kat pointed out to the deputy sheriff in Montezuma that

Fleming as well as Marcus should be charged with the murder at the Too Late. However, that was not to be, for Marcus never went to trial. He was found the next morning, hanged in the shaft house where the miners all swore they had left him locked up but alive.

Kat shivered when she heard. Perhaps she should not have gone about things as she had. The violence was escalating. She'd never know if her own employees had lynched him or some minion of Fleming had done it to protect his employer. The one explanation she did not consider feasible was that the cowardly Pel Marcus had hung himself.

"Noleen was the only one in the house, Daddy," said Jeannie. "Someone brought Kat a message; Kat said, 'The saints preserve us,' threw some clothes in a valise, told Noleen to look for her when she saw her, and left."

"Noleen didn't even find out where she was going?" Connor didn't like the sound of that.

"Well, she'll probably be back tonight, don't you think?" Jeannie was trying out chords on Ingrid's piano. "Sister Pauline says I ought to take lessons with her, that I've a real flair for music."

"Until Diederick finishes the repairs, there are too many people crowded into too few rooms for me to put up with inexpert piano playing."

"Kat would think I should get to practice."

"Then maybe you should have found out where she was going."

"She was probably trying to get away from all the visitors. Every lady in town has come to call—even the Protestants."

"Oh?" If his daughter had said every *man* in town had come to call, Connor wouldn't have been surprised. He wouldn't have liked it, but he wouldn't have been surprised. Then he reminded himself that he'd have to watch that tendency toward jealousy. After all, he had no proprietary rights where Kat was concerned.

*   *   *

"Mr. Macleod, I wonder if I might invite you to tea?"

Connor couldn't remember when he had been more taken aback. He knew who the beautiful, elaborately dressed woman was, although they had never been introduced, nor had he ever expected to be invited to the house of Medford Fleming. She had stopped him on the street in front of the confectioner's shop. "Your husband wants to speak to me?" he asked warily.

"No, this is not a business matter," said Eustacia Fleming. "I have a favor to ask."

Stranger and stranger. Connor accepted the invitation out of curiosity and appeared at the new Fleming house on Nickel Hill, amused because several of the more flamboyant Nickel Hill ladies yoo-hooed at him from their balcony as he rode toward his four o'clock appointment.

"Mr. Fleming is out of town at present," said Mrs. Fleming, tucking a honey-colored lock into her elaborate coiffure as she sank gracefully onto a brocade love seat and indicated the spot beside her.

Connor sat down. As far as he knew, the statuesque Eustacia Fleming was seldom in Breckenridge herself and rarely entertained natives when she was there. A maid appeared and served tea.

Eustacia murmured, "If you would prefer something stronger than tea, of course, I can provide it."

"Tea's fine," said Connor, who detested the nasty stuff. He kept his eyes firmly on his cup because his hostess was wearing some loose, floating garment, and he was quite sure that she was uncorseted. Could she have just risen from a nap? Was she wearing a dressing gown?

"Do have a biscuit." She offered him a plate of cookies, and her wide sleeve fell away to reveal a delicate wrist and rounded arm.

Connor accepted a cookie, thinking wryly that Eyeless would be surprised to be offered this "biscuit" to sop

263

up his gravy. Mrs. Fleming evidently had pretensions to English gentility. That thought was interrupted when her thigh pressed against his.

She looked straight into his eyes and said, "Dear Mr. Macleod, I wanted to consult with you about a problem concerning my house."

Connor politely shifted his leg, interested to see if she would renew contact. Perhaps he was misreading these signals, and she wasn't really entertaining him in her bedclothes. That thing she had on might be some fashionable kind of dress he'd never heard of.

"I am quite happy with the house," Eustacia was saying. "Of course, it's just a simple country place, but I did choose the site myself—for the fine view, you know."

So that's why Medford Fleming now shared a hill with Miss Marcie's house of ill fame. With difficulty, Connor controlled the amused twitching of his lips.

"Now I find that I have neighbors who are, shall we say, less than desirable."

He took a sip of tea and noted that her thigh was once again in contact with his and that she was now staring at him with soulful violet eyes, for all the world like a woman in the throes of romantic passion.

"Just because you and my husband are at odds, Mr. Macleod, is no reason why you and I cannot be friends." She smiled at him and laid her hand gently on his arm. Connor took another sip of tea. "Knowing how well thought of you are here in Breckenridge, I wondered if you might not use your influence to—ah, convince my undesirable neighbors to take themselves elsewhere."

"I doubt that your husband would like to think he was indebted to me in any way, Mrs. Fleming."

"Eustacia," she purred. "And I hardly think my husband comes into this. I, on the other hand, should not mind being indebted to such a . . . charming gentleman."

Connor studied her thoughtfully. The idea of bedding

his enemy's wife held a certain perverse attraction. But then maybe Fleming didn't give a damn what the beautiful Eustacia did. Also, there was the fact that she stirred no fire in Connor's loins. A glance from Kat would have been harder to resist than the prospect of a week in bed with Eustacia Fleming.

"Maybe you'd like a tour of the house," she suggested.

A tour of the house? Ending in a bedroom?

"Are we understanding each other, Connor? I may call you Connor, may I not?"

"Certainly, ma'am."

"And you must call me Eustacia. Dear me, *ma'am* is so quaint. If you have—ah, scruples because I am a married woman, perhaps you are unaware that my husband's name and that of your—goodness, I'm not quite sure in what relationship Mrs. Fitzgerald stands to you, Connor. At any rate, their names are quite closely linked in town gossip."

Connor felt a jolt of startled anger, then the certainty that Kat would never have anything to do with Medford Fleming. In Eustacia's eyes shone a gleam of spiteful pleasure. Why? Because she was planning to cuckold her husband? Or because she had just blackened Kat's name?

"Thank you for tea, Eustacia. I think I'll pass up the house tour, but I'll look into your problem."

"Oh dear, I hope I haven't offended you. People *will* gossip, you know."

He nodded noncommittally, wondering just what her purpose had been in inviting him to tea. Was she attempting to drive a wedge between him and Kat? Or perhaps tempt him and then say that he had made improper advances to her? He wouldn't put it past Fleming to have thought up either plot or both. Or she might really think her husband unfaithful and Connor, her husband's enemy, a good candidate with whom to seek her revenge. Connor rose, anxious to escape a distasteful and possibly dangerous situation.

"You're going?" Eustacia affected a look of sweet

disappointment. "We must meet again soon."

Connor left, still unsure as to whether he'd been propositioned or set up. He'd have to be very careful of that lady, and in the meantime, where was Kat? If both she and Fleming were out of town, and gossip linked them— no, he'd talk to her before he reached any conclusions of that sort. It would have been like a knife in the heart to think that what Kat had given him, she might have given elsewhere—especially to a man he despised, a man he'd thought she despised. But he didn't believe that of Kat.

If Connor had had any serious doubts, they were resolved before Kat ever returned to Breckenridge because everyone he met as he conducted the last of his day's business was eager to ask what he intended to do about Medford Fleming's dastardly treatment of Mrs. Fitzgerald.

"Of course," said Fred McNaught, who accosted Connor on his very doorstep, "she did pretty well protectin' herself. Most folks think Fleming left town because everyone knew how he'd got that cut an' lump on his forehead."

"How did he get it?" asked Connor.

"The way I hear it, she flung that gold nugget that come from their mine on Farncomb Hill right in his face."

"How is it everyone in Breckenridge knows about this, Fred?" Connor asked.

"Oh well, them ladies at the Methodist Ladies' Aid Society wormed it out of her. She was that scared afterwards that she went straight to Lucinda Dyer an' burst into tears, poor girl. Be a terrible shock to hear that kinda talk from a man 'sposed to be a gentleman. 'Fore he left, Fleming made out like nuthin' had happened, high an' mighty as ever. That's what I hear. But you kin bet he ain't got a friend left in town. Not the way he acted."

Connor nodded thoughtfully and went into his house, heading toward the miserable little room he now shared with Eyeless. He'd have to get the full story from Kat, but it seemed to him that her shocking experience, whatever it had been, had worked out to their advantage. Of course, it wouldn't win them the apex suit—or would it?

Before he could explore the implications of that thought, the unnatural silence in the house caught his attention. "Diederick!" he roared, striding through the corridor toward his own side. He checked every room without finding the carpenter at work, although the kitchen was still fire-damaged.

"Diederick!" he shouted as he shoved open the hall door and stuck his head out into the back yard. At last he discovered his do-nothing employee. Diederick was standing beside the outhouse that served Kat's side. If the fellow had been using it, Connor might have forgiven him, but Otto Diederick was sawing an opening into the side wall. "What the *hell* are you doing?" Connor demanded.

Diederick turned around, having finished the job, and knocked the small square through the wall. "I saw dis fine vindow in ein necessary house down on Ridge Street, unt I thought Missus, she'd like to have vun for her—"

"God give me patience," muttered Connor, and said, with what he thought of as remarkable calm; "Get back to work on my house before I kill you, you idiot."

"Missus, she ain't gonna—"

"Go!" shouted Connor. Diederick went.

"Just the lady I've been looking for," said Sister Freddie. "Jeannie hasn't been in school for two days, yet I didn't find either of you at home when I called yesterday."

Kat sighed wearily. She'd just got off the train from Keystone, only to encounter another problem. "I've been in Montezuma, Freddie. I'll have to check into it."

"Sister Fredericka," corrected her friend, grinning. "You don't want to offend Reverend Mother any more than you already have, and she does not want to hear me called Freddie."

Kat smiled back and trudged wearily home, where she caught Jeannie just coming in. "Where have you been?" she demanded, "and don't tell me you were in school. I just talked to Fr—Sister Fredericka.

"I was sick."

Kat frowned and closed her parasol, carefully folding in the pretty lace awning that decorated its edge. "Then why aren't you at home in bed?"

"I—I went over to ask Mrs. Finding what to do because—because I had my monthly, and I—hurt."

"Oh, Jeannie, you could have asked me."

"But you were out of town."

"Have you had this trouble before?"

Jeannie nodded, not meeting Kat's eyes.

"You should have told me."

"You're so busy, and I didn't want to act as if—well, as if you were neglecting me."

"Oh my dear, have I been?" Jeannie looked so embarrassed that Kat felt terrible. The poor child couldn't even meet her eyes. "Heat helps. Let me put you to bed."

"I feel better now," said Jeannie hastily. "And here's Daddy. He's been ever so worried about where you were."

"Leave the room, Jeannie," said Connor, stalking into the house.

"Well, goodness, Connor, why are you angry with Jeannie?" asked Kat. She unpinned her sailor hat with the green ribbon.

"I'm angry with you, not Jeannie. Why the devil would you disappear without telling anyone where you were going?"

"I didn't realize that I hadn't, but my trip *was* an emergency."

"And what's this story I'm hearing all over town about you and Medford Fleming?"

"I'm not going to talk to you about that, Connor. It's too

268

humiliating." She raised her chin defiantly.

Connor looked alarmed. "Did he do you an—an injury?"

"Of course he did," said Kat and then, seeing the look of fury on Connor's face, added quickly, "What he said was unforgivable. The man's a scoundrel."

"What he *said?*"

"Yes."

"Could you give me just a—general idea?"

Kat thought a minute. "He suggested that I should direct my—my passions away from causes and toward—" her lips compressed angrily, and she flushed.

"Toward?"

"He invited me to be his mistress."

Connor had never seen a look of greater distaste on anyone's face.

"I hit him with a nugget."

"A proper revenge," Connor murmured, wishing he'd been there to see it. "And then you evidently denounced him to the Methodist Ladies' Sewing Circle."

"Aid Society," she corrected. "They just happened to be there when I went to Lucinda Dyer for—moral support."

"My dear Kat, you are a truly extraordinary woman."

"You don't seem the least bit worried about my honor," said Kat stiffly.

"I'll go over and shoot him if you like," Connor offered. "I doubt, given the state of public indignation, that Will would arrest me for it."

"Oh, of course, I don't want you to shoot him." Kat sighed. "And I'm afraid he's no longer content to deal in rumors." She explained events at the mine in the Snake River district and the measures she had taken to trap the culprit.

"My God, Kat, do you know how to use a pistol?"

"Not really," she admitted. "But Marcus Pel didn't know that."

"It was a very dangerous thing to do."

Kat didn't dispute him. "We've got to warn all our superintendents. We don't know where he'll strike next."

"I'll start tomorrow. The mines here, then the Ten Mile District."

"I could visit the local ones."

Connor shook his head. "Too dangerous. He has reason now to hate you, and as you've found out, he's no respecter of womanhood."

Kat shivered. If anyone had told her last year this time that she'd be involved in a dangerous mining feud, she'd have thought it some unlikely tale from a romantic novel, but as she'd known for some years now, romance was no generator of happily-ever-afters.

"That's a pretty dress you're wearing," said Connor at dinner that evening. She had on a regular frock that didn't cause a man any qualms or confusion, he noted approvingly, but she still looked beautiful in it. The apple green sprigs all over the material matched her eyes, and the white lace on the front looked pretty and respectable. Besides which, he was sure she had on corsets. No woman's waist could be that small without them. He felt a rush of anger at the Flemings—Medford for daring to insult Kat, Eustacia for dressing and acting so provocatively. What were they up to? And why was Kat giving him that odd look? As if he'd never told her how pretty she was?

Chapter Nineteen

"Connor, there's a hole in the side of my outhouse," said Kat, furling her parasol and taking from her reticule some papers she had picked up for him at the bank. "Now who would play a trick like that?"

"Your idiot carpenter wants to make you a fancy window."

"A window?" Kat looked astonished. "But—"

"I told him to get back to work on the fire damage."

"But what about the hole? Anyone could come along and look in." Her face turned red as she realized that she was discussing—indirectly—bodily functions with Connor.

Connor sighed and stuffed a clean shirt into his valise. He was packing to go to Ten Mile Canyon, where the hoist at the Sister Katie had fallen, injuring two men. "We've got to get rid of Diederick, Kat. He never follows orders, just ignores me and starts on any fool project that comes into his head."

"But what if I can't find another carpenter? You'll be out

271

of town, and I'll be left with that hole. And why would he want to put a window in an outhouse?"

"He saw one on Ridge Street. I guess it had scrollwork."

"Really? Scrollwork on an outhouse?" She looked intrigued as she removed her gloves.

"Listen, Kat, we've got more important things to discuss before I leave."

"Maybe more important to you, but—"

"The judge has finally set a trial date."

"Then why is Fleming still making trouble?" They both assumed that Fleming had engineered the accident at the Sister Katie. "He'll only turn every prospective juror in the county against him by—"

"You've already done that, my girl," Connor interrupted, chuckling. Then he sobered. "Maybe Fleming wants to frighten the jurors—or force us to give up before we go to trial. We've got to hang on another month, and even then, if the judge lets him, he could delay further. He could get a stay on our operations at the Ingrid's Ring while he drives a tunnel into our ore and cleans us out."

"Can we hold out long enough?"

Connor shrugged. "I think Fleming underestimates us." But he admitted uneasily to himself that he might be underestimating Fleming. Eustacia had lured him once again into her house with the message that her husband wanted a meeting. Connor had been cautious enough to take Charlie Maxell along. She was quite unapologetic about having lied, but with Charlie present, they talked about her desire to have the house of ill repute removed from Nickel Hill; there were no thigh nudgings or offers of tours. Charlie was sympathetic to her problem, Connor suspicious, and Kat still unaware that Eustacia had become a player in the game, a loose piece whose uncertain loyalties made her all the more dangerous.

Kat fretted for two days. She had wanted to go to the Ten Mile district with Connor and resented it when he sent no word. Miners from the Breckenridge and Snake River districts stopped by the house every few days, hats in hand, mumbling that they'd heard she'd had a bit of trouble with Medford Fleming and assuring her that they were men who didn't hold with such disrespect of women. Kat always thanked them for their support and introduced them to Noleen or told them about Mary Beth, who was still reigning queen of the Ingrid's Ring mine and kitchen. Kat supposed she was helping with labor relations, but she wanted to do something positive, so she sent for Pat Morrisey, the leader of the miners' association in Summit County.

"You've turned my men to spyin' on each other," Morrisey said accusingly. "Oh, don't look surprised, Miz Fitzgerald. I know you've got 'em lookin' out for Fleming's troublemakers."

"Well, it's for their own protection."

"Miners got to depend on each other. Now they don't."

"But—"

"It's an owners' fight, not an association fight."

"But it's the miners who are getting hurt. One died at the Too Late."

"Yep, we're all beginnin' to see it as too dangerous—workin' for you an' Connor."

Kat felt a jolt of fear. If they lost their work force through her interference, their cause would be hopeless, and Connor would never forgive her. She had to change the subject while she thought of some new way to approach Morrisey. "Are you a church-going man, Mr. Morrisey?" she asked at random.

"That's none of your business, ma'am," said Morrisey.

"Well, I just thought—because of your name," Kat stammered, taken aback, "that you might be Roman Catholic."

"Like I say, my relationship with God is my own concern."

"Well, of course."

"And I don't aim to discuss whether or not I like a drop of whiskey from time to time neither."

"Oh, Noleen, here you are with the coffee!" Kat had never been so glad to see anyone in her life. "Sit down and join us, won't you?" Pat Morrisey rose politely until Noleen had taken a seat on the dark green sofa Kat had bought for the corridor parlor. Then, introductions having been made, they all sat tongue-tied for the moment.

"Cream and sugar, Noleen?" asked Kat.

"Just sugar, ma'am." Noleen fussed with the cake as Kat poured coffee.

"Noleen is from Chicago," said Kat brightly.

"Likely it's a terrible place," said Pat Morrisey, accepting a piece of pound cake from Noleen.

"Indeed it is," said Noleen. "Miz Fitzpatrick and Miss Kat just about saved my life, bringing me out here," and Noleen, never a backward girl, described with relish the horrors of life in Chicago for a single woman, after which Pat Morrisey described the horrors of life in Boston, from which he had come, for anyone of Irish descent. Ten minutes later, the two hardly noticed when Kat excused herself. *Noleen and the hard-boiled Mr. Morrisey,* thought Kat. *Mother will be so pleased. Especially since, no matter how cagey he is about it, he must be Roman Catholic.*

"I can't prove it," said Connor, "but that lift cable was frayed by human hands, not normal wear. I'm as sure as I am of my own name. If it hadn't given out when the lift was close to the bottom of the shaft, we'd have more dead miners. And no matter how it happened, our people are scared."

"They surely don't blame us?"

"It doesn't matter to them whether we're negligent or Fleming's responsible. Their lives are on the line either way."

Kat sighed. "Pat Morrisey's taken with Noleen," she offered as the only piece of good news in a week of trouble.

"Lord, how can you think about romance when our whole operation is falling apart?"

"Don't blaspheme," she snapped. "And I'm not thinking of romance. I'm thinking of labor relations."

"I should have known. You wouldn't know true love if it bit you on the nose."

Unaccountably hurt and then angry because she couldn't help caring so much, Kat, who had been kneading bread dough as they talked, turned impulsively and flung a handful into Connor's face.

He staggered back, peeled it off, and emerged looking as surprised as she felt.

"Connor, I—"

"Guess I should be glad it wasn't baked," he interrupted, grinning. "I'd have been knocked out cold. In fact, if it were yesterday's bread, you'd probably have killed me."

"What's that supposed to mean?" He was the most perplexing person. How many men would make a joke after being hit in the face with a blob of dough?

"Well, Kat, we all know a loaf of your day-old bread would bring down a moose."

"It would not," she retorted, starting to grin. "Well, maybe a baby moose." They each broke into laughter.

"Mr. Morrisey, have you heard any rumors of high grading at the Rose Laurel?" Kat and the labor leader were sitting in the parlor while Morrisey waited for Noleen to appear and accompany him to a lecture at the G.A.R. Hall.

"No, ma'am," said Pat Morrisey. "I'd have sworn every man out there was dead honest."

Kat nodded. "That's what I thought, but someone arrived this morning, whispered with Connor, and off he went to check it out."

"If I might change the subject, ma'am, an' you bein' in the way of family to Noleen, I'd like to ask your permission to court her with a mind to marriage."

Kat gave an inward sigh. It was sort of depressing— all these young lovers and weddings. "Of course, Mr. Morrisey. If Noleen is amenable, I think you'd make her a fine husband."

"I appreciate that, ma'am. An' I will say that there are many men in the association on the lookout for wives."

"Well, I'm sure you can count on my mother to keep the supply of eligible females flowing from Chicago." *Why do I feel so down?* Kat wondered. *This is just what Mother and I wanted.* She bestirred herself and offered the labor leader more coffee. *It must be the strain of all our business woes,* she told herself.

Before she could give Noleen her blessing, a stranger burst into the parlor, crying, "Just heard that Connor's comin' down on the long bucket."

"What? What does that mean?" She turned anxiously to Pat Morrisey.

"It's also called the dead bucket," he replied somberly. "It's the bucket on the gravity tram they use to bring down the dead or injured."

"Oh, my God." Kat grabbed her bonnet and headed for the door, Morrisey close at her heels, Noleen wringing her hands behind them in the parlor.

Kat had never ridden so fast in her life, galloping recklessly through town without a thought for the mayor and his miserable, potholed streets, the only civic issue on which she'd ever agreed with Colonel Fincher of the *Summit County Journal*. She and Pat Morrisey made record time to the mine outside of town, arriving as the first bolts of lightning cracked across the August sky. From the foot of the hill, they could see the long bucket gyrating wildly on the gravity tramway and the men shouting, cheering, and making bets on its progress. Kat was horrified both at the sight and at their conduct.

"Is he dead?" she gasped.

"Is who dead?" The miner beside her was jumping up and down with excitement. "You still got time to place a bet, Pat. Connor's comin' down first. Then Phyllo."

"He cain't bet now," shouted another. "We already know Connor ain't gonna win. Be lucky if he don't git dumped out, what with the dead bucket swangin' like it is."

"Is he injured?" asked Kat, confused.

"Not yet, ma'am," replied the miner who had invited Pat to bet.

"But I don't understand," she whispered as she watched that bucket swinging dangerously as thunder rolled overhead. Why was Connor in it?

"We're timin' 'em, ma'am, an' damned if I didn't put my money on Connor. Ain't like him to git the bucket swangin' like that. Keepin' it steady, that's how you win."

"He's doing this for a bet—a contest of some sort?" She couldn't believe her ears, but at last the tram reached the bottom of the hill, and Connor hopped out.

"You idiot!" she screamed. "How could you do such a stupid thing?"

"Well, I didn't figure on those gyrations." He turned to watch the long bucket start back up, pulled by the weight of loaded ore buckets coming down.

Kat punched him in the arm to get his attention. "I thought you were dead!"

"Why'd you think that?" he asked as a man at the top climbed into the bucket.

"You—you dreadful person! If anyone ever tells me you're hurt again, I won't budge from the house. If the whole mine blows up, I won't come to your funeral."

"Bite your tongue," said Connor, glancing nervously at the miners surrounding them.

Kat burst into tears.

"Reckon she's sweet on you, Connor," said Pat Morrisey, grinning. "No wonder she doesn't entertain suitors."

"That shows how much you know," shouted Kat as the wind picked up and rain began to plop against their faces. "I wish that bucket had dropped him on his stupid head—right on top of the tailings. I wouldn't even dig him out."

Connor had begun to laugh. Uphill at the shaft head his opponent started down, and again the bucket began to swing. "What the hell's the matter with that tram?" he muttered. "Shouldn't be doin' that."

"It's God's punishment for man's stupidity," said Kat.

Connor put an arm around her and said, "If you'll just simmer down, I'll give you some good news."

"What?"

"Mary Beth is engaged to Manfred Oppenheim. They figure to marry next week. And he's a papist, you'll be happy to know."

"Oh, wonderful," snapped Kat. "Pat here wants to marry Noleen. Now I'll be left without help again."

"Well, for God's sake, Kat, there's just no pleasing you." As he turned to Pat Morrisey, the rain began to fall heavily. "You probably think she's bringing all these girls to town out of the kindness of her heart. The truth is, she hates housework and cooking."

"Just so she keeps 'em comin'," said Pat, "no one's goin' to complain about her motives."

"Oh, my God," Connor gasped. The tram cable had snapped, dropping the long bucket onto a ledge where it teetered precariously, half on, half off, midway down. Still, had the bucket not been gyrating, it would have fallen to the bottom of the hill, probably killing its occupant. They watched, breathless, as the storm worsened and the men ran to try to rescue Trapper Phyllo.

Kat slipped her hand into Connor's. "That would have been you if you'd gone second," she whispered.

"I *would* have gone second if Trapper hadn't wanted to flip for it," Connor replied soberly. Then he and Pat went to join the rescue effort, and later, when the storm had abated, to check the cable for signs of tampering.

No one could remember who had suggested the contest. A fellow from another mine, some thought. As with the lift cable in Ten Mile Canyon, the tampering, if it had been that, was carefully done. The damage could have resulted from wear, except that Connor swore he'd inspected that cable the week before. The superintendent said the same. They got Trapper Phyllo down safely, and he insisted that he had won because he ended his trip quicker than Connor. Those who bet on Connor refused to pay off. Kat thought they were all crazy and said so.

"You get to takin' the danger for granted," said Pat Morrisey, but he didn't look as if he were taking anything for granted. In the meantime, they had another mine shut down. The Too Late was back in operation; the Sister Katie, with luck, would reopen two days hence; but their most profitable gold mine would slow to near stoppage without the tramway. And the rumors of high-grading had been just that—rumors. Had Connor been lured to the mine in the hope that he'd die in some set-up contest? Kat shuddered at the idea.

"Take a coat," Kat called after him. "It's getting nippy out for August." She turned away from Connor's departing figure. "I don't remember it ever being this cold in Chicago, do you, Noleen?"

Noleen didn't. "I hope it'll be fair for my wedding."

"You'd think they'd have stayed to help make the plans." Connor had left with Pat Morrisey.

"Oh, there's a big labor meeting this afternoon," said Noleen.

"And Connor was invited?" asked Kat. "But not me?"

"Now Miss Kat, if they invited you, you'd be giving them a talk on the dangers of drink, when they're for tapping a keg of beer and using foul language not fit for ladies' ears. Or so Pat tells me. You'd not have liked it at all."

"They're not going to be happy I've invited you, Connor," said Pat Morrisey as they rode to Fireman's Hall.

"I appreciate the opportunity to speak my piece," said Connor, who had been appalled when he heard that his work force, including representatives from Ten Mile and Snake River, was gathering to discuss the growing danger of working for Connor Macleod and Sean Fitzpatrick.

"And I," said Pat morosely, "bein' a man on the brink of matrimony, would hate to have my honeymoon cut short for a strike."

"You think they'll strike?"

"Don't know, but Noleen will have my hide if they do, she's that loyal to Miz Fitzgerald. She was all for continuin' to work after we marry. Said she was afraid you folk would starve to death without her."

"You're both welcome to move in. We'd never notice one more," said Connor dryly.

Pat's mouth quirked in a seldom-seen smile as he refused the offer. When they had climbed the stair to the hall, there was some grumbling among the men because Pat had brought along a representative of management, but Pat insisted that Connor be allowed to speak.

"I've two things to say to you, and then I'll leave you to your discussion," said Connor. "First, I know it's been dangerous of late, but by keeping our eyes open, we haven't had any accidents in a week now, so maybe we've got the bastard stymied."

"Who's to say it's Fleming? Who's to say the trouble isn't that you're cuttin' corners on safety?"

"Fleming does that, not I," said Connor, "and if you

need proof, talk to the men from the Too Late up beyond Montezuma. They know who's to blame for the death up there."

"Pel confessed all right that he was in Fleming's pay," said Sweet Holsen of the Too Late. "Course, Miz Fitzgerald had a gun on him."

"If you hadn't a hung 'im—"

"We lost three men," said Sweet indignantly. "Two hurt, one dead, but we didn't hang the murderer, an' you've my word on that."

"The one who had the most to gain in keeping Pel Marcus from going to trial was Fleming," Connor pointed out.

The men muttered among themselves, but Connor thought on the whole that they agreed with him. "The second thing I got to say is that if you put me out of business—and a strike could do it—then you're out of jobs, which means the wages will go down for those who can get work elsewhere. I'm running some marginal mines as it is, and the price of silver is rotten. No way I could keep the silver producers going, and I'm not sure I could sell them."

Connor then left, their mutters and shouts following him down the stairs. He hoped to God Pat could keep them working. No one would profit but Fleming if they went out. As he stepped into the street, snow flakes drifted down into his upturned face, and Connor chuckled, thinking how surprised and pleased Kat would be at the unusual spectacle of snow in August.

Not pleased, however, was Father Eusebius Geiger, whom Connor saw on Lincoln Avenue, shivering visibly with one hand tucked under his armpit and the other holding his valise. The priest must be newly returned from one of his preaching journeys through the mountains, Connor decided and, taking pity on the poor man, offered him a ride to the rectory.

Teeth now chattering, Father Eusebius stared at the

horse nervously. "A priest's robe isn't suited to riding," he murmured unhappily.

Connor studied the priest's long black skirts and replied. "Well, I've no sidesaddle to offer you, Father. You'll just have to swing astride behind me with your skirts hiked."

"My limbs will show," said Father Eusebius.

"'Fraid so," Connor agreed. "What do you usually do?"

"Ride the train and walk." Since Connor was already astride and holding out his hand, the priest, shivering in the snow with no coat to protect him, allowed himself to be helped. When his gown pulled up, his bright green socks were exposed, and he heard Connor's snort of laughter. Father Eusebius sighed. "They were a gift from a parishioner, and all mine had holes," he confessed. "I'm not much of a hand with a darning needle." They rode two blocks in silence, and then the young priest said, "I never expected snow in August. I wonder if it's a penance from God because I've so enjoyed the beauty of the summer and written pridefully of it to the Benedictine brothers back home."

"We all try to enjoy summer, Father," said Connor. "It lasts so short a time. Maybe God keeps it short so we'll appreciate it the more."

"A profound thought," said the priest. "I must pass it on to Father Rhabanus. He says that, no matter how blue the sky or how many flowers in the field, this pastorate is ruining his health."

"One thing you might oughta consider," said Pat Morrisey as the shouting match among the miners wore down. "If you want to marry, Miz Fitzgerald controls the only steady supply of respectable females on the Western Slope. An' she can be a hard woman when crossed."

"Oh hell," said the representative from the Too Late. "It's a dangerous livin' anyway. When's the next batch of girls comin' in from Chicago, Pat?"

The vote went against a strike.

* * *

"Why does she keep sending two at a time?" Connor asked. Margaret Mary Hubble and Olga Karlsdatter had appeared at their door, having disembarked from the Denver train and found their own way to the house.

"Sh-sh. Because at least one always gets married," Kat whispered. "Your side of the house is done. Why are you complaining?"

"I'm not complaining. With two, if one's no good in the kitchen, I still won't have to eat your cooking."

"Father Eusebius thinks I'm a wonderful cook. I took him some chicken soup just today, and do you know what he said?"

"Bless you, my child?"

"Well, that too, but he also said he was beginning to think my idea about Christ changing the water to chicken soup wasn't so bad after all."

"When did Christ ever do that?"

"He didn't. It's just a little joke between me and Father Eusebius. By the way, it was nice of you to give him a ride the day it snowed. He'd probably have caught pneumonia instead of a cold if you hadn't."

"Always glad to help out a priest wearing bright green socks and gaiters."

"Connor, he was not!"

"Word of honor."

Kat started to giggle. "Oh, I wish I'd seen it."

"Our room's just fine, ma'am," said Olga, bustling in, "but I did notice that one of the rooms has no ceiling and the story above it's got no roof."

Kat sighed. Diederick, once forced to finish Connor's repairs, had eliminated the ceiling in the room that had housed, first, Phoebe and Sean Michael and, later, Connor and Eyeless. In fact, he'd done it before Connor got his belongings transferred. Sometimes Kat just didn't understand Diederick. He hadn't done anything about the

283

hole in the outhouse wall either. Kat had had to tack muslin over it.

"What happens when it snows?" asked Olga. "Mrs. Macleod that was Mrs. Fitzpatrick did say it snows something fierce here in Breckenridge come winter."

"Yes indeed," said Kat. "In fact, it snowed last week."

"In August?" Margaret Mary Hubble, a tall, full-breasted young woman who had been a teacher in a small town whose school closed, looked very interested to hear it. "Is summer snow a common phenomenon here on the frontier?"

"Not in the valleys," Connor replied, "although you probably noticed that many of the high peaks are snow-covered."

"I did indeed notice that."

"Don't she talk fine?" marveled Olga. "We shared a room in Baltimore and in Chicago, and I learned ever so much just listening to her. Better'n going to school." Olga was a pretty girl with rosy cheeks and pale blond hair who had come from a farm in Pennsylvania to make her fortune in the city.

"*Doesn't*, Olga," said Margaret Mary. "*Doesn't* she talk— and *fine* is not an adverb, so you must choose another word."

"Good?" hazarded Olga.

"Preferably one with an *l-y* on it."

"*L-y?* Finely? No." Olga went off toward the kitchen, trying out various *l-y* words. "Goodly? That don't—doesn't sound right. Fancy? No *l*."

"You may not think so, but Olga is a very apt student," said Margaret Mary.

"Maybe you ought to take on my daughter as well," said Connor.

"I'd be delighted to."

Kat frowned. Teacher or not, Margaret Mary was supposed to help around the house, and Connor was taking an unusual interest in her. "Maybe we ought to find a teaching position for you, Margaret Mary," said Kat.

"That's very kind of you, Mrs. Fitzgerald, but first, of course, I must work off my debt to you, and then I believe I'd prefer to marry. Teaching has not proved to be the secure profession I once thought it."

"Oh." Kat didn't know what to say, but with Margaret Mary smiling at Connor, Kat had the unhappy thought that the former schoolteacher might be viewing him as a more secure profession than housemaid or teacher.

As the *Summit County Journal* said, Dave Braddock came to town "yelling like a Comanche," and Kat was delighted to see him. She waved down his wagon and inspected his fresh vegetables. Today there were radishes, turnips, carrots, and rutabagas with the valley soil still clinging to them, their colors peeking through lusciously. Margaret Mary would be ecstatic. She was a great one for healthful meals and especially insistent on vegetables, which earned her a lot of grumbling from Eyeless. Not that Margaret Mary, a woman of conviction, paid the slightest attention. "Eat your carrots, Mr. Waterson," she said, "or I'll not be reading this evening."

"I ain't no kid to be read a bedtime story," muttered Eyeless. Nonetheless, he was always in the parlor when Margaret Mary took up *Bleak House,* the Dickens novel she had chosen as suitable for a family involved in a lawsuit.

"I think that Esther is really boring," said Jeannie.

Kat thought so too. Of all the dreary characters in *Bleak House,* Esther was the dreariest.

"Damn, if lawsuits really go on that long, we'll be broke before the apex suit ever gets settled," was Jamie's opinion, something they were all afraid of.

"Don't blaspheme," said Kat.

"Don't she read beautiful," said Olga.

"Doesn't and beautifully," corrected Margaret Mary and went on with the trials of the protagonists in *Bleak House*. Kat wished the schoolteacher had chosen another book, but since Connor didn't seem to object, Kat hadn't protested. *He* wasn't at home every night to be sunk in Dickensian gloom. But where was he?

"Oh, lettuce," Kat cried now, pulling her thoughts away from Margaret Mary and the lawsuit that loomed over them.

"Yep," said Dave, "an' I got peas too. Had to try three different kinds 'fore I found some that would grow here in the high valleys."

"You are a many-talented person, Dave," said Kat and began to fill her basket with lettuce. "If I pay you now and pick out other selections, could you drop them by the house?" Dave only came three times a week, and given Margaret Mary's penchant for vegetables—she not only served them, but canned them—Kat could hardly buy enough to last the two or three days until Dave or his son Frank came to town again.

"Glad to, Kat. You folks are my best customers. Don't suppose Connor'd be home? I'm fixin' to run for sheriff, an' I wanted to see if I had his support."

"Well, you certainly have mine," said Kat, who was still miffed that Will Iliff had arrested her.

"Thank you, ma'am, but you can't vote."

"Well, I can talk," said Kat. "I shall talk up your candidacy."

"Say, there's Connor." Dave pointed across the street toward Finding's Hardware. "Oh well, I see he's occupied with a pretty lady."

Kat spotted him too, Connor and a blond woman wearing a Gainsborough hat with dramatic feathers and a bronze silk dress with brown velvet dots and an asymmetric skirt of the very latest style. Kat had seen such gowns in a fashion magazine but never on the streets of Breckenridge. When she considered her own bonnet, whose chief purpose was to keep the sun from her face, and her everyday dress, she felt quite dowdy. "Who is that woman?"

"Couldn't say," said Dave. "Looks too fancy for Breckenridge, but not fancy enough to be a painted woman." He laughed uproariously at his own joke while Kat frowned. "Now, if you'll just say what you want, I'll set it aside for you."

Kat found it hard to concentrate on turnips when that strange woman had her hand on Connor's arm, smiling into his face as if they were long-time friends. Could his evening absences mean he was courting her when he'd sworn—both he and Kat had sworn—that they never wanted to marry again?

"Rutabagas are good today," said Dave.

The woman and Connor walked off down the street together, and Kat, stuck with a wagon full of vegetables and a family to feed, couldn't follow and inveigle an introduction.

"I know you'll want radishes," said Dave. "Miss Hubble dotes on radishes. Says they're good for the blood. How many bunches you want?"

"Twelve," said Kat absently.

"Twelve bunches?" Dave looked nonplussed.

"Oh, no. I meant twelve radishes." Who *was* that woman?

Chapter Twenty

Kat sat at the head of the table, Connor at the foot, Margaret Mary on his right, Eyeless on Kat's right. Margaret Mary had arranged that seating after a proper consideration of the ages and positions of the people involved, stating at their first dinner, "I realize that I am in essence a housemaid, but on the other hand, I am the oldest female except for yourself, Mrs. Fitzgerald. Perhaps you would consider some other arrangement more suitable."

Kat didn't like being described as the oldest female, but she couldn't very well insist that the dignified Margaret Mary eat in the kitchen. Jeannie liked the arrangement because she sat by her father. Jamie sat to Kat's left and told her jokes, the point of which she didn't always get, especially when she was concentrating on the conversation between Margaret Mary and Connor, something to do with Medford Fleming and his new lawyer.

"Gosh, Kat, I'd thought you'd really like that one," said Jamie.

"Hush," she murmured. "What was that you said, Connor?"

"Are your ears tingling? I said Fleming's fancy out-of-town lawyer had no more than arrived in Breckenridge than he saw you on the street and asked Fleming who you were. Remembering what happened with Harrison Ponder, Fleming decided his new lawyer had to stay up on Nickel Hill."

"Lotsa men wouldn't mind stayin' up on Nickel Hill," said Eyeless and laughed into his soup, making a wave that sloshed over onto the tablecloth.

"What is the attraction of Nickel Hill?" asked Margaret Mary.

Kat glared at Eyeless and shoved a bowl of radish-and-lettuce salad into his hands. Just the thought of eating lettuce quelled Eyeless's good humor.

"The Flemings have a house on Nickel Hill," said Connor. "Fleming wants the lawyer where he can keep an eye on him. They say he's refused to let the man go to the ball this weekend."

"He's afraid the lawyer will fall in love with Kat," Jeannie explained. "The other two did, both ours and Fleming's."

"It must be a trial to you, Mrs. Fitzgerald, to be so embarrassingly attractive to men," said Margaret Mary.

What did she mean by that? Kat wondered. "I wouldn't know Medford Fleming's lawyer if he—if he—"

"—fell at your feet?" Connor suggested.

Kat glared at him, and Olga said, "Miss Kat's just about the prettiest lady I ever did see—except for you, Margaret Mary."

"I prefer to be admired for my intelligence, not my looks," said Margaret Mary.

Snob! thought Kat. And she didn't believe that Medford Fleming was keeping a guard on his lawyer; that was just Connor teasing. He never teased Margaret Mary. Did that mean he had too much respect for her? Did he tease that beautiful blond woman in the gorgeous hat?

While Margaret Mary and Olga were in the kitchen, cleaning up after dinner, Kat managed a minute alone with Connor. He was sitting in the parlor reading the newspaper when she joined him, unable to contain her curiosity any longer. However, she planned to be subtle in her approach. "Perhaps you'd like to bring your new friend to dinner some night," she suggested.

"What new friend?"

"Oh, I saw you walking with a blond lady this morning. I couldn't help noticing," she added hastily, "because I was down on Main buying vegetables from Dave Braddock."

"Well, you'd better quit buying lettuce."

Ah ha! He was trying to evade the subject. "Why, doesn't your friend like lettuce?"

"Eyeless doesn't like lettuce."

"Well, I'm sure Margaret Mary would be glad to cook whatever your friend likes if you invite her to dinner."

"You mean as long as it suits Margaret Mary's idea of a healthful menu. I don't like lettuce myself."

Very cagey, she thought. Did that mean he didn't like Margaret Mary either? "Who is she?" Kat blurted out, afraid Connor would keep changing the subject until she couldn't ask without making a fool of herself, although actually she'd just done that.

"Who is who?"

Kat stood up with a flounce and started to leave, at which Connor relented. "She isn't a friend. That was Medford Fleming's wife." Kat looked so astounded that he felt the need to defend himself. "Up on Nickel Hill there's a house—ah, besides Fleming's, there's this—"

"I know about the house of ill repute," Kat snapped. "You told me, or had you forgotten? And what's that got to do with you?"

Good lord, worried Connor. *Does she think I patronize*

Marcie's place? "Mrs. Fleming doesn't like having her own house near—"

"Then why did she build up there? And why's she talking to you about it?"

"She wants me to use my influence with the town officials to boot Marcie—er, the house—"

"Marcie?"

"The woman who owns the house."

"You're on a first name basis with a—with a—"

"Everyone knows her first name."

"I didn't."

"Well, you're the only person in town who doesn't. Also the only woman who'd mention it."

"What's that supposed to mean?" Kat demanded.

"It means respectable women don't talk about women like Marcella Webber." Connor hoped that he'd diverted Kat from the subject of Eustacia Fleming, who had dragged him up the hill and kissed him beside her grandfather clock, just after explaining that it came from France and was very expensive.

"Well, I'm sure Mrs. Fleming is quite capable of handling that problem herself," said Kat sharply. "She was flirting with you."

"She's a married woman."

"How can you consort with the enemy like that?"

"I wasn't consorting," said Connor defensively.

"*I* didn't consort with Medford Fleming. I hit him with a rock."

"Nugget," he corrected. "Probably had a couple of pounds of gold in it."

"I'm sure I don't care."

"That's what made it so heavy."

"Stop changing the subject."

"And why it raised such a big lump on his head." Connor was grinning.

"Why were you flirting with Mrs. Fleming?"

"What do you care?" He didn't think *he'd* been flirting. And he couldn't very well tell Kat what Eustacia Fleming had wanted.

"Time for *Bleak House*," said Margaret Mary, marching into the parlor with her book. In minutes the whole family assembled, and Kat had to give up her inquisition.

As the trial date approached, Kat was heartened to find that the Flemings were becoming a source of great amusement to the town. First, Fleming refused to allow his lawyer, Boniface Denton, III, to go to church unless accompanied by Eustacia, who, after attending one makeshift Episcopalian service in the G.A.R. Hall, declared Breckenridge worship "not what she was accustomed to" and refused to stand guard over the lawyer on any future religious occasions.

Then the sporting house of Marcella Webber began its trip downhill and across the river toward West Breckenridge. The rumor mill whispered that the Flemings had had to pay the madam a huge amount to induce her to move. *Good!* thought Kat. Having solved her problem, Eustacia Fleming would no longer have any reason to flutter her long eyelashes at Connor. Kat also assumed that public opinion was against the Flemings, since they had been unable to influence the town government to intervene on their behalf. Didn't that mean that the jury would be unlikely to find for Trenton Consolidated? She wanted to ask Connor but couldn't bring herself to mention the beautiful Eustacia again.

In mid-September, the town was rocked by the death in Denver of one of its pioneer citizens, Judge Silverthorne. Kat, although she had never met him, called on his daughter, Mrs. Finding, to express her condolences, taking a reluctant Jeannie along. "Of course, you must go," she told Jeannie. "The Finding girls are great friends of yours. You're over there studying most afternoons after school."

However, Kat discovered in her conversation with Mrs. Finding that the girls were missing Jeannie's visits.

When questioned later, Jeannie said, "You must have misunderstood. Where do you think I've been?"

Kat couldn't imagine and didn't like to call Jeannie a liar. Trouble always seemed to come in threes, she thought dispiritedly—the impending trial, the problem of Jeannie, which Kat didn't want to take up with Connor when he had so much on his mind, and now Margaret Mary, who had stopped reading *Bleak House* and taken to leaving as soon as the dinner dishes were done. Remembering her mother's lectures on her responsibilities to the young women in her care, Kat asked Margaret Mary where she was going.

"Out," said Margaret Mary. "I have an engagement."

"With whom?" asked Kat. Margaret Mary gave her an offended look. "Well, I have a responsibility to see to your welfare," said Kat defensively. "How can I do that when I don't know where you are or who you're with?"

"Whom," said Margaret Mary. "*Whom* I'm with."

Kat scowled at her.

"You need not concern yourself, Mrs. Fitzgerald. I am a woman grown, sensible and intelligent, and hardly in need of anyone to oversee my manners or morals. I shall not, I assure you, disgrace your family in any way."

"Well, I didn't think you would," Kat mumbled.

"Then why are you concerned?"

What could she say to that? Margaret Mary hadn't even admitted that she was meeting a man. She might be going to some women's study group, some group she thought too intellectual for Kat. Or some group meeting to plan good works. *I'm interested in good works,* thought Kat resentfully.

But as the trial date loomed, Kat could think of nothing else. Connor predicted that the jury rocking chairs he had purchased would help their case. Charlie Maxell was sure no jury would give the decision to the scoundrel who had insulted Kat. Kat was terrified that they'd lose. Everyone she talked to said that the Flemings' lawyer retired to his room each night to pore over law books and case notes and left instructions that no one was to so much as knock on his door. She didn't think Charlie was that diligent. He kept coming over to call on her.

There was a hard freeze the night before the trial. The next morning Kat saw for the first time the glory of aspen leaves turned gold and shivering in the late September breeze. "It must be a good omen," she said to Connor as they walked to court, Margaret Mary following behind.

"I don't see how," said Connor. "It happens every fall."

"Belief in omens is the mark of a primitive mind," said Margaret Mary.

Kat wished she hadn't granted the woman's request to attend the trial. For one thing, it wasn't fair to Olga, and Kat was beginning to see that Olga often got the short end in that friendship. Olga had evidently found Margaret Mary, an out-of-work schoolteacher of good family, destitute on the streets of Baltimore and taken her in, gotten her work at a meat-packing plant, and showed her the ropes. The two women had then saved enough to travel to Chicago in the hope of better wages, only to be robbed of their luggage by a dishonest cabman whom they had hired to take them to the rooming-house district. The story sounded like the working-girl romances Kat used to read. Had they made it up?

Tomorrow, thought Kat, *Margaret Mary will have to stay home, and Olga can come to the trial.* Realistically, however, she knew that Olga would never deprive Margaret Mary of anything she wanted.

Once in court, it didn't take long to impanel a jury. Each time the opposition lawyer objected to a juror, the judge said, "We ain't got that many folks in Summit County that you can afford to find fault with anyone who's willin' to serve. This ain't the big city, you know."

"I don't think he's all that good a lawyer," Kat whispered to Connor.

"I think Mr. Denton cuts a very fine figure," said Margaret Mary and, when Kat gave her a surprised frown, added, "One can tell he's an intellectual and a gentleman. You'll note that his grammar is much better than the other lawyer's and certainly far superior to the judge's."

"Whose side are you on anyway?" asked Kat.

"Be quiet out there in the audience," shouted the judge. "You females can't keep from gossipin', I'll send you back to your kitchens. Now let's get on with this trial. It's lasted too long already."

"Too long?" echoed Boniface Denton, looking surprised, presumably because jury selection had been completed in less than an hour. "Before I make my opening statement, your honor, my client would like to object to the jury's sitting in chairs purchased by Mr. James Connor Macleod."

"You boys wanna give up them rockin' chairs?" asked the judge.

"Well, hell, your honor, this looks to be long an' dull," said the foreman. "If we gotta be uncomfortable too, ain't none of us gonna stay."

Mr. Denton conferred with Mr. Fleming and addressed the judge. "My client, representing Trenton Consolidated Mining Corporation, wishes to say that he is not opposed to a postponement, since we have such reluctant jurors."

"Excellent diction," murmured Margaret Mary.

"Well, I got objections," said the judge. "We got a jury; we got the litigants an' their lawyers in court; so we're goin' ahead with this trial, an' don't you worry, Sep, it ain't gonna take all that long."

"That mean we gotta give up the rockin' chairs?" asked Septimus Embry, the jury foreman. "'Cause if it does, we ain't gonna take kindly to Trenton Consolidated depriving us of our comfort."

295

"What did I tell you?" Connor whispered. Kat smiled and nodded.

"My client will concede the rocking chairs," said Mr. Denton after another conference with Medford Fleming.

The two lawyers made their opening statements, and then the judge recessed court for the midday meal and his customary postprandial nap. Kat, Connor, and Margaret Mary went to Barney Ford's Saddle Rock Cafe, where Kat called to the owner, "Here I am at long last, Mr. Ford, come to visit your restaurant. I hope you still have chops." Barney Ford assured her that he did. "How's Mattie doing?" she asked, referring to the Negro girl who had come west with Hortense.

"Oh, she's married and living in Denver," said Barney Ford. "Julia was sorry to see her go."

"I'll have to write my mother. She always likes to hear that one of her girls has married."

"You must bring her a lot of joy then," said Barney Ford. "Seems like every other day I hear about some Chicago girl getting married."

"That man is a person of color," whispered Margaret Mary when Barney Ford had returned to his place by the till. "In Baltimore, persons of color do not intermix socially with white persons."

"He owns this restaurant," said Kat, pleased to note that Margaret Mary looked stunned to hear it. "Well, how are we doing?" she then asked Connor.

"I would judge that for oratorical presence and rhetorical sentence structure, Mr. Boniface Denton, III, far outclasses Mr. Charles Maxell," said Margaret Mary.

Before Kat could become alarmed, Connor said, "That may be, but two jurors fell asleep during his speech."

"Did they? I'm afraid I didn't notice." Margaret Mary asked for a vegetable plate and received a bowl of beans, at which she looked askance. Connor and Kat feasted on chops, mashed potatoes, and cream gravy, quite indifferent to their schoolteacher-maid's warnings that gravy was not healthful.

"Oh, don't worry about us, Margaret Mary. You've got enough to do, fishing all those chunks of unhealthful fatback out of your beans," said Kat cheerfully.

On the third day of the trial, a strong wind came up and blew all the golden aspen leaves away. "Hope that's not a bad omen," said Connor, grinning. Actually he thought the trial was going very well. The jury had stayed awake for Connor's testimony about how Fleming had salted the mine he now wanted to reclaim. On the other hand, they dozed off during Boniface Denton's many geological witnesses. Of course, they dozed off for Charlie's geologists too, but Connor explained to Kat on the way home that he figured they were even on geologists and ahead on Fleming's chicanery.

The fourth day, Kat dozed off, having heard more about mine geology than she thought one woman should be exposed to in a lifetime. When she woke up, her head was cozily tucked against Connor's shoulder, and Boniface Denton was saying, rather huffily, "Your honor, I must protest. One of the jurors is snoring."

"Right," said the judge. "I'm gittin' pretty sleepy myself. We'll recess for the noonday meal, an' maybe you could try to be a little more interestin' this afternoon, Mr. Denton."

"I find the geological points *quite* interesting," said Margaret Mary as they left.

Kat was sick and tired of Margaret Mary and told her to go home and do the ironing. Then Kat accompanied Connor to the Saddle Rock, where they had lamb chops instead of pork chops and chatted with Barney Ford, which they couldn't have done if Margaret Mary had come along. Goodness knew what she'd have said to sitting down with a "person of color." "Do you like her?" Kat asked Connor when the schoolteacher-maid's name came up.

"I think she's a pain in the neck," said Connor over a piece of Julia Ford's famous mountain cherry pie, "but she's a real housekeeper. She's got the mop out to clean up after you before you can get your muddy boots off."

"I think that's rather rude of her," said Kat.

The trial had to be postponed that afternoon because two jurors drank their midday meal and came back noticeably inebriated. Mr. Boniface Denton was horrified. The judge said, "Not the first time it's happened. Won't be the last," and went home for his second nap of the day.

"Well, I think that's enough testimony," said the judge toward noon the fifth day.

"But your honor," cried Boniface Denton, "I have more witnesses."

"How about you, Charlie? You gonna insist on more witnesses?"

Realizing that the judge was getting testy, Charlie Maxell said, "I'm willing to call it quits, your honor."

"Well, I'm not," cried Denton.

"Look, son," said the judge, "we've heard about how the claim got sold, an' we've heard from damn near every geologist in the state of Colorado. Any you boys wanna hear more?" He raised his voice but still failed to awaken the most persistent sleepers on the jury. The other jurors signified that they'd heard enough. "Right," said the judge. "We'll have closing arguments at, say, two-thirty. Hope you realize I'm cuttin' short my nap for you, Denton."

"But your honor—"

"Now don't try my patience. We been here—how many days? Even Fitzpatrick's sister can't stay awake."

"I'm awake," said Kat.

"Well, you weren't fifteen minutes ago. When two fine-lookin' bachelors like you lawyers can't keep a pretty woman awake, especially a pretty woman who stands to lose money if her side don't win, then you know you're boring ever' one else half to death. Closin' speeches at two-thirty. Don't make 'em too long. Keep in mind the winner gives the dance afterward." The judge slammed down his gavel and stamped out.

"What dance?" asked Kat. "Do we get to have a dance?"

"That's the custom," said Connor. "If we win, we pay for it."

"Margaret Mary, you'll have to go home and start baking."

"But I'll miss the closing arguments. And you don't know you're going to win."

"If we don't win, we'll all stay home," said Kat.

"I'm impressed," said Connor. "I didn't know you took this trial seriously enough to give up dancing."

"Your honor," said Septimus Embry. "We find for Connor. Fleming tried to cheat him, an' then when he found the tables turned, he jus' tried it another way. Abalone Wilson here"—The foreman nodded toward a juror who had slept through most of the trial.—"he knows more about where an apex lies than any a them fancy geologists, so he jus' went out last night an' looked. Connor's got the apex on the claim he bought from Fleming, which gives him the whole vein. That bein' the case, Fleming's gotta pay him for what he took out on Consolidated's side of the property line. Besides that, Abalone says looks to him like Fleming's been mining on Connor's side."

An enthusiastic hurrah went up from the audience with Boniface Denton, III, shouting over the tumult, "We intend to appeal, your honor."

"That's your right," said the judge. "Course, if you do, I'll take that verdict Sep jus' give us as a fraud conviction an' slap your Mr. Medford Fleming right in jail. You gonna try to tell me I cain't do that, city boy?" There was a hurried conference, followed by a more gracious acceptance of the verdict. "Right," said the judge. "Dance at seven sharp. Your treat, Connor, an' you kin stop huggin' Miz Fitzgerald. I don't like women in my courtroom, much less huggin'."

Kat felt a bit disappointed when Connor obeyed the judge, but still they'd won, and she hoped Medford Fleming stewed in his own bile. "We don't have to invite *them*, do we?" she asked.

"Certainly," said Connor. "If the jury had voted to hang him, he'd still have to be invited. It's the custom of the country."

"Connor, someone's brought beer," said Kat, breathless from a dance with Septimus Embry, who had told her he'd have voted for her side just on the strength of her pretty face. In fact, she had danced twice with the whole jury.

"I bought the beer myself," Connor replied. "Folks are here to help us celebrate, and I'm not serving them temperance beer. Let's dance." And he whirled her out onto the floor.

"I don't imagine the Flemings are here to help us celebrate," she retorted, although Eustacia Fleming certainly looked festive in her lilac and purple ball gown with its elaborate beadwork embroidery. Didn't she know this was a just a dance, not a fancy dress ball? Kat felt that she herself was much more appropriately dressed in a simple coral twilled silk with coffee lace accents and a proper high collar. Look at that neckline on Eustacia Fleming's dress—heart-shaped and cut very low. Connor, who fussed if Kat or Jeannie showed an inch of bosom, ought to say something to his friend, Mrs. Fleming, thought Kat.

"The Flemings are here so they won't look like sore losers, would be my guess," said Connor, who didn't seem at all put out by Mrs. Fleming's cleavage.

"She hasn't taken her eyes off you once this evening," Kat muttered.

"You're imagining things."

I'm sounding jealous, Kat realized with alarm and changed the subject. "Margaret Mary has danced three times with Mr. Boniface Denton."

"Swept off her feet by his oratorical presence, no doubt."

Kat started to giggle. It was hard to stay bad-tempered when Connor was whirling her around the floor as if he actually enjoyed it. However, later in the evening when she saw him dancing with Eustacia Fleming, Kat found it very easy to recover her pique. She didn't see that being a gracious winner extended to dancing with the enemy or, in this case, the enemy's wife. When Medford Fleming bowed in front of her, Kat felt no obligation to be a gracious winner. She said, "Get away from me, you foul-mouthed scoundrel."

Fleming gave her a look of frightening malice.

"Oh, Miss Kat," Olga cried. "Margaret Mary's disappeared."

"Now Olga," said Kat soothingly, "I'm sure she's around someplace."

"No she isn't. I've looked."

"Well, maybe she stepped outside for a breath of air."

"No, she hasn't. I looked."

"Well, maybe she's gone home."

"She wouldn't go home without me."

"Well, if a gentleman escorted her—"

"She'd tell me." With Olga on the verge of tears, Kat began to feel a bit uneasy herself. Still, Margaret Mary was nothing if not reliable. She wouldn't have left without telling someone. Could this be some Fleming plot? Had they set their lawyer to lure her maid away?

Kat turned on Medford Fleming, who had been viewing the scene with supercilious amusement. "What have you done with my maid?" she demanded.

"Madam, what *would* I have done with your maid? We have our own maids."

"Indeed," said Eustacia Fleming, who had been danced in their direction by Connor when he saw a confrontation taking place. "I have no need to kidnap your maid, Mrs.—Fitzgerald, is it? Is that Irish?" She said Irish as if it were a dirty word.

"Margaret Mary's disappeared and was last seen with their lawyer," Kat explained to Connor.

"Yep, they climbed in a buggy and headed up the road to Braddock," said Septimus Embry. "Elopin', I'd say."

"She hasn't paid off her passage," said Kat. Now she remembered all those evenings when Margaret Mary had been absent and unwilling to account for her whereabouts. Had she been consorting with the enemy?

"By God, you've done it again," raged Medford Fleming. "Here I take steps to protect my lawyer from *your* wiles, and you sic your maid on him."

"Don't be ridiculous," snapped Kat.

"I'm going to demand a retrial." Fleming grasped his wife's arm and stalked away.

"Did you know she was seeing their lawyer?" Connor asked suspiciously.

"She couldn't have been," said Kat. "He's an Episcopalian."

Chapter Twenty-One

Olga remained frantic for two days until Margaret Mary informed them by telegraph that she had become Mrs. Boniface Denton, III. Then Olga moped, her rosy face pale, her blond hair lank, her eyes red from secret weeping. She burned the last of the season's fresh vegetables and then had to start using the jars of produce she and Margaret Mary had put up, the sight of which sent Olga into fresh tears.

Kat decided that, even if she were left without household help, she must find Olga a husband, so she took the girl in hand. First, she provided material for a new dress. Olga couldn't believe that such a gown was to be hers, a fashionable combination of apricot silk with a cream waistcoat and cream tassels. Kat approved of waistcoats because they could be changed, making an old dress look new. Olga was so delighted with her gown that she cried less and corrected her own grammar now that Margaret Mary was no longer there to do it for her.

Once the dress was under way, Kat detailed Jeannie to

303

Elizabeth Chadwick

research the latest hairstyles recommended in the ladies' magazines. After that she bought a dressing table with a large mirror from the wife of a mine superintendent who was moving to Aspen, sat the two girls down at the mirror, and instructed them to try out on each other every new coiffure Jeannie discovered. Two days of giggling ensued, during which Olga hardly remembered that her friend Margaret Mary had deserted her without so much as a good-bye.

When Connor remarked at breakfast that Charlie Maxell wanted to have a meeting with them, Kat said, "Invite him to dinner tomorrow night." She'd try the new Olga out on Charlie. She ordered Olga to fix all her best recipes, standing over her to be sure that the girl didn't fall into melancholy and destroy the dinner. On Kat's instructions Olga appeared at the table wearing the new apricot and cream silk dress and the new hairstyle, which Jeannie, seldom home these days, had been ordered to recreate.

When Charlie tried to flirt with Kat, who was wearing her oldest dress and plainest hairstyle, Kat turned the conversation to Olga, pointing out the girl's cooking prowess, talents with a needle, scores of admiring swains. The last was an exaggeration. Before Kat redid her, Olga had been too shy to attract more than ordinary male attention, which she had ignored because she was more interested in Margaret Mary's doings.

In the midst of pork shoulder and roast potatoes, Charlie's smiles were transferred to Olga. Kat felt quite pleased with herself. Before the last piece of pie had been consumed, Charlie was talking exclusively to the blond housemaid. He had to be reminded that he had asked for a business meeting.

Connor murmured, as Kat tugged him through his own parlor into the corridor room with its cozy new love seat, "I think Charlie's flirting with Olga to make you jealous."

"He'd better not be," said Kat. "If he's toying with her

304

affections, I'll make him very sorry."

"This is the first time he's even noticed her," Connor protested.

"Which just goes to show what a little planning will accomplish," Kat murmured and turned to their guest. "Do try out the new sofa, Charlie," she suggested and all but pushed him into the love seat. "Now, what was it you wanted to talk to us about?"

"Well—" Charlie looked embarrassed. "I know the Ingrid's Ring is a good mine, and it's not that I don't appreciate your offer of a percentage in return for my services."

"Shall I have Olga bring you another cup of coffee? She does make wonderful coffee, doesn't she?"

"Ah—yes, she does."

Kat had left the door open for just such an opportunity and called the coffee request to Olga.

"And I'm not trying to back out of the deal if you're hard up for money," said Charlie.

"Here's Olga now. Why don't you sit by Charlie, Olga." Connor was staring at her in puzzled amazement, but Kat felt that she might as well make the most of her opportunities while she had an eligible bachelor in the house.

Charlie edged over so Olga could join him on the love seat. "But on the other hand," he resumed, "if you could pay me now, I wouldn't mind giving up the percentage. Not of course, if it puts you to any—"

"Of course, Charlie. Connor, you'll see to it, won't you?" Kat pulled him out of his chair, saying, "Now, why don't we leave the young people to get acquainted?"

"What was that all about?" Connor asked once she had edged him out of the room and into Ingrid's appalling red parlor. "Just because I said he was flirting with her—"

"I'm so glad you brought it to my attention. I think they make a lovely couple."

"Olga and Charlie? Why would a lawyer want to marry your maid?"

"She's a beautiful girl."

"And why the devil did you say we'd pay him hard cash?"

"Now Connor, if that's what he wants, I'm sure we'll profit by keeping the percentage we offered him."

"In the long run," Connor agreed, "but—"

"And the long run is what counts. Do you think we can leave them alone together for, say, a half hour without offending the proprieties?"

"How should I know? My courtship was spent traipsing along behind Rose Laurel's father while he tried to shoot every wild animal in Colorado."

Kat returned from an afternoon of campaigning for Dave Braddock to find a business crisis awaiting her and Connor gone to Denver.

"I'd like to go to Denver some time," said Kat wistfully to Eyeless. "I haven't seen my brother since last spring, and he's not much of a correspondent. You don't suppose he blames me for Ingrid's disappearance, do you?"

"No one would blame a female for anything Ingrid did," said Eyeless. "Anyways, Connor's gone, and the messenger said Hortense is gonna quit the Ten Mile Canyon mines."

"Why would she do that? I thought she was happy there. And I know the miners are happy with her."

"You put your finger on the problem. Dang fools keep proposin' to her."

"Oh? Well, that's different."

"She don't like it. That's why she's quittin'."

Kat sighed. "I guess I'll have to go up there myself."

"I'll go with you."

"But Eyeless, who'll look after Jeannie and Jamie?"

"I ain't no nursemaid. Olga can hold the fort for a few days."

Kat was doubtful, but she dared not let any labor troubles escalate in Ten Mile Canyon. Connor was already upset because she'd told Charlie they'd pay him in cash. With any luck, she thought smugly, Charlie would use the money to marry Olga and set up housekeeping. He'd taken to calling at least three times a week. "I don't see why you have to go, Eyeless."

"Connor don't like you travelin' off into rough minin' country by yourself," said Eyeless.

"Did he say that?" Kat asked eagerly.

"Didn't have to."

"Oh."

A journey with a one-eyed, one-legged, cripple-handed miner was not the easiest arrangement Kat had ever endured, and they had to visit all three mines in Ten Mile Canyon, advising the men at each that they'd have to stop proposing to Hortense if they wanted to continue eating like royalty.

"She don't want to marry any a you fellers," said Eyeless to every miner he met, many of whom denied any romantic interest in Hortense. When they finally caught up with Hortense at the Dead Wife, they were able to assure her that she would be receiving no more unwelcome proposals.

"Well, that's a relief," said Hortense. "I served notice that the next one who bothered me would get a punch in the nose, an' then I'd quit."

"You cain't blame the poor fellers," said Eyeless. "You're a fine figger of a woman, Hortense."

"Ah, git on with you, Eyeless. They're just after havin' a good cook to themselves."

"Cain't blame a man for wantin' to corral the best cook on the Western Slope. Hell, I reckon you're the best cook in the whole danged country, an' that's a pretty fair compliment comin' from a fella like me who knows a thing or two about cookin'."

"Ah, git on with you, you old fool."

Were they flirting? Kat wondered.

"Have another piece of pie, why don't you?"

"Thanks, Hortense, but I'm stuffed," said Kat.

"I meant Eyeless."

"Don't mind if I do," said Eyeless.

"Why do you care who gets elected sheriff, Miss Kat?" asked Septimus Embry. "You can't vote." They had met in front of the Summit County *Journal* office.

Kat was tired of being told that she couldn't vote. Still, she kept campaigning for Dave Braddock. "The man who developed temperance beer and vegetable farming on the Western Slope deserves our support," she told people.

"Myself, I don't care for either," said Abalone Wilson, who had come out of Bradley's Saloon and stopped to pass the time of day. "When a man comes up from a mine after ten hours a hard work, he wants real beer an' meat, not temperance beer and turnips."

"Dave would still make a fine sheriff," said Kat, stifling her normal desire to defend temperance beer and temperance sentiments. Dave said she was better than an ad in the newspaper and almost as good as a brass band. And Abalone had voted for them at the trial. In fact, his apex opinions had swung the other jury members.

It was unfortunate that she couldn't solicit votes by inviting bachelors over to the house to meet a prospective wife, but Olga, the last eligible female in residence, was now being courted assiduously by Charlie Maxell. Kat hoped the wedding could be delayed until after Christmas, but that was just selfishness. Christmas was two months away.

She ducked into the Chinese laundry to leave Connor's shirts and, coming out, saw Fred McNaught. "Hello, Mr. McNaught. I hope you're planning to vote for Broncho Dave."

"Election ain't till next month," said Fred McNaught. "An' what do you care? Womenfolk ain't got the vote."

"That doesn't mean we're not interested," said Kat through gritted teeth. "Hello, Mr. Crane. Getting your laundry done, are you? I hope you're planning to vote for Dave Braddock."

She'd have to write to Mother for more girls. Particularly, one for Diederick, who had been sulking around the house, getting very little done because he was hurt that Kat had danced twice with each member of the jury and not once with him. In Kat's opinion, Diederick needed a wife, someone bossy to keep him moving; he was taking forever with the tower room. Yet the girl couldn't be terribly bright lest he feel inferior. Men were so touchy about things like that. Some nice Germanic farm girl. Kat wondered how Maeve would feel about special ordering a bride for Diederick.

She continued down the street and, passing Mr. Faro's confectionery, was tempted to buy herself some of his lovely chocolates but decided against it; Connor was being rather difficult about money lately. "Good afternoon, Mr. Collins. Did you know Broncho Dave Braddock is running for sheriff?"

Connor should be back from Denver any day now with news of Maeve and James and of Sean. Was Sean better?

"Good afternoon, Mr. Finding. Isn't this a lovely October day? I'm soliciting votes for Dave Braddock."

"Tell Connor, he owes me for last month's bill," said Mr. Finding.

"He does?" Kat felt a little stab of alarm. Connor was very prompt about paying bills. He liked to deal with local merchants and pay on time.

"You sold the First Strike and your mine on the Snake River?" Kat was unnerved by Connor's announcement.

"Sure did. Found some eastern investors and sold out lock, stock, and barrel."

"You didn't ask me."

"You didn't ask me, Kat, when you promised Charlie we'd pay him cash."

"Oh, Connor." She looked stricken. "We didn't have the money? That's why you sold two mines? I just wanted to leave Charlie and Olga alone together. I didn't think—"

"That's a bad way to do business."

"Sean must be furious with me."

"No, he thought selling the First Strike was a good idea. He helped me arrange the deal, and it wasn't too easy. Silver's below a dollar now, and that mine's not a big producer anymore. I expect the vein's pinching out."

"But what about yours?"

"The Too Late? It's a good mine, but it costs too much to get the ore to a smelter. The Easterners have more capital. They'll keep both mines open so the men won't lose their jobs, and we'll have more cash money."

"Is that why you didn't pay Mr. Finding? Because we're poor now?"

"We're not poor, Kat. We're just temporarily short of funds. Where's Jamie?"

"Playing baseball."

"And Jeannie?"

"I don't know," said Kat absently. "At Finding's I guess." But then she remembered her conversation with Mrs. Finding a month ago. If Jeannie wasn't going to Finding's, where was she—

"Eyeless has a surprise for you."

"Eyeless?"

"He and Hortense want to open a restaurant here in town."

"Eyeless and Hortense?"

"Pay attention, Kat. You've managed to marry off another of your Chicago girls."

"Eyeless and Hortense!" Kat's mouth dropped open.

Kat was getting tired of arranging wedding parties. How many had she given? Bridget, Jilly, Mary Beth, Noleen,

Hortense. Of course, the dancing was lovely, but since Ingrid left, she had to hire someone to provide music. Well, not for the little party to celebrate Coleen's acceptance as a novice at St. Gertrude's; Reverend Mother Hilda had said no dancing at that one. Margaret Mary had taken care of her own wedding, and Olga would be next, but money was tight. The apricot dress with a little restructuring would have to do for the wedding, but who could she get to play the piano for free?

Kat sighed. She'd ordered a girl for Diederick, and her mother had sent the specifications on to Genevieve in Chicago. Eyeing her tower room as she left the house, Kat decided that the five sides looked stupid. Of course, she hadn't seen the original tower in Aspen, but she was sure eight would have looked better. Diederick had the window frames in, but he'd done nothing on the balcony. Nor had he built the stairs. Slowpoke carpenter! He probably hadn't even ordered the leaded windows.

Kat was going out to campaign among the ladies for Broncho Dave. At least the ladies wouldn't remind her that she couldn't vote, and they could influence their husbands. Maybe she'd stop by afterwards to visit Sister Freddie. That always cheered her up.

The Methodist Ladies Aid Society, of which Kat was the only Roman Catholic participant, met without Lucinda Dyer the afternoon Kat attended to talk up Dave Braddock's candidacy. The ladies were encouragingly supportive because of Dave's temperance beer, although fearful that sheriff's duties might keep him from the cultivation of vegetables.

"Oh, Connor says Dave is capable of running half the businesses in the valley without missing a step," said Kat.

"How is Mr. Macleod?" asked one of the women. "It must be so difficult for you, my dear Mrs. Fitzgerald, now that everyone's talking about him."

311

"They are? Oh, I suppose you mean about his selling the mines. Well, you know silver prices are—"

"Goodness, that was the least surprising of his activities in Denver. At least, that's what we hear."

"Well, he visited the family," said Kat, puzzled.

"And Mrs. Fleming."

"Mrs. Fleming?" Her heart gave an anxious bump.

"Why yes, Mr. Haprod saw them coming out of a hotel together. We thought maybe you'd know all about it."

"M-maybe it had something to do with settling the l-lawsuit," Kat stammered. But it wouldn't have. Although Trenton Consolidated owed them money for ore taken from Connor's vein, Eustacia Fleming wouldn't be involved in the arrangements to pay that debt.

"I suppose it could have been business," said Mrs. Haprod, "but I've heard several people say Mr. Macleod's been seen leaving the Fleming house on Nickel Hill in the middle of the day, when Mr. Fleming would have been away."

Kat swallowed down tears. She wasn't going to defend Connor to these women, and she wasn't going to cry. "I guess you'll have to ask him," she said in a steady voice. "I've no idea what his connection with Mrs. Fleming is."

"Well, my dear, maybe *you* should ask him. After all, you're living in the same house."

They wouldn't act this way if Lucinda were here, Kat thought. *Or Gertrude. They wouldn't say those things in front of Gertrude.* The conversation moved on, and Kat was left to think about Connor and Eustacia Fleming. He'd been in Denver with her? And at her big, fancy house here in Breckenridge when her husband wasn't home? He'd said that Mrs. Fleming only wanted to talk about moving the sporting ladies down hill, but the sporting ladies were gone, so what business did he have with Eustacia Fleming now?

The more Kat thought about it, the angrier she became.

312

And hurt. She was hurt, remembering the two occasions when she and Connor had been intimate. He'd used her, with no honorable intentions, and then he'd found someone who was safer for a confirmed widower. He could dally with Eustacia and never have to fear that she'd demand marriage. That must be why Connor had taken up with Eustacia Fleming. Or maybe he just liked her better than he did Kat.

"And I'd like to make a toast to Miss Kathleen—" said Charlie Maxell at the wedding feast.

"Here, here!" shouted the male wedding guests.

"—who's done more for the happiness of men in Summit County than anyone since gold was discovered in '59."

"Here, here!"

"I reckon us men don't deserve it—"

"You certainly don't," said Kat.

"—but we're sure grateful," Charlie finished, looking confused, as did her many admirers in the crowd.

"Considering how little character the average male has," said Kat, "they get much better than they deserve. In fact—"

"In fact, Kat thanks you for that handsome toast, Charlie," Connor interrupted, "and now I'd like to propose a toast to the bride and groom."

When the dancing began, three gentlemen, in defense of the impugned male character, told Kat they were thinking of giving up drinking, and four mentioned that they figured to attend church more often. "I'm glad to hear it," she replied coldly to each. Connor, the hypocrite, never even asked her to dance. Not that she cared. She wanted nothing to do with a man of such frayed moral fiber. Maybe she ought to move out. With Olga and Eyeless gone, she could hardly live unchaperoned in a house with a man like Connor.

In fact, she was now sorry she'd given away in marriage all those innocent young women to creatures as detestable as men. She'd have to write Mother and tell her to stop sending girls, that Kat was abdicating her role as matchmaker to Summit County.

"What the hell did you mean by that remark about the average male having no character?" asked Connor when the last guest had gone.

"Figure it out for yourself," snapped Kat and flounced off to her room.

"Well, it wasn't very festive," he called after her.

The next day Gretel Baumeister arrived—sturdy, blond, opinionated, a little slow, and perfect for Diederick. And Kat had a change of heart about Connor. She decided that the affair must have been Eustacia Fleming's fault and that it was her duty to see that he didn't remain in the clutches of such a person, an evil woman and a Protestant. Perhaps it was her Christian duty to divert his attention to herself. If she only knew how.

Kat had never considered deliberately setting out to entice a man. Her problem had been getting rid of them. Of course, Connor was different from her usual admirer. She and Connor lived together. He saw her every day and obviously took her for granted. And why shouldn't he? He'd been in her bed twice. Was that an advantage or not? Kat wondered. He'd seemed to enjoy it, but on the other hand, he hadn't tried for a third encounter. By now he must consider her part of the domestic scenery, which meant she had to make him notice her.

Kat sighed dejectedly. She'd never in this world manage to look as stylish and seductive as Eustacia Fleming. She couldn't think of any woman in Breckenridge who did. Except Marcella Webber! The woman whose Gentleman's Sporting Club had been forced to move to West Breckenridge at Eustacia Fleming's insistence. Now *there* was a woman who knew a lot about men! *She'd* know how to turn Connor's head. But would she be interested in taking on a part-time student?

I'm not seriously considering this, Kat told herself. *It would be a shocking thing to do.* She looked at herself in the dressing table mirror she had bought when she wanted to help Olga entrap Charlie. That had worked. Why not this? *Nothing ventured, nothing gained.* Mother always said that. And Mother thought Kat and Connor should marry. "He's the kind to put food on the table," Mother had said.

If Mother could snare a will o' the wisp like James, Kat felt that she ought to be able to snare Connor. With a little help. She'd rather not have to use her mother's method to do it. Not that she didn't want children. Kat smiled wistfully, then extracted herself from that brief daydream. After they were married—that was the proper time for children. But the problem was marriage. Did she really want to take that kind of risk again? She could be initiating a course of action that would wreck her life—and all because of a transient jealous impulse.

"I believe half the wedding party turned up at mass this week," said Father Eusebius. "The male half."

"I've had three parishioners ask if I thought they were men of little character," said Father Dyer. "I told them there wasn't a Christian alive who couldn't stand improvement."

"I quite agree," said Kat.

"I expect they were feeling guilty because they'd been dancing at your house."

"I'd like to have invited you and Mrs. Dyer to the wedding, but you know how we papists are." Kat grinned at him. "Always dancing."

"If it weren't for the dancing, you'd have made a fine Methodist," said Father Dyer. "Is Connor Macleod still insisting that you give up temperance?"

"Who cares what he says? Do you want to go out Sunday?" she asked on impulse.

The Methodist clergyman sighed. "I'm not as young as

I used to be. Actually, I'm thinking of retiring."

Kat was sorry to hear it, but his retirement did let her off the hook. It would be hard to entice Connor, even with expert guidance, if she were fluttering her eyelashes at him on weekdays and attacking saloons on Sundays.

Chapter Twenty-Two

She managed to find her way to the Gentleman's Sporting Club in West Breckenridge without asking directions. After all, a respectable woman couldn't stop a stranger and say, "Pardon me, sir, but could you direct me to Marcella Webber's house of ill repute?" Finding the house wasn't difficult; she'd seen it in the middle of various streets for a week while it was being moved from Nickel Hill across the river.

Then, having found it, she suffered the indignity of knocking at the door, which was answered by a maid wearing an outfit such as Bridget might have worn when she was being pinched by her employer in Chicago, only this uniform had a skirt that ended at the knee and a ruffled apron with no standard bodice underneath. Kat tried not to stare at the maid's knees and bosom. And she got through the embarrassment of asking for an interview with the proprietress and having the maid gape at her and ask in return if she was sure she'd knocked at the right door.

But when Marcella Webber appeared, Kat lost her tongue completely, silenced by the sight of all those honey-colored ringlets and the garment her hostess was wearing. She'd never seen anything like it. Was it a nightgown and robe? If so, it exposed a lot of bosom for the chilly nights of Breckenridge. But then Mrs. Webber worked at night, so she probably slept by day when one wouldn't need as heavy a nightdress. That was why Kat had chosen late morning for her visit, hoping to arrive when the lady was awake but before customers started to arrive—at least, Kat hoped no customers visited in the morning. Wouldn't that be embarrassing! And the robe—a gossamer thing, very beautiful but offering no cozy warmth. Perhaps the garments were—what? Evening wear?

"You wanted to speak to me?" Marcella Webber prompted.

"Oh, yes," Kat stammered. "I'm—ah, my name is Kathleen Fitzgerald."

"I know."

"You do? How?"

"Why you're the chief source of gossip in this town."

"Me?"

"Of course, You live with Connor Macleod, causing all the old biddies to cackle, yet not a one of them really believes you're sleeping with him, and all the miners grumble about your temperance campaigns, yet there's not a one of *them* who isn't in love with you."

"Oh." Was that how people saw her?

"If you're looking for Ingrid, she didn't come here. I haven't seen her since she left to marry Sean."

"Left where?" Kat gasped. Suddenly she noticed the room, looked at it closely instead of noting peripherally that it made her uneasy. It was red! As red as Ingrid's parlor. "Left where?" asked Kat again.

The woman's large hazel eyes narrowed. "Anywhere. Left anywhere."

At last Kat thought she understood. "Ingrid worked for you, didn't she?" That explained a lot, but she'd think about Ingrid later. "I'm not here about Ingrid."

Now Marcella Webber looked surprised. "What then? If you want me to ban hard spirits from the Sporting Club, I'll have to disappoint you."

"Well, that would be nice," said Kat wistfully. Temperance would have been a less embarrassing errand than the one on which she had come. "But I wasn't going to suggest that. Actually, I—I'm in need of expert advice, and I thought you—" She studied the beautiful, voluptuous, intimidating woman seated regally in a red velvet chair, and wondered if any advice from Marcella Webber would be something Kat could implement.

"First, I'd better ask if you are—ah, indebted to the Flemings, or in any way their—friend." Rumor had it that Fleming had paid this woman a huge amount to move her house. She might be grateful. "I do hope you'd tell me if you—" Kat stopped because she saw the light of pure fury shining in Marcella Webber's eyes.

"You're asking if I'm grateful because they offered me such a generous choice—move or be burned out?"

Kat's mouth rounded. "Most people thought they paid you a lot of money."

"They paid for moving the house," said Marcella bitterly. "They didn't pay for the loss of business while my premises were in transit."

"I always thought Medford Fleming had my house burned," Kat confided.

"He probably did. So it seems we have something in common, Mrs. Fitzgerald. However, I assume this isn't a social call. You did mention advice, although I can't imagine what knowledge I'd have that you need."

"Oh, but you do. You know all about men," said Kat earnestly.

Marcella's lips quirked. "You seem to do quite well in that respect yourself. Half my customers have proposed to you."

Kat was certainly surprised to hear that. She hadn't realized that so many men visited places of this sort or imagined that any she knew would do such a thing. "Do you know Connor Macleod?" she asked.

"Of course." Then at the look on Kat's face, the madam added, "Not as a customer." Kat looked so relieved that Marcella asked, "Is it Connor you want to attract? Goodness, you've got the man right in the house with you."

"But he doesn't notice me," said Kat. "He's interested in someone else."

"He's courting someone?"

"No, she's married."

"Ah, you want to take him away from Eustacia Fleming."

"Oh, well—"

"And you want me to help you." Marcella burst into laughter.

"I guess you think that's impossible."

"Not at all, and it's a challenge I'd love to take on," said Marcella. "Any injury I can do that snobbish bitch will give me great pleasure."

Kat had to bite back the impulse to reprimand the madam for bad language.

"And you're twice the woman Eustacia Fleming is—both for looks and character. Your only problem would be an excess of character, whereas she has none."

"By character what exactly do you mean?" asked Kat.

"Oh, morals, that sort of thing. Maybe we'd better establish what it is you're after. You just want to see that she doesn't keep her claws in him, or do you want him for yourself? Do you want to marry him?"

"Well—yes." It still frightened Kat to give up her long-held defenses against marriage, but she did want to ally herself more securely with Connor, and marriage seemed to be the only option. "It's really my duty, don't you think?" she added defensively. "In order to keep him away from such an evil woman."

"Duty? Well, it's not going to be much fun for Connor when you get him—"

"Do you think I can?" Kat interrupted.

"Sure. But a wife who's just doing her duty—that's what sends the husbands to my place. Don't you love him?"

Kat thought about it. She'd *loved* Mickey. She'd just had to have him. Thought him the most romantic, handsome man in the world. Whereas what she felt for Connor—well, she admired him. She enjoyed his company. Of course, she liked his looks too and found him physically attractive. All this she tried to explain to Marcella, admitting with some confusion that what she felt might not be love.

"You're in love," the madam assured her. "What you felt for the other one—that was just infatuation. Kids' stuff. Connor will be a lucky man to get caught by you."

"Oh, I'm so glad you think so."

"Except for one thing."

Kat looked at her anxiously.

"Coming here will ruin your reputation. Women like you don't associate with women like me."

"Oh, that's no problem," said Kat. "We'll say I'm coming for Christian conversation."

"Christian conversation?" Marcella looked amused.

"That is, if your employees wouldn't mind some. I could just—well, give them an inspirational message, a Bible verse or something. I wouldn't take too long. As far as I know, they don't go to church, so it would be a very good thing for them."

"Is that what you're up to?" demanded Marcella. "What for? Our kind aren't welcome in the churches. If you're looking to reform a few fallen women—"

"Truly, it just occurred to me," said Kat. "As a reason

for coming. But I couldn't explain my presence here that way unless I really were actually saying something inspirational."

"No, I don't suppose you could." Marcella Webber frowned thoughtfully. "And you're probably the only woman in town who could protect your good name that way. Folks'll just say it's another one of your crackpot notions."

Kat was about to protest that she wasn't given to crackpot notions when Marcella continued, "So that gets you past the problem that respectable ladies don't come to West Breckenridge for any reason, much less to visit my place."

"Oh, I think you're wrong. I come over all the time to meet the train."

"You're supposed to use the stop at the edge of town. That's what it's for—to keep respectable ladies from being contaminated."

Kat started to giggle, remembering her chagrin when the depot agent tried to make her go away. "I had no idea." Before Kat could explain why she was laughing, the maid knocked and announced that breakfast was about to be served.

"Well, do you want to join us?" asked Marcella. "Bring the gospel to a few unrepentant soiled doves?"

Breakfast? At this hour? Kat shook off her surprise and opened her mouth to say she hadn't prepared any inspirational message, but then she realized that she had to start sometime. It might as well be today.

"I'll have you out of the house before the customers arrive," Marcella promised.

"Thank you for the invitation," said Kat. "I'd love to." She noted Marcella Webber's surprise.

Marcella was not, however, nearly as surprised as the six women to whom Kat was introduced in the dining room. "Mrs. Fitzgerald is going to visit us from time to time to bring the—ah, word of God," said Marcella. Her

322

employees looked at Kat as if she were the circus come to town and about to perform for their entertainment. "Mrs. Fitzgerald, would you like to say a prayer before we eat?" asked Marcella politely.

Kat bowed her head. "Holy Mary, Mother of God, bless this food—no matter how it was come by. And bless all of us women, who have such a difficult path to tread in a world where men have all the advantages. Amen."

A chorus of amens, some of them loudly heartfelt, followed her little prayer.

Kat was sitting next to a woman named Babette, who said, "You're the one who went into the saloon that time, aren't you?"

"Yes, I am," said Kat. "I think drinking is very unhealthful."

"And the sheriff arrested you?"

"Yes, he did."

"This woman up on Nickel Hill wanted to have us arrested. I suppose you do too."

"No, I don't," said Kat, after giving the subject some thought. "Maybe your customers should be arrested. They don't have to come here—"

"Let's not spread *that* idea around," said Marcella.

"—but I can see that women and girls might have to choose between hunger and homelessness and—and well, your life," Kat forged on. "My mother takes girls in, in Chicago, to prevent such—such choices."

"I'm from Chicago," said a young woman named Birdie. "I wish your mother had found me."

"I wish she had too," said Kat sadly. She wasn't really sure how many women took up a life of sin because they wanted to and how many had no choice.

The conversation then became general, if somewhat stilted. Kat could see that her presence put a damper on the meal, so she concentrated on her food, which was very good.

323

"Maybe you'd like to give us your religious message at this time, Mrs. Fitzgerald," said Marcella as she served Kat a second helping of pudding. There was a gleam of amusement in her eyes.

Kat had been savoring the creamy dessert, marveling at the idea of dessert with breakfast, and was caught unprepared when she realized that she had to come up with something beyond the prayer. She stared at the sugar bowl for inspiration, then said, "Perhaps the most important thing to remember is that there is always hope of salvation. Take St. Mary Magdalene, for instance. From what I understand, she's the patron saint of—ah—"

"—whores," said Red Melba helpfully.

"Um—yes," Kat replied. "And yet she was the one who discovered that Jesus had risen. She saw the angels at his tomb and took the word to the disciples. I think St. Mary Magdalene is a lesson to us all, that Jesus casts out our devils—she had seven—and forgives our sins."

"Seven?" Babette's eyes lit with interest. "What did they look like?"

"Well, I suppose like their pictures."

"I never seen a picture of a devil," said Birdie. "I've known a few, but they're just your ordinary Saturday-night-on-the-town type devil."

All the girls laughed at that, and Marcella, to Kat's relief, didn't insist that the religious instruction continue. Kat thought the girls looked rather wistful when she said good-bye. Were they hungry for female company outside their profession?

"How often you planning to come by?" asked Marcella as they walked back to the parlor to retrieve Kat's mantle.

"Would once a week be all right? I don't have a lot of extra time."

"So I've heard. You really going to try to get women the vote?"

324

"Why not?" said Kat defensively. "Why shouldn't we vote?"

"No reason that I can see. Well, I'll give you a bit of advice to tide you over with Connor until next week."

Kat's heart sped up a little.

"Brush against him now and then. Put your hand on his arm. Nothing too obvious, but men like to be touched. And when he talks to you, duck your head a little, look at him under your lashes and think about making love with him."

Kat flushed.

"Well, surely you've thought about it before now. You said you want to marry him."

Kat wasn't about to admit that she'd actually done what Marcella suggested she think about. "What good would that do? He won't know what I'm thinking."

"Just do it. See what happens. Then next week we'll talk about your clothes and hair."

"What's wrong with my clothes and hair?"

"They're fine for the Ladies' Altar Cloth Society, but they're not going to inspire passion," said Marcella dryly.

"Oh."

From the Gentleman's Sporting Club to the bridge, Kat dutifully practised thinking about making love with Connor. She began to feel a little flushed. From the bridge to Lincoln Avenue, she tried to imagine having such thoughts while actually looking Connor in the eye. The idea made her uneasy. Yet she had gone to the trouble of asking advice; she'd be silly not to try it.

From Lincoln Avenue to French Street, she tried to come up with an inspirational message for her next visit to West Breckenridge. After all, she did have a Christian duty to take that aspect of her visits seriously. Was there any other saint who had been a prostitute? She couldn't ask Fathers Rhabanus or Eusebius or Reverend Mother Hilda, but she could ask to borrow a book of saints' lives.

She detoured to the rectory where Father Eusebius lent her such a book and mentioned that masses in the mining camps had been very well attended lately and that five communicants had particularly asked that he mention their names to Kat as men of character. She nodded. Goodness, it had been a just passing remark—her reply to Charlie's toast. Now it seemed that she'd started some sort of religious revival.

With the book under her arm, she remembered that she had an errand on North Main, which she carried out and walked up Wellington Road, again rehearsing love-making thoughts. She was hardly half a block off Main when she noticed a huge beast standing in a field near a log cabin. Kat gasped. That was a buffalo! What was a buffalo doing in the town of Breckenridge?

Terrified, she took to her heels and ran all the way home, sure the animal was stampeding after her. Did buffalo bite? Or did they just trample one to death? She sprinted up the steps and yanked open the door to the house, tumbling into the corridor room where she confronted Connor.

"What's wrong?" he demanded.

"I'm being chased by a buffalo." Kat collapsed into his arms, shaking in every limb.

"Kat," he said soothingly, "that's not very likely."

"I *saw* it," she gasped.

"Where?"

"Near Main Street on Wellington Road. Look out the window. It's probably trying to get up the steps."

Connor led her to the window. "See. No buffalo," he said, drawing aside the curtains.

"Well, I saw one."

"Wellington near Main." He grinned. "Reckon Professor Edwin Carter was airing his buffalo."

"Airing it?"

"It's stuffed. He's got a museum of stuffed animals."

326

"Buffaloes?"

"Some. I reckon they get to smelling from time to time, so he airs them out."

"Oh." Kat dropped into a chair. She should be looking at him under her lashes, thinking of lovemaking, but she didn't feel up to it. All that practice, and she was going to have to pass up this opportunity. And Marcella had said to brush against him. Subtly. Throwing oneself into his arms in fear of a stuffed buffalo wasn't very subtle—or romantic. He'd think her idiotic instead of enticing.

Kat studied Ingrid's parlor and shook her head. All these months she'd endured sleeping next to a room that took its decorative motif from the parlor of a sporting house. Well, at least she could remove the fringed red velvet scarves on the tables and piano. She did. Changing the wallpaper had helped some, but there was still that strange picture on the wall in its gaudy frame. She studied it from several different angles. Superimposed on two rather awkward-looking, naked baby bodies were the photographed faces of Phoebe and Sean Michael. The mismatch was obvious. Still, those were the only pictures she had of the children. She'd keep them no matter how bizarre the whole. But the awful red velvet furniture was another matter.

With determination, Kat went in search of paper and pen. "Dear Sean," she wrote. "Now that we have the larger parlor provided by the corridor room, I wonder if you'd mind my storing or even selling your red velvet furniture . . ."

Feeling like a sneak, knowing Jeannie would realize what she was up to, Kat made an after-dinner call on the Findings, where Jeannie had said she would be studying. Kat needn't have worried about Jeannie's reaction; the girl was not there, and a few casual questions proved that Jeannie hadn't been there in over a month. Kat felt quite grim as she walked home and then waited on the cold porch to see from which direction Connor's daughter would come. Kat obtained not only that information but the name of the young man Jeannie was with—Tommy Weston, the miner they had met last spring at Gertrude Briggle's Dillon picnic.

The young couple was taken completely by surprise when they began to say good-bye on the corner of French and Lincoln only to be invited to the house by Kat, who had sprinted the half block to confront them.

"We—we just met by accident when I was walking home from—"

"I've been *there*," said Kat.

"You've been spying on me," Jeannie accused.

"And you've been lying to me."

"Ma'am, we weren't doing anything we shouldn't," said Tommy. "I mean we weren't—"

"We're in love," said Jeannie.

"At sixteen? Take my word for it; you're not."

"I am too."

"Then why didn't you bring him home?"

"Because I knew you'd make a fuss," Jeannie mumbled resentfully. "He's not Catholic."

"Well, if you want to keep seeing each other, you'll do it where you can be properly chaperoned. And as for you, young man, if you ever hurt her—"

"Oh, Miz Fitzgerald, I'd never."

That night as she got ready for bed, Kat thought that she shouldn't have said what she had about love. Not everyone was as stupid about love as she had been at that age. But then, some people were even more stupid. Diederick, for instance. He wouldn't pay any attention to Gretel. Kat sent Gretel to him with coffee, with cookies, with a mustard plaster when he caught a cold working on the tower room in the nippy October wind. No reaction.

"Have you been doing what I told you?"

"Yes," said Kat grudgingly. Just yesterday afternoon

before dinner she had put her hand on Connor's arm while he told her about production figures at the Sister Katie. She had watched his mouth and imagined his kiss.

He'd said, rather impatiently she thought, "Are you listening, Kat?"

The day before they'd had a moment together in the corridor room, and Kat had sat opposite him, knitting and glancing at him, remembering the feel of his body on hers in the farm house. Connor had been talking about the profit figures from the restaurant Eyeless and Hortense had opened. "Maybe I'll bank that fire," he had said.

"Are you warm?" she'd asked hopefully.

"No, but you look flushed."

"I don't see that I'm having much success," Kat admitted to Marcella Webber. "Maybe it's hopeless."

"Why hopeless? We've hardly begun. Now I want you to go to Mrs. Luella Mitchum. She's a dressmaker. Get yourself some new clothes, and be sure they show off your figure. Tight waists and bodices."

"It takes time to have clothes made," said Kat.

"In the meantime, I have this nightgown for you." Marcella shook out the garment.

"I'd freeze to death," said Kat. It had a very low neckline. "And he never sees me in my nightgown."

"Then you'll have to arrange it."

"And then what?"

"And then see what happens. Be receptive. Of course, you don't want him to get you with child, so don't go to bed with him. Just keep him all hot and bothered."

Kat felt quite glum. She'd already been to bed with Connor, and no declarations of love had been forthcoming, certainly no marriage proposals.

"Have you been brushing up against him?"

Kat nodded.

"What part of you? What part of him?"

"Well, I brushed some lint off his shoulder, and I straighted his tie." Marcella was looking disdainful. "And once I touched his cheek."

"How did he react?"

"He jumped."

"Good. As soon as you get home, stand just to one side and in front of him, then turn as if you didn't realize he was there and let your breast rub against his arm. Don't look shocked. Try it."

Kat swallowed.

"If you have a sofa or love seat, sit beside him so that your thighs are brushing. Then shift around as you talk. Cause some friction. After you've done that a few times, and if you seem to be making him uncomfortable but he hasn't grabbed you yet—"

"Grabbed me?"

"In a manner of speaking. If he hasn't made a move, try the nightgown on him. And continue thinking about making love. Every time he's in the room—"

"Marcie, there are two children in the house, not to mention a maid and a carpenter, various visitors—"

"Breakfast, Miss Marcie," said the maid in the short skirt.

"Time for your inspirational message," said Marcella.

Kat's heart sank. She'd read Father Eusebius's book and then borrowed one from Reverend Mother, and she couldn't find a single additional saint who had been a prostitute or even a flirt. They all seemed to have been *born* saintly except for Mary Magdalene. She managed a creditable prayer, but as she enjoyed the delicious meal, she wondered desperately what she'd say when Marcie called on her for a message.

They didn't want to hear about temperance, and they probably weren't interested in woman suffrage. She realized that they were all looking at her expectantly, so Kat swallowed hard and said, "Today I'd like to tell you about St.—ah, Genevieve." There was a St. Genevieve, but Kat couldn't remember a thing about her. The name had sprung to mind because of loyal Genevieve in Chicago, running Maeve's rooming houses. "St. Genevieve was a—a prostitute who went with the crusaders to the Holy Land." Well, that had got their attention. "And she—well, she didn't see anything sinful about—er, selling her favors to Christian knights."

"How much did she get?" asked Babette.

"I don't know." This improvising was hard enough without being asked questions for which she couldn't begin to make up answers. "Then one afternoon there was a great battle, and she was captured by the Saracens."

"Who are they?" Birdie was wide-eyed.

"Heathen warriors with harems and swords so sharp that they could cut silk."

Kat got in deeper and deeper, having to explain to her fascinated audience what a harem was and then what a concubine was.

"Let her finish," snapped Red Melba. "I want to find out what happened to St. Genevieve. Ain't that a fine name. Think I'll call myself Genevieve."

"*Saint* Genevieve?" hooted Dolly.

"So Genevieve—she wasn't a saint at that time—realized that being captured by the cruel and dreadful heathen Saracens was God's punishment because she had sinned."

"The harem doesn't sound so bad," said Babette.

"You don't get paid in a harem," Dolly pointed out disdainfully. "Only dummies and wives do it for free. Beggin' your pardon, Miz Fitzgerald."

"Yes, of course. So when the Saracen wanted to—well, have his way with her, she refused, and he was just about to cut off her head when the Holy Mother appeared in the heavens wearing a beautiful blue gown"—Kat was warming to her subject. —"and around her head was a halo that glowed like fire and melted the Saracen's sword."

"Oh," breathed Birdie, eyes round. "It was a miracle, wasn't it?"

"Yes," said Kat. "Then a party of Christian knights rode by and rescued Genevieve and carried her to a—a convent in the Holy Land, where she spent the rest of her life in prayer and good works and converting the heathen. And even today St. Genevieve is an inspiration to us all."

"That was a wonderful story," said Babette.

"Oh yes," Birdie agreed. "Just like a fairy tale."

"I'll bet the knights cut off the Saracen's head," Red Melba guessed.

"Probably," Kat agreed. "There wasn't much he could do after his sword melted. Now I think I'd better be getting home." She bade the ladies of the Gentleman's Sporting Club good-bye and hurried across the Blue as fast as she could, straight to St. Mary's where she cornered Father Rhabanus and made her confession.

"Forgive me, Father, for I have sinned."

"And what is your sin, my child?"

She could see that the poor priest was looking terrible and probably wanted to go home to bed, but she felt that she had to clear her conscience immediately. "I lied, Father."

"About what did you lie, my child?"

Kat had hoped he wouldn't ask. "I made up a saint's life," she whispered.

Silence greeted her statement. Then he said, "Why in the world would you do that? No, don't tell me. You're a very peculiar young woman, Kathleen Fitzgerald."

He was supposed to pretend he didn't know who was confessing, she thought resentfully.

"The church has hundreds of saints, all of whose lives are instructive to us lesser mortals. I can't even imagine a situation that would tempt one to *fabricate* a saint's life."

Kat sighed. Little did he know. "I'm sorry, Father. Truly contrite." And it had been such a melodramatic saint's life! On the other hand, they'd liked it.

"I want you to pray every night for the next month to be forgiven for this—this peculiar fall from grace."

"Yes, Father," she said humbly. "I'll start right now."

"So you should." He went away mumbling, "Made up a saint's life? What next?"

Poor Father Rhabanus, thought Kat. Life in Breckenridge was really too much for him. Sometimes she thought it was too much for her.

She went home, having said a number of prayers asking for forgiveness, and while standing beside Connor at the window in the corridor room, she turned slowly, brushing her breast against his arm as Marcella had told her to do. She found the experience electrifying. Her nipple sprang erect immediately. He evidently felt something too, for his hand closed over her forearm. She looked up at him and thought of how his hand had felt on her breast when he made love to her in his room the night she had come looking for Jeannie. Connor swallowed visibly and jerked his hand away as if her skin had burned him.

"I think dinner is ready," said Kat, disappointed.

When she sat down beside him after dinner, thigh to thigh, he got up and left the room. Kat sighed. Tomorrow she'd have to go to that dressmaker. And in her room, hidden under her flannel nightdresses, was the gown Marcie had given her. It probably wouldn't fit, she thought. She was almost afraid to try it on.

Chapter Twenty-Three

Connor was in town, Jeannie and Jamie at school, Gretel at choir practice, and Diederick outside the tower room nailing up scrollwork. He'd be leaving any minute because snow was imminent. This was as close to an empty house as she was ever likely to get, so Kat slipped into her room and drew the door silently shut, as if someone might hear and follow if she weren't secretive. She glanced at her window; the heavy winter curtains were drawn. *Safe*, she thought, lifting out the nightgown Marcie had given her. Then, feeling both daring and embarrassed, she quickly slipped her clothes off.

Once Olga was married, Kat had moved the dressing table with its pier glass into her own room. She pulled the garment over her head, walked on bare feet to the mirror, and, peeking in, gasped at what she saw. The bodice, what little there was, hugged the round curves of her breasts, and her nipples showed pink through the unlined white lace, which was caught below the breast by a band of blue ribbon. From there sheer white silk fell in folds, but through those folds her hips and legs and the triangle of curly hair were revealed, as if through a silken mist. It was a shocking gown, not something she could ever wear in front of Connor. She remembered her own horror when he had walked into that ranch house while she was bathing. No, Marcie was wrong to think that Kat, wearing such a garment, could display herself in front of a man.

But still Kat was mesmerized by her own reflection. She touched one breast, then drew her fingers away quickly and raised them to her hair, taking out the pins. The curls tumbled free, and the image in the mirror stared back, a wild, voluptuous woman like none *she'd* ever known. Certainly not like ordinary Kat who went to mass, ran the house, solved labor problems at the mines, married off her mother's protégées, and tried to stop people from ruining their lives with drink. Not Kat whose best friend was Sister Freddie and who had a taste for reading books about saints or about Colorado and who'd never even *known* that there were gowns which revealed a woman's nipples.

"Kat!"

She froze. Connor was home, and he sounded very irritated.

"Kat!"

But he didn't know she was here. She'd just keep quiet. Afraid to move or breathe, she stared at herself, wide-eyed, in the mirror.

"God damn it, I can't find a shirt," he shouted.

Always a blasphemer, she thought. His footsteps sounded in the corridor room, but her door was closed. He'd never come in, never see her in this disgraceful gown. And she'd never go back to West Breckenridge, she decided, not even to return the nightie.

"Kat!" His fist slammed against her door, and it flew open. Appalled, she watched him loom up in the mirror.

"I can't find the clean—" He stopped, his face stunned

335

as he caught sight of her reflection. "God in heaven what are you—where did you get that—" He couldn't seem to finish.

"They're in the basket in the kitchen," she whispered.

"What?"

"Choy delivered your shirts this morning." Her voice wavered.

Connor towered over her, still staring at her reflection. Marcie had said Kat should think about his body, that bodies were important. He was certainly looking at hers—as if he'd never seen her before. When he put his hands tentatively on her shoulders, she tried to edge away, but his fingers tightened, and the pressure of her arms, clinging protectively to her sides, deepened the exposed cleft between her breasts.

She heard him inhale sharply. Then, breathing out, he said, "My God, Kat," and turned her, holding her at arms' length, staring. His body was there for her to study too. He was wearing his long winter underwear, as all mining men did. It hugged every powerful muscle and outlined the tell-tale projection at his loins. She hadn't but a second to consider the significance of that before he stepped forward and wrapped his arms around her, leaning her back against the low edge of the dressing table. "You can't imagine how you look," he muttered.

But of course, she knew. She'd been looking at herself when he burst in. As if he could read her thoughts, he glanced over his shoulder at the open door, picked her up, and took her with him while he kicked it shut, after which she found herself pressed between Connor and the smooth, hard wood. "Where's Gretel?" he asked hoarsely.

"Choir practice," she whispered.

"We're alone." There was a note of wonder in his voice, and he lifted her until they were pressed hip to hip.

Kat trembled violently at the rush of heat that swelled from that intimate contact. She thought dazedly that he might thrust right through the thin silk of the gown.

"Missus." The voice sounded distant.

She had forgotten Diederick and looked up into Connor's eyes with confused dismay.

"Don't say a word," he whispered and pressed harder, holding her against the door with his hips while he slid a hand between them, fingers seeking her nipple.

"Missus."

Diederick had descended the ladder. She could tell that he was at first-floor level.

"Sh-sh-sh." Connor covered her mouth, squeezed the swollen bud of her breast between his thumb and forefinger. Her body jerked, and he thrust a knee between hers, reached down to fumble briefly, then pressed himself between her thighs with only the thin silk between his seeking manhood and her swollen hunger.

"I'm leaving," Diederick called.

Connor was rocking against her. Already lifted away from contact with the floor, she braced the bare soles of her feet against the door. Connor groaned against her mouth, mumbled something rueful about her beautiful dress. *Marcie's dress,* she thought, and didn't care. Because of Marcie, she'd been teasing him all week, and now she had her reaction—this volcanic passion that had erupted at one sight of her in a mirror. Wearing a whore's gown.

If she'd wanted to run, she couldn't have because Marcie's dress was so long. She'd have tangled her feet in the hem and fallen to her pursuer. Kat had no doubt that he'd have pursued. If she'd run. But she too was caught up in Marcie's snares. She too found the silken barrier between them unbearable.

"He's gone," said Connor harshly and dragged the silk up around her waist.

Kat had forgotten about Diederick. She could think only about Connor, who, like some demon lover, took her against the door with one deep thrust. The bursting heat spiraled inside her—up and up and up. He was like the Saracen captor she'd made up, but there'd be no knightly rescue. Connor, carrying her to the bed, still impaled, was captor and lover, sword and miracle, because inside her body he caused that irresistible, spiraling glory and death—even when he fell on top of her and she ached with the force of his lovemaking. Her head tossed, and she curled her fingers desperately around the bedposts to hold onto the rapture, to let it go on and on until she died of it. And when it ended at last, she was too dazed to speak or think or do anything but hold him tightly with eyes closed.

And I thought I wasn't in love, she marveled.

When she awoke it was dark, and late, and she was alone. What had he told the others when they got back from ordinary, everyday pursuits—choir practice, school? Kat didn't care. He'd tucked the covers around her. She was warm and content and, for once, she didn't care about appearances or daily responsibilities. She turned on her side, smiling, and drifted back into sleep.

"Reverend Mother says the bishop will arrive on the twenty-second," said Jeannie.

Kat nodded and smiled over her oatmeal.

"I'm sorry you were sick last night," said Jeannie. "We missed you at dinner."

So that's what he'd said. Very inventive.

"Minnie Brandt is taking the veil," Jeannie resumed, all atwitter. "That's why he's visiting."

Jeannie certainly seemed to have changed her attitude toward the bishop. On his last visit, the girl had fled to Findings' house, her unexplained absence precipitating Kat and Connor's first fall from grace. Kat smiled secretly at her oatmeal and took another spoonful. It tasted wonderful.

"Sister Freddie says he's ever so old and doesn't travel

much anymore, but he'll be here for the ceremony. Are we going to have a party for him?"

Kat nodded. She could see from under her lashes that Connor, in his usual place at the head of the table, was eyeing her seriously, as if she were an invalid newly risen from her sickbed.

"Can I invite Tommy?"

"Who's Tommy?" asked Connor.

"My beau."

"Why haven't I met him?" Connor had turned his attention from Kat to Jeannie, at whom he was frowning.

"Well, he's come to call three times, Daddy. You just weren't here. But Kat was," Jeannie added hastily.

When the breakfast group broke up, Connor pursued Kat into the corridor room and asked in an undertone, "Are you all right?"

Kat tipped her head and smiled into his eyes, thinking joyously, *He's mine. He'll never look at Eustacia Fleming again.* Connor's hand closed over her arm, and she winced because last night, in holding her against the door, he'd left bruises. Of course, simple jealousy of Eustacia Fleming didn't begin to cover the way Kat felt about him, she decided. She loved that hair burnished with its copper highlights, that rugged face, the solid, muscular body—especially that. Connor seemed very flustered.

"Damn it, Kat," he muttered. "Don't look at me like that."

Goodness, Marcie was certainly right about one's thoughts influencing one's lover.

"You're driving me crazy. You've been driving me crazy all year."

One's lover. What an exotic idea for a girl raised by Maeve and the sisters at St. Scholastica. Father Rhabanus was going to be appalled when she went to confession. First the fictitious saint's life. Now this.

"Sweetheart, are you sure you're all right?"

She nodded, thinking, *There probably won't be time for confession before the bishop arrives. First the party, then the wedding. Maybe the bishop can marry us. No, that would be too hurried. Like Mother's wedding. And Mother's baby is due in December. Maybe Connor will agree to a honeymoon in Denver so we can be with them for the arrival of our new sister or brother.* It occurred to Kat that the new baby wouldn't be much older than the children she and Connor might have. How bizarre! What was he saying? Good-bye obviously. He had leaned forward to kiss her, changed his mind, and tramped out.

Kat drifted happily back to her room. Men were so funny. And dear.

"I had the most peculiar visitor," said Reverend Mother after their discussion of the bishop's visit. "A woman named Babette called to ask me if there was a holy order that devoted itself to converting heathen Saracens. Can you imagine? Saracens no less!" Reverend Mother laughed as Kat experienced a rush of anxiety. "She said she was interested in joining."

"What did you say to her?"

"I said I knew of no such order, although she might consult the bishop when he comes on Friday."

Kat tried to imagine Babette and the bishop discussing the conversion of heathen Saracens.

"Then I advised her that if she was seriously contemplating life in a religious order, she would need to repent her sins and take a vow of chastity. She was, I assure you, a young woman no better than she should be. Such clothes!" Reverend Mother tut-tutted. "I don't think she'd realized chastity would be a requirement."

Poor Babette, thought Kat. *Her first impulse toward a better life—foiled by the thought of chastity.* Kat herself wasn't much interested in chastity these days. She hoped her friends at Marcie's would not be too disappointed when she didn't show up this week, but with the bishop's arrival, there simply wouldn't be time. She'd even had to give up campaigning for Broncho Dave. That was a shame with the election so close, but perhaps she could get in a few good words for him at the party.

Kat looked beautiful, her hair pulled up and back in some pretty arrangement of curls, loops and green ribbons, her dark green dress molding her breasts, cut square and low in front with a small white ruffle calling his eyes to the hint of cleavage. Connor shifted uncomfortably, unable to look away as she moved from one guest to another with a radiant smile. She reminded him of a Christmas present, temptingly wrapped and festive, with delights yet to be revealed. Every other male eye in the room followed her progress.

How had he got himself into this fix? A year ago his life had been all mapped out, and the map did not include marriage. Now he wanted nothing more than to wed Kat as quickly as possible lest someone take her away from him. He considered every man in the room a potential rival.

But what did Kat want? He had no idea. In her peculiar fashion, she was the most devout woman he'd ever known, yet she'd allowed him to make love to her three times. Allowed, hell! She'd participated with enthusiasm. Kat was wonderful! He wished he could drag her off to bed this instant, although no doubt she'd object.

Then he sobered, remembering the dismaying reality of his situation. Last January, as they made that disastrous train trip together, she had been quite clear about her feelings on remarriage—she'd been more adamant against it than he, and back then he'd had no doubt that romance was not for him. He'd changed his mind, but Kat had never said anything in the interim to indicate that she had changed hers, never hinted that she loved him or wanted to spend her life with him.

341

If he brought up marriage, she might laugh or be furious. He hadn't forgotten the time she'd hurled the bread dough in his face. The woman had a temper. And Connor couldn't bear the thought of her refusal. If he asked and she refused, she might move out. She might go to her mother in Denver or back to Chicago where he'd never see her again. In helpless frustration, he clenched his fists because he didn't know what to do.

And in the meantime, while he fretted, Kat was smiling at Abalone Wilson as if he were the most interesting man in the world. Could she be taken with Abalone because he had swung the jury in their favor? Surely she wouldn't fall in love with a man because he'd helped her win a lawsuit. Connor edged closer to them, trying to look as if he weren't pursuing her, and then, damn her, she moved on with a gay smile over her shoulder for lucky Abalone Wilson.

"Did you hear that Father Rhabanus is being sent to Boulder?" asked Sister Freddie.

Kat couldn't help but feel a bit relieved. Maybe she'd delay confession until after he left.

"And the bishop congratulated Reverend Mother because the school is doing so well—forty boarders, as well as the day students."

"What good news," said Kat. "I must write to Mother Luitgard Huber."

"And did you hear that I've been reprimanded for the temperance campaign?"

"By whom?"

"The bishop."

"That's outrageous!"

"Well, don't, for heaven's sake, talk to him about it," said Freddie quickly. "It wasn't that bad. He just said that women, especially nuns, shouldn't be interfering in such matters, that it wasn't proper."

"Well, of all the old-fashioned, uninformed—"

"Now hush, Kat." Freddie started to laugh. "Don't take on the bishop. The man must be eighty. He's not up to being reformed by you. You need an opponent who'll offer more spunk and less power."

"Like who?" asked Kat.

"How about Reverend Mother? The bishop's not liable to whack you with a ruler for being a newfangled woman, although he might excommunicate you for consorting with Methodists, but Reverend Mother—she's already offered to take the ruler to your backside."

They grinned at each other.

"Hello there, Diederick," said Kat. "Having a good time?"

Connor tried to edge away from Mrs. McNaught, who was telling him some tale about Jamie and her boy. Kat was smiling at Diederick now—that idiot carpenter. Connor couldn't stand him. He was always hanging around, staring at her. Didn't Kat notice that? She couldn't like Diederick! Who had those empty blue eyes and that messy yellow hair. Always up on some ladder peeking in a window.

But no, she wasn't stopping to talk to Diederick, whose face flushed with anger. What did the man expect? He was the carpenter, not part of the family. She was headed for the bishop. Connor breathed a sigh of relief. He thought it would be a fine idea if she spent the rest of the evening smiling at the bishop. A good man, Bishop Machebeuf. A little, wizened, *celibate* man.

"Some very interesting women have taken up social issues in Colorado," Kat told the bishop. She didn't see any harm in trying to modernize his opinions at least a little. "Take Mrs. Van Cott. She was here in Breckenridge just last year, holding religious meetings."

"She's a Methodist."

"Well, yes." Maybe the Widow Van Cott hadn't been the

343

best example. "And there was Susan B. Anthony. I've heard she drew huge crowds to her woman suffrage meetings in Lake City ten years ago. Men mostly, and they were very enthusiastic."

"Women should not have the vote," said the bishop.

"Why not?"

"God put women on earth to be wives and mothers."

"And nuns," Kat reminded him.

"Yes, that is a fine vocation for a woman. But voting? Absolutely not."

"I'll bet I can change your mind," said Kat slyly.

The bishop smiled at her. She was such a merry girl, and short, like him. He liked Kathleen Fitzgerald. The idea that she could change his mind was amusing, and an old man, even a bishop, didn't mind being amused by a pretty young woman, as long as she was a devout Catholic.

"What if the Holy Mother wanted to vote?" asked Kat.

The bishop smiled. "The Holy Mother is not here."

"All right," said Kat, not to be deterred. "What if—" She thought a moment, then asked, "What if, at the Second Coming, God sent his only begotten Daughter? Would you deny Her the vote?" Kat grinned triumphantly.

"Daughter? His only begotten *Daughter?*"

"Well, it was just a thought," said Kat hastily. The bishop looked positively apoplectic. She had a sudden vision of him dropping dead in her parlor. "Have a cookie, won't you, Bishop Machebeuf?"

"Daughter?"

"They're really quite delicious. Gretel makes them herself."

"That's heresy," said the bishop.

"If you'll excuse us, sir," said Connor, moving in and grasping Kat's arm firmly, "Kat is needed in the kitchen."

"Are you two still living together?" asked the bishop.

Connor whisked her away before she could answer.

344

"Daughter?" he asked and started to laugh as soon as he'd got her out of the room.

"I don't see what's so funny," said Kat.

"Did you really tell the bishop Jesus Christ was a woman?" asked Marcie.

"That just goes to show how gossip distorts what really happened," said Kat irritably. "I said no such thing."

"Then what did you say?"

Kat told her, and Marcella Webber laughed long and hard. "By God," she gasped at length, "I've got a real live anarchist coming to call."

"I'm no such thing."

"What did *he* say?"

"He said it was heresy." Kat began to giggle. "And Sister Freddie had just warned me he might excommunicate me for consorting with Methodists."

"I thought you weren't supposed to call her that."

"Do you know *everything* that goes on in Breckenridge?"

"Everything," Marcie assured her. "You can't so much as horrify an elderly bishop without my hearing about it. And I must say, I'm proud to be a fellow Chicagoan."

"You're from Chicago too?" asked Kat, delighted.

"I am, and don't get any ideas about marrying me off like the rest of them."

"Sister Freddie said exactly the same thing." Kat was feeling exhilarated. Now that all the hullabaloo of the bishop's visit was over, she expected Connor to find the opportunity to propose.

"Well, let's get down to business," said Marcie. "Have you been driving Connor crazy?"

"So he says," said Kat smugly.

"When was that?"

"The day after he made love to me."

Marcie looked astounded. "You mean he actually—"

"Yes, he did."

"But I haven't told you anything about that."

"We managed on our own."

"How was it?" Marcella was frowning.

"Wonderful!" said Kat enthusiastically. "Why don't you look more pleased?"

"Well, Kat, you don't seem to realize that sex doesn't always lead to marriage."

"Well, it wasn't just—sex," Kat protested.

"Unless you have a ring on your finger, that's all it is, and he can get that anywhere."

"B-but I thought—"

"Did he say he loves you?"

"No."

Marcie sighed. "How naive can you get? You should have waited until I told you exactly what to do."

"Like what? You just—just do it together."

"Well, Kat, there are ways and ways of—just doing it," said Marcie scornfully. "There are ways so that he wants to *keep* doing it. Why else are you coming to me? You don't just want to *get* him. You want to hang onto him."

"This wouldn't be anything—unnatural, would it? Like a mortal-sin type of thing?"

"For heaven sake, Kat. You're already guilty of fornication. Now we've got to get to work and be sure you're good at it."

Kat turned bright red.

"For instance, when he—"

They were interrupted by a terrible commotion—weeping and screaming beyond the closed parlor door.

Marcie jumped up with an exclamation and strode out with Kat at her heels. They found Birdie in the hall, shivering, dripping and sobbing, two men holding her limp body between them.

"She tried to drown herself, Miss Marcie," Babette explained.

"Where?" asked Kat.

"In the Blue," one of the men answered. He was gaping at Kat.

She paid him no mind. "There's only eighteen inches of water in the Blue," she pointed out. "Although I'll admit it's ice cold."

"Birdie isn't one to plan ahead. If she wants to do something, she just jumps in, as it were," said Marcella.

"Why *would* you do such a thing, Birdie?" Kat asked.

" 'Cause I realized there wasn't no troop of knights comin' to rescue me," said the weeping Birdie.

Kat rolled her eyes and told the men to carry Birdie upstairs. She climbed behind them, telling Birdie that suicide was a sin, and that she'd catch her death of cold, and that it was a good thing Kat had experience with pneumonia; she'd just take precautions before Birdie got it. "I'll need enough beer bottles to outline her body," Kat called to the downstairs maid.

"I'll have a beer," said one of the men who was carrying Birdie.

"That's just what Father Eusebius said," Kat muttered.

"Now I know you! You're that Roman Catholic woman who told the bishop God was female," said the second man.

"I said no such thing."

"What are you doin' here?"

"Good works," snapped Kat. *Nosy busybody,* she thought. She hoped he wasn't a gossip as well. "And lots of hot water to fill the beer bottles," she called over her shoulder. Marcie directed them to a room, a tiny little room with a bed, a chamber pot, and a few gaudy dresses hanging from pegs. It was so pathetic that Kat felt like weeping for poor Birdie.

Instead Kat said, knowing that sympathy wasn't what Birdie needed at this juncture, "I can't believe a Chicago girl would do such a thing. You're a discredit to your place of birth, Birdie."

Birdie sniffled and stammered that she was sorry.

One of the rescuers said, "Hell, ma'am, she's a whore. It ain't as if she knows any better."

"Watch your mouth," snapped Kat.

Chapter Twenty-Four

Marcie had been right; making love with a man did not prompt a marriage proposal. None had been forthcoming from Connor. Instead there was a strange waiting quality to him. What was he waiting for? Sean to come home, separate the households, and get Kat out of the way so Connor wouldn't suffer any more embarrassing, if momentary, passions for his friend's sister? Kat had just about given up hope, and she hated to go back to West Breckenridge, afraid that Marcie would say, "I told you so." Except for her inspirational mission, there wasn't any need to return. Marcie's lessons hadn't worked with Connor—not in the right way—and Kat certainly had no intention of pursuing another man—ever.

In the meantime, and in the face of her own disillusion, love was again flourishing in the house. Jeannie, only sixteen, seemed deeply involved with her young miner, who wasn't even Catholic. Of course, Jeannie wasn't actually a Catholic herself, but Kat had hopes for her.

She was doing wonderfully at St. Gertrude's, but if she married Protestant Tommy Weston, she'd never join the church. And she was too young to marry.

Besides, spending all her evenings chaperoning two young people who couldn't take their eyes off each other got on Kat's nerves. Their repressed passion quivered like heat lightning in the air of the parlor, making Kat want to burst into tears. She almost hugged Tommy with relief when he announced that he would be out of town for a week.

However, Tommy's absence gave her no respite because Gretel suddenly acquired a suitor—Gretel, who was supposed to marry Diederick, except that stupid Diederick wouldn't look at her. It would serve that custard-brained dolt right if he died a bachelor. Still, Tommy had no sooner left town than Kat's presence was required in the parlor to chaperone Gretel and Bas Mestre, a miner from the Too Late.

While those two sat making awkward conversation on either side of a table with a fringed, embroidered *green* cloth, Kat knitted and worried about Birdie at the Gentleman's Sporting Club. Her conscience told her that in missing her weekly visits she was letting Birdie down. What if Birdie tried to commit suicide again? She might find some more viable method than attempting to drown herself in eighteen inches of icy water. Then her immortal soul would be lost, and Kat would feel responsible.

"I sure do admire you, Miss Gretel," said Bas Mestre.

What could one do for a poor, fragile soul like Birdie? Kat wondered.

"You have my respect as well, Mr. Mestre," said Gretel.

Marriage would be a solution. Birdie evidently had some domestic skills. Marcie had mentioned that Birdie liked to take over on the cook's day off.

"I was talkin' about more than respect, Miss Gretel," said Bas.

"Please stop pulling at the tablecloth fringes, Mr. Mestre," said Kat. Goodness, the man was nervous.

"Yes, ma'am." Bas Mestre flushed a miserable red.

Kat sent him a forgiving smile and returned to her thoughts about Birdie. Marriage might be a good solution for Birdie, but who would want to marry her?

"Bein' as I'll be gittin' a considerable raise in salary," said Mr. Mestre, "I'm lookin' to marry. Figger I can afford a wife an' even some young 'uns."

Kat's attention sharpened. Gretel, however, didn't appear to be very excited about the impending proposal.

Mr. Mestre cleared his throat, looking twice as nervous, and said, "What I mean is, I'd like to marry you, Miss Gretel, and take you off to Leadville with me."

Gretel stared at him thoughtfully. "I don't love you, Mr. Mestre, so I—"

"Oh, that's all right," he interrupted quickly. "I don't mind. I'm looking for a wife is all."

"And there's your ears," Gretel continued, unperturbed by Mr. Mestre's unromantic marital requirements. "I just can't see spending the rest of my life with a man whose ears stick out the way yours do."

Mr. Mestre looked stricken, and the offending ears turned brick red.

"So thank you just the same." Gretel stood up, shook hands, and left him in the parlor looking crestfallen.

"Dang," said Mr. Mestre. "I sure did want to git married. My new job comes with a house, an' now I ain't got a wife to put in it. This is a real disappointment, bein' as you ain't got no more girls at this time. You wouldn't be expectin' any durin' the next week, would you, Miss Kat? I got but a week more in Summit County."

"How particular are you, Mr. Mestre?" asked Kat.

"Well, not too. Course, I wouldn't want no old woman. Nor one too ugly."

"Well, I might have a candidate. She's young and quite pretty."

Mr. Mestre brightened and tugged at one protruding ear. "Sounds good to me," he said. "She lookin' to marry?"

"Oh, I think she might be persuaded. There's just one problem," Kat murmured. "She's slightly used. But on the other hand, she can cook."

"Well, you cain't have everything," said Mr. Mestre when Kat had told him who and where the candidate was. "Ain't as if I'm stayin' in town where other fellers might make remarks to hurt my feelin's."

"Just what I thought," Kat agreed, and she invited him to meet her at Marcie's the next day. After he left, Kat trekked disconsolately to her room. Another marriage, and it wasn't hers. She didn't even know where Connor was.

Connor hadn't been at dinner last night. He hadn't been at breakfast this morning. Everyone assumed that he'd had to leave early. Kat wondered whether he'd been home to bed at all, but she could hardly ask. Instead she went to her own side of the house and snapped at Diederick, who was installing beautifully turned spindles to support the stair rail to the tower room, although he had yet to make the inside of the room habitable.

Then she shut her door and dressed for an outing which involved errands in town and the walk to West Breckenridge. She planned, for one thing, to choose wallpaper for her new room in the hope that Diederick might, during her lifetime, get around to hanging it. She had left him with his usual whipped-dog expression, which didn't make her feel nearly as guilty as it once had. He'd almost lost his chance to marry Gretel. Kat decided that she'd have to make a greater effort to get those two together. Gretel did seem to like Diederick, probably because his ears lay flat to his head.

Once warmly dressed, Kat braved the brisk November temperatures. It hadn't snowed again since August, but she assumed it soon would. Not today, however. The sky was clear and cold, like a sheet of blue ice. She was going to

Morgan's, which advertised that they had four thousand rolls of wallpaper in the "most magnificent patterns ever seen." However, when she began to cross the street to her destination, she changed her mind. With a heavy heart, she watched Connor holding the door for Eustacia Fleming, then following her into Morgan's. When a man and a woman looked at wallpaper together, even if the woman was married, Kat considered that a pretty intimate thing.

Maybe the beautiful Eustacia planned to divorce Mr. Fleming. There were whispers about him at the Sporting Club. Marcie had once said that she hated to see him at her door, that he was a cruel man with women. Kat shivered, remembering the leering contempt he had shown her during that visit to his office.

She turned sadly, stopped at Kaiser's butcher shop to put in an order and called at Finding's Hardware to look at a new supply of table lamps about which she had heard from Mrs. McNaught; they were handsome models with shades made up of stained-glass petals, and she ordered one for the corridor parlor. Then she bought a length of fine blue wool for Jeannie and delivered it to the dressmaker with a pattern, purchased from Watson's a cap Jamie had mentioned at the dinner table the other night, checked by Mr. Eli Fletcher's to arrange for repair of some slight damage to her skis—skiiing season would soon be upon them—and at last, having wiled away the time she would have spent looking at wallpaper samples, crossed the bridge to West Breckenridge.

Mr. Mestre awaited her on the porch of the Gentleman's Sporting Club, shifting from foot to foot, his mammoth ears red with cold. Kat hoped Birdie wouldn't be put off by them. Otherwise, he seemed to be a good enough fellow with excellent prospects.

"No gentlemen allowed in until afternoon," said Marcie severely when the maid had summoned her to the hall.

Kat whispered a quick explanation before Marcie could

turn away the now very nervous suitor.

"I might have known you couldn't leave my girls alone," muttered the madam, but she did send the maid for Birdie.

When Birdie came down the stairs in what Kat considered half a dress, Kat whispered, "Doesn't she have anything to wear that's—that's more appropriate to the occasion?"

Marcie's eyebrows rose sardonically. "If he marries her out of my house, he knows what he's getting. Why pretend otherwise? Anyway, he doesn't look offended."

Kat glanced at Bas Mestre, who was beaming as Marcella whispered into Birdie's ear. Eyes opening wide, Birdie looked at Mr. Mestre as if she had never seen a man before. "Why don't you two sit in the parlor and get acquainted," suggested Marcie. "Unless you want to chaperone them, Kat?"

Kat shot her a frown and headed for Marcie's apartment. "Well, you've been a stranger," Marcie remarked as she followed her through the door. "Don't tell me you've got married and I haven't heard about it."

Kat blinked back tears, remembering Connor's hand on Eustacia Fleming's arm as they entered Morgan's.

"Oh, oh. What happened?"

Kat told her.

"Well, not much can happen in a wallpaper store. I don't think you need worry."

"It's not funny. He had his hand on her arm."

"Has he made love to you again?"

Kat shook her head. She didn't want to talk about making love.

"Good. You want him to propose. Once he's done that, you can let him back into your bed."

"He's not going to propose."

"You don't know that. I think what you need is a romantic dinner for two. Candles, a low-cut dress that shows a lot of bosom. You did go to the dressmaker? Good. Get everyone out of the house and ply him with food, liquor, and cleavage.

Once he's full of good food, he'll think, 'Well, if I ask her to marry me, I can spend the rest of my life having wonderful meals across the table from a beautiful woman who'll let me make love to her afterwards.' That's the kind of misconception that makes a man propose."

Kat saw three immediate problems. First, arranging to be alone in the house would be almost impossible. Second, no one would propose to Kat on the strength of either her cooking or her cleavage. Third, unless the dining room was full of people generating body heat, it would be cold, and the cleavage Marcie had mentioned would be covered with unromantic goose-bumps.

"Now Kat, you don't want to give up, do you? You don't want to say, 'All right, Eustacia, he's all yours'?"

"No," Kat mumbled.

"Good. Now we get to the interesting part. Dinner's over—"

And he has indigestion, thought Kat.

"—he's been stunned by your beauty—"

Or else he's decided that I'm not nearly as pretty as Eustacia Fleming.

"—he's begged you to become his wife and you've agreed, after a suitable amount of demure hesitation—"

Kat thought that if Connor ever did propose, she wouldn't hesitate a second. She'd probably cut him off in mid-offer to say yes, only to discover that he'd been proposing that she fire that "damned Diederick," or that she get rid of the Turkey carpet that tripped him up when he came in late at night, or that she tell Jeannie that he wasn't having a new piano shipped over the mountain no matter how much talent Sister Whosis said Jeannie had.

"Then, if he really insists, you can make love again. Now here are some things you ought to know about."

Kat turned pink and suggested that, for propriety's sake, they look in on Birdie and Mr. Mestre.

"We'll talk about body-kissing first."

Body-kissing? Kat gulped.

"Have you ever thought about how many places you could kiss a man that he might like?"

"Of course I haven't."

"Well, think about it. Let's say you start by kissing him on the chest. Nipples are good. Many men like that. Some don't. For instance, it takes a lot to get an old man aroused. So if you used some of those tricks on a young man, think how it would affect him."

Kat stared at Marcie.

"You've kissed his nipples, and he seemed to like it. Maybe he groaned."

Kat glanced anxiously at the door.

"So you're encouraged. You continue kissing him, moving down—"

"Down?"

"Yes."

"Why not up?"

"You want this to be something he never forgets."

Kat knew that this would be a conversation *she'd* never forget. She must have been crazy to come here.

"You move down—slowly—to his navel. Linger there. He'll like that. In fact, you may get a pretty unmistakable reaction."

Kat thought she could guess at the reaction. "Shouldn't this sort of thing be—well, spontaneous?"

"Of course not." Marcie frowned at her. "Now, you're moving down from his navel. Use your tongue, and—"

"Is this going to get unsanitary?" Kat blurted out.

"Kat, we're talking about sex, not—"

A timid knock sounded and Kat, thinking, *Oh thank, God,* flew to the door to admit Birdie and Bas Mestre.

"Sissy," Marcella Webber whispered in Kat's ear as Mr. Mestre announced that he and Birdie were engaged and planned to marry immediately.

"And just a few weeks ago, I thought a knight would

356

never come for me," Birdie marveled. "I'll bet I'm happier than St. Genevieve when the crusaders rescued her from the Saracen."

Bas Mestre, who had never thought of himself as a knight, beamed at his prospective bride.

Marcie muttered to Kat, "I certainly never thought of myself as a Saracen."

The maid announced breakfast, and they had an impromptu engagement party, at which the other girls wept sentimental tears, made tasteless jokes about the state of matrimony, and asked Kat if she didn't have another saint's story to tell them. She told them about St. Denis, the first Bishop of Paris, who, having been martyred by having his head chopped off, picked up the head and walked six thousand steps to a place where he fell dead and was buried. The girls thought it was an amazing story. In fact, several didn't believe it could be true.

How ironic, thought Kat. They'd believed the made-up story about St. Genevieve, who had actually been a French saint—Kat had looked her up after attributing to her a completely bogus history—but they hadn't believed the real story of St. Denis and his miraculous, headless trek. *Well, at least I don't have to confess to another falsification of sacred history*, she thought.

Kat didn't give Marcie's intimate-dinner-for-two suggestion much thought because she knew she'd never find herself alone with Connor. Then, on Friday morning Jeannie mentioned that she had been invited to dinner at the McNaughts'. Kat would have been suspicious had she not known Tommy was gone. And tonight Gretel had choir practice, preceded by a covered-dish dinner. She'd be gone three hours, weather permitting. From November on, all plans included the proviso "weather-permitting." That left only Jamie.

357

Was Connor still seeing Eustacia Fleming? Was there any use in—

"Kat, can I spend the night with Bennie? Mrs. Fletcher invited me, and if you let me, I'll bring your skis home tomorrow morning," offered Jamie with an engaging grin.

"Well," said Kat, her heart beginning to pound, "it's Friday. No school tomorrow. I suppose—"

Jamie let out a whoop, dropped a kiss on her cheek— he and Kat had become good friends in recent months— and grabbed his book bag.

Jeannie called, "Wait for me, Jamie," and sped after him.

"Looks like my children have become interested in education," said Connor dryly. "Jamie mentioned the College of Mines the other day. I couldn't believe my ears."

Kat nodded, thinking of the dinner she would prepare.

"I have you to thank."

She looked up in surprise at the compliment.

"Why don't we just have something cold for dinner," he suggested. "Then you won't have to cook."

"That's very thoughtful of you, Connor," she murmured with a secret smile. She knew he was thinking cold leftovers would be more edible than anything she prepared.

"Promise now."

Kat nodded, her fingers crossed. She hadn't followed Marcie's advice about getting a dress, but she did have one with a collar and oval insert in front. If she hurried, she could take out the insert, sew in some lace edging—

"I have to go out to the Rose Laurel this morning, but I should be back by afternoon."

"Will you want a midday meal?"

"No, I'll eat at the mine dormitory."

As soon as Connor left, Kat raced to the store without even glancing at the sky. She got caught in a cold rain coming back and took shelter at St. Joseph's, getting a high-altitude cake recipe from Sister Angela Quinlan while she waited, shivering, in the hospital kitchen. When the rain showed no sign of abating, she borrowed an umbrella and ran all the way home, arriving with muddy boots, a wet hem, and a short temper.

"Why are you still messing around with that stairway?" she demanded of Diederick but didn't wait for his answer. She changed her clothes, rushed over to the stove on Connor's side and, with the utmost care, made Sister Angela's cake. It came out of the oven a jewel among cakes. *It's going to work,* she thought happily. *For once, I'm going to prepare a wonderful dinner, and he's going to propose, and we're going to live happily ever after.*

She heard Connor enter the house around two and quickly hid the cake in the cold box, which jutted through the back wall of the pantry to the outside. Perishables were kept there during the winter.

Connor came in dripping with a bundle under his arm and a grumpy look. "I thought I told you not to bother cooking." He had touched the cooling stove. "Stay away from the stove this afternoon, you hear."

"All right, Connor," she replied, smiling gaily.

"Sorry I snapped at you," he apologized. "You're looking pretty."

"Why, thank you." Kat was wearing an old dress, nothing like the one she had been slaving over for several hours. When a man told you you looked pretty for no reason at all, that was a good sign. Eustacia was always dressed up, yet he liked the way Kat looked in her old, ready-made house dress. She beamed at him and thought for a moment that he meant to kiss her.

"Missus." Diederick appeared at the door. Kat could have kicked him. "I'm gonna build you a vindow seat. You gotta tell me vat vindow." Kat was torn. She didn't want to leave Connor when he was in such a good mood, but on the other hand, the idea of a window seat in her tower room sounded wonderful. Someday, she and Connor could sit there together, looking toward the mountains, but if she left it to Diederick, he'd pick the wrong view. He'd have her looking at the smelter stack across the river, or the outhouse in the backyard.

"Go choose your window," said Connor good-humoredly. "I'll see you at six."

Kat nodded and sped off toward the new stairs. Connor was gone when she got back, but he'd built a low fire in the stove. How thoughtful. He must have been worried about her fixing a cold dinner in an unheated kitchen. Rather than taking any chances with untried recipes, Kat planned to make her mother's Irish stew and then put a pie crust on it and pop the pie in to brown just before Connor got home.

Consequently, she put together the stew and let it simmer all afternoon while she finished the dress, set the table with linen and pewter candlesticks, and made the pie dough. At four she sent Diederick home and had a bath, using a perfumed soap Sean had sent for Christmas two years ago. Then she dressed in the renovated, abbreviated dress and checked her stew and the cold box to see that the cake wasn't freezing. At five thirty she inspected her cleavage— no unromantic goose bumps, she was happy to note—and put up her hair in curls and matching ribbons as she had done the night of the bishop's party.

What a story that had become! Every few days someone stopped and asked her if she had really said this thing or that to the bishop, if he had really excommunicated her for heresy, if she would like to join their church—Methodist, Congregational, Episcopalian—as if she'd ever worship in the same room with the detestable Eustacia Fleming.

Five forty-five. She dashed to the kitchen, built up the fire in the stove, put the final touches on the table and, when she heard Connor at the door, balanced her meat pie in one hand while she opened the stove door with the other.

"Kat?"

She slid the pie in, giving it a good shove.

"Right here," she called and, flushed from the warming oven, started for the kitchen door before he could come in and discover that she had cooked him a special dinner.

The force of the explosion hit her in the back and blew her into the dining room. Connor rushed in from the corridor room to find her dazed and trying to rise. "Damn!" he swore and picked her up, his face white with fear. "Are you all right?"

Kat tried to nod. She was trembling all over and didn't know what had happened in the kitchen. She didn't even want to look. Had the butcher or the grocer sold her something else with bullets in it? Had they spoiled her dinner and all her plans? Tears welled in her eyes. "If they'd just close the saloons, things like this wouldn't happen," she said, lower lip trembling.

Connor looked at the kitchen door, half off its hinges. He could see part of the stove, now misshapen, door hanging open, tilted to the side. The only good news was that the house wasn't on fire. "Did you mess with that stove when you promised you wouldn't?"

"It was going to be a surprise," said Kat, tears falling faster, "but the meat pie must have blown up."

"The dynamite blew up," said Connor.

"What dynamite?" gasped Kat.

"The dynamite I put in there to dry out."

"You put dynamite in my stove?"

"It's perfectly safe with a low fire, unless some fool comes along, after promising, and throws more wood—"

"You blew up my meat pie and ruined the dinner I planned just for you!"

Connor had never seen so many tears in his life. They were running down her face and dripping onto—he noticed for the first time the fetching sight of her low-necked dress. Connor swallowed hard, realizing that finally she'd been

361

ready to give him the signal he'd been waiting so long to get, and he'd ruined it by drying out dynamite in the kitchen stove. She'd never forgive him. He might have killed her. If she'd been standing in front of that stove when it blew . . .

Kat had turned away from him. "There's meat and gravy all over the walls," she sobbed.

"And we'll just leave it," said Connor soothingly. "I'm so sorry I ruined your surprise."

"We can't leave it. It'll dry and—"

"We pay Gretel to take care of that stuff. Come on, I'll take you to dinner at Barney Ford's. We'll have your favorite, chops with mashed potatoes and gravy."

Kat sniffed. It sounded tasty, and she'd forgotten to eat at midday. But he wouldn't be proposing at Barney Ford's while a bunch of hungry miners and businessmen slurped up food and shouted at one another.

"Come on, sweetheart." Connor put his arm around her waist, noticing with a sinking heart that the back of her skirt was in rags. "You can change your clothes, and we'll walk downtown."

Kat looked at him, then over her shoulder at the dress, and began to cry again.

"It was a beautiful dress," he assured her. "You look like a—like a storybook princess."

Kat felt even worse, because she had to change into something he saw all the time, and she wouldn't look like a princess any longer. But she changed, and they walked to town and had a delicious dinner, and Connor was so sweet to her that she began to hope again. Not for tonight. Gretel would be home when they returned. And Jeannie. "Maybe we ought to stop by the McNaughts' and walk Jeannie home—save one of the McNaught boys the trouble."

"She's not at the McNaughts'," said Connor.

"But she said she was going there for dinner," said Kat, "right from school."

"I stopped there to return some tools Fred lent me. They were having dinner, and she wasn't there."

"But I—" Kat felt dismay sweep over her. "I thought it was safe to let her go since Tommy was out of town."

"What does that mean? Why wouldn't you let her go if he were in town?"

"Because she lied to me before," Kat admitted in a tiny voice. "She said she was going to the Findings', and I caught her with him."

"And you didn't tell me? You let them keep company?"

"Well, I—I chaperoned them, Connor. I saw to it that they were never alone."

"Why the hell didn't you tell me?"

"She's only sixteen."

"Exactly."

"I thought she'd get tired of him."

Connor sprinted toward French Street and his house, leaving Kat behind, taking with him their umbrella. By the time she got home, wet clean through, her boots squelching where she had splashed through puddles in her hurry to follow, he was reading the note he had found in Jeannie's room.

"They've eloped," he announced ominously.

"We'll catch up with them."

"How?" he snapped. "They took the morning train to Denver. They could have got off anywhere along the line. If not, they're almost there, and no way in hell can we catch up before they marry. And you let it happen."

"Miss Kat?" asked Gretel timidly, having come in when she heard voices. "What happened in the kitchen?"

"She blew up the stove," said Connor grimly.

"I wasn't the one who put dynamite in it," retorted Kat. She felt terrible about Jeannie, but she didn't see why she should take all the blame. "And I'm not the one who told all the lies. Jeannie did. Maybe if you'd got married instead of selfishly ignoring your children and leaving their upbringing to an old reprobate who never sets foot in church, maybe this wouldn't have happened. You're every bit as culpable as I am, Connor Macleod, so don't you blame me."

Gretel was gaping at them. Connor was struck dumb in the face of Kat's attack.

"What should I do about the kitchen?" Gretel whispered.

"Ask Mr. Dynamite here," said Kat. "I'm going to bed."

Chapter Twenty-Five

Connor had taken the morning train to Denver in an effort to catch up with Jeannie. Kat, feeling very blue, decided to visit Sister Freddie for comfort and a good cry. *You plan a romantic dinner, and what happens?* she asked herself as she trudged along. *Stew all over the kitchen walls, the back of your skirt and even your petticoat in rags, the object of your affections blaming you for the explosion and his daughter's clandestine marriage. What's the use?* Maybe the anticipated proposal had been a case of wishful thinking. After all, neither of them believed in romance, so why had she been trying for the impossible?

Kat felt guilty about Jeannie. She hadn't set a very good example for the girl—living with her father, falling in love with him. Kat sighed, knocked on the door to St. Gertrude's, and asked for her friend. Instead she got Reverend Mother Hilda Walzen, scowling ominously with a copy of the *Summit County Journal* in her hand.

"I don't know why you read that, Reverend Mother," said Kat, following her into the office as ordered. "Colonel Fincher is a mean-spirited man."

"So you've read this week's edition."

"Indeed, I haven't. Since Colonel Fincher attacked my temperance campaign, I read only Mr. Hardy and the *Leader*."

"In that case you'd better look at this article, and then explain to me what you were doing in West Breckenridge at a house of ill repute."

Kat's eyes widened, and she took the paper from Reverend Mother. As she read, her anxiety turned to anger. Colonel Fincher stated that a certain scandalous rumor had come to his attention when a busybody lady, who thought herself qualified to interfere with the behavior of others, had been seen in a brothel on the west side of the Blue. Suspecting that such a story about a woman of well-known religious conviction, if little sense, might be false, he had ignored the rumor. Now, however, another such occurrence had been reported by a citizen of impeccable stature. What would a lady be doing in such a place? asked Colonel Fincher. Moreover, on two occasions. The colonel suggested that people who set themselves up as moral arbiters should examine their own conduct before passing judgment on that of others.

"Is this story true, Kathleen?" asked Reverend Mother.

"Well, I was there," said Kat. "He just didn't bother to find out why. And what citizen of impeccable stature would know about the Gentleman's Sporting Club?"

"Kathleen, have you no concept of how much damage this story will do your reputation?"

"Certainly," said Kat, "and I shall deal with the slanderer first thing."

"And create a greater scandal. He says you entered this house with a man."

"Oh, goodness, that was Mr. Mestre," said Kat. "He was

looking for a wife, and Gretel wouldn't have him because of his ears. On the other hand, Birdie, poor thing, had tried to drown herself and would have succeeded and ended up in hell if there'd been any water to speak of in the river. I just saw the opportunity and got them together." Kat folded her hands in her lap and smiled at Reverend Mother.

"Now Mr. Mestre has a wife who thinks he's a wonderful man instead of a jug-eared undesirable, and Birdie can repent her sins and have a respectable married life. She's promised to go to church in Aspen. What could be better?"

Reverend Mother looked quite taken aback. "You're a continuing source of amazement to me, Kathleen. I do believe in the redemption of lost souls. Was that Birdie person some project of yours? I remember now that you borrowed a book of saints' lives."

"Of course," said Kat. "The lives of saints were a source of comfort and inspiration to Birdie and her colleagues. I told them about the life of St. Denis the last time I visited. And St. Genevieve the time before." Kat didn't mention the revision in the life of St. Genevieve.

"Any particular reason you're choosing French saints?" asked the bewildered Mother Superior.

"Well, our bishop is French," said Kat.

"Oh, yes. Poor Bishop Machebeuf must still be in shock if the reports of your conversation with him are true. I hope you're not telling those poor souls across the river that they should work for woman suffrage because it's the wish of the Blessed Virgin."

"I've hardly mentioned woman suffrage to them."

"Well, I'm sure you meant well, Kathleen, but I hardly know what to advise you in this matter and must pray to the Blessed Virgin for guidance."

"I will too," said Kat. *But first I'll pay a call on Colonel Fincher.* Kat knew how slanderous editors were treated west of the Mississippi. She went straight home and got her horsewhip. By the time she had reached the *Journal* offices on Main between Lincoln and Wellington, she had accumulated quite a following of people who had read the newspaper.

I shall be very dignified and formal, thought Kat. *I shan't scream at him, but on the other hand, I shan't make any wishy-washy, ladylike attempt to disguise my indignation.*

"So, sir," she said, flinging the door open and flourishing her whip, "you have seen fit to slander a woman for doing her Christian duty."

"Eh?" Colonel Fincher looked up from his desk.

"I intend to horsewhip you, Colonel," said Kat. "You probably think I don't know how these things are handled, but I am well acquainted with Colorado history."

Two of the colonel's three daughters, all of whom helped him publish the paper, looked alarmed. It wouldn't be the first time their father had been attacked by an irate reader, but never a woman. How he could defend himself? The third daughter was grinning.

"However, as a peaceable Christian woman," Kat continued, "I shall give you a chance to apologize by telling you that had you bothered to inquire, you would have found out that I was visiting the Gentleman's Sporting Club for inspirational purposes."

"And were you inspired, madam?" asked the colonel.

"Your humor is misplaced and ungentlemanly, Colonel Fincher," said Kat. "I have been so far successful that one of the young women is now married and living a respectable life. Can you say that your scurrilous newspaper has ever achieved as much? You can't even get the holes in the streets filled."

Kat heard a cheer from the street. Perhaps public opinion was with her. "And now I intend to horsewhip you—unless, of course, you would like to solicit my sympathy for an elderly person such as yourself by telling me just what so-called citizen of stature told you such a misleading tale."

"Medford Fleming," said one of the daughters. "I told you you shouldn't believe him, Father."

"Irresponsible journalism at its worst," said Kat. "You'd take the word of a man who cuts mine cables, who pays villains to drown innocent miners, who sets fire to private houses—and who, incidentally, has a reputation for violence even among the very women with whom you have accused me of consorting. I can't imagine what you thought I was doing there if it wasn't good works."

"I'll write an apology in next week's paper myself," said the tallest of the daughters.

"The devil you will," cried Colonel Fincher.

"What are you going to do, Daddy, if she horsewhips you? Punch her in the nose?" asked the middle daughter.

"If we're not allowed to write the story, we'll go out on strike," said a third daughter. "And you know that with your rheumatism, you can't run the press by yourself, Papa."

"Women can always be trusted to do the decent thing," said Kat, relieved that she didn't have to horsewhip an old man with rheumatism.

"Did you find her?" Kat felt awkward with him, the memory of their anger and her dashed hopes still fresh in her mind.

"Not a trace."

Connor looked so tired that she felt a pang of sympathy, even though he had treated her so unfairly.

"They got on the D.S.P.& P. at the edge of town, but no one saw them get off. I asked at every station and siding from here to Denver."

Kat sighed. "I do believe they will have married." *I sound as if I don't care, as if we're strangers.*

"They probably did, but look at what it got the two of us, marrying that young."

So he was back to that, Kat thought sadly. More proof

that he'd never intended to propose.

"I heard a story I could hardly credit when I got in," he continued. "Were you really seen over at Marcie's place?"

Kat nodded, too dispirited to care what he made of that tale.

"What the hell were you doing there?"

"My Christian duty," she replied. *Wasting my time as far as you're concerned,* she added silently.

"Only you would decide that it was your Christian duty to visit Marcie's," he remarked while taking off his coat. "Well, I'm going to bed. Maybe after I've got some sleep, I'll go over and horsewhip Jonathan Cooper Fincher for you. He should have known better than to think you'd be doing anything at Marcie's but pursuing some crackpot crusade."

Kat, although touched by his offer to discipline the choleric editor of the *Journal,* didn't care for being called a crackpot crusader. "Thank you, Connor," she said politely, "but you needn't bother. I threatened to horsewhip him myself. His daughters, who are very sensible women, will be printing the apology next week."

"Completely self-sufficient, aren't you?" said Connor and turned toward his room.

What did he mean by that? Kat wondered. He'd sounded almost sad.

The streets of Breckenridge were covered with snow once more. Six inches had fallen overnight and then frozen hard toward morning. *Winter's here again,* thought Kat as she got out her newly repaired snow-shoes. These were shorter than the ones on which she'd skied down from Boreas Pass last January, made especially for her by the king of snow-shoes, Eli Fletcher. She carried them down the steps, poked her boots in between the block and the strap and pushed off into French Street.

Connor was still asleep, and Kat was off to employ

Charlie Maxell. She made it safely to Washington and slid downhill toward Main at an exhilarating pace, waving to friends and calling out greetings as she went. *What a lovely morning,* she thought. *All crisp and white!* The mountain tops were heavy with snow, and white cushions padded the branches of the evergreens in front of Barney Ford's house. She waved to Julia, who was sweeping snow off her steps. *I'll have to find another Negro girl for Julia,* Kat decided. Barney had said the night the stove blew up that Julia was very short of breath these days.

Kat used her pole to steer around a cluster of little boys throwing snowballs. In doing so, she slid into the mayor of Breckenridge, knocking him and herself flat. As they picked themselves up, Kat made it to her feet first and gave the mayor a hand. "You should watch where you're going, young lady," he said angrily.

"It was just last summer that you told me what terrible riders ladies are," she replied. "Don't you remember? When my horse fell in one of your potholes? Well, you can hardly expect us to be better snow-shoers than we are riders. If I were you, I'd stay off the streets when you see a lady on snow-shoes." Having got her own back on the mayor, she pushed off again and made her way safely to Charlie's office without knocking over any other citizens.

Charlie Maxell told his wife Olga that night that he'd be able to give her the sofa she coveted. He'd had a flurry of business that day. Kat Fitzgerald had come in with two legal problems. First, she had asked his advice about running for a vacant position on the school board. Charlie had felt honor bound to tell her that, as a woman and a Catholic, she had little chance of winning. To his knowledge, Breckenridge had never voted a woman onto the board, and people hadn't forgotten that Bishop Machebeuf had wanted state money for Catholic schools and had been defeated soundly. "Folks will say that your children—well, Connor's and Sean's—

don't go to the public schools, so why should you have a say in their running?"

"Of course, she didn't listen to me," he told Olga. "And even worse, she wants to sue Medford Fleming for slander. Seems the information for that piece in the *Journal* came from him."

"You'll be famous," said Olga.

"Who'm I goin' to get to testify? Miss Marcie? Her girls? This is going to cause a terrible scandal, and Kat's a Roman Catholic. The jury's bound to be mostly Protestant and all men, who don't want the whores reformed any more than they want the saloons closed."

"Charlie Maxell!" exclaimed Olga. Then she got a dreamy look in her eye. "I'm going to have the finest parlor in town when I get my new sofa."

"And Connor now wants instant payment from Medford Fleming. He says either he gets the money by next Friday or we go back to court."

"Wonderful," said Olga. "We'll be able to buy the matching armchair."

Kat had decided to give Diederick a last chance to fall for Gretel. When Gretel admitted that she thought the carpenter handsome, Kat invited him to tea. As she told Connor a week later, when they had reestablished friendly, if somewhat wary, relations, "The tea party was wonderfully successful. Both Diederick and Gretel were downright animated. I'm sure they're falling in love."

"You're getting more successful at this marriage business all the time," Connor remarked.

Kat's spirits plunged. She might be successful with Mother's girls, but she hadn't been able to do anything for herself. "Diederick has to be in love," she continued with less enthusiasm. "Ever since I invited him to tea, he's been a whirlwind of activity, putting in the leaded windows, hanging wallpaper."

"Tacking up more scrollwork on that tower," Connor muttered. "Three women have stopped me to complain that you're monopolizing the only carpenter in town who'll do that kind of work. Elias Nashold certainly won't."

"I know," said Kat uneasily. Somehow or other Elias Nashold's structures always looked tasteful, but one couldn't help feeling that Diederick put up one piece of decoration too many, sometimes even four or five too many. "Well, he should be through before Christmas, and then he can get married and go to work for someone else."

"That sounds good. You realize, don't you, that this could turn out to be a great waste of money? I've already had to sell off two mines. If any more play out or turn unprofitable, which could happen the way the silver market is, we'd have to sell the house and move."

"Really? You mean to another town?"

"That's right." Connor watched her closely, knowing that women hated instability. Rose Laurel had forced him to stay in Sts. John long after he should have moved on.

"That sounds exciting," said Kat. "Where?"

"Wherever the next strike is. I listen for rumors, look at the area when something sounds good, maybe grubstake someone or buy a claim. It's a hedge against the future."

"I had no idea," said Kat. "Wouldn't that be fun—going to a new place? Starting a whole new enterprise?"

Kat went away hugging herself with relief. She didn't mind moving if Connor planned to take her with him, and he'd said *we*. Perhaps there was hope for them after all.

Connor marveled at her adventurous spirit. She would be just the woman for him if she'd only get over her unwarranted prejudice against marriage. But her attitude was exceedingly unconventional. She had been ready to move to another town with him, yet she showed no interest in marriage. Did she imagine they'd live together for the rest of their lives, unmarried? Maybe making love once or twice a year? He couldn't think of a respectable woman anywhere who'd contemplate such a future with equanimity.

Kat knew that Charlie worried about their chances in court because the jury was solidly Protestant except for one Roman Catholic who was known to spend his Sundays in saloons rather than churches. Kat's view was that if she didn't win, she'd at least get a chance to defend herself against the rumors that were flying. The courtroom was packed. Connor and Jamie were there, Gretel and Diederick, and most touching, Jeannie and her new husband had come from Aspen to lend their support. Kat felt quite optimistic even if her lawyer didn't.

And she was wearing a favorite dress—gray, green and white plaid moire silk with a handkerchief overskirt that fitted in points over a pleated underskirt. She'd chosen it in a spirit of defiance, imagining that Eustacia Fleming would appear in the very latest fashion. Kat's dress was four years old, but becoming nonetheless. She felt that she was making a statement against women who were slaves to every new fashion fad that came along. Also, the judge had been so prompt in setting a trial date that there'd been no time to acquire a new dress.

Medford Fleming's attorney told the judge that his client considered the suit frivolous. "Mr. Fleming himself saw the plaintiff leaving the premises of said house of prostitution, and an employee of his mentioned to him that Mrs. Fitzgerald had been on the premises a week or so earlier. Mr. Fleming simply mentioned these circumstances to Colonel Fincher in casual conversation. The colonel chose to write about them in his newspaper. Consequently, the suit is misdirected. If Mrs. Fitzgerald wants to sue, it should be the newspaper."

One of Colonel Fincher's daughters, who was sitting behind Kat and Charlie, covering the trial for the *Journal*, bristled, leaned forward, and whispered loudly, "Call me, Charlie. I'll testify for Kat."

The judge glared at her and said to Fleming's lawyer, "Where is your client?"

"Mr. Fleming is a busy man. He did not feel that his presence was necessary since his lack of culpability is obvious."

A mutter of disappointment ran through the crowd. Kat, glancing around, discovered that Eustacia was absent as well. The judge refused to throw the case out and told Charlie to call his first witness. Charlie, after a hurried conference, called Miss Fincher, who said Mr. Fleming had more than just mentioned the matter to her father; he'd made it sound as if Kat were working at the Gentleman's Sporting Club. Everyone gasped. "I told Papa that was silly, but he was still mad about the saloon business. Anyway, we've printed an apology."

"Is it true, Miss Fincher, that Mrs. Fitzgerald threatened to horsewhip your poor old father?" asked Fleming's lawyer.

"Poor old father!" Colonel Fincher could be heard rumbling angrily from back in the crowd.

Miss Fincher chuckled and said, "Wouldn't that have been a sight? She's no bigger than a minute."

The lawyer cleared his throat and raised his voice, "So one might say that the apology was coerced?"

"Don't be silly," said Miss Fincher. "My sisters and I wrote the apology, and we weren't coerced. There's not a one of us who isn't a full head taller than little Mrs. Fitzgerald. And Papa's not afraid of anyone. The whole town knows that, even if you don't."

Babette had been chosen to represent the Sporting Club contingent, her grammar adjudged the best in the house except for Marcie's. Of course, Marcie couldn't testify because she knew what Kat's initial motivation had been. However, when Kat got her first look at Babette's idea of a gown suitable for a court appearance, she had second thoughts about her witness. The outfit had a low, square neckline that caused several jurors to lean forward for a closer look. The gown was a bright yellow silk, and the skirt featured wide bands of bright blue ruching that matched a blue hat with huge yellow feathers. Kat sighed as, with a glowing smile, Babette took the witness stand and began to answer Charlie's questions.

"It was ever so much fun having her come to visit," said Babette enthusiastically. "She gives a really good prayer, like asking God to look out for all us women who have such a hard time of it, and if you don't think working in a sporting house is having a hard time, you don't know anything. We all want to run and hide when Mr. Fleming comes to call. He's mean." She nodded flirtatiously to the jury, causing all those yellow feathers to wave and flutter.

"Your honor," cried Fleming's lawyer. "I will not have my client defamed by a person of this ilk."

"Elk?" cried Babette. "I'm no elk. I'm not fat at all, just nicely rounded." She ran her hands over her tightly corseted waist. "Ask my customers if you don't—"

"Oh, pipe down, both of you," snapped the judge. "You want to ask this witness anything else, Maxell?"

"She wasn't finished testifying, your honor."

Charlie, Kat noticed with amusement, was very embarrassed to be questioning a lady of the night, but the jurors were wide awake. There had, in fact, been competition to be included on the jury.

"Anyway," said Babette, tilting her nose in the air as a snub to the lawyer she thought had insulted her figure, "Miz Fitzgerald not only gave fine prayers, but she told us all about St. Denis, who walked six hundred steps carrying his chopped-off head. Now if that isn't a miracle, I don't know what is. And the best one was St. Genevieve, who was a lady of my profession and was kidnapped by a heathen Saracen, but she wouldn't have anything professional to do with him, so he was going to chop off her head. Then St. Genevieve was rescued by a horde of Christian knights, and after that she lived a virtuous life, converting heathens and such. We all found that pretty inspiring, I can tell you," Babette confided. "Old Meddie Fleming ought to be ashamed of himself, saying bad things about Miz Fitzgerald. Not many Christian ladies care what happens to girls like us, but she did. I think that's real nice."

Charlie thanked Babette for her testimony.

Fleming's lawyer rose and said, "Mrs. Fitzgerald's visits seem to have had little effect on you, Miss—ah—"

"Babette," said Babette helpfully. "Hey, I went over to see the nuns' madam. I thought maybe if there was a house that converted Saracens I might join up, but she said I'd have to repent my sins and take a vow of chastity first and she didn't know of any places like that anyway. But I'm aware of the Saracen problem now. If a Saracen comes to Miss Marcie's, I, for one, won't take his money, and I'm sure the other girls feel just the same."

"Admirable," said the lawyer sarcastically. "Would you say the reformation of—ah, soiled doves would require Mrs. Fitzgerald to go upstairs at the Gentleman's Sporting Club? Just answer yes or no, please."

"No," said Babette sullenly.

"Yet Mrs. Fitzgerald did go upstairs on at least one occasion, didn't she?"

"Yes, but—"

"It is basically upstairs where business is conducted, isn't that so?"

"Yes, but—"

"And Mrs. Fitzgerald was upstairs, was she not?"

"Yes, but—"

"Thank you, Miss Babette."

Shocked whispers filled the courtroom as Kat took the stand. "Mrs. Fitzgerald, did you in fact go upstairs at the Gentleman's Sporting Club?" asked Charlie.

"Certainly," said Kat. "When Birdie tried to drown herself, I assumed that she'd catch pneumonia, so I had them carry her upstairs. My mother always says, 'An ounce of prevention in matters of health is worth a pound of cure.'"

Various ladies in the audience nodded at that well-accepted piece of wisdom.

"So I used the beer bottle treatment, which I first heard of here in Breckenridge. I got Father Eusebius well with that treatment when he had pneumonia, and I do believe that it kept Birdie from becoming seriously ill."

"You women stop that talking," shouted the judge, since various ladies in the audience were discussing the innovative idea of applying the beer-bottle treatment before the patient fell ill.

"Then seeing that Birdie's soul was in jeopardy—suicide being a mortal sin—I found her a good husband. She's now happily married and living a virtuous life elsewhere. Mr. Fleming's lawyer was being sarcastic about my efforts across the river, but I call that success."

"Weren't you aware when you took up this cause, Mrs. Fitzgerald, that you were putting your reputation in danger?" asked Charlie.

"Certainly," said Kat, "and if I hadn't thought of it, Mrs. Marcella Webber, who owns the Gentleman's Sporting Club, told me so."

"Then why did you do it?"

"When I feel that something needs doing," said Kat, "I do it." She sighed, remembering her futile hope of winning Connor. "It doesn't always work out, of course, but that doesn't mean we shouldn't try. Which reminds me—" She now addressed the spectators. "I'm running for the school board, and I hope you'll all vote for me. Being as everyone on the board's Protestant, I feel that I would bring a unique experience to public education, having myself been educated by the Benedictine sisters in Chicago. Those are the sisters who do such a fine job here in Breckenridge at St. Joseph's and St. Gertrude's. I'm sure Reverend Mother Hilda would be glad to advise me, should I—"

"Look here, Miz Fitzgerald," the judge interrupted, "you're supposed to be testifyin' in this case, not makin' a campaign speech."

"Well, I just thought, since everyone is here, that I'd add a few words about my candidacy," said Kat. Then she smiled at the crowd and said, "Thank you for your attention."

"Just what I always say," muttered the judge. "Women got no place in a courtroom."

Kat turned to the opposing lawyer. "Did you want to ask me anything? I don't think Charlie has any more questions."

The lawyer, who was still trying to assimilate the fact that the plaintiff had used the witness stand to campaign for a position on the school board, looked confused and mumbled, "What can one say to a woman who doesn't care about her own reputation?"

"I think you do the people of Breckenridge an injustice," said Kat. "I'm sure my fellow citizens understand that I was simply doing my Christian duty—as my mother taught me to. She runs boarding houses in Chicago for working girls, you know. To see that they have a good home environment and proper chaperoning when they're all by themselves in the big city."

"Your honor, I didn't ask her anything about her mother."

"I consider my efforts here in Breckenridge an extension of my mother's work."

"I haven't asked her anything at all."

"Why, several of the women at the Gentlemen's Sporting Club are from Chicago. Birdie was, and my mother was delighted to hear of her marriage. Mother believes that marriage is—"

"Be quiet, Mrs. Fitzgerald," the judge snapped.

"Well, really," said several ladies in the audience, while others said, "Did you hear that?" and "That was certainly rude." Kat was happy to note the support of the Methodist Ladies' Aid Society and the Ladies' Altar Cloth Society. Too bad they weren't on the jury.

"Quiet!" roared the judge, so angry that he refused to let the lawyers make closing speeches. He sent the jury out immediately. They stayed long enough to smoke a cigar each, provided by Medford Fleming's lawyer, then returned a verdict for Kat in the amount of three hundred dollars.

She later discovered, as she was accepting the congratulations of various well-wishers, that the wives of jurors had instructed their husbands to vote for Kat, who was probably the only woman in town who had thought of a way to close down the houses of prostitution.

"Marry them off, and send them out of town; that's the way to do it," said a woman Kat had never met. "Keep up the good work, Mrs. Fitzgerald."

Kat supposed she'd have to.

Also, the Protestants were intrigued with the stories about her confrontation with the bishop. She was asked numerous questions about what she had really said.

"I just said *if*," Kat insisted. "*If* the Blessed Virgin wanted to vote, *if* the Second Coming was God's only begotten Daughter."

The real story caused a greater scandal than the rumors. Kat realized that, had she been Protestant and said such things, she'd probably have been ostracized, but as a Roman Catholic, which all the Protestants thought a bizarre religion anyway, she was simply considered a fascinating eccentric. Kat didn't consider herself an eccentric. Why shouldn't God have a daughter? He could do anything he wanted. Including seeing that the jury awarded her three hundred dollars of Medford Fleming's money.

"You're certainly looking smug," Connor murmured as they walked home.

"I'm thinking of how angry Fleming will be when he discovers that he has to pay me three hundred dollars," she replied gleefully.

Chapter Twenty-Six

"And I can support her, Mr. Macleod," said Jeannie's new husband. "I have a job selling mining supplies, and I'm doing some prospecting around Aspen."

"We have a room at a boarding house for now, but we're looking for a house to rent," said Jeannie.

"That's what I'll do with my three hundred dollars from the lawsuit," said Kat. "You can use it to set up housekeeping."

"Fine," said Connor, his voice heavy with sarcasm. "My sixteen-year-old-daughter runs off, sends me traipsing all over the countryside looking for her—"

"Did you go to Denver?" Jeannie started to giggle.

Connor scowled. "Then Kat, who never bothered to mention that you'd been seeing him secretly, wants to reward you for running away by giving you three hundred dollars. Your mother and I never had any three hundred dollars to—"

"Oh, all right, Daddy, if you want me living in a cold,

382

drafty room—if that will make you feel better—"

"He doesn't want any such thing," exclaimed Kat.

"How do you know?" Connor muttered.

"Daddy doesn't know what he wants, Kat. If he did, he'd marry you instead of acting grumpy all the time because everyone else in town is proposing to you and he's too stubborn to do it."

The room went still, Kat waiting for Connor to deny any marital aspirations. She couldn't even look at him.

"What makes you think she'd have me?" Connor mumbled.

"Of course, she would. You're in love with Daddy, aren't you, Kat?"

Kat flushed and looked down at her hands. She was sure Jeannie meant well, but Kat had never been more embarrassed in her life.

"You shouldn't interfere in adult affairs," Connor said gruffly.

"Why not? I'm a married woman. Goodness, Daddy, if *you're* ever going to get married, you'll have to hurry. Pretty soon you'll be a grandfather and too old."

"A grandfather! Is that why—"

"No," said Jeannie hastily.

Kat breathed a sigh of relief. Connor would *never* forgive her if she'd let his daughter get pregnant. And he hadn't denied wanting to marry her when Jeannie made the suggestion. He'd said, "What makes you think she'd have me?" If only he'd said, "Will you have me?" But now the moment had passed.

Jeannie and Tom left the next morning, anxious to get back to Aspen and start looking for a three-hundred-dollar house. "You'd didn't have to do that," said Connor. "I'd have helped them out."

"Good," said Kat. "You can buy their furniture."

"It's not as if she's your daughter."

"No," said Kat sadly.

"Although—" He looked at her searchingly. "That suggestion she made. Have you ever thought about—our getting married?"

What was she supposed to say? "I never think about anything else?" Or "Why do you think I've been to bed with you three times if I don't love you?" Or "Please, please, please, marry me, Connor"? She hadn't the nerve. She could enter a house of prostitution, something no other respectable woman in town would do. She could argue woman suffrage with the bishop, something no other Catholic woman would do. She could march into a saloon to support Sunday closing, something not even many Methodist women would do. But she couldn't propose to Connor.

"Kat—" He extended his hand slowly, tentatively, and lifted her chin with one finger.

Kat swallowed and took a step toward him.

"You're so beautiful."

Did he really think that? Here she was in another ordinary day dress. No cleavage. No ribbons in her hair. Connor stepped closer and bent his head. The touch of his mouth sent a shiver of pleasure through her.

Then someone rapped at the window, and they jumped apart, turning simultaneously to see Diederick's scowling face, bent sideways because he was halfway up the ladder.

"That damn carpenter!"

Connor was stamping toward the outside door when Diederick burst in, crying, "You can't kiss her!"

"Diederick, what are you talking about?" And why was the *carpenter* trying to interfere in her personal life?

"You invited me to tea."

"I invited you for Gretel," Kat replied, astonished.

"Gretel? Vat I vant mit Gretel?"

"You mean you've been leading Gretel on?"

"He's not in love with Gretel, Kat," said Connor. "The idiot's in love with you."

"Of course, he isn't."

"Yah, unt you love me too, Missus. Vy else vould you gif me all dat vork unt invite me to tea?"

"Well, the work part is an easy misconception to correct," said Connor. "You're fired. What do we owe you? Seventeen-fifty, isn't it? Here." Connor counted it and slapped the money into Diederick's hand. "Now, clear out."

"I vork for Missus, not you," said Diederick.

"Maybe it would be better if—well, if you didn't work for us anymore," said Kat. Diederick thought she was in love with him? Strange Diederick? She felt a little sorry for him, but she had *never* given him reason to think that she loved him. What a dreadful idea! Now she wondered how she could have wished him on poor Gretel, who was standing, red-faced, in the doorway with her hands rolled in her apron.

"I wouldn't have married him anyway," said Gretel. "You don't have to worry about me, Miss Kat. Plenty of better men than him like me."

"I'm sure they do, Gretel," said Kat soothingly. Placid Gretel looked furious. This whole thing was dreadful. Diederick was looking at the money in his hand as if it might bite him, then at Kat as if she had betrayed him. Without another word, he turned and left, snatched his ladder from the side of the house and marched away with it, his breath puffing into the December air in exploding white cloudlets. Kat had to close the door. He'd left it open.

Connor stamped into his room, grabbed his coat, and announced that he wouldn't be home for dinner.

"Don't you cry, Miss Kat," said Gretel. "There are better men than him too. Everyone who doesn't want to marry me wants to marry you."

There might be better men than Connor, but Kat didn't know any. That kiss before Diederick peeked in the window had been so nice. *I wonder if we're star-crossed lovers?*

she speculated glumly. Considering what the carpenter had interrupted—and the moment had certainly held promise—Kat thought she'd like to give Diederick a kick in the shins. She hadn't kicked anyone since she was eight years old and Mary Alice O'Brien threw mud on her pinafore at St. Scholastica. But that Diederick was *dumb!* Dumber than Mary Alice O'Brien. He'd better not show his face around here again!

It had been a long time since Connor had too much to drink—not since Rose Laurel's death. However, the night of his near proposal to Kat, he spent six hours at the Ingrid's Ring dormitory drinking himself into a stupor, fell into someone's bed, and awakened the next morning with a terrible headache and the conviction that he had to get himself cleaned up so that he could go home, apologize to Kat for stamping out like a sulky schoolboy—it wasn't, after all, her fault that every man who saw her fell in love—and once he got all that behind him, he'd propose. She could only say no. It would break his heart, but at least he'd find out where he stood.

He arrived back in Breckenridge feeling a little better. She was certainly right about drinking. The stuff was poison. He pulled his horse up in front of the house and walked straight in, calling her name. No answer. Had she gone to town on some errand?

"Gretel?" Gretel would know. No answer. God, Kat hadn't taken Gretel and left, had she?

"Jamie?" Jamie would be at school. No, it was Saturday, and Jamie had spent the night with the Fletcher boys. Connor remembered that now.

The silent house made him uneasy. He walked slowly over to Kat's side, where he found her door open and an unusual state of disarray inside. It looked as if there had been a free-for-all in her bedroom. Had she thrown a temper tantrum? Or—panicked at his thoughts, he hurried to Gretel's room. She was there—trussed up, eyes wide and staring, making muted noises behind the gag.

"Who did this?" he demanded once he had freed her mouth. She didn't know. She'd been gagged with a knee in her back before she was fully awake. She'd heard the struggle in Kat's room but had been helpless to intervene.

"Whoever he was, she got him good," said Gretel.

"But she's gone." Connor freed the maid and raced out of the house, looking for the sheriff.

"You promise not to run avay, I untie your hands. Unt you gotta promise not to bite me neither."

"Nincompoop," snarled Kat. "I wouldn't promise you a warm coat in a snowstorm." His nose was swollen, and he had bite marks and two bruises, one on his cheek and one on his forehead. Her fist still hurt, but it had been worth it.

"You marry me now. I got tree huntret dollars."

"Where would you get three hundred dollars?" asked Kat disdainfully.

"Got it vor taken you avay."

"Someone paid you to kidnap me?"

"I vant to. Just don't hurt none to get paid."

"Who paid you?" He didn't answer. "Three hundred? Medford Fleming."

"I didn't zay dat."

"You're both slimy villains," said Kat.

"No, you love me now I got tree huntret dollars."

"I wouldn't love you if you had more money than Guggenheim and—and General Palmer put together."

"Ya, you love me now. Ve get married."

"Never. You missed your chance. I had Gretel sent out specially for you."

"I don't vant Gretel."

"Now you won't have anyone."

"I got you."

387

"You'll go to jail." She looked around the miserable little windowless cabin, wondering where she was. She'd been blindfolded, bumping around on the wagon floor under a pile of blankets all the way to wherever they were. Well, it didn't matter. She'd get free. Diederick wasn't bright enough to keep her long. If she had to, she'd tell him a pack of lies so that she could escape. If she could make up a saint's life, she could lie to Diederick. Mother wouldn't approve, but *she'd* never been kidnapped.

"I have to use the outhouse, Diederick," said Kat craftily. *Just you wait,* she thought. *I'll get you.*

"Just like you thought, Connor," Sheriff Will Illif said, "Diederick's gone. You're the last person to see him. An' another person gone is Medford Fleming. Him an' his wife closed up the house and left on the train last night. May not mean anything, but a fella who works for him says he was that mad when he heard Miss Kat won her slander suit."

"I'm rounding up men at the Rose Laurel and Ingrid's Ring," said Connor.

"I'll recruit as many as I can in town," said Will. "We'll find 'em."

When Connor thought of Kat with the crazy, pale-eyed Diederick, it made his skin crawl.

The outhouse trick hadn't worked. She'd hit him with a stick of firewood, but he had a thick skull—she should have anticipated that. He'd turned around and knocked her down. Then he'd tied her to a chair.

Kat sighed. Her wrists hurt, and her hand hurt where she'd hit him. Her face was sticky where he'd tried to feed her some slop he'd cooked up. And she was tired! And cold. How would he react if she burst into tears? No, that was out. She wouldn't give him the satisfaction.

* * *

"All right," said the sheriff to the assembled men, "we know this Diederick rented a wagon, and he was flashin' money, more than Connor paid him. So if he took Miz Kat, maybe someone hired him to do it."

"Like Fleming," said Connor, his voice grating.

"Then a miner saw a yellow-haired fella drivin' a wagon toward Hoosier Pass last night late. So Connor an' his group gonna head that way, bein' as that's our best lead. The rest of you will divide up and ride in different directions in case it wasn't Diederick that took her. Ask everyone you see. We figure we're lookin' for a man with some bruises on him an' a woman who's givin' him trouble."

"Reckon he's sorry he took Miz Kat," said one of the miners. "I was at Engle's the day she come preachin' temperance, an' I sure wouldn't wanna git on her wrong side."

Connor scowled at him. "I don't see this as any joke."

"Hey Connor, Otto Diederick ain't all that smart," said Septimus Embry. "We'll catch up."

"You ready to get married yet?" asked Diederick.

Kat had stopped talking to him, which seemed to bother him more than being hit with a stick of firewood.

"You vant some dinner?"

She stared at him malevolently.

"Use da outhouse? You vant to go to der outhouse?"

She did want to, but she wasn't going to say so.

"How ve gonna git married if you don't say nuthin'?"

Once untied, Kat went into the outhouse and stayed. After fifteen minutes, he called to her, but she lurked beside the door silently, waiting to see what he would do. The place smelled, and the indignity of being stuck in this disgusting place made her even angrier. Finally he gave up calling and cautiously opened the door. Kat waited. He stepped in, and she gave him a mighty shove toward the hole and ran. Diederick caught her at the edge of the clearing. He was fast for such a dumb man. *Oh well, next time,* she thought as he dragged her back.

"Dat vas wery bad," he said once he had her tied up again. "Vifes shoult treat husbands better. Mit respect."

Kat stared at him in silent anger, and he shifted uncomfortably. "I'll make zum foot."

"I'm Septimus Embry, an' this here's Miss Augustina McCloud. I found her at the railroad station when I got back to town."

"Did you find Miss Kat?" asked Gretel anxiously.

"Nope. My, you're a pretty thing, ain't you?"

Gretel smiled at him. "Would you care for a cup of coffee after your efforts, Mr. Embry?"

"Don't mind if I do. Miss McCloud, she's another a them Chicago girls sent by Miz Fitzgerald's mother. Former schoolteacher, she says."

Talking all the way, Gretel showed Augustina McCloud to a room. "There was another schoolteacher, but she ran off with a lawyer. No one liked her. I hope you're not the snobbish kind because I've been lonely, especially since Miss Kat got kidnapped. Mr. Macleod is out looking for her. They think the carpenter did it."

Augustina McCloud looked astounded at this unusual flood of information, but she followed Gretel into the kitchen to get coffee for Mr. Septimus Embry, who regaled them with tales of the net of searchers that was spread over the countryside searching for Kat.

Diederick heard the voices before Kat did. He came running in and gagged her. Then he lifted her chair, hauled her to the outhouse, and threw a blanket over her. Wedged into a corner and gagged, she couldn't call attention to herself, although she could hear the questions they asked. They were looking for her. However, she didn't hear Diederick's voice. What was he doing? Why didn't they make him answer their questions? The tears began to slip down her cheeks when she heard them leave. *I'm here*, she thought wildly. *I'm right here*. How could they not know?

"See," said Diederick when he got her back in the house. "Dey kum. Dey go. Now ve git married."

She shook her head wearily.

When Connor returned after two days of futile searching, he found that no one had been any luckier than he. More than fifty men had gone out, and no trace of Kat was found, nor any of Diederick. Red-eyed from lack of sleep, he went home for a meal and a few hours in bed. At home, he found that he had yet another Chicago girl in residence, another schoolteacher. Happily, this one didn't try to lecture him on vegetables or insist on correcting everyone's grammar, but still Connor didn't want to deal with her. He left it to Gretel and Jamie.

Then Connor and the sheriff interviewed every searcher who came in, hoping to find something they'd overlooked. Nothing turned up except a report by two miners from the Rose Laurel of a deaf mute chopping wood at a remote cabin near Mohawk Lake. They'd peered into the cabin and found it empty.

"Fella was wearin' one a them knitted caps on his head," one miner remembered. "Couldn't see his hair. Didn't take that cap off, did he, Penrose?"

"Nope," said Penrose.

"How tall?" asked Connor. "What color were his eyes?"

"Didn't hardly look up," said Penrose, "so I don't recall. How about you, Malcolm?"

Connor didn't think Diederick was smart enough to feign being a deaf mute, but there'd been no sign of Kat, and no one knew of any deaf mutes in the vicinity. "I'm going up to Mohawk Lake," Connor told the sheriff. What other hope had he, if she wasn't there?

"I'll stay here and keep the search goin'."

Connor nodded.

* * *

"Tomorrow ve start marriage," said Diederick.

Kat, who hadn't spoken in two days, stared at him with hatred and contempt.

"You shoult be afraid of me," he said, his pale blue eyes gleaming in the firelight. "I set fire to your house. You don't marry me, maybe I set fire to dis vun."

Kat swallowed hard. She was tied to the chair. Did he mean to start the fire and leave her here?

"He paid me. Zwei hunnert dollars. Supposed to catch *him* dere. Vas terrible you come home instead of him."

The man had meant to kill Connor. Had almost killed Jeannie. Kat wondered how she could have thought Diederick so innocuous.

"I tell Herr Fleming about you unt vomen voting too. Vomen shoultn't vote. I don't vant vife voting. Too bad he didn't die—dat Macleod. His fault you don't love me."

Diederick, thwarted in love, might well kill her, Kat realized. Even yesterday, she wouldn't have believed him capable of such a thing. Today he was withholding food and water. She swallowed against dry thirst and fear. Perhaps defiance had been the wrong way to handle him, but she had been so angry.

"You got till tomorrow morning to change your mind. Marry me or get burned mit dis cabin." He rolled up in his blankets between her and the door and went to sleep. Kat hadn't had a lying-down sleep since he'd kidnapped her. If she could just get a few hours of real sleep, maybe she could decide what to do.

She heard the sound of the door first, squeaking on rusty hinges, but Diederick stirred immediately thereafter. Her eyes darted from the dark shadow frozen in the doorway to the waking figure of her captor. *Let him go back to sleep,* she prayed, but he didn't. He sat up.

"Diederick," she said sharply. "Wake up."

The carpenter stopped rubbing his eyes and turned to her, away from the door. She concentrated on him, never looking at the unknown man, praying he was a rescuer. "I've changed my mind," she said to Diederick. "I'll marry you."

"How do I know you ain't lyin'?" he asked. "How do I know ve get to der priest, unt you zay—"

"Because I don't want to die," she interrupted as the figure moved silently toward her captor. "We'll do whatever you say tomorrow."

"Tonight—" he began, and then some sixth sense must have alerted him. His head was turning when the rifle butt hit him.

Kat let out a trembling breath. What had he meant to do tonight, she wondered, and who—

"I'm going to tie him first."

Kat went limp with relief. It was Connor. "How did you find me?"

"We didn't know of any deaf mutes in the mountains," he replied as he bound Diederick's hands and feet.

The answer meant nothing to Kat, but Connor was untying her now, helping her to stand. "Can you hold the gun on him while I look for his horses?"

Kat flexed numb hands, then took the rifle, inspecting the trigger mechanism.

"Just pull that if he makes a move." Connor showed her, then strode out. He was back very quickly to drag Diederick out the door by his heels.

"Do you need a hand throwing him in?" Kat asked as she trailed behind.

"Nope." Connor picked up the carpenter and heaved him into the back of the wagon. "You'll have to keep the rifle while I drive. If in doubt, shoot him."

Kat nodded and allowed herself to be helped up onto the wagon seat. Then Connor retrieved the blankets from the cabin so that she could wrap up. During her entire captivity she'd had only the warmth of her heavy flannel nightgown and some bed socks her mother had knitted for her years ago, the garments in which she'd been kidnapped. "What about him?" she asked. "Should we give him a blanket?"

"Since he took them all for himself when he was in charge, we'll let him shiver now that we have the upper hand," said Connor. He sprang onto the seat, using the wheel for leverage. "I've got one question for you, Kat."

"Oh?" If he asked whether Diederick had had his way with her, Kat knew she was going to be very angry.

Instead Connor said, "Will you marry me?"

Turning sideways on the seat, she stared at him, unable to believe that he'd proposed at long last. "What about Eustacia Fleming?" she asked cautiously.

"What about her?" Connor looked surprised.

"Everyone in town says you're having an affair with her."

"The devil I am! She's married!"

"She was chasing you."

"Well, maybe," he admitted. "But I didn't get caught. Anyway, I always figured Fleming put her up to it."

"Oh." Kat thought his answer over and, reminding herself that Connor was a truthful man, said, "In that case, I'll marry you."

"Good." Connor flicked the whip over the horses' backs and turned the wagon toward Breckenridge.

Chapter Twenty-Seven

As they pulled away from the cabin, a gray dawn rose above mountains heavy-laden with snow. Then a few streaks of opalescent pink appeared, like the pearl on the inner side of a drab seashell. Mohawk Lake stretched before them, a deep, secretive blue-black, bordered with tall pines. Connor drove along the lake shore, then turned the wagon onto a rutted back trail that cut through the forest to follow Spruce Creek.

Kat, although she had been unable to sleep while tied to that chair, couldn't bear to close her eyes. She looked at each view with the sharp sense that she might have died and never had the chance to see it. Almost a year she'd lived in these mountains, yet the things she knew best were houses, streets, stores, and people.

Now she marveled at the humps of snow that dotted the creek like vanilla icing on the rocks. She spotted a deer with big, butterfly-wing ears, its dark nose thrust inquisitively from between slender pines. One moment it was there, the next its white tail bobbed away into the gloom. "Mule deer," Connor said.

In a snow-blanketed meadow as they approached the Blue, she saw a bull elk with immense antlers overbalancing its head; it stood as immobile and statuesque as one of Professor Carter's specimens. Behind it the trees were dim with mist as they faded up the mountain, which, in turn, was almost indistinguishable from the gray sky. "There's snow coming," Connor predicted.

She hated to miss a minute of the trip home. Everything she saw seemed precious and beautiful, but her eyes kept closing. At last she gave up, snuggled against his side, and slept, waking only once when she heard Connor say to Diederick that he'd end up in the shaft of a flooded mine if he made just one more noise and woke Kat. After that the only sounds were those of creaking harness, horses blowing, the bump and rattle of wagon wheels, and the *whish* of a cold December wind in the high tree tops. Kat went back to sleep and woke when they approached the town.

"A new girl turned up while you were gone," said Connor once she was fully awake. "Another schoolteacher."

Kat groaned, remembering Margaret Mary Hubble.

"This one's nicer. Slim, pretty, red hair, never mentions vegetables or grammar." He smiled sideways at Kat and saw tears on her cheeks. "What is it, honey?"

"Nothing," she mumbled. She didn't like Connor talking about pretty girls. "I haven't married off Gretel yet."

"Well, if that's all that's worrying you, Gretel and Sep Embry seem pretty taken with each other. Got one other piece of news for you," Connor added as they drove up Main Street to deliver Diederick to the sheriff. "Maeve's presented us with a new baby sister."

"But I was supposed to be there!" exclaimed Kat. "What did you tell Mother?"

"I wired that the weather was too bad for traveling."

"I'll have to leave for Denver right away."

"The devil you will. You'll stay home safe and sound and not turn my hair gray with worry. Anyway, it's started to snow again. I hope you haven't forgotten the avalanche that hit our train last year." Flakes were indeed beginning to fall. "My father can take care of Maeve and the new baby," he concluded. "Sheriff!"

"Well, Miz Kat. There you are," said the sheriff, coming out of his office to greet them. "Now all them fellas out lookin' for you, hopin' to find you and win your hand in marriage, are gonna be disappointed."

"Her hand's been won," snapped Connor. "Can you haul Diederick out of the back? He's roughed up some, but he should be fine to stand trial. Kidnapping and arson."

As they continued home, word spread through town that Kat had been rescued. The townsfolk began to show up before she could finish her bath and put on clean clothes. Ignoring the deepening snow, the women brought food and good wishes, the men tales of the hunt for Kat, which most of them had participated in. Diederick's crimes were discussed, Augustina McCloud introduced around as she cooked and passed food to the guests. Furniture was cleared from the corridor room so a fiddler could take his place, and between dances, Gretel and Sep Embry announced their engagement.

"You want to announce ours?" Connor asked Kat when they had finished a set, breathless.

"We haven't agreed on a date or spoken to the priest or reserved the church," she demurred.

"The church? Kat, we can't get married in that church." Connor was edging her toward the door.

"Well, I certainly wouldn't get married anywhere else. The sisters' chapel isn't big enough."

"And the church is too cold. Our guests would catch pneumonia, and so would we."

"Where do *you* want to get married?" asked Kat.

397

"Fireman's Hall. I've been a volunteer fireman since the early eighties."

"For heaven sake, Connor, be reasonable. Even with summer flowers I couldn't make that hall look good."

"Well, we'd have to wait until next summer for the church to be warm enough." His mouth was set stubbornly.

"I'm the bride. I should have—"

"You're tired," Connor interrupted. "We'll discuss it when you've slept. In fact, why don't you turn in early?"

"Turn in early yourself. I'm going back to dance." Was he trying to delay the wedding? she wondered angrily.

"Say, Miz Kat, anyone told you you won the school board election while you was gone?" asked Fred McNaught. "Reckon you'll be the first Roman Catholic to serve on the public school board in this town."

"Well, shu-ee, Fred," cried his wife. "She'll be the first woman. That's what counts."

"Oh my," said Kat, beaming. "I won? Connor, did you hear that? I won. Why didn't you tell me?"

"I completely forgot about it." He was frowning and murmured to her, "Now that we're getting married, maybe you ought to reconsider taking that post."

"Why?" she asked, astonished.

"Because you'll be busy. You might not have the time."

"But—" She stared at her new-minted fiancé uneasily. He sounded like Mickey when she'd announced that she intended to spend two days a week doing charity work for the church. Mickey had said her place was at home, not out waltzing around the city, playing Lady Bountiful. Or her father. When Maeve brought the first working girls into the house and pointed out that there was a profit to be made in boarding them as well as a good deed to be done, Liam Fitzpatrick had said that women had no business making money; that's was what husbands were for. He'd sent those first two boarders packing.

But Connor wasn't like that; he'd hardly ever tried to

curtail any of her activities. She smiled at him, then whirled away, laughing, when Charlie Maxell asked her to dance. "Did you hear that I won the election, Charlie?"

"Sure did," said Charlie. "Did you hear that Fleming finally paid up on the slander suit?"

"Oh, wonderful!" said Kat enthusiastically and passed into the arms of her next partner, Thomas Wintermute, the banker, who smiled when she told him about the school board and looked a bit disconcerted when she told him that she and Connor were engaged. Probably she shouldn't have mentioned her impending marriage; Thomas was still mourning his wife.

Gretel got married in the church, and Connor shivered ostentatiously throughout the ceremony. Afterward he said to Father Eusebius, "You don't have to marry people in the actual church building, do you, Father? Couldn't you have a religious ceremony somewhere else? Somewhere warmer?"

Father Eusebius sneezed.

"Hell would be warmer," Kat suggested sweetly in an aside to Connor. Why was he being so difficult about where they got married?

"Kat, would you sit down for a minute?"

"I haven't got a minute, Connor." She was wrapping a scarf around her head and neck for the trip downtown. "I'm already late for the school board meeting."

"Damn it, Kat—"

"Connor Macleod, watch your language!"

"Look, I have to go to Ten Mile tomorrow morning, and I'd like to have this talk before I go."

"But the board—"

"What's more important? The damned school board or the house we're going to live in after we're married?"

"I'm beginning to think you don't really want to get married," said Kat. "If you did—"

"You're the one who won't compromise. But whenever we get married, and even if we don't, we need to do something about that tower room."

Kat laced her fingers together tightly to conceal their trembling. "Knock it down then," she whispered. "I never want to see it again. It—it reminds me of Diederick." Face pale, she reached for her cloak. "And now I'm going to the school board meeting." And she did, worrying about Connor's priorities. He thought some little domestic discussion was more important than her responsibilities as an elected public official—the only woman in Summit County elected to public office. Maybe that was it. Like a lot of other people, he didn't think women, even his future wife—or was it especially his future wife?—should be allowed to vote or hold office. Was she planning to marry a man who wanted her to stay home dusting the bric-a-brac? But no. Connor wasn't like that. Was he?

Connor was shaken by the look of remembered horror on her face. Kat never said much about the time she'd spent with Diederick, but evidently the carpenter had frightened her badly. And now they were stuck with that room, which she wanted him to have torn down. That would be a waste of money, not to mention the ruination of his plan, which was to turn it into a private place for the two of them once they were married. A place where they could get away from their often overflowing household.

Connor scratched his head. It was still a good idea, but how was he to get the tower room prettied up on his own? He'd figured Kat could do it—sort of work it in around the school board, the spiritual visits to Marcie and company, and the church work and business affairs and temperance campaigns and woman suffrage. Well, maybe expecting Kat to find time for decorating had been overly optimistic, he admitted to himself, chuckling.

"Now, what are you laughing about, Mr. Macleod?"

asked Augustina McCloud, who whisked into the room with a mop and bucket.

"Say, Augustina," said Connor, seeing her as the answer to his problems, "I've been thinking of fixing up the tower room—as a sort of surprise Christmas present for Kat. How are you at choosing furniture and stitching draperies or whatever you have to do to make a room look fine?"

"Well, I think of myself as a woman with tolerable good taste," said Augustina. "It's to be a secret, is it? As busy as Miss Kat is, we ought to be able to manage."

Connor beamed at her. "I'm off to Ten Mile Canyon tomorrow. I'll stop downtown and tell them you can charge on my accounts."

At first Kat had been suspicious of the butter-machine man, a wispy little fellow with a pot belly and thinning hair, combed in careful but separate strands across a bulging forehead. Beneath that protrusion were rosy cheeks and eyes sparkling with the enthusiasm of a good-natured fanatic.

"It's the wave of the future in the dairy business, Mrs. Fitzgerald." That's what he told her, and Kat thought of Mrs. Landis and her eldest daughter on the ranch near Dillon, churning butter by hand. If the butter-making machine worked, they could increase their output and supply every mining camp in Summit County. The more she thought about it, the more grand her ideas became. She remembered anticipating, half in jest, that she might sometime become the queen of milk and mines on the Western Slope.

But she wasn't buying a pig in a poke, as her mother liked to say, so she told the butter-machine man that she'd only consider the hefty purchase price if he actually freighted his miracle invention out to the Dillon ranch so she could see it at work.

He jumped at the chance. "Which one do you want?" he asked. "The one with the wood-powered engine or the one run by animal power?"

401

Kat didn't know much about the mechanics of engines, but she did know that the river valley around Dillon had few trees and that it would cost her considerable to have firewood cut and transported from the surrounding mountains. Therefore, she asked, "What animal?"

"Why, whatever animal you can get to walk in a circle, running the machine," said Mr. Huckleby. "Mayhap you could use one of the cows, although I've never tried it. For sure a horse or a mule would do the trick. The cotton compressors in the south, they ran that way in the old days.

You couldn't prove that by Kat, but she nodded and looked knowledgeable, and when Mr. Huckleby had gone off to arrange for shipment of his machine to Dillon, she went in search of Connor to tell him about her exciting prospects in the butter business.

"I've never heard of a butter machine," said Connor. "I imagine you'll be making yourself a lot of work and a load of grief if you take up such an untried project."

She glared at him. "That's the way people make money," she replied curtly, "taking up untried projects. Aren't you the one who thought it would be a good idea to electrify our hoists and trams?"

"Well, that was *just* a thought since we have no electricity."

"All I need to produce butter in quantity is the butter machine and a beast to run it." In the face of opposition she was more and more sure that Mr. Huckleby's invention would prove a great money-maker.

"And more cows to provide the milk," Connor reminded her. "Cows are expensive. And you've got to have folks to milk them."

"Every one of the Landises knows how to milk a cow," said Kat. "Why are you being so negative? Well, don't tell me, because I'm going to Dillon tomorrow with Mr. Huckleby to see the butter machine at work."

"To Dillon?" Connor looked surprised, then thoughtful, then said, "Well, why not? Can't hurt to have a look, as long as it's at his expense."

"It is," said Kat. Would Connor want to go with her? She remembered their last visit to the ranch with a little shiver of excitement.

"Have a good trip," said Connor.

Kat stared at him suspiciously. Why had he changed his mind? Why was he sending her off to see this butter machine in action if he had no faith in it or in the potential of the butter market in Summit County? Nonetheless, the next morning she was on the train to Dillon with Mr. Huckleby, his machine safely stowed in a freight car. She planned to stay overnight and return the following day.

"Is that furniture here yet, Augustina?" Connor asked as soon as Kat left the house.

"Yes, sir. It came in on the train from Denver just yesterday. I guess I'll have to leave it at the depot."

"No need," said Connor. "Mrs. Fitzgerald is off to Dillon and won't be back until morning."

"In that case, I'll arrange to have it freighted across town immediately if you're sure she won't be going upstairs."

"We'll have to make that room an entirely new place if she's ever to climb those stairs again."

"Well, I've some fine ideas," said Augustina. "I always have liked decorating a house, though I've never had a free hand where money's concerned. Would you like to hear what I have in mind?"

"I'll leave it to you," said Connor. "And I appreciate your effort."

"Not at all, sir. I've not that much to do with my evenings," and Augustina took up a heavy cloak and went off to arrange for the furniture while Connor, pleased with his acumen in getting Kat out of town, headed for his office.

* * *

Mr. Landis was very doubtful about the butter machine. He'd never heard of such a thing. Mrs. Landis, on the other hand, was determined to be pleased with it, as she and her older daughter had no great love for churning butter. However, the machine didn't work with a cow because the cow couldn't be convinced to walk in a circle. Then they attached Mr. Landis's work horse to the poles. Lo and behold, the machine made butter. In fact, it made a great deal of butter. Then Mr. Landis argued that he had other uses for his horse, whereas his wife had plenty of time for churning butter. The look he got from Mrs. Landis would have curdled milk.

"How am I to get to town with the butter if my horse is tied to a pole making it?" he asked defensively. "And how am I to move the cows from one pasture to another and bring in feed and supplies from town? No, 'twill never work. The cows won't do it, and the horse hasn't time." He stared stubbornly at the three women.

"Then we can buy a mule," said Kat, "along with the extra cows." She and Mr. Landis fell to arguing about what his share of the new profits would be since he wasn't putting money into the new venture and she was.

"I'll be putting more work in," he pointed out.

"The *mule* will be putting more work in," said Mrs. Landis. "And as for you, when did you ever do any churning?"

"The butter has to be delivered," said he.

"Only to Dillon," Kat retorted, "for with that much butter, I'll have to set up a distribution system and find new customers—or were you thinking of doing that yourself?"

He scowled at her, but over dinner they came to an accommodation, and she and Mr. Huckleby agreed on a handshake that she would buy his butter-making machine. She got a good price by offering to give testimonials to its efficacy, which he could use in selling it to other dairy farmers on the Western Slope, should he be so lucky as to find additional forward-looking entrepreneurs of her stripe.

So Kat went back to Breckenridge satisfied with her new business prospects. When she arrived, bowing to convention by getting off at the edge-of-town ladies' siding, a heavy snow had begun to fall, and she had to beg a ride on Christ Kaiser's grocery sled or she'd never have made it home. Then, when she opened the door to the corridor room, there were whispers and rustlings and thumpings elsewhere in the house but no one to greet her. She had removed all her winter wraps by the time Augustina and Connor, looking flushed and flustered, appeared at the door to her side of the house. She eyed them uneasily.

"Well, Kat, how did your trip go?" asked Connor while Augustina whisked off to the kitchen with only a hello.

"Very well," said Kat. "I've bought the machine."

"What!"

"Well, I've *agreed* to buy it."

His frown deepened when she told him what it would cost, in addition to the price of a mule. "Where do you think you're going to get this money?" he asked.

Kat hadn't truly thought about that. Somehow or other she'd assumed that Connor would arrange it, but she could tell from the look on his face that he had no such inclination. If he so disapproved of the idea, why had he rushed her off to Dillon? Then she remembered those guilty looks on the faces of her fiancé and her maid. *What you're thinking is just silly,* she told herself. But to test the waters of love, as it were, she asked, "Have you given any thought to what day we should reserve the church?"

"I have not," said Connor, "since I don't intend to be married in the church. Are you, by any chance, trying to blackmail me into financing a project I have no faith in by reminding me that we're engaged?"

Much good that would do, she thought. *He's putting off the wedding. Perhaps he's changed his mind.* That idea and his accusation made her so angry that she said, "I'll arrange to finance the machine and the mule myself then."

"And how will you do that?" he called after her, for she was heading toward her own room, back stiff with anger.

"What business is that of yours?" she replied without turning her head. "It isn't as if there aren't profits coming to me from the Chicago Girl."

"Those profits are being plowed right back into the mine. We won't have spendable money again from that investment for at least six months."

Kat whirled at the door and glared at him. "Then I'll borrow it," she said.

"Banks don't lend money to women."

"Well, we'll see about that," she exclaimed, seething.

"So when's the wedding to be?" asked Marcie, once they were ensconced in her private apartment, Kat having given the employees of the Gentleman's Sporting Club a rousing tale of saintly derring-do over their late breakfast.

"We can't even agree where to have the wedding," said Kat, "although I can't imagine why he should think a good Roman Catholic like myself would agree to be married anywhere but in church."

"Where does he want to get married?"

"Fireman's Hall."

"Well, plenty do," said Marcie easily. "If I were you, I'd not let him slip through my fingers. Hell, you'd be wasting all those lessons I gave you." She glanced slyly at Kat, who didn't look amused. "You're not changing your mind are you—about marrying Connor?"

"No, of course not," said Kat. *Or am I?* she then asked herself, although it seemed a foolish question. She'd wanted to marry him for such a long time before he asked. "It's just that I don't think a husband should have his way in everything. What kind of married life would we have together if he expects that?"

"Most men do want things their way," said Marcie, "and

most women find tricks to get around it."

"Tricks! That's not the kind of marriage I want."

Marcie shook her head. "I'd not have taken you for a girl with impractical notions about marriage. Maybe it's something else. Isn't he any good in bed?"

"He's too good," muttered Kat.

"Well, you can't keep sleeping with him, unmarried, if that's what you've been doing. You'll end up pregnant."

No fear of that, Kat said to herself, remembering that he'd not so much as kissed her since he proposed. Maybe he *was* backing out, thinking that she wasn't a traditional enough woman for him, that she wanted to lead her own life, not walk demurely in his shadow. And in truth, she did expect to lead her own life, marriage or no marriage. What a conundrum.

"Well, you'd best make up your mind whether you want him or not," said Marcie, "but if you'll take my advice, Connor Macleod's as good a man as you're likely to find and better than most."

Kat *knew* that, but still he seemed to have changed since they got engaged, as if activities he didn't mind when she was just Sean's sister and Connor's business associate became unacceptable when she was to be his wife.

Connor, who was supposed to have picked her up at Marcie's, failed to arrive at the appointed time, so Kat stamped angrily through snow turned gray and ugly by fallout from the smelter stack and workmen tramping about. Crossing the bridge, which was slick with ice, she took two falls and was a sorry sight by the time she got back to Main Street and found herself accosted by a dandified fellow, obviously no citizen of Breckenridge if she were to judge by the fine fur coat that kept him warm.

"Have I the pleasure of addressing Mrs. Fitzgerald—Mrs. Kathleen Fitzgerald?" he asked.

"You have," she · replied sharply, quite ill-tempered

because she hated to be caught looking so damp and frowsy.

"Madam, if I may presume to introduce myself, I am Emmet M. Statler, and I have a fine business proposition to offer you."

"Indeed?" Kat didn't stop her determined progress up Main Street.

"Perhaps we could sit down somewhere. Might I buy you dinner at the Saddle Rock Cafe?"

"I don't take meals in public places with strange gentlemen," said Kat.

"But madam, I hope to become better acquainted."

She glared at him.

"In a business way," he added hastily.

Kat stepped off the board sidewalk, waded through a pile of snow at the edge of the street, and made her way to the corner of Lincoln and Main, as Mr. Emmet M. Statler scurried behind her. "My proposition would bring you a lot of money, ma'am."

Kat paused, thought of the butter machine, climbed up onto the sidewalk in front of Finding's Hardware, and turned to Mr. Statler. "Money for what?" she asked.

"For your share of the Chicago Girl mine," he replied. "We could offer you—well, I think my principals might come up with twenty-five thousand."

Kat looked at him with contempt. They'd already poured twice that into developing the mine, and besides, Connor would never forgive her if she sold out. Still, it was something to think on, what with Mr. Statler keeping pace, smiling at her with the glistening teeth of a snake-oil salesman and raising his offer ten thousand dollars per block as they progressed up Lincoln. He was just one more man who thought he could take advantage of her because she was a woman.

"Go away," she ordered as she turned onto French Street. She could always find Mr. Statler again if Thomas

Wintermute at the bank refused her a loan, although, no matter what Connor said, Kat didn't think that would happen. And if she had to deal with Emmet M. Statler, she'd make him pay for trying to hornswoggle her. She knew what that mine was worth. She left Statler standing on the corner, looking confounded.

Every day Connor told her what the temperature was. His smug expression on December twenty-first, when he announced that the overnight low at four a.m. had been forty-two degrees below zero, was not to be borne. "Today would have been a fine day to get married in church," he remarked. "The sacramental wine would have frozen."

"Wine doesn't freeze," Kat retorted and went off to keep her appointment at the bank with Thomas Wintermute. Connor seemed to be quite unaware that she and Thomas were friends. Wintermute had lost his beloved young wife before Kat ever got to Breckenridge, a fact which Kat first discovered in casual conversation at a G.A.R. ball. The poor fellow had been dying to talk about his Clara and, out of mistaken sympathy, none of his friends would let him. Kat, however, on three different occasions had listened to his grief and encouraged him to reminisce about his idyllic marriage, now lost.

"How lucky you are to have such wonderful memories," she'd exclaimed during one of these conversations. He'd seemed surprised that she should think him lucky in anything but changed his mind when she gave him a sample of her own recollections of marriage to Mickey.

"Kathleen," he exclaimed, a smile lighting his solemn face when she was shown into his office. "What a pleasure to see you."

"How are you doing, Thomas?" she replied. "Feeling more cheerful I hope?"

"Not really." His face fell. "But it's good of you to call on me."

"Actually, I'm here on business, a venture I think could be profitable to both of us."

"Really." He looked surprised but listened intently to her proposition. When she'd finished, he said doubtfully, "We don't usually lend money to women. How does Connor feel about this?"

"Thomas, I'm disappointed in you," said Kat, giving him a humorously reproving smile, although she felt more like snarling at him. Men were really impossible! "I own the ranch at Dillon," she continued, "and Connor's not at all interested, so you must judge my proposition on its merits, although you might remember that I prospected and found the Chicago Girl and own half of that venture."

"True," said Wintermute, looking thoughtful.

"I suppose I could offer an interest in the mine as collateral, or in the ranch, but first you must tell me whether or not you think I can sell the butter."

"Oh Lord," said Wintermute, "there's never enough butter. I'm a prospective customer myself. In fact, I don't know why I'm hesitating." Then an unbankerly smile lit his face, and he said, "Our resources are at your disposal, my dear Kathleen."

In that way she not only got her loan but was escorted like royalty across the bank's fine tile floor by bank president Wintermute himself. She wondered uneasily, as she trudged home, whether the availability of credit had really been the result of her canny plan to exploit the miners' taste for butter or because she had been such a sympathetic listener over the period of her acquaintance with a man who had money to lend. Now that she thought of it, at her welcome-home-from-kidnapping party, Thomas had looked disappointed when she mentioned that she and Connor planned to marry, but of course that could be her imagination.

"Never look a gift horse in the mouth," her mother always said, and in the matter of this bank loan, Kat didn't intend to. If Wintermute had given her the money because he was suffering from an extreme case of unrequited love, she'd still take it. And now she'd have to begin soliciting butter customers at every mine kitchen, dormitory, boarding house, and grocery in the county. No doubt Connor would object, the weather being abominable, but Kat intended to pursue her project no matter what he said. Thought she couldn't get the loan, did he? Ha!

"Tom let you have the money?"

"Well, after all, we're good friends," she replied smugly.

"You and Tom Wintermute?" Connor scowled at her.

"Why not? He's a nice young man. Lovely manners, and he sees the potential in the butter market—which, incidentally, I intend to explore immediately. I think I'll start off with Ten Mile Canyon."

Connor nodded, and she caught an exchange of glances between him and Augustina McCloud, as if they would be glad to see her go. She was hard put to suppress the flame of jealousy that sprang up in her heart. Three days she'd be away, and Connor didn't seem to care a bit. He'd probably have shrugged if she said she'd have to miss Christmas.

Chapter Twenty-Eight

Kat arrived home on December twenty-fourth, a fair day, bitter cold with no sign of snow. That which had fallen was frozen hard. When no one answered her call from the corridor room, she unwrapped her outer wear and went into Connor's parlor to write, at his desk, a short Christmas note to her mother describing the new butter business and explaining, in answer to Maeve's inquiry, that no date had been set for the wedding because of Connor's stubbornness in the church-versus-fire station controversy.

"Well, it's about time."

Kat jumped. She hadn't expected Connor to be home at this time of day and anticipated with resignation that he would criticize her butter venture and the banker who had financed it. On the morning she'd left, Connor had muttered that Thomas Wintermute hadn't been the same sensible businessman since Clara died.

Kat was surprised when he grasped her arm and said, "Come along," hustling her across the house.

"I'm not going up there," she protested. "You know it reminds me of him."

"Humor me," said Connor and urged her up the stairs. At the top she found the room completely transformed. The dark moldings, window and door frames had been painted white, Diederick's wallpaper replaced with a pale green parchment. The used furniture she'd installed before the kidnapping was gone. Now the room held carved, golden oak wardrobes, and at the windows and the balcony door hung white lace curtains and rich green drapes with golden fringe and tassels. A large four-poster bed of matching oak with a green, white and gold coverlet stood across from the window seat on which now rested cushions covered in the same fabric. The room was handsomely carpeted and lit with stained glass lamps and a chandelier. Kat, turning in a slow circle, stunned at the beauty of the chamber, glanced questioningly at Connor.

"My Christmas surprise," he explained. "I still think we'll freeze up here, but at least I wanted it to be pretty for you."

How did he manage all this without my knowing? she wondered.

"Maybe I'll have a stove put in," he mused, drawing the drapes over a view of snow-covered mountains. Then he turned and said, "Alone at last," putting two large hands around her waist and bending for a kiss which, caught by surprise, she tried to avoid. "What's wrong?" he asked.

"Nothing," she replied. The kiss had left her breathless and quivering.

"Good. Come to bed."

"Connor, it's the middle of the afternoon!"

"I know."

"Someone could return any minute."

"They won't."

"Well, we can't—"

"Why can't we? We have three times before this. If you

won't marry me, you'll just have to satisfy my manly lusts without benefit of clergy."

"I'll do no such thing," said Kat, her voice weak in the face of his teasing laughter.

"And then there are your womanly lusts." He picked her up and carried her over to the new bed. "Which I freely admit took me by surprise the first time I discovered them."

"You're trying to embarrass me."

"I'm trying to have my way with you, or your way with me." He had her pinned to the coverlet, looming over her with a look of humorous determination.

He's not serious, thought Kat, and then he kissed her again and came down on top of her, knocking out her breath in a whoosh and convincing her that he was in earnest. His hands were everywhere, tugging at snaps, laces, buttons, kissing, inflaming her senses until she could think of nothing but joining her small body to his big one—and quickly.

"Ah, that's better," he sighed, and it was done. They were floating, quivering on a flood tide of love, the rapture bursting over them before Kat could even get her fill of him. "Just a taste, love," he whispered. "So you won't be willing to wait so long again."

Kat opened her eyes and smiled at him, expecting that now he would agree to the church. What else could he do when Fireman's Hall was about to be moved away from its present location to a new one on Main Street? Did he want to wed while the building squatted at some intersection?

To her disappointment, he said nothing about marriage, and Kat, as the glow of physical love dissipated, tried to comfort herself with the luxury of his expensive Christmas gift. The trouble he'd taken had to mean something. "How in the world did you manage to accomplish all this without my knowing? I've never seen such a beautiful room."

"Well, Augustina did the choosing and buying," he

explained, "not to mention the sewing."

Kat frowned and sat up. His confession offered a more palatable explanation for the whisperings between Connor and Augustina, but where had Augustina found the time? "How has she managed to keep up with her own work and do all this?"

"Well, she put in a few evenings," Connor admitted.

"In that case, I hope you paid her extra."

He looked surprised. "Why she did it for kindness, sweetheart. Is that so surprising? I've no doubt Augustina would have been insulted had I offered to pay her."

Kat swung her legs over the side of the bed, thinking that Augustina's donation of time and effort was the sort of unpaid labor that had been expected of Kat all her life. Had a man run her father's saloon during his last illness, the man would certainly have been paid, but Kat was not, nor even mentioned in her father's will. Liam Fitzpatrick's estate had gone to his wife and son. How unfair it seemed, when she reflected on it, that women's work was taken for granted and men's rewarded. Only Sean, by putting Kat in his own will, had recognized her contributions to the family. *Well, I'll pay Augustina,* Kat decided and rose to dress. Connor followed suit, looking puzzled.

As she descended the stairs, Marcie's words echoed in her mind: "You can't keep sleeping with him. Sooner or later, you'll find yourself pregnant." The thought was frightening, although not a month ago she'd been thinking happily of having her own children. In fact, a shroud of depression fell over her spirits that did not lift until her brother and his two children, bubbling with Christmas excitement, appeared on the doorstep. Thereafter, the holiday, which might have been an uneasy occasion, turned into one brightened by the laughter of the children.

On December twenty-fifth, at Christmas mass, which they all attended bundled up in heavy clothing, Connor whispered in her ear, "Can you really imagine marrying in this icebox? We might as well hold the ceremony down on the corner of Lincoln and Main or out in the middle of the street—"

"—where Fireman's Hall will soon be," she interrupted.

"—or better yet, on the bridge where we'd all freeze, the respectable ladies on the east side and your protégées from West Breckenridge on the other."

Kat gritted her teeth and ignored him.

"Augustina," said Kat, as they joined forces to clean up after the Christmas feast, "I want to pay you for the work you did on the room upstairs."

"There's no need, Miss Kat," said Augustina with her serene smile. "It was a labor of love."

"I believe you," said Kat, "but nonetheless, it's a labor for which you could earn a tidy living."

Augustina looked astounded. "I don't see how," she remarked, rinsing a piece of Kat's china.

"There are plenty of folk in town and around the county with more money than taste. Why shouldn't they pay you to make them fine rooms? Take that parlor on my side of the house. Sean had enough money to buy decent furnishings, yet he let his wife decorate it. Believe me, it's better now than when I first came, but it's still a dreadful room. And if Ingrid returns, I'm sure she'll restore it to its original tasteless condition."

A cloud settled over Augustina's face. "I thought his wife was dead."

"Oh no," said Kat. "She ran off. No one knows where."

"I see." Augustina busied herself again with the dishes. "Well, I've never heard of anyone being paid to fix up a stranger's house, other than painters or carpenters."

"It's done in the big cities," said Kat. "Maybe you'd like to give it a try."

Augustina looked dubious.

"You could put an ad in the newspaper, and then you could show the room you've done here to prospective customers."

"If they come," said Augustina.

"Well, if they don't, there wouldn't be much money lost, and if they do, you can sell them the furniture and drapes for a percentage over your own cost."

"I have no money to buy furniture and fabric."

"I'd advance it to you," said Kat. "I've been thinking lately about all the girls for whom I've found husbands. Yet perhaps not all of them wanted husbands; I certainly didn't. It occurs to me that I've been short-sighted. I think women should have other options—than marriage I mean—and so in the future, I want to provide business opportunities to the women coming out here from Chicago."

. "'Tis no terrible fate to be married," said Augustina wistfully, then, sighing, added, "but perhaps I should take you up on your kind offer."

"Good," said Kat, puzzled at Augustina's lack of enthusiasm. Such a talented woman should be ecstatic at the prospect of owning her own business. "We'll put the notice into the next issue of the *Leader*."

Augustina nodded and handed Kat a dripping gravy boat.

As Kat dried the piece, she thought of the offer she'd made Augustina and the reasoning behind it. Had she been thinking of herself? she wondered—and her own options? Of late Connor had seemed so disapproving of all her activities. For instance, she'd had to tell him that she couldn't attend a dinner party because she had a school board meeting. He'd greeted this announcement with decided coldness. Were they always to be at odds, he convinced that his activities should take precedence over hers?

And by going upstairs with him, she might well have cancelled out all her own options except marriage. The thought caused a pang in her heart, and she realized sadly that she was very confused, torn between love and her desire for independent action. Why did it have to be that way for women? she wondered miserably. Because she truly did love Connor. She wanted to spend the rest of her life with him, but not at the expense of every other hope she had for her future.

"And here's a picture of the new baby," said Sean. "James took it."

"Oh, isn't she beautiful?" murmured Kat. She did so want a baby. That was the problem; she wanted everything—her causes, her business ventures, marriage to the man she loved, a baby—yet she and Connor were no closer to agreement than they'd been when he first objected to marrying in an icy church. In fact, their areas of conflict widened every day. When Augustina's first customer appeared, Connor took the whole business amiss, telling Kat that, by encouraging the venture, she'd made him look like a cheapskate because he hadn't paid the girl.

"I paid her," Kat assured him, thinking that he'd be relieved to hear it.

"I see," he said coldly. "You paid for your own Christmas present." That had made Kat feel terrible. Nothing she did seemed right anymore in Connor's eyes.

"Sean," she said hesitantly, "did you realize that Connor refuses to be married in the church?"

"And you want me to side with you, right?"

"Of course."

"Settle it between yourselves," Sean advised. "I'm not spending the rest of my life mediating between two mule-heads like you and Connor. Which is not to say I disapprove of the marriage. In fact, I planned it—"

"You what?"

"You and Connor were made for each other. I saw that last January."

"Insufferable lout," she cried, laughing and throwing a pillow at his head as she had when they were children.

Then she sobered. "If we're made for each other," she asked, "why aren't we married?"

"Only you can answer that, little sister. As long as you're married by a priest, I don't see that it makes a difference where the ceremony takes place. You're not getting cold feet, are you?"

"Why accuse *me?*" she replied defensively. "He's the one who's always finding fault. He doesn't want me on the school board, and he doesn't want me going into the butter business—"

"Maybe he's jealous."

"Nonsense. I've never looked at another man."

"Jealous of all the calls on your attention."

"But that's silly. I don't complain that he spends most of *his* time pursuing business."

"Well, why would you?" asked Sean. "Connor just wants to support you in a grand style."

"I can support myself," said Kat resentfully.

Sean frowned. "You haven't, by any chance, discovered that what you felt when you said yes was more passion than love, have you?"

"I was assured by someone who knows the difference that I'm in love," said Kat drily.

"Oh, and who would that be?" Sean had looked quite serious when he asked Kat about the real nature of her feelings, as if he himself had made such a mistake. Had he been thinking of Ingrid? Kat wondered. Now he was laughing again, but she had no intention of telling him that her knowledgeable source was Marcie Webber. She'd not embarrass her brother by mentioning his wife's former employer. Still, she was moved to say tentatively, "I don't suppose you've heard from Ingrid?"

"Not a word," he replied. "What about you?"

Kat shook her head. Ingrid might have disappeared off the face of the earth for all they'd heard of her in Breckenridge.

"Then I guess I'll clear out her clothes," said Sean moodily. "Think Augustina would like them? She's almost as tall as Ingrid was."

Kat didn't want to say that ladylike Augustina McCloud wouldn't be caught dead in Ingrid's flashy clothing.

"No, I guess not," Sean answered his own question and changed the subject. "I haven't coughed in two months now. The doctor says I'm a certain cure."

"Sean, I'm so glad." She hesitated a moment, then added, "Mother says you must divorce Ingrid, but surely the church won't let you. I know it's unfair, but—"

"No worry there, little sister. I've already started the proceedings." Sean looked somewhat sheepish. "The fact is that we weren't married by a priest, so neither Maeve nor the church will object to the divorce."

Why had Sean taken up with Ingrid? Kat wondered. Passion? Loneliness? It wasn't a subject she wanted to discuss with her brother, any more than she could mention that she knew what Ingrid's profession had been.

"Well, no time like the present," he said, rising. "I'll see to Ingrid's clothes."

A few minutes later she heard him coughing, and her heart turned cold with dread.

"It was her," said Sean, appearing at the door. "I opened her wardrobe, took a deep breath, and started to cough." He lifted an arm load of clothes, buried his face in them, and dropped into a rocking chair, coughing uncontrollably.

"Perfume!" said Kat, snatching the garments away from him. "She was always drenched in perfume."

"My God," he said, "All that time I thought I was going to die, thought I had miner's lung, and it was that damned scent she wore. I can't believe it."

"I'll air these out and give them to the church," said Kat. Then it occurred to her that it might be better to sell them at Marcie's and give the money to the church.

*   *   *

420

"Where the devil are you going, Kat?" asked Connor, who was himself preparing to leave the house with Sean. "I suppose you're off to attend another school board meeting or turn your butter-making business into a national corporation."

Actually Kat was on her way to St. Gertrude's to see Sister Freddie, who had sent a note saying that they needed to talk about the wedding. However, with Connor taking that sarcastic tone, Kat didn't want to mention the wedding.

"In case you haven't noticed, there are two children in the house who need adult supervision," he continued, wrapping his neck in the muffler she'd knitted for him. "Who's to look out for them while you're—"

"Whoa there," Sean intervened quickly. "Augustina can see to Phoebe and Sean Michael."

"Augustina hasn't time for child minding," said Connor. "Kat's set her up in business."

"Well, I'm not that busy yet," said Augustina, smiling at Sean.

Kat eyed the two of them, puzzled at the intensity in their exchange of glances. Then, turning her mind to her errand, she left. Reverend Mother Hilda had vetoed Kat's request to have Freddie as her Maid of Honor—or Matron of Honor; there didn't seem to be any precedent for what to call a nun in one's wedding party. Reverend Mother said Benedictine sisters couldn't be in weddings, that it simply wasn't done. Not that it made much difference now, thought Kat. It didn't look as if she and Connor would need bridal attendants, and she told Freddie as much when they were sitting on the cot in Freddie's room at St. Gertrude's.

"Then why am I bringing the wrath of Reverend Mother down on my head if you're getting cold feet?"

"He wants everything his own way," said Kat resentfully. "He says the church is too cold and we must marry in the fire house, and he expects me to give up my business interests and my political aspirations and my—"

"Well, that's a woman's lot, isn't it?" asked Freddie.

"It's not yours," said Kat. "You'll be running a convent someday. Why shouldn't I be able to do things like that?"

"Why indeed? If you begin your novitiate immediately, you'll be a mother superior before you're fifty."

Kat gave her a look of surprised horror.

On December thirty-first, Maeve arrived with James and baby Bridget. Kat was taken by surprise and wondered uneasily what the occasion of this visit might be. She welcomed her mother and installed her in Sean's room, telling Sean, when he arrived home, that he would have to occupy Jeannie's little cubbyhole on Connor's side of the house since Kat herself was sharing with Phoebe and Sean Michael.

"Well, my girl," said Maeve briskly, once she had bedded Bridget down, "What's this about you and Connor being unable to settle on a wedding date? How long do you plan to live with the man, unmarried, before you—"

"We're not living together in that sense, Mother," Kat interrupted, crossing her fingers because of those sins of the flesh.

"You say it's a matter of the site," Maeve persevered, ignoring Kat's disclaimer. "Well, 'tis no fine church; he's got the right of it there, but what of the priest? Is Connor refusing to be married by Father Eusebius?"

"No, and it's not even entirely the church, Mother," Kat admitted. "I'm not sure Connor still wants to marry me. If he truly did, why would he be so difficult about everything?" Although she had once thought of the room upstairs as an expression of his love, she now saw it as a place of assignation—where he could have her in privacy without agreeing to her marriage terms.

"And why would he have changed his mind?" asked Maeve. "I did gather, from your letter, that he proposed out of affection rather than any more sensible consideration."

"And there's me," Kat forged on reluctantly. "I'm not sure that *I* want to marry."

"Kathleen Fitzgerald!" exclaimed her mother. "Sure you're not back to that old bit of foolishness. How many times do I have to tell you that a woman must marry to keep food on her table—unless she is, as I, a widow well provided for by a husband deceased."

"I don't need a man to feed and clothe me," said Kat resentfully. "I'm perfectly capable of doing it myself."

"How? With your butter business? You don't know that's going to prove a steady source of income."

"I own half of a mine for which I was offered fifty thousand dollars just before Christmas," said Kat.

"Fifty thousand dollars!" Maeve thought about that for a minute. "Still, mines eat up capital and then run out of whatever metal they've got in them, and then where will you be? A lonely, impoverished spinster. And I hope you're not thinking to live with Sean forever. He's already taken steps to free himself from that scandalous woman who deserted him. And sure he'll be looking for a new wife. Why else would he have married the first time if he weren't a man who needed a woman in his house? So there you are, Kathleen. You must marry Connor however you can get him, even if it means that the priest joins your hands in your own front parlor like some heathen Protestant couple."

Kat stared despairingly at her mother. She didn't know what she wanted to do. She didn't know what Connor wanted. The one thing Kat did know was that she couldn't let Maeve make this decision for her. "Mother," she said, "we're talking about the rest of my life. This is the one time above all that I must make up my own mind."

"The one time above all?" said Maeve. "As if I'm responsible for the foolish choices you've made in the past—like marrying Mickey. Was that my idea?"

"No," said Kat, "but you can be sure I've learned a lesson from my mistake."

"It appears to me, Kathleen, that you've got the lesson wrong."

Chapter Twenty-Nine

On New Year's Day, as they raised their glasses of temperance beer in toast to 1888, Kat thought wistfully of how confident she'd been, how elated and joyous, not a month ago when she had said yes to Connor's offer of marriage. Now all was confusion. She suspected that Connor, who hadn't said a word about marriage since taking her to bed in the tower room, now wanted to retract his proposal but was held back by the awkwardness he'd cause if he jilted his best friend's sister.

She looked around the room, which still displayed the Christmas greenery that Augustina had put up. Augustina and Sean stood in front of the stove, deep in earnest conversation. Jamie had invited a friend, and they, in the way of teenaged boys, were eating up the last of the buffet supper. Over by the door to Connor's side of the house, Kat's erstwhile fiancé was in conversation with Maeve and James, James laughing, probably telling some story,

Maeve flushed with pleasure, Connor with his arm around his father's shoulders. *How happy they all are*, thought Kat, *and I'm the specter at the feast.*

Then Connor looked her way, and she put on a smile, which brought him to her side. "If I had any sense, *I'd* kidnap you," he whispered into her ear. "I haven't had a moment alone with you in days. We no sooner got rid of Gretel, than Augustina arrived; then your brother moved back in, and—"

"Half of this house is his, Connor."

"I guess we could go up to Dillon and kick those people out of the ranch house."

Kat bit her lip. It would seem that Connor still felt something for her, but it was lust, not love. "We'd have to milk all the cows ourselves—and in a cold barn," she pointed out, determined to circumvent any plans he might have for getting her into bed again.

"And make love in front of a warm fire. Or have you forgotten our night in the ranch house?" he murmured.

Kat shook her head. No, she hadn't forgotten—not that night, nor the afternoon upstairs in this house. In fact, the memory made her stomach flutter, and not just with the thought of the love-making. If her monthly didn't start by tomorrow, she'd be begging Connor to marry her, no matter where the ceremony was performed or how reluctant he was.

"Now, I've agreed to be married by Father Eusebius," said Connor, "but I don't intend to make all the concessions."

He didn't intend to make any concessions, she thought. He had been wary of marriage a year ago, and he still was. "They're about to slide Fireman's Hall out into Lincoln Avenue and move it to Main Street," she pointed out. "We can't get married in a building that's being hauled across town on ropes."

"All right. How about the G.A.R. Hall?"

"The church," Kat insisted. As a good Roman Catholic,

such insistence was her duty, and he knew it. He just wanted to dominate her—

"Fireman's Hall," said Connor. "And I don't care where it's sitting at the time."

—or force *her* to break the engagement.

"Still quarreling, children?" asked Sean. "What a way to start the new year."

On January second, Kat knew that if she wanted to remain single, she could; she wasn't pregnant. James and her mother had taken the baby and gone off to Braddock to spend the night and revisit—Kat thought wryly—the scene of her mother's seduction. James had said to Maeve, " 'Twill be a second honeymoon, my dear." Second honeymoon indeed! The first one had preceeded the marriage. Not, Kat admitted to herself, that she and Connor were any better, and for them there might be no marriage.

Then when the parents were out of the house, Sean and Augustina had taken Jamie with them to pay New Year's calls. Kat found herself alone with Connor, who smiled and said, "Shall we look at the new room again, sweetheart?"

Kat pulled away from him sharply. The man wanted to put her through another month of anxiety, another month of terror that she'd find herself pregnant and unmarried.

"No," said Kat.

"No?" He looked hurt. "Kat, have you stopped loving me?"

"Why would you ask me that?" she mumbled.

"Well, you're in no great hurry to get married."

"Neither are you," she retorted.

"Yes, I am. I'd happily elope this very day. Put on your coat, and we'll—"

Kat had dropped into her rocking chair. Here it was; he *did* want to marry, but only on his own terms, and Kat was unsure of how to say what had to be said. "Connor," she interrupted hesitantly, "I'm no longer sure that I'm the

Elizabeth Chadwick

woman you should marry. There are things I want to do with my life, and you seem to be against them all."

"I don't know what you're talking about," said Connor. "What is it you want to do that I've objected to?"

"Better ask what I've ever done that you supported," she muttered, then said firmly, "Connor, I do love you, and I do want to spend my life with you, but I don't want to spend it being your housemaid."

"Well, who asked you to?" he responded indignantly. "We've got the Chicago girls for that. I don't suppose your mother intends to stop sending them."

"No, I don't suppose she does," Kat agreed, "but every time I try to do something interesting, you object."

"Like what?"

"Like everything. Like the temperance campaign; you didn't approve of that. Then the school board; you thought I should give it up because we were getting married. And woman suffrage. I think women should have the vote, and I intend to work for it."

"Well, I have no quarrel with that," Connor protested.

"Oh no? What if I should want to run for office? I mean what if I wanted to be mayor of Breckenridge or— or governor of Colorado, once women get the vote? What would you think of that?"

"I'd be mighty surprised," said Connor, "to hear that you, or any woman, could win such an office."

"But if I did?" she countered resentfully.

"I don't know what I'd think, Kat. Good lord, I doubt there's a man in the world who wouldn't be dismayed to picture himself as—well, the spouse of the governor. What would my place be—serving tea to the legislators' wives?"

Kat couldn't help but giggle at the thought, and he looked relieved. "But I'm serious, Connor," she added quickly. "I'm serious about woman suffrage—and business. I want to remain active in business and to pursue my own projects, like the butter sales and Augustina's decorating service, both of which you criticized. And there'll be more women coming from Chicago that I'll want to help, that I'll want to offer options other than marriage."

"Well, there it is," said Connor. "You never have changed your mind about marriage, have you?"

"I just don't want to give up everything else in my life for it," said Kat pleadingly. "Would you? Would you want to sell up everything you own so that you could devote all your time to me?"

"You mean sell the Chicago Girl and the mines up Ten Mile Canyon and—"

"—all of them," said Kat.

"My God, sweetheart, men don't do that. They work and support their families."

Kat nodded. "And they enjoy their work too. At least, you do, and I'm no different, Connor."

"Good lord." He looked shaken. "I guess I had no idea how you felt, Kat, and I don't know how I feel about what you've said. I'll have to think about it."

Kat nodded and turned away, tears in her eyes. She had a pretty good idea of the conclusions to which he'd come.

The next morning, Connor was gone, leaving word that he had business in Denver. Maeve, James and the baby left Breckenridge the following day, but Maeve said privately to Kat, before she boarded the train, "It doesn't pay, my girl, to set yourself against society's ways. Such newfangled ideas can only bring you unhappiness," and she took little Bridget, whom Kat had been holding, and added, "If you continue on the path you've taken, you'll never bear a sweet child like this one."

Kat swallowed hard and waved as the train pulled away. Her mother's advice had come too late. Kat was sure that Connor would return to Breckenridge and break the engagement. He'd remained unmarried nine years; no doubt, he'd decide to keep his life as it was rather than take on a woman with such unfeminine ideas.

Well, she thought unhappily, *best get back to business. Now I must make a success of my ranch at Dillon.* So she went home and packed her valise, preparing for another trip to drum up customers for Fitzgerald Sweet Cream Butter. *Perhaps,* she thought as she folded a change of undergarments and slipped them into the bag, *perhaps I should sell eggs as well as butter,* although she'd heard that chickens were given to diseases and sudden death. A tear slid down her cheek as she closed the door to the bedroom.

"Augustina," she called as she crossed the house and stuck her head into the kitchen. "Augustina, I'm taking the train to Robinson. You'll see to the children, won't you?"

"Of course I will. I do adore those two little ones." Augustina smiled wistfully. "I fear I'll never be the business woman you are; I seem to be more domestic than I imagined during my teaching days."

On the train ride to Denver, Connor's reflections were bitter. Why was he traveling in rotten weather on mine business that would make Kat richer—rich enough to spurn his offer of marriage? Women were supposed to want to get married—and without imposing a whole list of conditions on a man. Kat acted as if marriage were a prison and he proposing to be her jailer. He fumed all the way to Boreas Pass, took a nap, and woke up thinking of the things Kat had said, admitting that she *might* have made some valid points.

Perhaps he had, without quite realizing it, been trying to circumscribe her activities, to make her dependent on him, to make her into the "ideal wife." But what was an "ideal wife" like? He'd never given it much thought. By the time he disembarked in Denver, he'd formulated a few ideas on the subject. For instance, he supposed she'd be a devout woman and given to good works—like Kat—although not to the point of trying to close down saloons and reform soiled doves. In fact, now that he thought of it, where in the world had Kat ever got the idea of knocking on Marcella Webber's door?

And of course, he reasoned, as he registered at his hotel, an ideal wife wouldn't want to run for public office; she probably wouldn't care one way or another whether she had the vote, and she'd certainly never say to her husband that, if he expected her to give up her business activities, he should do the same. She wouldn't *have* any business activities; she'd expect him to make the money—as much money as possible. Dear God, he realized suddenly, he'd just described Rose Laurel! The woman with whom he'd been miserable! He dropped his bag on the floor of his hotel room and stared down at the bustling streets of Denver.

Maybe the "ideal wife" was just what he *didn't* want. Maybe he'd fallen in love with Kat because she was so different. Why should he want a wife who, as Kat put it, stayed at home dusting the bric-a-brac?

The more he mulled it over as he made his rounds in Denver, pricing mine machinery, the more he became convinced that he'd be bored to death if he managed to change Kat, and she would be more miserable married to him than Rose Laurel had been. Neither he nor Kat was suited to marriage as their contemporaries viewed it.

By the time he boarded the D.S.P & P. for the return trip to Breckenridge, he could hardly wait to get home and assure Kat that they could lead a good life together without her changing a whit, and they'd have to hurry if they were to work the wedding in before Fireman's Hall began its journey down the hill to Main Street. He smiled to himself. After all, even a modern-thinking man like himself couldn't be expected to make all the concessions, and he hated that miserable, cold church. Maybe later he and Kat could donate the money to make it at least reasonably comfortable.

* * *

"Where's Kat?" was the first thing he asked when he returned from Denver.

"Oh, she's gone off to Robinson," Sean replied.

"Damn," said Connor. "Did you know your sister's backing off from marrying me?"

"Well," said Sean slowly, "I think you've got that wrong, my friend. It's just that she's afraid."

"Yes," said Connor, "afraid I'm going to lock her up in the kitchen, although I never meant to give her that impression."

"You've got to remember," said Sean, "that life has taught Kat it's all downhill from the courtship."

"Life taught me the same thing," said Connor, "and I'm willing to take the chance. And by God, Sean, I intend to marry your sister—and to make her happy." He shoved his hands into his pockets and glanced toward the stairway that led to the honeymoon room he'd commissioned for Kat. Well, he was damn well going to spend his honeymoon there—with her! "I know just how I'm going to change her mind," he said, and dropping his carpet bag on the floor, he turned and stamped out of the house.

Sean shook his head. What was Connor up to now? The two of them were stubborn as mules. God knew if they'd ever manage to get together and, if they did, whether they could stay together without killing each other. Maybe his original matchmaking scheme hadn't been as brilliant as he'd thought.

"You can't be serious, Connor," said Charlie Maxell.

"Well, I am," said Connor. "Now, I want you to draw it up, and then I'll sign it in front of witnesses."

Charlie shook his head. "I've never heard of such a thing."

* * *

432

"Good morning," said Father Eusebius. "Are you ready?"

Oh dear, what meeting have I forgotten? Kat wondered. It was what? January twelfth. It must be the church renovation committee. "Just give me a minute to change, Father." As she hurried to her room, she wondered why he had looked so surprised. Did he expect her to wear her old house dress to the meeting? Actually, she had a new gown, a biscuit-colored serge with a sapphire vest and tunic and sapphire mohair braid trimming the skirt and plastron. She donned it quickly and whisked back into the parlor.

"Is that what you're wearing?" asked Father Eusebius.

Kat looked down at her dress. It was very pretty—in her opinion, more than good enough for a meeting of the church renovation committee. "Yes, why not?" she replied, wondering just when Father Eusebius had become interested in women's fashion. She put her coat on, wrapped a warm scarf around her head, and picked up a large muff. "It's not at the church?" she asked as they turned downhill at Lincoln.

Father Eusebius gave her a puzzled look. "I thought that was all agreed to, the church being so drafty."

"Well, I think you're right," said Kat. "You've had so many colds this winter."

"I didn't realize it was for my sake. That's very considerate of you, Kathleen."

What a strange conversation, thought Kat. She said, catching sight of Fireman's Hall, "Doesn't that look ridiculous, squatting there like some giant, lethargic snow toad? They ought to move it faster." The building was temporarily and inconveniently perched in the middle of Main Street.

"Well, I hope they don't move it today," said Father Eusebius whimsically.

"Why not? The sooner the better, I'd say. Leaving it in the middle of the street is dangerous."

Father Eusebius seemed to find that confusing. He shook

433

his head and guided her around the building.

"Well, goodness, we'd begun to think you weren't coming," said Sister Freddie.

"To tell you the truth, I forgot all about it."

"Of course you did." Sister Freddie laughed.

"Here you go, Katie." Sean lifted Kat up into the doorway of Fireman's Hall, then did the same for Sister Freddie.

When Kat looked back, wondering why Sean and Freddie were attending the meeting, and why the session was being held in an itinerant building, her brother was helping Father Eusebius before hopping up himself.

"Most unusual," said Father Eusebius as he began to climb the stairs to the second floor. The nun urged Kat to precede her, and Sean brought up the rear.

"This is a bad choice," said Kat. "What if the building falls over while we're in it?"

"Then half the town will be tumbled together like turnips in a stew," said Sean. They stepped into the second floor hall where they found what Kat took to be more than half the town seated in rows, a makeshift altar in front, Connor waiting for her there, Maeve weeping in the first row with little Bridget in her arms, and James beside her with his tripod and camera. Across the aisle were Jeannie and Tom. Jamie stood with Connor.

"Sean," hissed Kat, "I never agreed to this. What kind of trickery are you up to?"

"Here," he said and placed a heavy roll of parchment in her hand. "He's given you everything you asked for. If you don't marry him now, it's because you don't love him."

Everything she asked for? She stared in confusion at the document in her hand.

"Read it," said Sean, "before the wedding guests start getting restless."

Slowly Kat unrolled the document and began to read.

I, James Connor Macleod, Junior, being of sound mind

and body, do undertake, in the expectation of marriage with Kathleen Margaret Fitzpatrick Fitzgerald, the following:

That I will love her all my life.

(Tears rose in Kat's eyes when she read that.)

That I will not expect of her domestic activities beyond those required in any emergencies that may befall our household.

That I will not belittle her political beliefs nor discourage her political aspirations.

That I will not interfere with her religious activities or projects of good work, unless said projects should spell financial disaster for the two of us.

(Kat frowned at that one, although she could see a certain justice and practicality to it.)

That I will encourage and support her business ventures when it is in my power to do so.

And that I will attend mass with her on any Sunday when the church is open and the snow is not above eighteen inches in depth nor the temperature below zero.

So say I.

(And there was his signature, bold and positive, *James Connor Macleod*) and below that:

Attested to on this twelfth day of our Lord, January, 1888, Breckenridge, Colorado.

Then the signatures of Charles Maxell and Septimus Embry with the seal of the Clerk of Summit County.

"Satisfied?" asked Sean.

She rolled the parchment carefully and tucked it into her muff, which she handed to Sister Freddie along with her coat. Then she raised her eyes to meet Connor's across the width of the room, took her brother's arm, and made the short walk that would end in her marriage.

Father Eusebius, who had already taken his place at the altar, beamed down upon them.

"Eighteen inches?" Kat whispered to Connor. "The snow's that deep nine-tenths of the year."

435

He smiled and whispered back, "Surely you can allow me some concessions."

"I'm going to be married in Fireman's Hall, aren't I?"

"Is there some problem?" asked Father Eusebius, looking alarmed.

"No problem at all, Father." Kat tucked her hand into Connor's arm, and in that fashion she took her vows in Fireman's Hall, after which the chairs were cleared away, temperance beer and refreshments served, and dancing followed. Both papers thought the occasion a fine one, although Colonel Fincher decried the lack of a proper tipple for gentlemen. Sean announced his engagement to Augustina McCloud, and Kat whispered urgently, "You can't become engaged. You're still married."

"I'm taking care of it," he whispered back.

Thus the last of the 1887 crop of Chicago girls was accounted for. During the reception, twenty-seven unmarried men applied to Maeve for first choice of the 1888 crop and were told they'd have to wait their turn.

Connor said to Kat when they'd kissed over the wedding cake, "Did you feel the earth move?"

"That was the building," she replied, "and I must say, it's not that much warmer than the church."

"Well, we have a fine stove in our tower room."

Kat smiled to herself. She was looking forward to revisiting the tower room.

Author's Note

Although many of the characters and most of the events in *Reluctant Lovers* are fictitious, Breckenridge is a real town and some of the characters actually lived there in 1887–1888 and might have acted as they do in the book had they met the Chicago girls. For instance, the Breckenridge Temperance League is a product of my imagination, but Father Dyer and Gertrude Briggle are real people who held the sentiments that I ascribe to them. Sister Freddie is fictional, but Fathers Eusebius and Rhabanus, abbess Hilda Walzen and the other Benedictine sisters are historical.

Kathleen Fitzgerald and her family, Connor Macleod and his family, plus all the Chicago girls and their suitors, are imaginary, but many of the townsfolk, people like Eli Fletcher, the ski-maker; restauranteurs Julia and Barney Ford; Sheriff Will Iliff; the Engle brothers and their saloon; banker Thomas Wintermute; the Finding family and others were citizens of Breckenridge.

Books like J.L Dyer's *Snow-Shoe Itinerant* and Isabella

Elizabeth Chadwick

Bird's *A Lady's Life in the Rocky Mountains*, which Kat read, and Mark Fiester's *Blasted Beloved Breckenridge* and Mary Ellen Gilliland's *Summit*, which I read, not to mention the week I spent in Breckenridge in the library and exploring the historic district with Marta Wallace of the Summit County Historical Society, made the town and the era come alive for me, as I hope this book will for my readers.

I also owe a debt to Carolyn Heilbrun's book *Writing a Woman's Life* and her ideas on role models in women's fiction and on compromises in marriage that portend greater happiness for the women who insist on them, as well as to *Women Adrift Independent Wage Earners in Chicago, 1880–1930* by Joanne J. Meyerowitz for fascinating information on working women in Chicago. *Women Adrift* inspired the creation of Maeve Fitzpatrick, rescuer of young women.

N.R.H.

LOVE SPELL

THE MAGIC OF ROMANCE
PAST, PRESENT, AND FUTURE....

Dorchester Publishing Co., Inc., the leader in romantic fiction, is pleased to unveil its newest line— Love Spell. Every month, beginning in August 1993, Love Spell will publish one book in each of four categories:

1) *Timeswept Romance*—Modern-day heroines travel to the past to find the men who fulfill their hearts' desires.

2) *Futuristic Romance*—Love on distant worlds where passion is the lifeblood of every man and woman.

3) *Historical Romance*—Full of desire, adventure and intrigue, these stories will thrill readers everywhere.

4) *Contemporary Romance*—With novels by Lori Copeland, Heather Graham, and Jayne Ann Krentz, Love Spell's line of contemporary romance is first-rate.

Exploding with soaring passion and fiery sensuality, Love Spell romances are destined to take you to dazzling new heights of ecstasy.

COMING IN JANUARY!
TIMESWEPT ROMANCE

TIME OF THE ROSE
By Bonita Clifton

When the silver-haired cowboy brings Madison Calloway to his run-down ranch, she thinks for sure he is senile. Certain he'll bring harm to himself, Madison follows the man into a thunderstorm and back to the wild days of his youth in the Old West.

The dread of all his enemies and the desire of all the ladies, Colton Chase does not stand a chance against the spunky beauty who has tracked him through time. And after one passion-drenched night, Colt is ready to surrender his heart to the most tempting spitfire anywhere in time.

__51922-4 $4.99 US/$5.99 CAN

A FUTURISTIC ROMANCE

AWAKENINGS
By Saranne Dawson

Fearless and bold, Justan rules his domain with an iron hand, but nothing short of the Dammai's magic will bring his warring people peace. He claims he needs Rozlynd—a bewitching beauty and the last of the Dammai—for her sorcery alone, yet inside him stirs an unexpected yearning to savor the temptress's charms, to sample her sweet innocence. And as her silken spell ensnares him, Justan battles to vanquish a power whose like he has never encountered—the power of Rozlynd's love.

__51921-6 $4.99 US/$5.99 CAN

LOVE SPELL
ATTN: Order Department
Dorchester Publishing Co., Inc.
276 5th Avenue, New York, NY 10001

Please add $1.50 for shipping and handling for the first book and $.35 for each book thereafter. PA., N.Y.S. and N.Y.C. residents, please add appropriate sales tax. No cash, stamps, or C.O.D.s. All orders shipped within 6 weeks via postal service book rate. Canadian orders require $2.00 extra postage and must be paid in U.S. dollars through a U.S. banking facility.

Name_____
Address_____
City _____ State_____ Zip_____
I have enclosed $_____in payment for the checked book(s).
Payment <u>must</u> accompany all orders.☐ Please send a free catalog.

COMING IN DECEMBER 1993
FROM LOVE SPELL
HISTORICAL ROMANCE
THE PASSIONATE REBEL
Helene Lehr

A beautiful American patriot, Gillian Winthrop is horrified to learn that her grandmother means her to wed a traitor to the American Revolution. Her body yearns for Philip Meredith's masterful touch, but she is determined not to give her hand—or any other part of herself—to the handsome Tory, until he convinces her that he too is a passionate rebel.

__51918-6 $4.99 US/$5.99 CAN

CONTEMPORARY ROMANCE
THE TAWNY GOLD MAN
Amii Lorin

Bestselling Author Of More Than 5 Million Books In Print!

Long ago, in a moment of wild, rioting ecstasy, Jud Cammeron vowed to love her always. Now, as Anne Moore looks at her stepbrother, she sees a total stranger, a man who plans to take control of his father's estate and everyone on it. Anne knows things are different—she is a grown woman with a fiance—but something tells her she still belongs to the tawny gold man.

__51919-4 $4.99 US/$5.99 CAN

LOVE SPELL
ATTN: Order Department
Dorchester Publishing Company, Inc.
276 5th Avenue, New York, NY 10001

Please add $1.50 for shipping and handling for the first book and $.35 for each book thereafter. PA., N.Y.S. and N.Y.C. residents, please add appropriate sales tax. No cash, stamps, or C.O.D.s. All orders shipped within 6 weeks via postal service book rate. Canadian orders require $2.00 extra postage and must be paid in U.S. dollars through a U.S. banking facility.

Name _____

Address _____

City _____ State _____ Zip _____

I have enclosed $_____in payment for the checked book(s).
Payment <u>must</u> accompany all orders.☐ Please send a free catalog.

SPEND YOUR LEISURE MOMENTS WITH US.

Hundreds of exciting titles to choose from—something for everyone's taste in fine books: breathtaking historical romance, chilling horror, spine-tingling suspense, taut medical thrillers, involving mysteries, action-packed men's adventure and wild Westerns.

SEND FOR A FREE CATALOGUE TODAY!

Leisure Books
Attn: Customer Service Department
276 5th Avenue, New York, NY 10001